Praise for
Promise Bridge

"Eileen Clymer Schwab's debut novel takes us to the antebellum South to offer us the story of a friendship between two remarkable young women: Hannalore Blessing, a Southern belle, and Livie, a runaway slave. Defying the casual brutality of slave hunters and slave owners, Livie and Hannah become fully human to each other, forming a bond that transcends the narrow categories of race and social class. *Promise Bridge* is a courageous novel that never ceases to surprise and delight with unexpected twists and startling revelations. In it we find life lived to the fullest, not by the motto 'what if?' but by the motto 'why not?'" —Mary Mackey, author of *The Widow's War*

"*Promise Bridge* is a stunning debut that is sure to become a classic. With gorgeous writing and characters you'll come to love, Eileen Clymer Schwab has written a beautiful story of a young woman's awakening during the volatile years preceding the Civil War."
—Maryann McFadden, author of *The Richest Season* and *So Happy Together*

"Schwab's promising debut puts an uncommon spin on a runaway slave story. Readers who are won over by the strength of Hannah and Livie . . . will be rewarded by some surprising twists and an eventually riveting narrative."
—*Publishers Weekly*

"A moving story of the power of friendship, trust, and learning to open one's heart to love and new possibilities. Very much recommended."
—*Historical Novels Review*

EILEEN CLYMER SCHWAB

SHADOW OF A QUARTER MOON

NEW AMERICAN LIBRARY

NEW AMERICAN LIBRARY
Published by New American Library, a division of
Penguin Group (USA) Inc., 375 Hudson Street,
New York, New York 10014, USA
Penguin Group (Canada), 90 Eglinton Avenue East, Suite 700, Toronto,
Ontario M4P 2Y3, Canada (a division of Pearson Penguin Canada Inc.)
Penguin Books Ltd., 80 Strand, London WC2R 0RL, England
Penguin Ireland, 25 St. Stephen's Green, Dublin 2,
Ireland (a division of Penguin Books Ltd.)
Penguin Group (Australia), 250 Camberwell Road, Camberwell, Victoria 3124,
Australia (a division of Pearson Australia Group Pty. Ltd.)
Penguin Books India Pvt. Ltd., 11 Community Centre, Panchsheel Park,
New Delhi - 110 017, India
Penguin Group (NZ), 67 Apollo Drive, Rosedale, Auckland 0632,
New Zealand (a division of Pearson New Zealand Ltd.)
Penguin Books (South Africa) (Pty.) Ltd., 24 Sturdee Avenue,
Rosebank, Johannesburg 2196, South Africa

Penguin Books Ltd., Registered Offices:
80 Strand, London WC2R 0RL, England

First published by New American Library,
a division of Penguin Group (USA) Inc.

First Printing, July 2011
10 9 8 7 6 5 4 3 2

 REGISTERED TRADEMARK—MARCA REGISTRADA

LIBRARY OF CONGRESS CATALOGING-IN-PUBLICATION DATA:
Schwab, Eileen Clymer.
    Shadow of a quarter moon/Eileen Clymer Schwab.
    p. cm.
    ISBN 978-0-451-23328-8
    1. Racially mixed children—Fiction. 2. Identity (Psychology)—Fiction. 3. Plantation life—North
Carolina—Fiction. 4. North Carolina—History—1775-1865—Fiction. I. Title.
    PS3619.C4845S53 2011
    813'.6—dc22   2011004015

Set in Bulmer
Designed by Ginger Legato

Printed in the United States of America

PUBLISHER'S NOTE
This is a work of fiction. Names, characters, places, and incidents either are the product of the author's
imagination or are used fictitiously, and any resemblance to actual persons, living or dead, business es-
tablishments, events, or locales is entirely coincidental.
    The publisher does not have any control over and does not assume any responsibility for author or
third-party Web sites or their content.

The scanning, uploading, and distribution of this book via the Internet or via any other means without
the permission of the publisher is illegal and punishable by law. Please purchase only authorized electronic editions, and do not participate in or encourage electronic piracy of copyrighted materials. Your
support of the author's rights is appreciated.

In honor and in remembrance of
America's Underground Railroad

Acknowledgments

As always, I count my blessings. Love and gratitude to my husband, Ray, and to my four wonderful children: Connie, Ray, Brian, and Griffin.

I love you, Mom and Dad. Thank you for always being there.

The evolution of this novel required many talented caregivers, beginning with my publisher, Kara Welsh, and editorial director, Claire Zion. Your team at NAL is the best!

Heartfelt thanks to my wonderful editor, Ellen Edwards, who makes this process so prolific and creative. Working with you has been a dream. Your guidance and expertise have made all the difference in this book and in my growth as a writer.

My sincere appreciation to the NAL sales team; managing editors Frank Walgren and Daniel Walsh; Ashley Fisher-Tranese and the advertising/promotion department; editorial assistant Elizabeth Bistrow; and my publicist, Elizabeth Tobin.

Thanks to Anthony Ramondo and the art department. Special thanks to Mary E. O'Boyle for the beautiful cover design.

To my agent, Kevan Lyon. I would not be here without you. Thank you for your continued support and guidance.

Endless gratitude to Robert Peek, whose respect and admiration for Dismal Swamp and Canal added a special magic to this book.

Many thanks to my friend and fellow author Maryann McFadden. You have been so gracious in sharing your experience and enthusiasm.

Special thanks to my niece Emma Schwab for sharing her love and knowledge of horses.

Last, and most important, I would like to acknowledge the profound inspiration stirred by the National Underground Railroad Freedom Center in Cincinnati, Ohio, and the many other sites found within our National Underground Railroad Network to Freedom. It is my privilege to honor and remember.

SHADOW
OF A
QUARTER
MOON

Chapter 1

"Jacy Lane, you are nothing more than a foolish quarter moon!" These words were the earliest recollection I had of my mother and me, spoken as she yanked my unruly hair in a fit of frustration, unable to wrestle my braids into perfection. More than twenty years later, as I wept in the glow of a full and brilliant July moon, I felt the sting of being dull and incomplete in her eyes. Much like the sliver of a quarter moon, I was a fragment of what she had hoped I would be. When the crunch of boots approached me from the rear, I shivered with dread and despair in the knowledge that I was a mere shard of the woman I dreamed of being as well.

"Don't turn around," he growled into my ear. His rough hands clamped over my hips and his weight pressed against me. I knew the routine and humiliation. How could I be promised in marriage to a man so vile?

"Please don't."

My words were small and futile. He would not be dissuaded. In his mind, he had rights as my betrothed. The fact that we remained clothed and the consummation was incomplete made the weekly act proper in his eyes. A release for him, a forced endurance to me. He played the perfect dinner guest with Mother, Papa, and Grandmother Mayme, but as after-dinner cordials were prepared he motioned his smoky eyes toward the door. His discreet command ordered me to go to our place in the shadows and wait. Like a bear scratching an itch against a cedar, he groaned with pleasure. Fortunately, the heavy flounce and ribbon adorning the back of my skirt buffered me from his exuberance, but nothing could protect me from the shame.

"Stop, Garrison," I begged as splinters from the wooden post I clutched pricked my fingers. He grabbed the back of my head and pushed it forward.

"Be still; I am nearly done with you." My braid unwound beneath his boorish touch and tangled in his hand. "Damn your thick mane," he said, shaking his hand loose and taking with it a healthy clump of my hair.

I willed my thoughts beyond the moment, but could not force them past my introduction to Garrison six months earlier. Our inauspicious start should have alerted me. He stood broad and shapeless, like the colonnade fronting the porch. The white, sticky film that collected in the corners of his plump mouth as he spoke distracted me when he first asked my name. His wide-set eyes and blunt features brought to mind a bulldog, as did his severe underbite, which jutted his chin beyond his upper lip when he laughed at me and said, "Jay . . . see? That's not a name. Those are letters carved on baby blocks."

His snide insult had infuriated me, because my name was given to me by my father. At the time, I had wished to slap Garrison's jowly cheek. But now, as I turned my eyes to the darkness of the lower pasture, I wished only for his completion. Subtle movement near the gate drew my gaze. A moonbeam revealed a figure crouched in witness to my indignation. The prowler rose from the grass, clear in the glow of a lantern he carried. Usually the appearance of a Negro in the night warranted suspicion, but it was only Rafe, a strong and strapping young man owned by my father. As he strode the rise of the pasture, the tinkle of iron stirrups draped from his shoulder caused Garrison to ease off me.

"Damn darky," he grumbled, clearly cut short in his pleasure. "Pin your hair and go into the house. I am too restless for casual drinks. This distraction has soured my mood, so fabricate an excuse for why I have turned in early. Tomorrow night I will make certain we are not interrupted."

"S'cuse me passing by, Marster Yob," Rafe said without looking at Garrison. His nonchalant steps carried him toward the barn. "Jes' checkin' on a foal we birthed up at the stable earlier today. The mother didn't make it, but we is determined to save the young filly."

As I scurried from the shadows, I heard the thump of Garrison's hand against the back of Rafe's head. His words were sharp with warning. "Don't ever cross paths with me in the night, boy. If you see me taking in the evening air, retreat to your cabin until twilight shows I have left the yard."

"Yas'sah, Marster."

I slipped through the front door, thankful for the reprieve that Rafe's appearance provided me, and equally glad to be spared having to witness Rafe being forced to grovel at Garrison's hand. The burden of degradation was lifted from me, as I knew that Garrison would likely stomp to the backyard to smoke his pungent cigar, as he often did when he was sulking. He would then retire to the guest room, using the rear entrance to avoid playacting a pleasant and proper good-night.

Mother and Papa stood near the hearth in the dining room. Their posture was stiff and uncomfortable, as it usually was when they were left alone. I prayed that my flustered demeanor would not reveal my intimate activity. Though I was not a child, nor the initiator, I could not bear the embarrassment of my father suspecting I was being held hostage to womanly duties. No father wanted to surrender his daughter's innocence, but I was old enough to know that being an adult came with expectations. Relief warmed me when Papa's shoulders eased and a broad smile lit his face as I entered the room.

"There's my girl," he said as he wrapped his strong arm around my shoulders. "We wondered where you had run off to. Where is Garrison?"

"He asked me to convey his regret that he cannot join us for drinks. Garrison has a pressing business matter that needs his contemplation, so he retired to the guest room to be alone."

Papa kissed my cheek tenderly. "What could be more urgent than sweeping my daughter off her feet?" Then with a teasing wink he added, "Obviously, the gentleman's manners are somewhat lacking."

If only he knew how close to the truth his humor had brushed. Instantly, Mother's face tightened. "The two of you are so cavalier with regard to Garrison. We should be thankful a man of his station has seen a benefit in our arrangement."

Papa's eyes flashed at Mother's words. "That's enough, Claudia. Jacy knows I am joking. Besides, it is Garrison who should be thankful for the company of such a lovely lady." His smile returned as he gave me a quick peck on the forehead. "Now I must ask you to excuse me as well. I have some paperwork to attend to while my eyes are still fresh and alert. The day after next, I shall deliver the palominos I bred for the Stevenses' stable up in Norfolk. Rafe and I will take them on the hoof as far as South Mills. Stevens will come down by flatboat through the canal at Dismal Swamp, and his stable boys will herd them along on the second half of the journey. There will be a handsome profit, so perhaps I will return with a new dress for my sweet girl."

Mother clucked with annoyance. "Perhaps more face powder and hair ribbons would be of better use."

"Claudia—"

Mother's words stung, but Papa silenced her with a frosty glare. His lips moved to scold her, though he held his tongue when our house servant, Jerlinda, entered the room to clear the dishes. He paused for a moment and then, with a parting scowl at Mother, Papa left the room.

"Jerlinda," Mother said, her cool eyes locked on mine. "Don't you agree that this reckless young lady should be grateful for the attention of a proper gentleman?"

Mother never spoke to Jerlinda except to give directions or orders, so the woman went still as she bent over the table and fixed her eyes on the dishes. Jerlinda's mulatto skin was light enough to flush with discomfort as she weighed Mother's question. "Yes, missus, if you say so."

"I should know what's best for my daughter, don't you think?"

"Yes, missus."

"Run along, Jerlinda. I want to talk to Jacy alone." The trembling woman rushed from the room, obviously glad to retreat from Mother's orchestrated banter designed to deliver a point for my benefit. "You see, even a lowly Negress has more sense than you in this matter. Do you think no one sees you shrink from Garrison when he is near? A woman can offer only beauty, wealth, and charm to secure a respectable husband. You are not overabundant in the first two qualities, so you cannot afford to lack in the third. I suggest you apply better effort in charming that man."

My cheeks tingled, hot with embarrassment. She and I did not share a close or comfortable bond; therefore the confession I hid had to be pried like a bad tooth from a flawless smile. "Mother, if you knew the entitlements he takes when we are without chaperone—"

Mother waved her arms. "Say nothing more. I do not want to hear your complaints."

"But, Mother—"

"Not another word, Jacy. Garrison is a good match and more than I hoped for, considering your advanced age. This may be your last opportunity before spinsterhood, so perhaps a degree of compromise is necessary to hold his interest."

"A degree of compromise?" My distress flowed from me like blood from an open wound. "Mother, you have paired me with a man who does not respect me."

"He has chosen you," she spat. "Is that not respect? Garrison values family. You want marriage and children, don't you?"

"Of course," I choked out. Mother was masterful at using this unfulfilled dream to keep me committed to my relationship with Garrison. Our mutual desire for a large family was our one true bond. Each of us was raised as an only child without the camaraderie of siblings. Garrison and I had talked at length about our hopes for a home that bustled with laughter and activity. In fact, it was his easy rapport with children at occasional social functions that ingratiated him to me after our rocky start. Garrison worked hard to curry favor with Papa and Mayme, but his strongest ally was Mother.

"Don't be naive, Jacy. Men expect compliance from their women, the same as they do their mules and field hands. Learn to defer to his wishes, and as his wife, you will reap a lifetime of reward for your acquiescence."

I spun on my heels and rushed from the room. Shouldn't a mother seek to protect her child? Instead, she added to my shame by using me as bait to lure a catch worthy of the net. My feet did not slow until I reached the hallway of the second floor. Mayme's door stood ajar. The golden glow of her oil lamp welcomed me to her.

"Come in, child," she said when I peeked into her room. I shut the door and sat at her feet, where she rocked near her fireplace. My father was blessed to have so gentle a mother. When I lowered my head to her lap, she stroked my hair as only a grandmother would do. "The evening has just begun, Jacy. Have you and Garrison said good-night so soon?"

"Yes," I whispered, desperately wanting to tell her why. Mayme had been struggling with poor health for nearly a year, and Papa had given us strict orders not to upset her. A bout with scarlet fever had weakened her heart and depleted her strength and spirit.

Once fiercely protective of me, she was now the one who needed protecting. And though Papa's decree against agitating Mayme was directed mostly at Mother, I felt a great responsibility in assuring that her needs were put ahead of mine. I closed my eyes and let her touch soothe me.

"I love you, Mayme," I cooed. "I remember a night like this one many years ago. Mother had clunked me atop the head with a hairbrush, as she used to do, and I came running to you for comfort."

Mayme's fingers slowed. "What would make you remember such a moment? Memories can be a hazy and painful commodity, Jacy. Don't dwell on snippets from the past. Why endure unnecessary turmoil over thoughts that are too far gone to remember with definite clarity?"

"Perhaps you are right," I said with a sigh. "But I feel every bit the quarter moon I was that night: foolish and undeveloped in the ways my mother values. She sees me as old and desperate because I am unmarried at twenty-two."

"Well, that is not your fault." Mayme chuckled. "She was determined to pair you with Louis Calvert even though everyone in the county could see he was full of wanderlust and not the marrying kind. When he ran off to chase a different life, the scandal rocked your mother as much as it did his own family."

"I admire Louis's courage. He dares to live the life he has chosen without the burden of expectation."

I smiled, remembering the dear friend who had never misrepresented himself to me. His desire for adventure could not be bridled even when he was a young boy. He would gallop his horse the three miles that stretched from his family's plantation to ours, just to explore the woods and highlands of our expansive property. Much to Mother's chagrin, Louis would drag me off to romp in the streams and thickets. He taught me to fish and showed me how to devise a snare to trap rabbits. It certainly was not the dainty behavior of a lady that was so often preached to me in Mother's biting words.

Even then, Papa and Mother's arguments centered on me. Papa indulged my tomboyish activity, I supposed because he had no son, but my penchant for rough and indelicate recreation made Mother seethe. Papa insisted my interests were harmless and made me all the more compatible with Louis. Our families may have thought us the perfect couple, but he and I knew our futures would never be joined. As I expected, when he turned eighteen, Louis's need to explore reached beyond the immediate North Carolina hills. So with an affectionate embrace, he bid me farewell and left behind a life that could no longer hold him.

I loved him as I would a brother and I cheered his courage to break free of tradition. Yet, in the aftermath of the scandal, I was viewed as a blemished woman, which kept other potential suitors at bay. After several years and much prodding from my mother, Garrison began an apathetic courtship. My dearth of suitors and deeply rooted desire for a home filled with children showered with maternal love made me lower my standards of decency. However, my wonderful dream soon became a nightmare.

"Am I foolish for not feeling indebted to Garrison?"

Mayme resumed stroking my hair. "Nonsense, child. You possess a natural and unassuming beauty that radiates from you, inside and out. Claudia's criticism and obsession with your appearance have made you self-conscious and unsure. Your golden complexion and rich mahogany hair are eclipsed only by the pull of your warm smile."

Her words were like a healing ointment rubbed into a wound. "You are sweet, Mayme, but you are also my grandmother. You view me through loving eyes."

"Surely Garrison sees all these treasures and more."

"I am terrified of him."

Mayme lifted my chin to study my hazel eyes. "What has he done to make you fear him?"

Immediately, I regretted letting down my guard. If I revealed my humiliation to Mayme, she would tell my father. But would his eyes reflect a father's outrage or a man's acceptance of the natural order? Either scenario would leave me flooded with shame. The delicate subject of intimacy was not meant for open discussion. Oh, how I wished I had a close female friend to confide in. Unfortunately, the social circle in our county was small, and one by one, the girls my age had married respectable suitors and relocated to places like Charlotte and Asheville. The only hushed conversation I remembered came a few years back, when Louis's sister, Mary Elizabeth, was about to wed Chester Frederick, a skinny cotton broker from Alabama. I overheard her whisper to the older girls, "Mama says it's a messy and vile deed. She told me if I remain still and do not interrupt, it will conclude quickly."

I looked now into Mayme's concerned gaze. Though temptation twisted in me, I could not reveal an indiscretion that would sicken her with distress. Even if presented casually and she was sworn not to tell Papa, she would surely confront my mother, as she often had when I was younger and left bruised by my mother's harshness. The two women had always had a tense relationship. I assumed it was because they were so different in temperament. Over time, they had learned to tolerate each other politely for the good of the household. I loved my grandmother too much to allow my discomfort to cause her anguish, so I tried to make light of my comment.

"Pay no mind to my fretful insecurities, Mayme. I am a coward who is terrified of *everything*. Garrison. Mother. Sometimes I even fear the thoughts in my head. Feelings stray within me that prove me to be inadequate."

Mayme took my hand as I stood to leave. "You are not inadequate, Jacy. Nor are you a coward. You are a young woman still discovering new and unseen pearls of who you are. Let them enrich you. Do not fear knowing yourself. When you face what you fear, you will be liberated. That includes your mother and Garrison alike."

I pondered Mayme's odd proclamation as I retired to my room. She was a wise old woman, but equally perplexing at times. Moonlight poured through every one of my bedroom windows. I stepped onto the second-floor balcony and gazed across the acreage of Great Meadow. The stable, barn, tack room, and pastures were bathed in the heavenly glow. The clapboard cabins of our slave quarters huddled within a modest grove of poplars in the distance. I guessed we had twenty-six slaves in all and the usual staples required to keep a plantation self-sufficient. We had cows for milk and butter. Our henhouses were filled with chickens, some to lay eggs and others to be plucked. The fields beyond the quarters were abundant with wheat, corn, alfalfa, potatoes, okra, turnips, and carrots. We had an orchard of apple and cherry trees, and a large pond that supplied catfish in the summer for frying and ice in the winter to maintain the icehouse year-round. Our smithy's forge lay beyond the barn. A busy cookhouse stood in the side yard, off the kitchen near the privy.

Despite the vastness of the property, it was the horses that made Great Meadow truly great. Papa bred palominos, pintos, Appaloosas, and quarter horses. All were considered the finest in the state of North Carolina. Papa had learned the intricacies of horse breeding from a slave named Cleon, who came to Great Meadow when Mayme and Grandpa were master and mistress. When Grandpa died of influenza, Papa expanded the stable with the help of Cleon. Tragically, Cleon succumbed to the bite of a cottonmouth when his son, Rafe, was only fifteen, but under his father's guidance the boy had already gained expert knowledge and understanding of horses.

In the eight years since his father's death, Rafe had grown into a dependable stable hand and skilled horseman who remained humble in spite of being a slave of high value and great demand. From the time we were children, Rafe had intrigued me. A year apart in age, he often played with me when we were youngsters. Mother was rather reclusive when it came to social activities with plantation families in the surrounding countryside, and even though she professed religion, I had no recollection of attending church on a regular basis. Therefore, the slave children were periodically brought from the quarters to play in the front yard under Jerlinda's supervision while Mother watched through the curtains of a second-floor window.

A chorus of snorts and whinnies stirred in the stable, pulling me from my reminiscence. I looked down and saw Axel, another stable hand, staring at me from the door of the tack room. He flinched as if he considered ducking inside, but he knew I had seen him. Instead, he stepped into the moonlit yard and walked along the fence where Garrison had pinned me earlier. As he passed the front of the house, he looked up at me and nodded. Something inside of me twisted. Twice in one evening I had caught a slave's eyes upon me. Mother would have him whipped for such a bold indiscretion, even though Axel had always been as docile as a puppy. I wondered whether Rafe had whispered to him of Garrison's power over me. Flushed with anger and embarrassment, I opted to shoo him away as I would a stray cat.

"Scat, Axel!" I backhanded my insistence toward the path to the quarters. "Go back to the quarters or I shall report you to Papa."

Axel frowned at my directive. His lips pursed tightly, giving the impression of disappointment and slight annoyance. I had never seen him unmask a negative emotion. Seeing it now pinched me with discomfort. It had been more than fifteen years since Nat Turner's slave rebellion slaughtered fifty-five white men, women, and children in Virginia, but the threat was still whispered among slaveholders as they bartered away unruly chattel or engaged in political debate.

I was never taught to fear the Negroes, but Mother had a deep distaste for them. I am not sure why, because I found them to be kind and diligent in their duties. However, Mother loved to mumble her distrust in the throes of a fit about Papa's lack of force when commanding our slaves.

"I sleep with one eye open because of your leniency," she often barked at him. "They have slain me in spirit and would finish me off in the flesh if given the chance."

Mother was always so dramatic in her proclamations. Unfortunately, her oft-stated accusations unsettled me. I should not have scolded Axel. It was not my nature to hurl unkind words. Had Mother's harsh demeanor hardened my heart?

Garrison and Mother were similar in their ambition to secure wealth and social prominence. It was Mother who first coaxed Garrison to call on me. We had met him at a cotillion on an estate near his home outside the town of South Mills. Satisfied with my physical and financial attributes, he began the courtship slowly. His carriage ride to our doorstep took several hours, so Mother sealed the bond by inviting him to stay in our downstairs guest room on Friday and

Saturday nights to accelerate the romance. Garrison had used his charm and wit to ingratiate himself with Papa, though he did not afford me the same effort.

Are all courtships this hollow?

I left the balcony for the sanctuary of my room. Peeking through my window drapes, I watched Axel continue along the path to the quarters. When he disappeared into the poplars, I climbed into bed. Sleep did not come for some time as thoughts of Garrison fanned my anxiety. Drained by ebbing emotion, I dropped into a deep slumber for what seemed like only a moment, when I was jolted awake by someone pounding on my door.

"Jacy, come downstairs immediately!"

Papa's voice was unusually brusque and forceful. The gray of dawn was warming to yellow with the rising of the sun. I pulled on my silk robe and descended the staircase. Something must be dreadfully wrong. My thoughts went to Mayme and her failing health. I braced for sorrow as I entered the dining room, but Mother's face was ripe with anger. To my surprise, Papa's scowl furrowed deeper than hers. They both stared at me, spurring my heart into a panicked gallop.

Finally, Mother turned her back to me as Papa crossed the room to grip my shoulders. "Jacy, is it true that Garrison has been forcing himself on you?"

"What?"

Mother spun around, her eyes wild. "There! Are you satisfied? Did you run off and whine to your father to spite me?"

"Claudia, I told you that Jacy did not alert me to Garrison's denigrating behavior," he spat with contempt. Then he looked at me, his eyes glistening with regret. "Although I wish she had."

"Lower your voice, Bradford," Mother pleaded. "He will hear you."

"Good," Papa said, his chin raised. "Let him face me, man-to-man, before I throw him from my home."

Mother gasped. "You wouldn't!"

"Rafe is hitching the lecher's horse to his carriage as we speak." The words had barely left Papa's lips when Garrison came strolling through the doorway, smoothing his dark hair behind his ears.

"Why so much commotion at this early hour?" He yawned nonchalantly, unaware he was the cause. "I thought I had overslept."

Before Garrison had taken two steps into the room, Papa bolted toward him and leveled him with one ferocious punch to his pompous face. Garrison yelped in shock as he hit the floor. Papa stood over him, both fists clenched, as Garrison lay sprawled on his back in the hall entrance of the dining room. "The wedding is off, you swine! Leave my property at once and stay away from my daughter."

Still dazed, Garrison struggled to sit up. Papa strode down the hallway to the guest room and returned with a hastily stuffed bag in his hand just as Garrison pulled himself onto his feet. Papa shoved him backward across the hallway as Garrison stumbled frantically to keep from falling until he slammed into the front door.

Garrison flushed with anger as he pushed Papa off of him. "You have made a grave mistake, Bradford," he snarled bitterly. His burning glare shifted my way. "You all have."

"Bradford, apologize to this man," Mother said, rushing to Garrison's side. "You are reacting to hearsay."

Papa yanked Mother from Garrison and swung open the door. "Get out of my house and never step foot on Great Meadow again or I will pummel you until you crawl from my land."

Garrison's bloody nostrils flared with fury. "I will not stand by and be disrespected by *any* man, Bradford. I shall answer your self-righteous tirade one day and then we'll see which of us is still standing and which of us is crawling. Have patches sewn to the knees of your breeches when next we meet."

My entire body quaked at the sudden turn of events. Through the open door, I could see Garrison mount his carriage and thunder away. Wild with anger, Mother turned to confront Papa.

"All my campaigning on her behalf is now laid to waste. What chance does she have, Bradford? She is nothing more than a qua—" The slap of Papa's hand against her face shocked me as much as it did Mother. Her eyes went wide and then drained of emotion.

"Don't you dare utter a word against my beautiful little girl." Papa took me by the elbow and guided me to the staircase. "Go on back to bed, sweetheart. I just wanted you to know that you will never again be victim to the likes of Garrison Yob. Now I must take a brisk walk to calm my anger."

"Thank you, Papa," I said as he patted my cheek with reassurance. When he left, I stood alone and disgraced by the discovered truth. How did he know what had transpired? The expulsion of Garrison from my life was an unequivocal relief. But the loss of my innocence in my father's eyes was one last degradation imprinted on me by Garrison, and by my mother in her willingness to sacrifice my happiness for her gain. It clung to me like the soot of a damp wood fire.

"You have no idea what you have done," Mother's voice hissed from behind me. She came around to bore her dark eyes into mine. "This is not finished, Jacy. I have done my best with you, but your feral ways cannot be dressed over. You have thrown away a life of security and you deserve what will come of it. In fact, you will be *shocked*. So don't expect to run to your mother when your life falls apart."

She started to walk away and then paused to indulge in a wry smile. "On second thought, that would be a perfect and fitting reward for my efforts. Then we'll see who has the last laugh. I guarantee it will not be you!"

I stood there stunned, feeling empty and confused by yet another verbal lashing from my mother. What made me so repugnant and flawed in her eyes? And why was it impossible for her to love me in spite of my imperfections? I would trade all of my finery and advantages if only my mother would open her heart and embrace me, but instinct told me she would despise me all the more.

Chapter 2

"*Mama! Mama!*" *The baby girl's frantic cries echoed in the darkness. A violent jerk numbed my body as if it were being kicked in the chest by an angry colt. Suddenly, Mother's face appeared in front of me.* "*It's Mother, you quarter moon. Say it . . . Moth-er!*"

My eyes sprang wide and were stung by the sharp rays of mid-morning. Still surging from the bizarre nightmare that had awakened me, my heart stuttered as I stared at the ceiling and composed my wits. The strange dream was familiar to me and popped often into the inevitable restless slumber that followed one of Mother's tirades. After all these years, the pattern was predictable. Mother would come undone in a vicious fit and then sink into melancholy for a few days or weeks. Eventually her spirits soared and she became overly attentive to me, as if making amends for her cruel outburst. However, the next round of fits would soon follow.

"Good morning, Mayme." Neither Papa nor Mother was present when I entered the dining room. I waited until Jerlinda poured my tea and left the room before I questioned Mayme. "Is it just the two of us this morning?"

"Your father is busy in the stable. Tomorrow he will be herding some horses to market."

"Yes, he mentioned he would be passing off a delivery at Dismal Swamp," I said, sipping my tea as I broached the true focus of my curiosity. "And Mother?"

Mayme glanced up over her teacup. "I heard about what happened earlier. Claudia is sequestered in her bedchamber with a migraine. I should have recognized something was amiss when you came to my room last night. I say good riddance to Garrison Yob. He doesn't deserve you, Jacy." Mayme reached to tenderly squeeze my hand. "Are you all right, dear? You look deeply forlorn, as so often happens after Claudia unfairly lashes out at you. I suspect she may not share my opinion that you are better off without that cad. What did she say to you?"

"Nothing that she hasn't said a hundred other times," I said dismissively. "Rehashing the incident with you would torment both of us. Besides, a great weight has been lifted from my shoulders."

Mayme studied me, her weary eyes filled with worry. "I don't want to add to your distress, child. My only wish is for your happiness."

I leaned over and kissed Mayme's wrinkled cheek. "What will make me happy is embracing the wonder of a new day. With Mother absorbed in her gloom, I shall take advantage of the momentary immunity and join Papa in his morning routine. There is a new foal at the stable. Perhaps he will let me groom her."

"You are a lover of all living things." Mayme laughed. "I am sure your father will indulge your tender heart just as his father did his. Be discreet, sweet girl. If Claudia finds you are tiptoeing in the manure and sunshine, you know what will happen."

"I know," I said with a mischievous grin. "She will sentence me to a long soak in lavender water and dust me with an extra layer of powder."

Mayme winked her encouragement. "Well, if it's worth the risk, then go and enjoy yourself."

On the porch, I breathed in the freshness of the day as I tied my bonnet snugly on my head. The length of the brim snuffed the sun from my face. Mother's insistence that I wear the widest of brimmed hats was an obsession. She often lectured me on the delicate appeal of clear, milky skin. I, on the other hand, thought colorless cheeks hinted at a sickly demeanor and reflected the natural appearance of a corpse, but when I did not comply with her "stay out of the sunshine" edict, I was forced to endure extended periods in front of the looking glass watching her coat my tanned skin with pearl-flecked face powder. As young as five or six years of age, I remember the dusty cloud swirling between us as I coughed and sneezed beneath the smattering of verbal jabs and powdered cotton bolls.

"Papa?"

The aroma and activity of the stable brought my senses alive. Horses scuffed and snorted in their stalls, awaiting their release to the fields. I was never one to shrink from outdoorsy delights, even when I had to shoo away an occasional field mouse or potato spider. So I strolled across the straw-covered floor without a care. As I neared the tack room, Axel appeared from inside, flinching at my sudden appearance. His undersized frame leaned to one side, the result of one leg being slightly shorter than the other and marred by a misshapen foot. The spark of recognition that glimmered in his light brown eyes quickly clouded over in discomfort. He lowered his gaze, lifted a bucket, and limped to the rear door.

When Axel disappeared into the outer corral, a wave of guilt washed over me. I had never reprimanded any of our slaves as I had Axel from my balcony the previous night. I had taken out my frustration and shame on him, yet it surprised me that he appeared to feel hurt in return. What a silly notion to detect in a slave. He had not been whipped or branded. Perhaps my guilt had me imagining deeply welling feelings where only a puddle could find depth enough to pool.

The low hush of a playful voice drew my attention to the far end of the stable. I peeked between the stalls and saw Rafe stroking an Appaloosa foal, its hide snowy white with chocolate brown spots of different sizes. The day-old horse stood on wobbly legs as one of Rafe's strong, lean arms cradled her withers.

"Go on now, lonely girl. Take ahold and suckle some milk. It ain't the same as a real mama, but it's gonna have to do."

I smiled in amusement at his gentle urgings. His slouch hat was pushed back on his head, revealing a smooth, chestnut face beneath a cap of knitted hair. His earnest eyes sparkled above his crinkled round nose as the foal latched onto the kidney sac he offered and found its nourishment.

"That's it, pretty thing." He grinned as he patted the base of her neck. "If you let ol' Rafe care for you, you'll grow into a fine filly."

I tried to remain hidden, but the sight of this serious, rugged man whispering in the speckled ear of a horse prompted a giggle from my lips. He straightened to his full height and twisted his head to scan the shadows of the surrounding stalls. His clear dark eyes fluttered when his gaze fell upon me. He turned quickly back to the horse.

"Sorry, miss. I didn't hear you come in."

"I am looking for my father," I said as I sidled toward the stall where Rafe coddled the orphaned foal. I could not help but be pulled toward the innocence exuded by both the needy animal and its gallant caregiver. Both Rafe and the foal jostled nervously when I approached the stall.

"Marster Lane took Titus down to the mill to sack some oats for the trip."

Rafe stepped back from the young horse when I reached out to stroke its muzzle. I pressed my cheek between the large, doll-like eyes. The gesture appeared to ease its jitters, and Rafe's as well.

"She is beautiful."

"Yes, miss, but she's without a mama to fuss on her."

I smiled. "She is lucky to have found warmth and a safe haven in your care. Have you named her?"

Rafe shrugged. "Thought the name Eclipse might suit her, since her color is a mix o' sunshine and shadows."

"It is, indeed." Patting her soft brown shoulders, I took notice of the makeshift udder he held in his hands. "How did you get her to take milk from that kidney sac?"

He lifted the dripping concoction. "I cut loose a teat from her poor dead mama and asked Jerlinda to sew it to the neck of the sac. Ain't very natural, but after coaxin' her all mornin' she finally got the knack of it."

I laughed as milk ran down his arm and onto his boots. "Not an easy feat, by the look of you."

His mouth relaxed into a soft grin. "Well, I ain't made for motherin'."

"Oh, yes, you are."

I wanted to tell him that I remembered how he had taken Axel under his wing when the boy was shuffled around because of his physical shortcomings. Rafe had worked with him many nights after the other slaves were dismissed to their quarters, until Axel was capable in his duties and eventually became one of Papa's favored stable hands.

"Jacy!" Papa's voice was warm with surprise and pleasure. "What brings you here?"

"Rafe was introducing me to the new foal. I love her tenacious spirit. Her gut-wrenching loss has not broken her will to survive."

"A life lesson for all of us, my dear." Papa smiled at my interest.

"Since you recognize the foal's special nature, I want you to have her. She is a gift from me to you."

"Oh, Papa! I shall prize her always!"

He laughed at my exuberance. I suspect the gift was his way of distracting me from my collapsed engagement to Garrison, but to me it was like sprinkling sugar on a gumdrop. Both brought me sweet satisfaction.

"Give some thought to the name you will give her, Jacy. When you decide, I will mark it in my log."

"With Rafe's help, I have chosen a name. We shall call her Eclipse."

Papa nodded. "Very well." Rafe busied himself at the rear of the stall, but I saw his lips turn up in a grin.

I stroked Eclipse's white mane. "May I attend to her while you are away?"

"I'm not sure that's a good idea," Papa said as his brow furrowed with doubt. "I don't mind you visiting the stable, but having you engaged in any kind of manly chore is unthinkable. You have not been raised to serve."

"But, Papa," I pleaded, "caring for Eclipse would not be a chore. It would be a pleasure, like painting or knitting."

Papa laughed. "Lord knows you are less squeamish and far more physically fit than any young lady in this county or the next. Your mother thinks I have cursed you by indulging your love of the outdoors."

"How could it be a curse, Papa, when I love it so much?" I smiled when I saw his expression soften.

"Well, I suppose I can have Titus prepare a kidney sac so you can provide her first feeding of the day. Anything more will set off your mother, so let's leave it at that."

"Thank you, Papa," I said, squeezing him around the waist. I glanced over at Rafe. "I shall take good care of her."

Papa kissed my forehead and hugged me to him. "You are a good-hearted girl, Jacy," he said, his voice hushed by emotional strain. "And you are born of strong, daring parents who do not fear an uncommon challenge. Don't ever let anyone break your spirit."

I sensed he was referring to Garrison and the dissolved engagement. "I won't, Papa, ever again."

Shame pricked my conscience when Papa excused himself. Awkward silence fell between Rafe and me as our unspoken knowledge of what had occurred the previous night became laced with our discomfort. I knew he would never speak of it, but I could not let the moment pass without comment. To maintain propriety, I focused on Eclipse and did not look at Rafe when I spoke with delicate discretion.

"Last night's interruption was a blessing. I am glad you came along when you did."

"So am I," he said, turning respectfully away to spare me further embarrassment. The thought struck me that perhaps Rafe had reported the encounter to Papa, but I quickly dismissed the idea that a slave would question the actions of a man who would one day be his master. Still, I left the stall with gracious proof that Rafe possessed more gentlemanly manners than Garrison could ever summon with regard to my feelings. Rafe's presence was a blessing indeed.

The next morning I went to the stable and mothered Eclipse. Without a word, Titus gruffly handed me the milk sac when I arrived. I generally felt at home around our slaves because most of them had been a part of Great Meadow's landscape for my entire life. The exception was Titus, who'd been purchased after Rafe's father died. He was twice Rafe's age, with a thick beard that contrasted with his thinning hair. He did not carry himself with the gentleness of Rafe or Axel.

In fact, Mayme said that Titus and his wife, Tess, often stirred trouble in the quarters by reporting the transgressions and shortcomings of other slaves. Their betrayal of their fellows did not impress Papa, but Mother rewarded Tess by plucking her from the fields and raising her station to the cookhouse. Mother wanted to displace Jerlinda in favor of Tess for house duties, but Papa was emphatic that Tess's tattling would not be her ticket into the main house.

Two days passed quickly as I stayed focused on the foal's needs, leaving me little time to fret over my discomfort around Titus. I secretly wished that Papa's return from South Mills would be delayed a day or so to give me more time to bond with Eclipse. She had become sturdy on her legs and seemed to dance with excitement when I appeared at her stall each morning.

"Even the dark patches and speckles on her creamy coat have deepened into shiny perfection," I boasted to Mayme over supper. "Eclipse may be the most distinctive Appaloosa on the farm."

Mayme laughed at my cheerful oracle. "Well, she must be special. The helpless little thing has captured your heart in no time at all."

"Who has captured your heart?" Mother's hoarse voice came from the doorway behind me. From my angle, I could not see her, but Mother's presence was reflected in Mayme's eyes, as a defensive veil draped their softness.

"No one," I said as Mother cleared her throat and came to join us at the table. She wore a wrinkled bed jacket and her onyx hair was pinned carelessly in clumps at the back of her head.

"Are you strong enough to be out of bed?" Mayme's question was neither harsh nor sympathetic, but Mother ignored it as she reached to pat my hand.

"The lilt of your voice coaxed me downstairs. What has you feeling so gay?"

Mother had obviously turned the corner from depression to remorse, and though I owed her no compassion, my heart could not help but mellow at her vulnerability. "I was telling Mayme about a precious foal that is new to our herd."

Mother's pale lips lifted into a faint smile. "Ah, horses are noble creatures indeed. There is no feeling equal to bouncing along with the rhythmic stride of a stallion."

Mother's confession surprised me. "I didn't know you liked to ride."

Her smile faded. "It feels like a lifetime ago, when joy was not so hard to come by."

There it was. The glimpse of her secret self that made me want to know more and to be closer to her. "Did your family breed horses too?"

Mother's eyes became tender with thought. "Tobacco was the cash crop of our plantation, but we had a fine stable of horses beyond those that worked our fields. My older sister, Sarah, and I were accomplished riders."

"I had no idea," I said. "You rarely mention Aunt Sarah."

"I have not seen her in years," Mother said as her gaze clouded with anguish. "She met a gentleman from Charleston, South Carolina, and moved there after they were married. Father died two years later after a short malaise. Debts accumulated quickly and Mother hoped Sarah's husband would lend his support. Unfortunately, he was not interested in saving the plantation, only in selling it. We lost our farm, our home, and life as we knew it."

Shaken by her tale, I reached my hand toward her. As subtly as Mother had offered her remembrance, she pulled herself away when Jerlinda entered the room with a tray of smoked ham and squash.

Mother remained quiet and detached during most of the meal, while Mayme smiled at my enthusiastic account of the young horse and her needs.

"I believe she thinks of me as her mother. She grows playful and nuzzles beneath my arm when I greet her."

"Of course," Mayme said. "You have nourished and nurtured her in her early hours. That initial attachment of the heart is quick and steadfast. You will always stir affection in her."

"And she in me," I said, warmed by love.

The clamor of a horse galloping into the front yard caught our attention. Mother rose from the table. "Who would call on us after dark?"

No sooner had the words left her lips than the rapid pounding of a fist against the door caused Jerlinda to hurry from the kitchen to the front entrance. She returned to the dining room with a middle-aged gentleman whose light windblown hair and dusty clothing marked a swift and urgent journey. The man's smooth face grimaced as he nervously cleared his throat, revealing teeth as wide and white as sugar cubes. Without waiting for Jerlinda to announce him, the stranger took a deep breath.

"Ladies, my name is Sylvan Firth from South Mills. Pardon the intrusion, but I come bearing tragic news."

My heart skipped in my breast at his pronouncement. Suddenly, Mayme was by my side, gripping my hand tightly in hers. "Tell us without delay, Mr. Firth. Please do not prolong our panic."

He cleared his throat again as if it would soften his decree. "I regret to inform you that Mr. Bradford Lane was killed while protecting his herd at the town livery."

My mind and body went numb as Mother gasped behind me. Mayme's hand trembled in mine. His voice continued, but his words echoed without form in my head, as though I were standing inside a cavernous, empty hallway where his sympathetic proclamations bounced from wall to wall. Mayme wobbled against me.

"Sit, Mayme," I said, easing her into a chair. Tears flooded her eyes and I knew my duty was to remain strong for her in spite of the heavy ache that sank within me. "Mr. Firth, please tell me you are mistaken. My father cannot be dead."

Mother glided between us as if she were keeping him from stepping toward me. "The man would not ride all this way unless he was certain." Her even shoulders and rigid back gave Mother an air of composed dignity, though her words were oddly curt as she addressed the shaken messenger. "Tell us what you know, Mr. Firth."

"It was a tragic turn of events," he said with earnest sympathy. "A rogue skunk wandered into the livery, causing a ruckus among the horses. When the animal released its spray, one of the palominos was blinded. In its madness, the horse kicked through the stable wall. Bradford tried to intervene, but before the animal could be put out of its misery, Bradford was trampled."

I burst into tears. Mayme gathered me into her arms and we sobbed together. Mr. Firth offered me his handkerchief as Mother continued questioning him. I could not bear to hear any further details, so I wept until I fell silent with exhaustion. Nearly an hour had passed and Mr. Firth still stood before us, never having been offered a chair.

"Please sit, sir," I said softly. "You have made great effort to deliver our heartbreak with care and kindness."

Mother's chin quivered as she struggled to maintain her composure. "I am sure Mr. Firth would prefer to begin his journey back to South Mills."

He looked at her with surprise and then nodded as if recognizing that he had overstayed his welcome. "Indeed, I should be on my way."

"Mother, the least we can do is to provide Mr. Firth with a night's rest. He has honored Papa by coming here."

Mother never shifted her eyes from our visitor, nor did she offer an invitation. He turned to Mayme and me. "It may comfort you to know that I administered last rites. I am a lockmaster by trade, but in my younger years, I studied at the seminary. I have the authority to oversee funeral and burial arrangements. If you wish, I can escort the body home and assist you with these delicate matters."

"That won't be necessary," Mother said as she brushed away a lone tear that trickled down her cheek. "I ask only that you direct my stable boys to bring him home in a sturdy coffin."

The muscles along the man's jawline clenched, but his eyes flickered softly when he extended his hand to me. "I have done what I set out to do. Your father was a good man whom I respected and admired. You have my deepest sympathy."

"Thank you, Mr. Firth."

Mother turned her back to him before he could address her. "See to it that my two servants find their way home and nowhere else."

Mr. Firth paused at the door. "They will arrive tomorrow by wagon with the body of your husband. With your permission, I shall conclude his business in South Mills as a final gesture of respect and friendship."

"I expect nothing less," she said without a word of thanks or farewell as she shut the door behind him.

My eyes burned with a mix of grief and anger at Mother's insistence on Mr. Firth's abrupt exit. How could her feelings be so cold and controlled in the face of such tragedy? Even poor Jerlinda leaned in the doorway of the kitchen, holding her apron to her face.

"Have you a heart of stone? The man was here on Papa's behalf," I said.

Mother pulled back the drapes to watch him ride away. "That

man is a viper. I know him only by reputation, but Sylvan Firth is said to be a treasonous dissident, no different from the Northern abolitionists who judge us from afar. He is not welcome in this house."

Mother's words sparked Mayme from her gloom. "How the man directs his compassion should be of no concern to us. We have lost Bradford. My son is dead!"

Mother fled from Mayme's cry and closed herself off in her bedchamber. Supporting Mayme by the elbow, I guided her up the stairs and into bed. Her thin frame was swallowed by the feather-stuffed mattress, making her look helpless and drained. I climbed beneath the covers and curled up beside her. A thousand thoughts of Papa rushed through my mind. I closed my eyes and conjured the image of his bright smile, which had always been a beacon of love. Pain settled into my breast with the weight of a boulder times ten. I could not breathe against the burden of it. The harder I tried to draw breath, the more panicked I became in my disbelief.

My papa is dead. How shall I bear it? What will we do without him? Don't leave, Papa. I love you.

"I have directed Jerlinda to search my trunks for the mourning attire I wore when my mother passed away the month after I was married," Mother declared as I descended the stairs the next morning. "It will require alteration for your lesser frame, but will be suitable enough."

Mother's affect was flat. What could have been mistaken for detachment appeared to be the result of drained emotion. She guarded her tears as closely as she had the struggles of her youth. I suspected she had been up most of the night preparing the black dress she now wore, complete with long, heavy veil. Crape covered the windows and the reflecting glass in the hallway, creating a shadowed gloominess that matched the veil over my heart. Mother peeked out the front door when the slow creak of wagon wheels came from the long lane that entered our property.

She smoothed her veil into place and stepped into the shadows of the room. "Your father has arrived," she said as if he were returning from the fields for dinner. "You must go and attend to him so I can maintain proper appearance."

The sight of the buckboard tore my heart in two. Rafe drooped over the reins next to a man I did not recognize. Axel sat in the bed of the wagon, his arm and head resting in sorrow on the wooden box carrying my father. The reality of the moment quaked my knees and shoulders so intensely it might have appeared I stood on the porch in the throes of a winter gale. But even the warm summer morning could not protect me from the chill of death.

When Rafe guided the wagon into the front yard, his cheeks were moist with tears. The stranger climbed from the bench seat and came to me with his hands outstretched. He was cloaked in a heavy black frock and wore a clergyman's hat. Long strands of thin, silver hair dangled across his shoulders.

"I offer my deepest condolences, Miss Lane. I am Parson Shull from Elizabeth City. Sylvan Firth called on me to escort the deceased home. I am experienced in the business of laying out the dead, and he asked me to do all in my power to ease your burden in this time of grief."

His words floated away on the breeze as I approached my father's coffin. Axel clutched the cedar lid as if unwilling to let go. He wiped his sleeve across his face when he saw my hand press against the smooth wood finish.

"We's sorry, Miss Jacy," he said in a voice tight with despair. "It was done and over before—" Axel's voice hitched. Unable to continue, he eased from the wagon and hobbled toward the stable as sobs ripped from his throat without pause.

Tears clung in heavy droplets on my lashes, but I did not release them. Here, in spiritual witness of my father, I vowed to honor him by remaining stalwart. Mother was consumed with her role as widow, and Mayme's days of matriarchal leadership on the farm were behind her. This left me to fill the void, though I did not know how to begin.

"Miss Lane?" The parson's gray eyes beckoned me for a response.

"Pardon me?" I muttered when his curt voice halted my pondering.

"Where should I instruct your slaves to carry the coffin?"

Emotion overwhelmed my thoughts. I felt abandoned in my sorrow and responsibility. Behind Parson Shull, Rafe climbed from the wagon and looked to me with steady eyes. Something in his rugged demeanor reassured me.

"Parson, perhaps you should pay your respects to my mother while I gather my thoughts."

"As you wish," he said with a nod.

When the clergyman disappeared into the house, Rafe stepped to the rear of the wagon. He crumpled his slouch hat in his hands, waiting for me to speak. My eyes shifted from him to the coffin and then back to him. Tears welled in my eyes from sorrow and uncertainty. Relief came when Rafe eased closer.

"Would you like me to gather some o' the men from the quarters and move your daddy to the parlor?"

"To the parlor?" I hesitated to consider his question and then realized he was gently offering his guidance. "Yes, the parlor would be the appropriate place."

"Axel and me will dig a hole over in the graveyard, next to your grandfather."

"Yes, a grave," I stammered. "We must prepare a grave."

He waited for me to say more. When no instructions followed, he gave me another verbal nudge. "Do you want me to call the slaves to the porch to be given the news or would you like me to talk to them myself, down below?"

"Um, perhaps you should deliver the news. Mother will want to address them formally at some point, but it may be several days before she is prepared to do so."

I was grateful that Rafe took on the burden of announcing the dreadful news. As we spoke, his face grew so ashen I thought he must be in physical pain. He shifted anxiously on his feet, waiting for me to excuse myself so he could attend to his duties. I ascended the steps of the porch, but Rafe remained in place.

I cocked my head. "What is it, Rafe? I sense there is more you wish to say."

He stepped forward to close the distance between us. "I share your hurt, Miss Jacy. Your papa believed that no creature deserves to be treated cruelly or with force. Not his daughter, not his horses, not even his slaves. All of us at Great Meadow will weep when I tell them Marster Lane is dead."

Tears glimmered in his eyes and I knew his words were genuine and deeply felt. An odd attachment tugged between us in our shared loss. "Thank you, Rafe."

The next two days blended into one long vigil of sitting in witness of the lifeless body dressed in his finest suit. Candles were lit around the room and flowers brought in, their fragrance slowly waning to the odor of rotting flesh. A stream of neighbors and business associates came and went as we awaited Papa's interment. Two distant cousins arrived by carriage and were of great comfort to Mayme, though Mother watched them suspiciously.

"They are probably here to poach my land," she said when I brought her a glass of lemonade. "Greedy vultures. No different from when my brother-in-law made our wealth his own after my father died."

"I am sure you are mistaken, Mother. They spoke to me with great affection for Papa."

"Well, I am one step ahead of them," she muttered under her breath.

Her state of mind concerned me. Perhaps it was caused by her grief, but Mother seemed preoccupied and defensive. "Mother, I would like to write a letter to Aunt Sarah to share the news of our loss. Having your sister come to lend her care and support in the coming months would be good for you."

"Listen to me, Jacy," she said, setting her glass aside so she could clutch my wrist. "I forbid you from contacting Sarah. I will not share my hardship with her."

"But, Mother, Mayme told me Aunt Sarah is a kindhearted woman."

"A kindhearted woman would not have allowed her husband to manipulate Mother and me into dire straits." Mother's pain was evident as tears slipped down her cheeks. "I vowed never to speak to her again."

"But, Mother—"

"Not another word, Jacy." She dabbed her eyes until her detached facade returned. "I have learned to protect what is mine. No outsider will ever again snatch what rightfully belongs to me."

As was the custom, Mother, Mayme, and I shared in the task of staying up through the nights to sit with Papa. However, by the third evening, Mayme was exhausted in mind and body.

"I will sit with him tonight, Mayme," I said as I led her to her room. It was still early in the evening, but her eyes were heavy with sleep.

"Do not carry the burden for both of us," she said weakly.

"Honestly, Mayme, my heart needs this final night to say good-bye. Papa will be buried tomorrow, and I have yet to give up on my hope that he will climb from his box to embrace me. Perhaps I will accept his fate in the coming hours, when at last he will prove to be at rest."

Mayme reluctantly agreed. The house was eerily still as I descended the stairs. Mother had retired earlier and was not expected to reappear until morning. However, as I entered the parlor, I heard light footsteps scampering down the hallway beyond the doorway across the room. They moved too quickly to be Mother's, so I followed them through the shadows of the house. The outer door of the kitchen creaked shut as I entered from the dining room. Spooked by the intruder, I peered from the window and caught a glimpse of a slight figure slipping into the wood.

My skin prickled at the bizarre occurrence. I remained at the window until I was certain the prowler was gone and harbored no threat. When my rush of fear subsided, I returned to the parlor and settled in the rocker that faced the coffin. The room was gloomy and stifled by the aroma of death. The comfort of having my father at home dissipated with his departed spirit. I felt guilty for feeling so, but burying what remained of him would be a relief. My eyes clouded with despair until the flickering candlelight revealed three rose petals scattered across the wooden floorboards. I followed their path to the coffin and looked inside. I could not bear to gaze upon my father's sunken cheeks, but there, tucked in his lapel, was a vibrant crimson rose, and for one brief moment he was my papa again. I pondered the unknown footsteps. Who would leave such a loving tribute in secrecy? The sweetness of the gesture resonated within me as I stroked my father's dark hair one last time.

Thump, thump, thump. The sound awakened me where I slouched in the rocker. The sun was barely over the horizon, yet I recognized the unmistakable sound of someone at our door. The early hour meant Jerlinda was still in the cookhouse, so I smoothed my clothing and crossed the entrance hall. When I opened the door, a sickening chill rushed through me.

"Garrison!"

His dull eyes shifted up and down my disheveled appearance. "Good morning, Jacy. I am here to pay my respects."

I tried closing the door, but his thick fingers caught my wrist as he stepped inside. "It is very rude of you not to invite me in."

"You are not welcome here. If you wish to pay your respects, do so by honoring my father's command."

His chin lifted in amusement. "I have come out of respect for your mother, not your father."

I pulled my wrist from his grasp. "You have no place here, Garrison."

Suddenly, Mother's voice came from the stairs behind me. "I asked him to come."

"Mother!" I was shocked when she greeted him with a welcoming smile.

"Come in, Garrison," she said as she glanced at me with an air of satisfaction. "Jacy and I are honored by your visit. Please make yourself at home."

Chapter 3

"Mother, how could you?" I implored when Garrison finished his biscuits and disappeared to the privy. Mayme had been equally shocked to see him sitting at our breakfast table. So much so that she had excused herself with teacup in hand to return to her bedchamber. Even Jerlinda flinched when she entered the room, but she recovered quickly, before Mother took notice.

"How could I *what*, Jacy?"

"Bring *him* here. Papa has yet to be lowered into the ground and you have already desecrated his memory."

"Your *papa* is no longer here. We must move quickly to secure Great Meadow. I will not lose my home and status a second time."

I tossed my linen napkin onto the table. "I cannot stand the sight of Garrison Yob. He stalks me like a wolf to prey."

"Hmm." Mother smirked. "You fancy yourself quite desirable, do you?"

"I do not feel desirable in his presence," I stressed. "I feel demeaned. You must have some idea of how he treats me."

"Jacy, you have obligations to me and to this estate. Garrison is a lot like me. He was born into a prominent family, only to lose that status when his father mishandled the family's shipping business. Yet, with fierce determination and clever business practices, he has reclaimed his station."

"If you think Garrison is so fine, then why not marry him yourself?"

"I am too old to bear him children," she said as her voice tightened with impatience. "He wants a young and capable bride. In the absence of a son, I need your cooperation to maintain our assets. You will find no better match. Garrison is a respected member of the local gentry and aggressive in his desire to increase his wealth."

"He is aggressive in *all* his desires," I countered as I stood and crossed the room, pausing at the window. I watched the horses roam the pastures and wished I could escape the emotional lasso she was attempting to slip around my neck.

"Am I interrupting, ladies?" Garrison stood in the doorway with his hands gripped on his lapels. He was in a position of power and seemed to know it. "With your permission, Claudia, I will walk to your family plot on the hill and check that the Negroes have dug a suitable grave. We wouldn't want a disagreeable ghost looking over our shoulder for years to come."

Garrison chuckled at his callous remark, which made me bristle with fury. His pretense of helping my mother served to ingratiate him all the more. Mother was unfazed as she thanked him for his forethought in confirming that all was ready for the day's funeral. I stormed from the room by way of the kitchen. Jerlinda watched with puffy eyes as I made my escape through the side door. A half dozen dark faces peeked from the cookhouse, their sweat-drenched expressions pulled as tight as the cloth bandannas knotted on their heads. I fled to the stable, where I could duck into Eclipse's stall. I meant to stay only a few moments, but when I heard Parson Shull's carriage arrive, I realized I had passed an hour lost in the comfort of brushing the young foal gifted to me by my father.

"Excuse me, Miss Jacy." The worn boots that scuffed in the straw outside the stall were Rafe's. "They are lookin' for you over at the house."

"I needed some time alone," I said as he opened the door of the stall to coax me out. "Solitude helps me sort out the thoughts that are awhirl in me. Mother has always thought of me as inadequate. I guess she is right."

"Don't sell yourself short, miss. Our world is turned upside down now that your papa is gone. We all gots'ta figure out how to go on. That's plenty enough to get your head a-spinnin'." He paused to wipe a sudden flow of tears from his dark cheeks. "I remember when my daddy died, I thought the sun was never gonna shine again."

Rafe's emotion took me off guard. How could he understand and articulate the feeling so clearly? It seemed his emotions were no different from mine, yet he was a slave. "You were so stoic after Cleon died. You went on with your chores like any other day."

"Steppin' into my daddy's shoes was my way of honorin' him. Your papa knew it and let me carry on. Outta sight of the main house, I had days when my thoughts spun low and tears fell."

I puzzled over him. "I had no idea."

"Maybe not in your head, but your heart sensed it," he said. "One low-down day, I sat down by the pond feelin' lost and alone. You showed up from nowhere and handed me a yellow daffodil. Then you was gone in a flash, because your mama screamed at you from the front yard, but I never forgot you showin' care about my daddy."

I thought back on those younger years and the days following Cleon's death. Rafe and I had grown from children who played together without noticing our differences into a teenage boy and girl who were no longer allowed to associate as friends. A social chasm had opened between us and we fell naturally into our proper roles. In fact, the day I walked the flower down the hill to give to Rafe as a gesture of sorrow was my last foray into the vicinity of the slave quarters.

Mother was livid when she saw me with Rafe, away from the neutral ground provided by the main house and stable. Papa had tried to calm her, but she shrieked.

"Rein her in now, Bradford, before she cuts loose like a wild horse trying to catch the herd!"

Papa whisked me to my bedchamber to escape her fury. The image of him pacing my room rekindled the confused feelings that had tormented me that day, as if I had done something dreadfully wrong. When Papa finally sat me on the edge of the bed, his words were gentle but firm.

"Though you are not yet an adult, Jacy, you are also no longer a child. There are certain boundaries you must abide by to maintain the status of your upbringing. Your mother is especially rigid in this area, and in this case, I must agree. While I wish you to be cordial and respectful, please limit your interactions with the slaves to the immediate property around the main house."

"Why, Papa?"

His expression softened. *"Because it must be so."*

"What about the horses?" I said, biting my lip to keep from crying. *"Can I still visit the stable?"*

He tapped his chin while pondering my question. *"Since the stable and barn are at the edge of the yard and in close proximity to the house, I will allow you to come and go as you please. I am usually there, but I advise you to step forward as a mistress or Claudia will clip your wings further."*

Papa's long-ago urging to step forward as a mistress snapped me from the remembrance. Panic clenched in me when I looked to Rafe. "I forgot about you and the other slaves. No one has given you direction in your tasks for the past few days. My goodness, how will I keep the farm going?"

Rafe's mouth softened into a sympathetic smile. "Don't fret about the chores. Nothing's left undone. We'll just keep on doin' what we've always done. The farm won't never suffer from idle hands."

My impulse was to reach out in gratitude. However, the warmth stirred by Rafe's sensitivity unnerved me and I stepped backward. "I'd better return to the house and make ready for the funeral."

Rafe opened the gate to let me pass. "You done a good job with Eclipse while I was in South Mills. She don't have the lonely eyes of an orphan. You must have cradled her with love."

Still off balance from the inappropriate pull of his kindness, I reminded myself not to confuse sympathy with affection. I raised my chin to reestablish my mistresslike demeanor.

"I would like to continue caring for Eclipse after things settle down. I feel close to Papa here in the stable."

Rafe's eyes glimmered sadly. "Axel said the same this mornin'."

By midday, a group of neighbors and friends had arrived at the house. Mother, Mayme, and I rode in an open carriage behind the wagon that carried my father's coffin along the upper pasture to the family graveyard beneath the willows. The fields and outbuildings were empty, as every slave of Great Meadow stood along the route with nary a dry eye. When the interment was complete, dinner was served to our guests on tables set up in the front yard. Mother sat on the porch, draped in her widow's lace, as Mayme and I mingled with our guests. Tess emerged from the cookhouse to assist Jerlinda in serving an array of dishes that included smoked ham, okra, sweet potatoes, and bread pudding. Garrison stood in the shade of a red oak, sipping brandy and watching me move through the crowd.

As the late-afternoon shadows stretched across the lawn, neighbors offered sympathetic farewells, and a steady stream of carriages began exiting the property until all were gone. Too tired to speak, Mayme and I sipped sweet tea and reflected on the day. Jerlinda led the cookhouse women around the empty tables and chairs, clearing dishes, linens, and unfinished food. From her perch between the colonnades of the porch, Mother rose and descended toward us. Her lined face was hardened into a frown and I braced for a confrontation. To my surprise, she walked past me and continued to where Jerlinda bent over a table, scrubbing a stain left by a spilled drink.

"Jerlinda!"

The woman immediately straightened, but lowered her gaze in obedience. Jerlinda was a quiet and abiding soul with soft features. She was close in age to my mother, but had a more youthful countenance in spite of the years of toil demanded by my mother. Jerlinda rarely had reason to smile, but when she did, she glowed. In the days since Papa's death, she had been weary and strained by the labor brought on by the interment rituals. Yet she had worked diligently as always.

"Jerlinda, your lazy work habits are unacceptable. Do you think that because the master of the house is gone you can take advantage of my grief by easing your efforts?"

Mayme interceded. "Claudia, do not lash out at Jerlinda. She has been steadfast in her service to all of us."

"Silence, old woman. I am the mistress of this property and will punish as I see fit."

Mayme's will to battle my mother appeared to drain away as Mother's words stopped every servant in the yard from their task at hand. We all waited for what would come next, and although I pitied Jerlinda for being Mother's target, for the moment it meant I was spared her anger.

"Off to the cookhouse," Mother said with a venomous smile curling her lips. "You are never to step foot into the house again. You cannot be trusted. If not for your skill in preparing a meal, I would send you to the fields. But I warn you, if ever I see you beyond the cookhouse walls, you will be reduced to threshing wheat with the common slaves."

Mayme and I held our breath, as did the slaves around us. I had never witnessed punishment doled out on our property. Mother was occasionally harsh, but Papa had handled all slave matters. He required no whips or chains to motivate or discipline. He used his words and actions as examples to follow and warrant respect. There were no overseers needed to drive our workers, because Papa often joined them in their efforts.

Mother scanned the dark faces around her. "Let that be a lesson to all of you. There will be no soft hand coddling you as in the past. Our survival depends on my making the most of your labor, and I will do anything necessary to thrive. Unproductive behavior will not be tolerated."

Mother moved close enough to Jerlinda to cast a heavy shadow over the woman's trembling frame. "Get out of my sight, you filthy wench."

Jerlinda ran across the yard and into the trees. No one else moved, afraid to draw notice their way. All were shaken, particularly Axel, whose mouth hung open in utter shock.

"Don't stand there looking stupid," Mother hissed. "Get back to your duties, all of you!"

The personality of the farm changed immediately. My father's gentle spirit was no longer reflected in the land or its people. Mother hired an overseer named Virgil McVey to supervise the work in the lower fields, which was critical in sustaining our personal needs as well as in maintaining the horse population. We produced no cash crops, so all that was grown was meant to feed the family, the horses, and the slaves—in that order, as decreed by Mother. To my dismay, Garrison also became a frequent visitor.

"Garrison will be calling on you this afternoon," Mother said as Tess awkwardly collected our plates in her arms, all the while clanking dishes and dropping silverware.

Mother had chosen Tess as our new house servant. She was young and feisty, a fact I surmised from her vicious teasing of Axel in their younger years. Tess was not soft and attentive like Jerlinda. She rushed through her tasks and showed no regret over Jerlinda's plight. Her gain was at Jerlinda's expense, a detail that seemed to make the prize all the more satisfying to Tess. I was disturbed that Mother continued to coax Garrison to our doorstep. I was not comfortable speaking with Tess as a witness, so I waited until she stumbled from the room.

"Mother, don't you think it is inappropriate to encourage courtship during our period of mourning?" I hoped the suggestion of impropriety would thwart her intentions.

"Garrison's visit is as much business as it is pleasure," she said without looking up. "I asked him to purchase a few items on my behalf in Elizabeth City."

"He has responsibilities to his family's enterprise," I stated flatly. "Entwining him in our activity will only encourage him."

Her gaze met mine over her teacup. "Exactly."

I refused to be baited into the same disagreement over Garrison that we discussed almost daily in the month since the funeral. This time was meant for mourning. As a widow, Mother had a full year before expectations could be made of her. I, on the other hand, had only six months and was already aware of her readiness to hand me over to Garrison as soon as it was considered proper. I was fast losing hope for a different future for myself.

Eclipse had grown considerably. Her stall had become my haven, and I often spent hours nestled on a bale of hay telling her my worries and sharing my tears. Though only a horse, she was warm and responsive to my touch. I fretted over Mayme, who remained secluded in her room in surrender to life. Lost in thought, I did not hear Rafe enter the stable. He stood outside the stall, holding a palomino by its bridle.

"Marster Yob has been askin' me what Eclipse might be worth in cash money."

I stood and smoothed my black dress, embarrassed to have him stumble upon me in such informal posture. "I don't understand. Why should Garrison care what she is worth?"

"Ain't my business to guess," Rafe said, though he was clearly troubled.

"His inquiry makes me suspicious of his intent. What did you tell him?"

"I told him she would be worth more if given time to mature and fill out. Is he workin' for your mama now?"

"Garrison?" I laughed with bitter sharpness. "His goals are far loftier and include me."

Rafe lowered his head to hide his discomfort. "Oh."

"Garrison's grandfather was a fisherman who made a tidy profit in waters off the coast of Elizabeth City. When the canal was completed through Dismal Swamp, the elder Yob invested in flatboats as commerce grew between the port at Elizabeth City and the interior at South Mills and on to Deep Creek, Virginia. It was quite a boon, especially when the canal was deepened to allow the passage of small steamers."

"Your papa told me Marster Yob owns the *Southern Gale*. I seen that river steamer a couple o' times when we were fetchin' supplies in South Mills."

"Garrison's grandfather had the steamboat built when the demand for timber increased his trade. The Great Dismal has an endless supply for those who can harvest and haul it. Well, the swamp delivered the grandfather his fortune, but it also delivered him a deadly bout of malaria. Garrison's father had neither the instinct nor desire to command the business, so it slowly dwindled to a couple of timber lighters and a steamer in ill repair. It still chugs along the canal delivering timber staves and cedar shingles to the ships that dock in Elizabeth City and occasionally up in Portsmouth."

Rafe looked at me, his eyes as rich and distinct as coffee beans. "I don't wanna speak out of turn, but I got a question to ask."

"Go on," I said as I stroked Eclipse's withers to maintain an air of nonchalance, even though my insides were twisted by the latitude I was allowing Rafe through this extended conversation.

"Is Marster Yob gonna be the marster around here?"

"Not if I have any say in the matter."

"Do you?"

"Do I *what*?"

"Do you have any say in the matter?"

The question hung unanswered between us when our eyes were drawn apart by the squeak of wheels rattling down the dusty road toward the house. Rafe tugged the bridle of the palomino. "I better get this colt to the pasture so he can stretch his legs."

They plodded out of sight just as Garrison steered his carriage into the front yard. "Ah, Jacy," he said as I stepped from the stable, "so good of you to greet me."

"Please do not neglect your personal duties by running errands for Mother," I said as politely as my annoyance would allow. "It is not necessary to call on us so often."

He dragged a large satchel from the back of the carriage. "Nonsense. I consider my outreach to you and your mother my most important personal duty. It benefits all of us to ensure that the plantation stays viable. Look and see what improved methods we will soon apply." He reached into the sack and pulled from it a long, heavy whip.

Nausea heaved in my belly. "That looks to be too cumbersome to manage the horses."

"Foolish girl." He howled with laughter. "This is for the slave force, not the horses."

"I know what it's for, you brute. Put that dreadful thing away, because it will not strike a single living creature on this property."

"Once again, you resist what is necessary," he said, emptying the contents of the satchel on the ground at my feet. Several whips, a branding iron, and chains attached to leg irons lay in the dirt like an unearthed treasure. "I was shocked when I surveyed the property at your mother's request and found not one whip or shackle."

"Did my mother authorize these acquisitions?"

"She sought guidance from me regarding some business decisions. I explained to her that increased profit could be had if the slaves were driven to higher yield."

"My father refused to employ these barbaric weapons, and so will I."

Garrison brushed a fingertip along my cheek. "The decision is not yours, Jacy. Your duty is to abide."

I pushed his hand aside. "You were told to stay away from me."

"I will say again, your *duty* is to abide," he spat back at me. "I have been patient while you mourned your loss, but your moment of submission to me is closer than you think."

I stomped away, but I knew I would face him again at the supper table. Without my father's protection, Garrison would grow bolder. I sought out Mayme for comfort, but she did not answer her door when I knocked; nor was she present at dinner. Tess hastily set a plate on the table with a thump.

Mother clucked impatiently. "Tess, you are not serving the picka-ninnies out by the trough. Our meal should be presented to us with delicate care."

"Yes, missus."

The servant's actions did not match her words. She had not made the distinction between a *chore* and a *personal service*. Nor did she appear inclined to try. Garrison was quick to intervene.

"I have a whip in the barn that might help you remember your mistress's instructions."

His blatant threat got Tess's attention. Her face tensed as she quickly cleared what was left of our meal. "I'll remember, sah."

When she rushed from the room, Garrison grinned. "You see? She will not have to be told a second time."

Mother paused, seemingly uncomfortable with the method used to obtain Tess's obedience. However, she could not deny the results. "Would you like some coffee or would you prefer something stronger?"

"Yes, a drink will be much appreciated," he said. When Mother went to the liquor cabinet, Garrison caught my attention and then motioned his eyes toward the door, signaling me to the fence.

I froze. When I did not move, he shifted his eyes again, this time with exaggerated insistence. I lowered my head and ignored him. Mother returned holding a snifter of brandy.

"Here you are, Garrison," she said. The moment she sat down, his boot nudged against my leg beneath the table. The memory of my father's words came to me. *"Don't ever let anyone break your spirit."* I raised my eyes to Garrison and shook my head in defiance.

His thick brows arched down against the bridge of his pug nose. "Let's go for a stroll in the evening air, Jacy."

"That's a wonderful idea," Mother chimed in from across the table.

"No."

"Jacy, don't be rude to our guest."

Garrison's eyes flashed with excitement. "You heard your mother; don't be rude." His sweaty palm clamped over my hand. I yanked it from his and grabbed his glass of brandy.

"I said *no*!" Defiantly, I tossed the golden liquid in his face, causing him to leap to his feet.

"You ungrateful—"

"Jacy!" Mother exclaimed.

Garrison flung a halting hand in the air to silence Mother's plea. He reached up and clutched my chin with enough force to keep me from pulling free.

"Do you think I can't tame you as easily as I did that uppity servant? She, at least, has value in her desire to please me. I will not waste time here without reward." He pushed me back into my chair, then turned to Mother. "This farm needs a man at its helm or it will sink into a murky grave along with your husband. Is that what you want? I will not be made a fool of by your impudent daughter!"

Garrison threw his napkin at my feet as he stormed from the room and out the front door. His carriage had barely sped from the yard when Mother flew across the room at me, squalling like a tomcat. "You have tossed our fate to the wind! Have you no sense or care?"

I stood my ground. "I will not be had by Garrison Yob!"

For a moment I thought she would grab me by the throat. "Jacy, you are in no position to deem a well-bred gentleman unworthy of your attention," she screeched, clawing in wild frustration at her hair and cheeks. "You are nothing but a quadroon dressed in lace. That's all you are. An ignorant, feral quadroon!"

I was dazed by her outburst and confused by her words. I moved to block Mother's exit from the room. "What did you call me?"

Her breaths heaved faster as she moved closer to me. "You heard me."

The insult had not been hurled at me since childhood, but now I understood its meaning. The innocent ears of a child had always heard *quarter moon*, when in fact she was calling me a *quadroon*, the child of a white parent and a mulatto slave. The room began to spin around me.

"Why would you call me such a thing?"

Mother's face peeled apart in a wicked grin. She pushed past me, leaving me alone and stunned. My legs wobbled beneath me and I sank to the floor.

Chapter 4

*S*ilence draped the house when I emerged from my stupor. I sat in the dark on the floor of the dining room. Embers smoldered in the fireplace at the back of the room, their orange glow a mere smudge within the pitch-black emptiness surrounding me.

I must speak to Mayme.

I drifted through the house like a sleepwalker, oblivious to sight and sound. Ascending the stairs, I paused outside Mother's chamber door. Eerie stillness sealed her in her cryptlike retreat. Mother often lashed out with words meant to wound, but this time had been different. Her outburst was akin to a boiling pot erupting its lid to spew what had become too torrid to be contained.

I told myself there could be no truth in her words. Mother was crazed with anger at my rejection of Garrison. She would say anything to rein me in. But calling me a quadroon was outlandish, even for her. I tiptoed down the hallway and slipped into Mayme's room. A low flame burned in the oil lamp on her mantel, allowing me to gaze upon her as she slept. Two abundantly stuffed feather pillows propped her up to a near sitting position. I sat on the edge of her bed and nudged her arm.

"Mayme." Her eyelids fluttered but did not open. I gently pressed my palm to her cheek. "Please, Mayme. I need to speak with you."

This time she blinked awake, startled. Her voice was weak and whispery when she spoke. "What is it, Jacy? What brings you to me in the middle of the night?"

"Mayme, I must ask you a question."

She studied my face. "Out with it, child. I can see you are troubled."

"I trust you will be direct and honest with me. Without Papa, you are the only one I can rely on to speak the truth with a loving heart." Mayme leaned forward and stroked my cheek, urging me to continue. "Mayme, is there merit to someone calling me a quadroon?"

Mayme's eyes bulged wide as she pressed a hand to her breast. "Jacy! Why would you . . ." Her breath caught in her throat. "Who would—"

"Mother told me," I said. My heart squeezed tight within me as she fumbled for words.

Mayme desperately wrung her hands in her lap to disguise their trembling. I stood to back away, but she reached out and pulled me to her side. "Please sit near me while I explain."

"Just tell me the truth, Mayme. Am I a quadroon?"

She took in a long, shaky breath. "Yes."

"No!" I gasped in disbelief. "I can't be! I can't be!"

Suddenly, the excessive face powder and wide-brimmed bonnets made painful sense to me. Mayme held on to my hand. "You were never meant to know, Jacy. It is not a simple matter."

"How can such an abhorrent thing be true?" I stammered, numb with shock. "How?"

Still reeling, I tried to pull away from her, but Mayme squeezed my hand tighter. "Claudia and your father were miserable in their childless marriage. You were seeded by your father and born of a mulatto slave. When you arrived, so pink and pale in skin color, he brought you into the main house to be raised as their legitimate off-spring. No one beyond the property suspected the ruse. Bradford wanted to give you the privileged life of a fully white child and hoped Claudia would embrace you as her own. He loved you so, but Claudia's resentment has never waned."

I twisted away from her. "You are lying! I am not a Negro!"

"You are more white than Negro, only half of one-half. Your appearance and upbringing have negated it altogether."

Mayme pleaded for me to stay as I fled her room. I ran down the stairs and out across the moonlit yard, then climbed into the loft of the barn and collapsed into the hay. It was as though a sorcerer had torn me from my body and turned me into a stranger. Nothing and no one were what I thought them to be. Angry tears stung my eyes as I realized my beloved papa had harbored the same forceful impulses as Garrison. I was proof of his faults and deeds. Rumors of disreputable masters engaging in sordid behavior with helpless Negro women had swirled in gossip circles near and far ever since I was old enough to understand them.

I rolled onto my side as a sudden surge of nausea heaved from my gut. I wiped my mouth, but could not rid my tongue of the vile taste that remained. Crawling over to the open hayloft door, I let the cool breeze of twilight soothe my moist cheeks. The sinking moon shimmered through the poplars that lined the far pasture, a thin veil between me and the cabins, turnip patches, and Negroes below. I vomited again, though it was more like dry retching this time. Drained of strength and emotion, I detached from my thoughts and sank with the crescent moon into sweet oblivion.

The whisk of a pitchfork through hay woke me. I was still curled in the straw, wrung out and chilled in the damp, gray morning. My entire world had been stripped from me. The frayed seams of my being continued to unravel as I grappled to understand my future and re-examine my past. I peeked down through the gaps in the loft floor and saw Axel tossing clumps of hay into an oxcart. He worked quickly despite his weakened leg, but filling the cart would take some time. Watching him limp through the straw mounds below me, I thought back to the day I first came upon him. I could not have been more than eight or nine years of age. He was barely four. Papa had taken Mother to visit a sick friend, leaving me in Mayme's care. As she dozed in the parlor, I followed Jerlinda into the kitchen. She took pity on me in my boredom.

"If you promise not to tell yo' mama, I'll let you watch the cookhouse women make molasses candy drops."

"I won't tell, Jerlinda."

She took me by the hand and led me through the brisk December air and into the warm cookhouse. My footsteps halted in the doorway when the roomful of black faces turned to study me.

"Don't be afraid, chile. You is among friends."

I shook my head, my eyes wide with fright. In truth, it was only six women seated in pairs pulling ropes of prepared molasses between them. The women stretched, braided, and folded the long strands together. A young girl, whom I eventually knew as Tess, sat at a table cutting hardened sticks of golden molasses into bite-sized pieces. Seeing the apprehension in my gaze, Jerlinda immediately regretted overstepping her authority. She took a piece of candy from the table and handed it to me.

"This ain't no place fo' a fine little girl." Her smile was bright and full of reassurance. "Let's get you back inside."

As I turned to leave, a little dark boy peeked from the corner of the kitchen. His almond eyes blinked up at me and made me giggle. "Pay no mind to Axel," Jerlinda said.

"What's he doing back there?"

"Stayin' warm and outta the way. He got one no-good leg and can't keep up with the other chilluns, so he stays up here with us."

I placed my molasses drop in the milky palm of his hand and waved good-bye. When the warm months came, Axel spent his days behind the cookhouse, out of the heat and out of sight of Mother. She was intent on selling "the damaged pickaninny" before he grew into a useless burden, but Papa wouldn't hear of it. He insisted that with some steady activity the boy's leg would strengthen. Axel's plight tugged at my heart, so I spent the better part of that spring and summer sneaking behind the cookhouse to stand him on his legs until he could support himself and eventually take a few steps. It all ended one autumn day when Mother noticed me disappearing into the side yard. When she found me using molasses drops to coax Axel to walk, she struck me with a hickory switch across the backs of my bare legs until Papa heard my cries and rescued me. My interaction with Axel lasted only a few months, but I could tell that, like me, he never forgot our time together.

Knowing what I did now, I wondered if Axel had instinctively sensed the rogue blood that had leaked into me. Mother had always made a great effort to keep me apart from the Negroes. Wasn't it odd that I would feel so compelled to help the lowly child? Papa said it was because I was good-hearted, but perhaps he knew I could not help but be drawn to the likeness of what was harbored in me like a hibernating plague.

When Axel took the cart of hay to the stable, I climbed down the ladder of the loft and went to the house. Inside, all was quiet, so I headed for the stairs.

"Jacy?" Mother's voice came from the dining room.

I was tempted to retreat without answering; however, I knew she would track me down until I was cornered. I did not know what to expect or brace for in our next encounter. Would I be attacked? Disowned? Would there be more secrets to topple me? The emptiness that hollowed me also numbed my defenses. I decided to face her head-on.

Mother watched me with hawklike closeness as I entered the room. I sat down across the table from her but said nothing. She held my fate in her hands and there was very little I could do or say, so I waited. I could feel her gaze upon me, but I could not bring myself to meet her eyes. Finally, she spoke.

"Mayme was looking for you."

"Oh."

"She is not happy with me," she said with little care. "But I cannot be faulted for speaking the truth."

My mind buzzed with exhaustion. "Why was I not told sooner?"

"Your father perpetrated the farce and therefore would not allow it revealed." She waited for a response. When none came, she continued. "If he had his way, you would never have known. I did my best with you, but your wild streak is inborn. My reason for telling you now is to keep you humble."

I looked at her composed expression. Questions and confusion throbbed in my head. "What do you mean by *humble*?"

"Jacy, you are cursed to cower like a mongrel for all eternity. Recognize the root of your inferiority and defer to your superiors as any Negro would do."

I shuddered, still unable to grasp the shocking revelation. "Mayme says I am only partially tainted."

Mother huffed. "One drop of colored blood makes you a Negro. On this, there is no debate."

Mother came around the table and took me by the elbow. She pulled me to the looking glass and pointed at my reflection. "Your fair appearance masks our secret. I will not bring scandal on our household as long as you cooperate in maintaining our reputation and social station. Garrison knows nothing of your mixed bloodline, so you can entice him with your womanly wares. I will repair the damage you caused last night with your outburst. In a few months, you will shed your mourning attire and a brief courtship will follow."

"Please do not ask me to wed Garrison."

Mother leaned close to my face to join her reflection with mine in the looking glass. "I am not asking you, Jacy. I am *telling* you."

"What about Walter Deboe?" I asked, frantically searching for alternatives. "Or the Chases' nephew over in Rocky Mount?"

Mother remained firm. "Walter is engaged to be married, and Jeremiah Chase is too dull to be of any use to us."

"There must be someone else we can consider."

"We do not have the luxury of time and choices, Jacy. Debts amass quickly if business goes unattended for even a few months. Besides, there is not an abundance of men in these parts who want a woman who can rope and ride better than they can."

"Can we take one trip to Raleigh to expand our social circle? I promise to be more genteel and sedate."

Unmoved, Mother shook her head. "I will not place my fate in the hands of a stranger. Garrison understands and respects my position in this household."

"But what about me?" I implored. "Have I no say in the decision?"

Mother leaned closer to hiss her response into my ear. "Jacy, you will wed Garrison Yob by autumn's end or I will turn you out to the Negroes. The choice is yours."

I withdrew to my room and spoke to no one for more than a week. Mayme pleaded with me to let her enter, but my door remained securely locked even to her. If not for Jerlinda's sneaking food to my room and emptying my chamber pot before dawn each day, I would have withered in my misery. She had been banned from the house, but risked punishment when Tess told her that I was not present for meals.

"Is you sick, Miss Jacy?" she asked, wringing her hands at my bedside. When I did not answer, the fretful woman smoothed my covers and scurried away before Mother stirred with the rise of the sun.

Though Mother was unaware of Jerlinda's coddling, I would not have been surprised to learn that Mayme had a hand in making certain that someone was watching over me. Still, my relationship with Papa and Mayme now seemed built on a charade. Despair swept me away, leaving me lost and alone in my fall from grace. Even Great Meadow's opulence mocked my unworthiness.

Who am I? Am I nothing more than a dirty secret? Not a daughter or granddaughter, but rather a pet brought into the fold to fill a void?

There was no end to my pain. The foundation of my identity had cracked and crumbled beneath my feet. I had always prided myself in being venturesome like my father. Now my earthy tendencies seemed wild and unnatural. It was no wonder Mother had fought so often with Papa about her reluctance to participate in social gatherings. She could not tame me to her world and feared the scandalous ruse would be discovered. I prayed I could find a way to kill or exorcise the Negro part of me from my being, but each morning I awakened to find it there, waiting to stalk me for another day.

Hours of despondent sobbing were followed by bouts of ranting into my pillow, but there was no escaping my imperfection. By the end of the week, dark circles shadowed my eyes, the result of sleepless nights passed pacing in fear of what the next sunrise would reveal.

"Jacy, Garrison is downstairs and willing to accept your apology." Mother's voice was direct, with no concern for my mental state. "Powder your face immediately. We will wait for you in the parlor."

When I opened my door, Mayme emerged from her room. "Jacy."

I walked past her as though marching to the gallows. My sanity splintered with each step I took toward the parlor. The aroma of Sunday supper wafted in through our open windows, but descending the stairs, I felt swallowed by the house I had no right to call home.

"Here she is, Garrison," Mother said, her voice chirping like a sparrow at daybreak. She was eager to reestablish our ties. "Say hello to Garrison, Jacy."

He stared at me, his arms folded across his chest. He took obvious enjoyment in watching me squirm. It required all my reserve to command my tongue, but finally I uttered a soft greeting.

"Hello."

He nodded, then lifted a glass of brandy to his lips. When he looked away to set his empty glass on the mantel, Mother reached over and pushed my chin upward to make me look squarely at him with the confidence he would expect. The smile I forced was as artificial as the powder on my cheeks.

Releasing a low belch, Garrison turned to me. "Your mother tells me that you wish to make amends for your offensive behavior."

How brash of him to accuse *me* of being offensive. I stared at his repugnant face until Mother delivered a verbal nudge.

"Jacy, I believe there is something you want to say to Garrison." Mother cautioned me with a glaring shift of her eyes.

Defer. Be humble.

Garrison's fleshy jowls puffed with impatience. Surrendering my dignity tore away what little of me was left. The words I spoke were banal and delivered slowly. "Please accept my apologies, Garrison."

"Very good," Mother chimed in. "I am glad we cleared up that silly mishap."

She continued to barrage us with pointless chatter intended to lighten the tension in the air. Garrison's hard stare remained on me. Then, as though challenging me to prove my resolve, he motioned his eyes toward the door. A chilling realization rocked me. I was defeated.

The yard was empty as I dragged my heels toward the fence. Except for feeding the animals, the slaves were not called to duty on Sundays. Of course, this rule did not apply to Tess and the cookhouse women, but all the others stayed in and around the quarters. They tended to their small vegetable patches, mended clothes, fished, and gathered for prayer meetings.

Slave. The word now frightened me with all it implied. Yet I prayed that one or two dark faces would busy themselves near enough to keep Garrison from cornering me. As I approached the spot where I was expected to wait while he fabricated a reason to follow, my footsteps did not slow. Instead, they picked up in pace until I was in a full sprint. I ran along the fence and away from the house and stable. Jerlinda and another cookhouse woman leaned out from the smoky doorway to watch me whisk by.

I dashed across a field of alfalfa without looking back. Life as I knew it was over. Mother was not my mother, nor did she care to play the role unless it served her purpose. Papa was dead, as was all I believed him to be. Was I a grandchild to Mayme or simply a dirty secret dressed in silk and lace? I clawed at my skin, wishing to release the blackness that stained me from within.

I cannot be Negro. I will not be Negro.

Darting through the trees of the highlands and across a clearing in the wood, I stumbled to a halt where the earth fell away with sudden abruptness. The toe of my boot toppled a pebble over the edge of the steep cliff. I had not run there with purpose, but looking down the rocky ridge at the boulders below, I believed purpose had been delivered upon me. The cliff dropped from the highlands that bordered our property, though the house and pastures were out of sight at the opposite end of the wood. Nothing but blue sky and distant farmlands stretched before me. I took in the view, knowing it would be my last. I fixed my gaze on a hawk circling above the boulders that would soon wear my spattered blood.

I am no more.

A voice emanated from within the trees behind me. "Don't move."

I did not turn, but stayed focused on the gliding flight of the carefree hawk. Its journey on the breeze beckoned me to follow.

"Step back before you stumble." I recognized Rafe's calm and deliberate assurance. He was closer now, but cautious in his approach.

"I have to go," I said softly.

The second voice startled me. "Please don't, Miss Jacy."

I looked over my shoulder and saw Axel five paces behind Rafe, who was three paces from me. Each man gripped a bamboo fishing pole; a string of trout hung from a rope tied around Axel's waist. Tears spilled over onto my cheeks.

"Go away."

Rafe tossed his pole aside and reached toward me. "We ain't goin' nowhere. Now give me your hand, Miss Jacy."

"I can't."

"Yes, you can. What is Eclipse gonna think if you ain't around no more? She'll think she is orphaned all over again."

My arms and legs began to tremble. "I am more orphaned than she."

Axel eased his way to Rafe's side. "That's nonsense, Miss Jacy. We all is heartbroke over your daddy, but you ain't no orphan."

I fixed my gaze on his panicked tawny face. "You know nothing about it, Axel." I lifted my face to the sun and spoke firmly. "You know nothing about *me*."

The hawk was gone. I turned to face the steep drop. Closing my eyes, I leaned forward.

"Yes, I do!" Axel screamed. His uncharacteristic force made me flinch. When I paused at his outcry, he yelled again, "I know about you. So does Rafe."

I turned to confront them. "You are only trying to distract me. Leave me alone!"

Axel limped closer and lowered his voice to a pleading whisper. "Believe me, Miss Jacy. I know all about you. And I know what you is feelin'. I know . . . because I am your brother."

My brother?

Instantly, my mind drained of thought and silence dropped over me.

Chapter 5

I floated in the deepest darkness I had ever known. Had I jumped? Muffled voices rose and fell in the abyss. At times my limbs were jostled, making me tumble about in a disorienting haze; then I would lift and float once more. All in all, it felt like only a few passing seconds and eternity both at once.

Eventually, the voices grew louder. My tongue remained still, though I desperately tried to call out. Slowly, the voices grew more distinct until miraculously they merged into one voice.

"Jacy."

The sound was tender and pulled me closer.

"Jacy."

A horizontal slice of light appeared in front of me. I ran for the brightness as it opened like a clamshell. All the while the voice beckoned me. Blinded as I entered the light, I blinked through squinted eyes until the figure hovering over me became clear.

"Jerlinda?"

At first I could not distinguish whether she was real or an apparition of my confusion. Then she reached down and touched my cheek. Her eyes were moist and sparkled with relief.

"You scared us half to death, miss."

I was tucked beneath a quilt on a straw-stuffed mattress. The interior of the cabin was barely larger than my bedchamber. The log walls were rough and dotted with pegs that held pots, cooking utensils, woolen socks, herbs, coats, hats, and bonnets. Rafe sat on a wooden stool next to a stone fireplace across the room. He leaned with his elbows on his knees, his expression distraught, though he grinned weakly when I looked his way.

"How did I get here?"

Jerlinda smoothed the quilt around me. "You fainted. Axel and Rafe carried you down from the mount. It was a stroke of fortune that their hankerin' for brook trout led them to the highland stream. Don't wanna think what could have happened to you if they hadn't."

Rafe raked his fingers across his head and face as if trying to excise the thought from his memory. He didn't speak, but watched intently as Jerlinda stroked my hair. She was less formal than I was used to seeing her while she was on duty. Her touch was easy and caring.

"I apologize for causing a fuss," I said as I shifted to a sitting position. "I must return to the house."

"Hold on now, chile. Can't let you run off till I know you is in yo' right mind."

"Thank you for your concern, Jerlinda, but I do not wish to air my problems and shortcomings. Now, if you will excuse me . . ."

I stood and walked to the door, but was surprised when it opened. Axel stepped in hauling a bucket of water. He looked at me, then to Jerlinda. "Where do you want the water, Mama?"

"Put it in the kettle and I'll brew us some sassafras."

Axel obliged. When he limped from the doorway, I tried slipping out, but a thought turned me around. "Axel is your son?"

Jerlinda nodded. "This is our cabin."

I shook my head to clear the haze. I followed my thoughts back to the cliff and re-created the scene in my mind's eye. Axel's words came back to me. *I know all about you. And I know what you is feelin'. I know . . . because I am your brother.*

My heart skipped and stuttered as I took note of her acorn skin and soft curls. I shook my head again, not wanting it to be true, yet needing to know. "Jerlinda, are you my mother?"

Her hazel eyes glistened. "Yes, Jacy. You are my firstborn chile."

"I don't believe you," I choked out.

"That's because you have never looked in my eyes," she said gently. "If you had, you would have seen our sameness."

I shivered at the plainspoken truth. She was tranquil in her delivery and lifted her chin with relief. Jerlinda held still, braced for any response that might erupt from me. But I was drained. Her confirmation should have torched me with shock and outrage, but I had already endured the worst. Unable to absorb her confession, I let it fall between us with no more fanfare than a puzzle piece dropped into place.

It is true. I am born of a slave.

Jerlinda took me by the hand and led me to a small table near the hearth. Rafe and Axel mumbled something about chopping logs and were out through the door before Jerlinda said another word. She placed a wooden cup in front of me and filled it with tea. She sweetened the brewed sassafras with honey, just as she had done a thousand times in my lifetime, only now I saw care in her actions rather than duty.

"It's a lot to chew on and mighty hard to swallow, but you ain't no different today than you was yesterday."

"Mother told me I am a quadroon, so I know what my father did to you."

"You know no such thing, Jacy. What you heard is missus's take on things. You been told the worst. Let me tell you the best."

I could not take my eyes from her as she set the kettle aside and sat down across the small table from me. "The best?"

"First off," she said, her voice soft and soothing, "I never liked that word *quadroon*. Makes you seem like a hunk of *this* and a piece of *that*. You is who you is, whole and complete. And secondly, yo' papa didn't *do* anything to me except love me and give me my two greatest gifts, you and Axel."

Her words startled and intrigued me. "How can you say that? He was your master."

"That's right, chile, but Bradford wasn't no carpet-gitter stalkin' his colored women for no good. No kinder, gentler soul ever walked this earth. We was drawn to each other when we was youngsters playing marbles and jackstones. Wasn't unusual for slave chilluns and little massas and missies to play together. But when we come of age and was forced to separate to our proper places, we was already in love. That boy thought of reasons every which way to come to the quarters." Jerlinda paused, lost in thought.

"Mayme and Grandpa Lane didn't object?"

"Oh, they didn't know our feelings welled deeper than the polite exchanges they witnessed at the main house. When I was old enough, I was brought in for house duties. Bradford was careful not to act in a way that would start folks eyeballing us, but our love kept a-growin'. We stole glances, and eventually kisses, every chance we got."

Jerlinda smiled, but her eyes glistened with emotion. "If Miss Mayme suspected any foolery, she never said so aloud. Prob'ly figured he'd outgrow it."

"If Papa loved you so, why did he wed?"

"Well, that's just the way of things, Jacy. When he came on marrying age, Bradford was expected to settle down and start a family. When he resisted, his daddy began to take notice of his constant visits to the quarters. He gave Bradford a long talking-to. Bradford never told me what was said, but afterward, he turned inside himself and barely looked at me. The kisses stopped. The visits stopped. But the pain that creased his face told me that the love in his heart still burned."

I sipped the tea and drank in the full portrait of my father as confided by Jerlinda. "Then he married Mother."

"Yes," Jerlinda said, lowering her eyes to her cup. "I could never expect it to be no other way. But Lord, it tore my heart in two, especially since I had to serve and attend to missus's needs. The truth is, missus was not as hard-hearted then as she is now. Disappointment and bitterness soured her soul. Bradford was miserable, and after a year or so, he started to show up on my doorstep after missus went to bed. At first, the visits were simply to talk by the fire or stroll in the moonlight, but soon our love couldn't be harnessed by thoughts of right or wrong. Within months, I was with chile."

"Me?"

Jerlinda nodded. "When you were born, you were as pale as a fresh-cut maple, the most beautiful baby I ever laid eyes on. Yo' papa adored you. He didn't want you denied or forced to live a life of hardship. It broke my heart to lay you in another woman's arms, but it was best for you and for yo' papa. In gratitude, he gave you a name that honored me."

"Jacy?"

Jerlinda traced her finger on the table to form the letters J and C. She smiled. "J.C. *Jerlinda's chile*, a name that would forever honor me as your mother, even though its meaning was only whispered to the heavens. Axel came later, but he was too dark to pass off; otherwise Bradford would have taken him too."

Jerlinda wept softly. With hesitation, I leaned forward and patted her hand where it rested on the table. Tears rose in my eyes when she entwined her fingers in mine, but the intimate gesture brought with it a flood of conflicting emotion that I was unprepared to navigate. Our fingers released, although our shared tears kept us joined in the moment.

"I miss Papa so," I said, drying my eyes with my sleeve.

"We all do, chile."

"Thank you for giving him back to me."

Jerlinda was puzzled by my words, so I explained. "When Mother—I mean Clau—" I paused, not sure what to call her.

"It's all right, Jacy." Jerlinda nodded with calm assurance. "She is yo' mother by law . . . and by appearance to all but a few."

I appreciated her tender care in putting me at ease. "When Mother pierced me with Papa's secret, she did so to wound me. Papa is dead, lost to me in body. Then Mother killed what was left of him in my heart and memory by destroying the purity of his character. I have been turned upside down and may never be upright again, but your honest confession has given me back the father whom I loved and cherished. He is forever gone, but you have returned him to my heart, where he will remain always."

Suddenly, the door of the cabin was flung open with a force so strong that one of its strap hinges tore loose. I jolted at the appearance of Virgil McVey, our newly hired overseer. He was a sturdy man with graying temples and tar black whiskers shading his cheeks and chin. His snarl revealed him to have only three teeth, two on the top and one on the bottom that wiggled when he spoke.

"What has this colored woman done to you, Miss Lane?"

Jerlinda leapt from her seat and stumbled backward into the corner of the room. In one glance, McVey took stock of my puffy eyes and disheveled appearance. His brow folded into a frown. With a quick tug of his belt, he disengaged a whip and let its length unravel along the floor. His fiery eyes looked to Jerlinda as he snorted.

"I don't know what you're up to, wench, but me and my whip will make you regret the day you were born."

Chapter 6

"**M**r. McVey, stop this gruff intrusion at once!"

My words halted the man's march toward the cowering Jerlinda. "Yob says you were dragged off and were nowhere to be found," he said. "Thought we might have an uprising on our hands."

"What a foolish notion," I said, shifting my position to block the path between him and Jerlinda. "I fell ill while taking a walk and was brought to the cabin to be attended."

McVey gave a contrite shrug of his shoulders. "Can't be too careful with these darkies."

"Put away your whip. My father would detest your excessive display."

"Miss, I don't take orders from a dead man," he said callously while reeling in his whip. "And I don't take orders from you, neither. Now, you better get on up to the house before Yob arranges for a cavalry search."

McVey was right. I needed to keep matters in hand at the house, but I hesitated at leaving him alone with Jerlinda. "Will you be all right?" I asked her.

"Don't worry about me, Miss Jacy. He knows I ain't no trouble."

I lifted my skirt and hurried home. When I entered the parlor where Mother and Garrison sat, he scolded me. "Where have you been? I thought a bear or buck slave ran off with you!" He shook me by the arm. "Or were you avoiding my command?"

"No," I said as fear pumped inside my chest. "I was overcome by a dizzy spell as I abided your wish and awaited you in the afternoon heat. In my disoriented state, I must have wandered into the countryside and fainted."

"She does look strained," Mother stated, but her gaze could not mask her air of suspicion. "We have reestablished our understanding, Garrison. Perhaps Jacy should rest. All our needs are served for today."

Garrison squeezed my arm until I whimpered. "*All* our needs are not yet served, but we shall leave them for another day. There will be no more foolishness, Jacy. Your mother has given me responsibility on your behalf. Great Meadow will soon function under my rule. That includes you."

Mother offered me no protection or sympathy. I was a pawn in her chess game, used to capture a king. I left the room and headed for my bedchamber. The upstairs hallway was quiet, but candlelight streamed from beneath Mayme's door. I tapped lightly and entered her room. Mayme dozed with her Bible open on her lap. Immersed in my self-pity, I had neglected her since Papa's death. She seemed shrunken in her bed jacket, her hands quivering as she slept. I knelt at her feet and rested my head in her lap.

"Forgive me, Mayme."

Her thin hands lifted with surprise, then stroked my hair and cheek. "My sweet Jacy, you have finally come to me."

"I am ashamed that I put distance between us, Mayme. I have

been so confused, and I blamed you and Papa for betraying me by pretending I am something I am not."

Mayme lifted my chin so I could see the despair in her eyes. "Our love for you has always been deep and real. There was never a moment of pretending with regard to our feelings. Please believe that. Your father's decision may pain you now, but he made it with a devoted heart and pure intent."

"Did you know it is Jerlinda who is my true mother?"

"Claudia told you?"

I did not want to worry Mayme with my near tragic incident on the cliff, so I told her only that I went to Jerlinda's cabin. "I figured it out on my own. Axel is my brother."

"Your father's one regret was that he could not provide Axel with the same level of privilege as you. But he loved that boy. Claudia was hell-bent on sending poor Axel to the auction block, but Bradford fought fiercely for his son and Jerlinda to remain together. Separation from her remaining child would have been the cruelest blow Claudia could have levied on Jerlinda, so she was furious when she lost the battle."

"Papa's choices must have shocked you."

"The household was in constant turmoil. When I learned of Bradford's involvement with the slaves, I was outraged. I believed only heartache and shame would come of it." She paused to kiss my forehead. "But in the end, it gave me you."

"Mayme, I cannot look at myself because of what I am."

Her distraught expression grew stern with intent. "What you are today is no different from what you were yesterday or the day before."

"Jerlinda said the same."

Mayme smiled. "She is a wise and gentle soul."

"Well, she is nothing like Mother, though now I understand why Mother despises me."

"Jacy, you have done nothing to warrant her scorn. You are innocent in this tangled mess. Her resentment has built over the years because other than her emotional remoteness, there was little that she could inflict upon you. Exposing the little girl she called her daughter as a slave's child would have brought severe judgment and ridicule upon her. Social status is the measure of Claudia's life. She will endure *anything* to sustain it."

"She frightens me, Mayme. I often have a dream in which I am calling out, 'Mama.' I usually awake with a jolt when Mother's nightmarish face appears calling me a quarter moon and forcing me to pronounce *Mother*."

"Dear girl, your night terror is not a dream. It is a remembrance. When you were a baby, Jerlinda tended to you here in the house. She suckled and coddled you. Do you remember what I told you about your care for the orphaned foal, Eclipse?"

I thought back for a moment. "You said that because I nourished and nurtured her in her early hours, her attachment to me would be quick and steadfast."

"Exactly. Claudia barely touched you. Bradford prayed affection would develop, because the charade could not be undone. However, your first spoken word was *mama*. That's when Claudia stepped in. She was determined you would not speak or act like a Negro, because it would reflect poorly on her. Jerlinda was no longer allowed to spend time with you as a mother. Claudia demanded she never be alone with you, so your natural bond could fade. Jerlinda was crushed, but she knew it was necessary for you to believe you were like any other little white girl."

I dropped my head back into Mayme's lap. "Now I know why Mother put so much care into powdering my face and taming my thick hair. The only time she smiled was when she had me looking like a porcelain doll. We would gaze into the looking glass and she would squeeze me with glee, saying, 'Now, aren't you a pretty little thing?' What I thought was love and pride was in fact her satisfaction in hiding my imperfection. Sadly, she cannot tame what is inbred in me."

Tears escaped my eyes when I looked up at Mayme. "I once believed Papa indulged my exuberant activities because he had no son. I was wrong. Now I suspect he let me run wild in an attempt to exhaust the unbridled Negro within me, much like we release the horses to the fields when they are spirited."

"Never doubt your father's devotion," she said as she brushed the tears from my cheeks. "He took great pride in the fact that you were not dainty and fragile. He would smile broadly when telling me of an outing where you did not shrink from a spider or snake. Remember how he would boast that you could hike up the mountain more swiftly than any boy your age? I think your father was just so happy that you were healthy and could run and play."

"Unlike Axel," I said with some newfound insight.

"Bradford felt immense guilt about Axel's infirmities. He feared Jerlinda had not gotten enough rest and nourishment while carrying the boy."

"Poor Papa. It must have been a great disappointment to have two imperfect children."

"Jacy, do not torture yourself. I know you are frightened and confused, but your life does not have to change. My hope is that in learning the truth you will no longer be pricked by Claudia's barbs. Take comfort in the knowledge that you were born of parents who loved you and who loved each other."

I kissed my sweet grandmother and wished her good-night. "Thank you for loving me, Mayme."

She pulled me to her bosom and embraced me more tightly than ever before. "I have always loved you, Jacy. You have been nothing less than my beloved granddaughter from the moment I first cradled you in my arms."

I was too restless to sleep. On the balcony of my bedchamber, I breathed in the warm night air and let the song of the crickets loosen the knot of tension at the back of my neck. Panic washed over me when I thought about the cliff. Axel and Rafe had saved me from my despair. Now, with the memory of my father restored and Mayme's love unquestioned, I did not feel so alone.

Yet I wondered how I would come to terms with my hidden shame. Mayme assured me that my life would be unchanged, but in truth, everything had changed. The Negro part of me could not be carved from my bones. It frightened me. I wondered if it was the reason I was not more guarded in Rafe's presence. The audacity to share a common interest with a slave no longer seemed so outrageous. Perhaps I had a natural impulse that drew me to him. I gazed down upon the quiet stable.

Can my conflicting emotions be locked away along with the secret that could change the course of my life, or has something feral been unleashed in me, as Mother has so often said?

The one certainty I carried was that she would not unmask my scandalous flaw as long as I could be used to maintain her status and wealth. Perhaps it was the price I was required to pay due to my inferior bloodline. Did not a slave abide? Only one drop of Negro blood decreed it to be so.

I walked through my well-adorned chamber with its silk drapes and crushed-velour rug. My downy feather mattress and fine cotton bedcovers snuggled me. Soft hands and a delicate upbringing made it impossible for me to imagine a life of hardship beyond the comfort of the main house. I thought of Jerlinda's cabin. Though tidy and well tended, its raw simplicity and rudimentary condition were appalling. Fate and a father's love had chosen me to rise above the circumstance of my birth. I knew no other way. Now, with my fate in Mother's hands, I could no longer defy her wishes. I was destined to abide like the slave she knew me to be.

My days of mourning continued to wane as summer neared its end. Since our encounter at the cliff, Rafe and Axel seemed ever present when I stepped outside the house. They remained at a respectable distance, hauling water or trotting horses, all the while stealing concerned glimpses as if gauging my state of mind.

Mother, on the other hand, showed no worry at all. With all revealed between us, she cared little about how or where I spent my time as long as I earnestly greeted and entertained Garrison when he came to call on me. Her years of obsession with keeping me separate from the servants were tossed to the wind. Mother no longer feared what I would discover; nor did she maintain the conduct set forth by my father. With the exception of meals and a ghastly lie, we shared nothing.

"Good afternoon, Miss Jacy. How is you today?" With a sack of oats balanced on his shoulder, Axel slowed to peek into Eclipse's stall as he passed.

"I'm fine, Axel," I said with a feigned lilt of assurance that had become my ritual. Neither he nor Rafe spoke of the cliff or of my visit with Jerlinda. To them, I was still the mistress and would dictate what would or would not be appropriate conversation to strike up with a slave. For a while I said nothing, even when Axel pulled a pink ribbon from his pocket.

"Mama says to give you this." He looked around to make certain no one else was within earshot. "She said Marster tied it in your hair the day you was born."

I laced the delicate ribbon between my fingers and felt its satin smoothness, then tucked it away in my pocket.

My restless nights continued, fraught with worries and fears that my secret would be exposed. Often weariness came upon me in the solitude of the stable and I would doze in the generous hay piled in Eclipse's stall. In one of these unguarded moments, Rafe came upon me.

"Eclipse is sproutin' into a fine filly," he said.

I sat up and rubbed my eyes. "Yes, she has grown strong and beautiful."

Rafe entered the stall and emptied a bucket of oats into her trough. He eyed me from under the brim of his slouch hat. "You all right, miss?"

The formality of the title dropped like a wedge between us. "You may address me as Jacy. We both know that *miss* does not apply."

"That's crazy talk," he said, staring at me over Eclipse's muzzle. "You is a good and proper gal with a gentle soul and a givin' heart. I'll call you what you like, but you will always deserve to be called *miss*."

"Thank you, Rafe."

"I'm just speakin' the truth . . . Jacy."

I smiled at the comfort brought by his speaking my name. "My gratitude is not only for your sweet compliment. I owe you my life. You saved me from tragedy."

Rafe removed his hat and wiped his brow. "We been mighty worried about you."

"The day you found me I was shocked and vulnerable. Though I have been struck down by a lifetime of lies, I assure you I will not seek the cliff again."

I saw in the glint of Rafe's eyes that he believed me. "Those words lift a hefty boulder of jitters off of me. Jerlinda and Axel will feel the same."

I was warmed by the care they harbored. It anchored me somehow. Suddenly Eclipse snorted and shimmied from side to side. "Whoa, girl," I said, reaching to pat her sleek neck.

Her prance became urgent and I thought she might rear up. Rafe's arms slid around her neck to collar her. "Easy does it, Eclipse. I got you."

I flushed when my hand got caught beneath Rafe's strong fingers as he pressed them against the unsettled horse. Eclipse jostled us slightly, then calmed. Rafe continued to whisper in her ear: "Easy, now. That's a good girl. Rafe's got you."

My breath quickened as his hand tenderly massaged mine. When Rafe realized he had more than the horse's hide in his touch, he pulled away. "S'cuse me, Jacy. I didn't mean . . . I was only tryin' to—"

I withdrew my hand and lowered my head to hide my flushed cheeks. "I know, Rafe. You were comforting Eclipse. No more was intended."

The reason for the horse's prickly outburst was revealed when Titus came around the corner. He was taller than Rafe, but as lanky as a scarecrow. I shuddered at how long he might have lingered out of our sight as Rafe and I spoke. We had remained discreet in our conversation, but our interaction had to have struck Titus as overly familiar and out of the ordinary. His stony face, always sculpted in a bitter and suspicious glare, did not divulge whether he had overheard our exchange. But Rafe and I knew the danger of unleashing gossip in the quarters. A vengeful slave would spare no one to better his position, just as a ruthless white would lie and cheat for his own gain. Titus and his wife, Tess, had no loyalty to the other slaves, and I was not the only one who would be hurt if our family secret was revealed. Therefore, I attempted to cover our transgression.

"Titus, fetch a bridle and take Eclipse to the pasture. Let her release her feisty mood with a good run. I am thankful Rafe was nearby when she nearly trampled me."

Titus glanced at Rafe as he stepped between us and bridled the unsettled horse. As they clopped from the stables, I turned to Rafe. "We must be more cautious."

Rafe nodded. "I better get to my chores, so Titus don't give us any more thought."

He picked up the empty bucket and started to leave. He paused in the doorway, then turned back to me, his eyes gleaming with excitement. "Sunday we is free from chores. Come to Jerlinda's for noontime supper. She is achin' to make certain that you ain't sufferin'."

"I'm not sure that's a good idea," I said as anxiety rushed through me, "especially after what just happened with Titus."

"How about a picnic in the pine grove by the cliff? Titus rarely wanders from the lowlands."

Rafe's care was so genuine, I could not cast it aside. Besides, months of isolation and loneliness made the innocent outing a prospect I could look forward to.

"We will be safe and away from scrutiny?" I asked.

Rafe's expression softened with a tender smile. "I would never put you in harm's way, Jacy. When you know me better, you will not doubt me."

I wanted to tell him that I had no doubts. He treated me with more respect and consideration than Mother and Garrison ever mustered between them. It made me feel good, but before I found the words to say it, I noticed Titus staring at us from afar through the stable window. It was a jolting reminder. For everyone's sake, I must not stray from my role.

Chapter 7

*S*unday came before I had the chance to fully digest Rafe's
invitation. It unsettled me as much as it intrigued me,
and I had spent the entire morning wrestling with reasons for why I should or shouldn't go.

"Mayme!" I exclaimed as the creak of the screen door drew me
from my conflicted thoughts.

I was thrilled to see my grandmother step from the doorway onto
the front porch. Guiding her by the elbow, Tess supported Mayme as
she hobbled to the cushioned bench on which I sat.

Mayme patted my hand when Tess disappeared into the side yard
toward the cookhouse. "There are not many warm days left. I want
to enjoy those that remain." She watched a group of starlings tussle
over some strewn sunflower seeds. I sensed she was reflecting on
more than the coming change of season.

"Are you feeling poorly?"

"Just worn-out, child. When the clock struck twelve, I decided to
breathe in some fresh air before retiring for a nap."

The noon hour had brought with it a twinge of guilt. Earlier, I had
seen Jerlinda leave the cookhouse when her contributions to Mother's

afternoon meal were complete. She had glanced over her shoulder to where I sat on the porch and probably wondered whether I would join them in the grove. I was ambivalent about the risk in venturing farther with them. Trepidation made me pause, much like wavering in the decision to open the door to a room I was warned not to enter.

"Jerlinda has reached out to me."

Mayme adjusted her spectacles to study me. "In what way?"

"Through Rafe," I said, leaning close to whisper to her. "She wants me to join them in the pine grove."

Her wrinkled eyelids fluttered with concern. "Why?"

"I think she simply wants to know me better."

"Do you want to know her?"

I rested my head on Mayme's shoulder. "I don't know. I believe so, but I am afraid. If my secret is discovered, my life will fall to ruin."

"Jacy, a harmless walk in the woods will hurt no one. Satisfy your curiosity, so you'll have no regrets. But be cautious. If you are discovered, say that I sent you to collect pinecones. Your mother knows I love their aroma when burned in my hearth. Simply say the Negroes lent you a hand."

"Does my interest in them shame you, Mayme?"

She took my hand in hers. "I will tell you what I told your father when he asked me the same question on the night he confided that Jerlinda was carrying his child."

"What did you tell him?"

"I told him my love was given without condition or requirement. Judgment is a godly deed and we should accept it from no other. Jerlinda, and then you, gave Bradford his greatest joys in life. How can I possibly condemn you?"

"You are an amazing woman, Mayme."

Mayme's eyes sparkled with wry humor. "That's exactly what Claudia says every time I cross her wicked path."

I burst out in giggles at Mayme's sarcasm. She chuckled too. Laughter was a rare commodity in our home since Papa died, and I think we both felt pieces of our souls heal.

"Why are the two of you in such a light mood?" Mother had opened the front door when she heard us. "Have you no respect for the period of mourning we are engaged in?"

Mayme's anger lit like a fire. "You? Mourning? That's a farce. You may be draped in black, Claudia, but you are dancing a jig within your hoop skirt. You can playact the tearful widow all you want, but don't dare think you fool me."

"Or me!" I spouted in support of Mayme.

Mother called out to Tess: "Come and take Mayme back upstairs, Tess. She's become disoriented." Mother grinned coolly at us. "Now it is I who will giggle with delight."

"Don't touch her," I said when Tess pulled at Mayme's arm. "You cannot order Mayme to her room, Mother!"

"It's all right, Jacy. I have expended my strength and must rest." Mayme leaned close to my ear as Tess corralled her toward the door held open by Mother. "Do not bring her wrath upon you. Allow me to be the target today so you can move freely."

Mother's triumphant smile angered me. "I invited Garrison for afternoon supper. Give extra effort when you powder and dress. We must do all we can to hold his interest."

The screen door banged shut and she was gone. With Mayme whisked away, I was left to brood alone. I wondered whether Jerlinda was still awaiting me in the pine grove. Was she disappointed? Were Rafe and Axel peeking through the trees, surveying the wood in hopes that I would turn up? My chest began to feel weighted like a wool blanket soaked in a downpour.

I will stay for only a few minutes, politely say hello, and be on my way.

I walked briskly through the field of alfalfa to where a thicket of trees welcomed me into the ascending forest. How strange it was to rush through the evergreens with anticipation rather than desperation, as I had a few weeks earlier. The hint of smoke on the breeze signaled that they had not yet given up on me. Near the far edge of the wood in a hollow of fern and azalea, the three sat on a blanket next to a crackling fire. They smiled when they saw me and stood to greet me.

"Thought maybe you decided against us," Rafe said as he removed his chambray coat and arranged it on the ground for me to sit on. "But Jerlinda kept sayin', 'Give her a little more time, Rafe. It ain't an easy walk.'"

Jerlinda waved me over. Using a stick, she poked at the glowing base of the fire. "Ash cakes is almost ready."

I stared blankly at her as she grinned. "I know you ain't got a taste for corn pone, so I brought you some biscuits from the cookhouse." When she handed me a linen cloth wrapped in a bundle, I saw a scabbed strap mark across her upper arm.

"How did you get that wound?"

She tugged at her dress sleeve to hide what I suspected was the cut of a whip. "Oh, that ain't nothin'."

I lifted her sleeve and saw that the raw line continued across her shoulder and out of sight beneath the back of her dress. "Did Virgil McVey strike you?"

Jerlinda lowered her eyes. "One lash to serve warnin' on me and the others. He said I shoulda fetched him the day you was at the cabin. Said I shouldn't be servin' you swill outta my kettle."

I turned to Rafe. "Why didn't you tell me?"

"It was already done," he said with frustration. "Mista McVey is new to the job and makin' an example every which way. We've all gotten the strap at least once since he's been here."

"First time for all of us," Axel said, as he used a flat rock to sift the charred lumps of cornmeal from the hot ash. I wished I knew how to reach out to him, as he had for me that day on the cliff. His gentle way reminded me so much of Papa.

Jerlinda pulled her sleeve back over her wound. "Let's not waste time talkin' about that rascal. Let's have a peaceful meal on the Lord's day."

Knowing they had been whipped made me awkward in their company. What must they think of me and my family? "I can't stay," I said quickly. "Garrison is calling on me this afternoon, so I am expected at home. However, your invitation was kind and I did not want you to think I had forgotten."

"Garrison Yob," Jerlinda muttered. She shook her head in disgust. "Thought we got rid o' him for sure."

My jaw dropped with surprise. "*Rid* of him? You mean *you* were the one who told Papa he was . . . ?"

Jerlinda looked at me with soft eyes, but lifted her chin with conviction. "When Rafe told me what he see'd Marster Yob doin' to you, I wasn't gonna sit quiet. He is lucky I wasn't near enough to wallop him with a fry pan. But I knew Bradford would take him in hand. Yo' daddy throwed a fit at the thought of that grubby man takin' liberties with you. Said he would never forgive himself for bein' tricked by Marster's fakery."

I stepped inside their circle to close the distance between Jerlinda and me. "I had no idea it was you. Thank you for intervening on my behalf."

Her chin quivered with emotion. "Just because you was took from my arms as a chile don't mean you is gone from my heart, Jacy. I wish I could do more now that Marster has wormed his way back here."

"Why do all of you address Garrison as a master?" I asked as I settled tentatively on the grass. "Is it because you believe he will own Great Meadow?"

"No, miss," Rafe said, speaking for the group. "It's jes' a show of respect. From the time we is babes, slaves is taught to let white folks feel that we know our place. Any white man who gots the means to buy or sell us is a marster by name, even if he don't own us."

"I see." I sighed. "I guess the challenges of a slave are not much different from those of a woman."

Rafe chuckled. "Don't know no mistress that could survive a day in the quarters."

I flushed. "Not a similarity measured by hardship. That could never be so, but perhaps in endurance of what is forced upon us. The privilege of choice is often had only by a man."

"Never thought of it like that," Jerlinda mused. "But judgin' by the fix you is in with Marster Yob, you ain't got much say."

Her words touched me. Jerlinda understood more than I thought was possible. Rafe and Axel excused themselves to fetch more logs for the fire, but I suspected they were giving us some privacy. Sitting opposite me, Jerlinda was a stranger, yet not a stranger at all. She had always been on the periphery of my life as nothing more than a servant, yet her presence had allowed her to maintain a finger in my care and an eye on my well-being. I was captivated by her gentleness and wanted to know more about her.

"All these years I never realized Axel was your son. I used to see him around the cookhouse when he was younger, but I never connected him to you."

Jerlinda smiled. "It warmed yo' daddy and me that you were so tender with Axel. At the time, Claudia was workin' me hard to punish me for bearin' another chile. He needed extra care because of his bad leg, but Claudia had me hoppin' from sunup to sundown. Little Axel stayed in the cookhouse and was mothered by all. In the commotion of our duties, Axel usually ended up in the corner or on someone's hip bein' carried instead of encouraged to walk. It was the easiest thing to do. We didn't know no different. All the gals fussed over Jerlinda's crippled chile, because they knew he was Marster Lane's chile too."

"I could never have imagined then what I know now."

"That he is yo' brother?"

I nodded, still unable to say it aloud.

"It was a miracle when you started sneakin' out behind the cookhouse like you was puffin' a tobacco pipe in naughty secrecy. Do you remember usin' molasses drops to coax Axel to walk, step by step?"

I laughed. "For a speck of hard candy, he would follow me anywhere."

"Axel loved the attention too. He limped and stumbled, but picked himself up just for the pleasure of makin' you clap with glee. Bradford said that yo' care was not rooted in pity, but was a sisterly instinct."

"Jaaa-cy!" The distant bellow halted us. I recognized the voice immediately.

"Garrison!"

No sooner had I spoken the name than Rafe hurtled through the underbrush. Axel hobbled quickly behind him. "Marster is comin' through the trees," Axel called. "We better scatter."

Jerlinda reached for me. "Go, Jacy. Don't let him find you with us."

"I won't let him hurt you," I said, squeezing her hands.

"I am not worried about what will happen to me. You stand to lose more than three lowly slaves put together. Run!"

Rafe grabbed me by the wrist. "Follow me!"

We tore through the flora as fast as we could. We ran far up the hillside, where the evergreens were dark and dense. "Call out to him," Rafe said, panting when we paused to catch our breath.

"What?"

"Call his name as though you are lost. It will lead him away from Jerlinda and Axel."

Without further thought, I hollered, "Garrison, I am here!"

Garrison shouted in annoyance, "Where, Jacy? What are you doing out here?"

Hand in hand, Rafe and I ran deeper into the thicket as I continued to cry out to Garrison. "I was gathering pinecones and can't find my way out of the forest."

Rafe pulled me behind a tree. He pressed my back against the trunk and leaned so close I could breathe him in. Quivering, I was aghast at how natural it felt. We held still and listened. Garrison's footsteps could be heard at a distance through the shadow of evergreen.

"Good," Rafe said. "He is followin' us."

Rafe's strong hands gripped my shoulders. I looked up at him as we shuddered in our nearness. We were so close that when his eyes fell on mine I could feel their pull. My breath hitched and eased beneath his touch. Common sense told me to push him away. Instead I was frozen by the pleasure that buzzed through me. He held me a moment longer until Garrison boomed, "Dag-blast, where are you, woman?"

My heart, already pounding within me, leapt when Rafe's hands drifted from my shoulders and down my arms until my hands were in his. He spoke with hushed urgency. "Will you be all right?"

I could barely unclench my throat to whisper, "Yes."

Rafe touched a tender finger to my cheek to gauge my certainty. With a nod of assurance, he backed away. Then, as swift and silent as a deer, he sprinted deeper into the wood. I did not take my eyes from him until he was out of sight.

When the distant march of boots snapped me to attention, I

scrambled for dropped pinecones on the forest floor. "I am here, Garrison!"

By the time Garrison escorted me back to the house, his disgruntled mood had faded. My convincing portrayal of a damsel in distress made him feel quite the hero. To my relief, Mayme's idea about pinecones made a quick and believable reason for me to stray from the farm. My activity was not under suspicion, although my dimwittedness was fodder for discussion later that night.

"She was so far out of the way," Garrison boasted, "she would still be there with the night creatures had I not tracked her down." Listening to his verbose account of my rescue was an easy concession to ensure that my questionable engagement would not be discovered. When Garrison had imbibed the last of his evening cordials, he leaned back in his chair, satisfied.

Or so I thought.

"The day has been eventful, don't you agree, Jacy?"

"Indeed," I said with humble deference. "My fatigue from the ordeal beckons me to retire early this evening."

Garrison stood. "Not before you and I take a brief stroll."

My heart sank. I had dodged Garrison's assaults for weeks. Now my reprieve was about to end. I attempted to politely excuse myself, but he already had me by the arm. Mother turned away when I glanced toward her for support, and I knew she had relinquished me to him.

The night was without moon or stars, its blackness an accomplice in Garrison's offense. "You owe me a debt of gratitude for today," he said as his fleshy hand pawed my cheek. I could not help but think how gruff his touch was in the wake of Rafe's gentle caress.

"Please don't do it, Garrison." He pushed his sloppy mouth against mine, leaving the taste of brandy and cigars on my lips.

"I am weary of being rebuffed," he said, jerking my shoulders. "I have given you margin during your period of mourning, but my patience cannot hold out. Soon we will be married, and I want assurance that you can be bridled."

He spun me around and pressed against me. "Hold still and be quiet."

I lowered my head, but immediately heard a heavy thud. Garrison released my waist. "What the hell?" Rubbing his shoulder, he looked around. "Something hit me."

"Perhaps the bats are flying low tonight," I said in hope of escaping once again. "Let's retreat indoors before we are bitten."

He pushed me harder against the fence. "Don't be stupid, Jacy. It was likely a walnut knocked from a squirrel's nest in the branches above us." He leaned into me again, this time with more force.

Then . . . *thump!*

The sound was clearly stone against wood. He bent over and picked up the plum-sized piece of gravel that fell at our feet. "Someone is throwing rocks at us!"

He scanned the night for an unseen assailant. "Who is out there? I demand you show yourself."

There was no way of telling from which direction the rocks were being hurled. The side and back yards were silent, as were the stable and nearby pasture.

"Get in the house, Jacy," Garrison growled. I ran to the porch while Garrison went to his carriage. I panicked when he strode across the yard with a whip in one hand and a shotgun in the other. "I'll put an end to this insolence," he mumbled as he paused to cock the hammer on his shotgun. Then he turned to bellow into the night.

"Man, woman, or child! You will die for your deed!"

Chapter 8

"Where is Garrison?" Mother snapped as she charged at me from the dining room, where she had been lurking. "I heard him raise his voice. You foolish girl, have you crossed him again?"

I did not know how to pacify her anger without agitating her further. "Someone—" I cut off my response to carefully choose my words. "We were interrupted."

"Interrupted by what? Why is he yelling?"

Garrison could still be heard roaring into the night. His bark echoed at the rear of the house, and although Mother could not discern what he was saying, I knew he would tell her soon enough. I needed to find a way to present the incident nonchalantly.

"He was struck by a small stone."

Mother's ivory cheeks flushed with rage. "By you?"

Before I could answer, a shot rang out in the side yard.

"Oh, no!" I screamed, pushing past Mother. Tess jumped from my path as I ran through the kitchen and into the darkness. Another shot was fired beyond the empty cookhouse. "Garrison, stop!"

When I reached him, he was pouring gunpowder down the muzzle of his shotgun. He shook me off when I clung to his arm, but I grabbed the barrel of the weapon before he could fire again. "Stop shooting! This is not an uprising."

Garrison seethed with each craggy breath he heaved. "We were attacked, Jacy. Stalked and targeted. That is how rebellion begins. Gracious luck spared your delicate face from being bruised."

Mother followed on my heels, her eyes wide with horror and confusion. Garrison explained that rocks had been thrown while he and I were *talking* in private. When Mother did not appear to be alarmed or frightened, I knew she surmised the truth: Someone had tried to protect me. She did not reveal her suspicions to Garrison, but she gave him the authority to seek out retribution in the quarters. I was sickened when he trod forth like a general to battle.

"Luck, indeed," Mother huffed. "Isn't it interesting that the rocks did not strike you?"

I offered no comment and returned to the house. Following me up the stairs and into my bedchamber, she did not let up on her inquisition. "Was it luck, Jacy? Or were the launched rocks aimed only at Garrison?"

I turned to face her. "Mother, it has been an upsetting day. I am weary and see no point in rehashing the event. Garrison is making too much of it."

With fierce warning, she poked her finger against my chest. "Do not misjudge my tolerance. I am not a fool, Jacy. One of your Negro kin did this. Probably that gimpy stable boy. I would have him hanged tonight if it would not raise the question of why in Garrison's mind. I will not risk our secret being discovered. All would be lost."

I refused to succumb to her intimidation. "You have no proof that the rocks were anything more than a mischievous prank."

"Keep your distance from Jerlinda and the other darkies," she said, clenching her jaw. "And do not rile them. Or you will regret it, as will they."

She slammed the door on her way out. At her exodus I murmured, "At least they care enough to get *riled* on my behalf."

Tension overtook Great Meadow after that night. To safeguard those in question, I did not leave the house for nearly a week. When I confided to Mayme what had happened, she agreed that maintaining a quiet, unassuming presence would make it less likely I would garner unwanted scrutiny from Garrison or Mother. I was forbidden from going to the stable or walking unattended. Garrison continued to rant and snarl, but the incident had shaken him. Not once since being plunked by the rock did he bid me to the fence. Alone in the dining room with Tess one morning, I sought assurance for my lingering worries.

"Is all as it should be in the quarters, Tess?" She stopped pouring my tea before my cup was filled. I carefully gauged her reaction as I continued. "Mr. Yob has been in a sour mood. He can be excessive at times."

Tess did not look at me. Nor did she answer. She curtsied politely and retreated to the kitchen. Anxiety nudged me from the house to the stable. The building was empty and oddly silent. Immediately I noticed the unkempt condition of Eclipse's stall. Manure lay in clumps around her hooves, and her water trough was nearly dry. When Axel limped in from the pasture, I could see by his bent frame that something was wrong.

"Axel, what has happened?" I said, helping him open the door to the stall.

"We all been movin' a bit slower the last few days, but we is gettin' caught up with our chores bit by bit."

He winced as he lifted a shovel to clean the stall. I touched the brown stain on the back of his shirt. "You have been whipped."

"Every slave on the property was strapped with ten lashes the night Marster came to the quarters. Him and Mista McVey been layin' a heavy hand on us."

"Oh, no." I pressed my hand to my breast. "Jerlinda and Rafe too?"

"We gots'ta bear the burden," he said evenly. "Just ain't used to it, is all. Never been beat by an overseer. Only thing worse than the pain is bein' forced to take it, especially when Mama is next in line for the whippin' post."

"I had no idea, Axel. Tess is the only servant I have seen and she seems fine."

Axel could not mask the glint of anger in his eyes. "Titus and Tess don't bear the mark of the whip. Those who act as Marster's eyes and ears is spared. We all gotta step careful in the path of Tess and Titus."

"Jacy, why are you here?" Garrison's voice boomed from the doorway. He strode toward us, his face purpled with fury. As Axel slipped from the stall, Garrison kicked him in the ribs, tumbling him into a heap. Garrison picked up Axel by the collar and tossed him into the pasture.

"Garrison!"

"You are forbidden to be in here with one of *them*. They can't be trusted."

I bristled at his command. "This is not your stable, Garrison. Not yet. I am here to groom Eclipse."

His eyes narrowed. "Then I will advise Claudia to sell the damn horse. That will keep you away from the muck."

"Eclipse belongs to me. She was a gift from my father and will remain here forever."

Garrison cornered me. "I don't know where you get your wild streak, Jacy, but I will tame it one way or the other."

"S'cuse me, Marster." Rafe's voice bolstered me. "Looks like rain. Do you want the foals brought in for the day?"

Garrison backed away from me and peered from the window, giving me the chance to look over at Rafe. The determination in his gaze made it clear his appearance was purposeful. Perhaps he had been alerted by Axel.

Garrison grumbled, "I see no storm clouds."

"Storm is comin', sah," Rafe said, his fists flexing at his sides. "I got an ache that tells me it's so."

"Damn Negroes and your superstitions." Garrison took me by the hand and dragged me from the stable.

"I was only looking in on the horses," I explained when he marched me straight to Mother.

"Claudia, it's bad enough that she traipses through the manure to stroke a beast, but then she chats with the stable boy like they are having high tea. I am beginning to wonder what I have gotten myself into."

Mother quaked with anger at the mention of Axel. I thought about his whip marks and quickly tried to undo the damage I had done. "I apologize, Mother. My intent was not to disobey. I was simply grooming Eclipse. Garrison is right. I did speak to the stable boy, but only to scold him for neglecting the stall. You must agree, Garrison, the stable was in disarray."

"Well, perhaps," Garrison countered. "But it is not your place to approach him. With all that has happened, I find it strange that you are not more guarded."

Mother interceded before he engaged in too much speculation. "It's not strange, Garrison, just dangerously naive. Jacy, you will concede to greater supervision. No more visits to the stable, no more walks about the grounds, no more chats unless granted permission by Garrison."

He inflated with satisfaction at the prospect of reining me in completely. I was not in a position to argue or object. I agreed, hoping my contrition would alleviate the doubt in Mother's glare. To demonstrate my obedience, I curtsied to Garrison. "With your permission, I will retire for the night."

Garrison smiled. "You are excused, Jacy. I must leave for Elizabeth City tonight on the *Southern Gale* for some pressing business. When I return the day after next, perhaps we will go riding so you can spend time with your precious mare."

I wondered if he was being serious or snide. It was uncharacteristic of him to give consideration to my feelings. Queasy apprehension turned in me as I ascended the stairs. I did not have to look to feel Mother's scorching eyes still locked on me. My uncertainty increased tenfold when I slipped into my room and found no reprieve from my worries.

Sleepless, I thought about what Axel had told me about the whippings inflicted in the quarters. Were Jerlinda and the others suffering? I paced the room, pulled between the entitlements that came with living in the main house and the endurance required of living in its shadow. Nothing about Great Meadow was familiar to me anymore. I missed my father. I was a part of him, but what was I a part of now? Rafe and Jerlinda had protected me when I was abused. Rafe even sheltered me when Garrison loomed. How could I not find a way to protect them?

I went to the balcony to escape the stuffiness of my room. A light in the stable immediately caught my eye. It alarmed me. If a lamp had mistakenly been left aflame, it could start a fire. I hurried through the darkened house, careful to make no sound. Dressed in only my nightgown and bed jacket, I entered the stable and followed the stream of light between the stalls.

"Eclipse!"

The sight of my beloved Appaloosa on her side horrified me. Kneeling next to her were Rafe, Axel, and Jerlinda. I rushed to her and stroked her mane. "What's wrong with her?"

"Axel came a-runnin' for me when he found her," Rafe said as he patted her distended belly. "Couldn't figure out what sickened her until I looked in her feed bag. Someone put chokecherry in her oats."

"Only a heartless demon would do such a thing," Jerlinda said. Immediately I thought of Garrison and his peculiar invitation to go riding when he returned. His ruthless intent was obvious now. What a cruel game of emotional manipulation.

Rafe threw hay on a puddle of vomit near the horse's snout. "As soon as I realized the poor thing was poisoned, I sent Axel to fetch Jerlinda and her herbs."

Jerlinda held up a half-empty jar of golden liquid. "A little brewed brak bush and pokeweed did the trick. Sly ol' Rafe got Eclipse to drink some usin' that kidney sac like when she was newborn."

"Will she survive?"

Sensing my distress, Rafe lifted his hand to my shoulder. "We don't know yet, Jacy. We gotta wait and see. Hopefully we got the poison out of her in time."

The fallen horse panted in shallow breaths. Her helplessness made my eyes overflow. Jerlinda wrapped her arms around me as soon as she saw my tears. "Hold on to me, chile. We'll get through it."

Jerlinda's warmth blanketed me. I folded my arms around her and held tight. She rocked me as I wept softly; all the while she stroked my hair and cheeks. When I settled, I remained in her embrace until I realized my hands were clutching her back where her flesh had been torn by the whip.

"Oh, Jerlinda," I said, easing my grip. "I am so sorry. Did I hurt you?"

Jerlinda's cheeks were moist with emotion. "Sweet Jacy, love is worth the pain."

I marveled at her devoted care. Rafe and Axel went to find rope that was strong enough to help the weakened animal onto her feet. Jerlinda stayed fixed against me as I patted down Eclipse. When we were alone together, I could feel her eyes watching me. "You been through a lot lately," Jerlinda said softly. "It must get your head a-spinnin'."

Her fretful gaze unlocked my heart. "I no longer know who I am," I said aloud for the first time. "I am not wholly white, as I once thought. Nor am I Negro. I am nothing."

Jerlinda turned my face to hers. "Chile, you ain't *nothing*. You are like this Appaloosa. Some folks look at Eclipse and see a white horse with patches of brown. Others look and see a brown horse with patches of white. But we know she is the same beautiful creature no matter which way you look at her." She touched my cheek. "Just as you are the same beautiful Jacy."

Her words filled me with hope that I was not meant to drift in a sea of in-between. I soaked in the maternal warmth I had lacked for as long as I could remember. It flowed so naturally it embraced me as tightly as her arms squeezed me. I could have stayed there forever had Eclipse not jostled her front legs. Jerlinda and I leaned back from her. Again she kicked, this time her back legs as well. Her colorful body bucked and flailed until suddenly she popped up onto shaky legs. Rafe and Axel came running when they heard the commotion.

Rafe rubbed his hand down the revived horse's muzzle. "Well, look at you standing there fine and pretty."

I laughed and combed my hand through Eclipse's mane, so grateful to see her upright. When I smiled up at Rafe standing opposite me, I blushed when he winked playfully. "That goes for you too, Jacy."

I laughed again and felt bonded by our shared affection. Rafe was serious and compassionate, yet in intimate moments a child's innocence sparkled in his gaze. He had first captivated me within the evergreens the day of the picnic, and here again in the stable within a halo of lamplight.

"Daybreak will creep up on us soon," Jerlinda said. She brushed her hand down the length of my hair. "I best get on back to the cabin."

Axel nodded to Rafe and me. "I'll walk down with you, Mama. We done all we can for the night."

"I'm gonna stay for a spell," Rafe said. "Just to make certain she is comfortable."

I hugged Jerlinda tightly. "Thank you for saving her. You possess the perfect healing touch."

What I did not say was that her wisdom and clarity of vision had saved me as well. She urged me to simply continue to be who I had always been, regardless of the color pattern imprinted within me, instead of being tormented by what I was or was not. I was embraced by the love of a true mother. Perhaps fate had brought her to me as a gift, not as a curse.

"You better scoot back to the main house too," Rafe said to me when Jerlinda and Axel had gone. "If missus catches you here—"

I moved around the horse to where he stood, running my hands along the length of her withers. "A few more moments will do no harm," I said with a hushed voice. "How shall I ever repay you for saving Eclipse?"

"We all did our part."

I stroked more slowly while finding the courage to speak what was in my heart. "Rafe, I am grateful that Eclipse's special nature and circumstance of birth brought us together."

Rafe lifted his hand and rested it near mine on the back of the horse. He was testing the water of our emotion and seemed to sense that a bigger move on his part might frighten me. All I wanted was to touch his hand again, as we did in the woods when running from Garrison. The memory of our brush with tenderness that day still tugged at me. I wondered if Rafe could hear the wild thump of my heart or see the blush on my cheeks. His fingers pressed lightly over mine. I raised my eyes to him as he stepped closer, but the only intimacy I had ever experienced of this kind was my twisted encounters with Garrison.

Instinctively, my defenses went up and I pulled away. Still holding my fingertips, Rafe winced with confusion. I saw in his hurt expression that my hesitation wounded the trust and tenderness between us. Before I could explain, a bright lantern was raised to our faces. Rafe and I pulled apart with a gasp, exposed by the burning wick and illuminated globe. Horrified at being discovered, I flung my hands over my face and braced for swift retribution.

Titus smirked at us through the fiery glow. "What's goin' on here?"

Chapter 9

"*T*itus!"

The man's eyes fluttered with disbelief. To him, we were a slave and a white mistress engaged in the worst kind of impropriety. My mind whirled with snippets of ideas to explain our indecorous exchange. However, the transgression was too serious and could not be dismissed as innocent, or misconstrued.

Rafe pushed the lantern away from our stunned expressions. "Step back from us, Titus."

I shifted between the two men to prevent a scuffle. Rafe's protective instinct poised him for battle. Titus could not be trusted; that much I knew. But I believed he could be enticed by reward and favor.

"Titus, you stumbled onto a delicate matter. I am sick with grief and commanded Rafe to take my hand. He could not refuse his mistress. Do you understand?"

Titus stared at me with knowing eyes. "If you say so, miss."

"You cannot refuse me either. I demand your silence and in return I will have Mother appoint you as lead horseman and carriage driver. Your higher station will mean no more shoveling manure, and an increase in wardrobe and ration."

Titus glanced at Rafe and then studied me. I gave him a determined nod, hoping my effort at insistence hid the doom swelling in my breast. Grudgingly, he returned my nod.

"It is agreed, then," I said. Rafe's ashen expression pained me. I wished to reach for him, but an abrupt end to the encounter was best for all. Without glancing at either man, I rushed from the stall and into the house.

I sat in the dark parlor, waiting for sunrise. A new day was soon to come, and I feared it would not end well. When Mother descended the stairs, she went directly to the dining room with no notice of me in the parlor. Voices coaxed me toward her. My heart sank when I peeked through the crack of the door. Titus's wife, Tess, already had Mother's ear. With her back to me, Mother gripped the chair. She wobbled slightly and leaned onto the table. I thought she might faint until a venomous cry tore from her throat, causing Tess to back away. In a sudden outburst, Mother clawed the table linen and yanked it with both hands. Two place settings of china crashed at her feet. "Damn that girl!"

"Jes' thought you would want to know, missus."

"You were right in telling me, Tess," Mother said, her voice tight but eerily controlled. "Now, go upstairs and bring her to me."

Dread overtook me. My indiscretion had crossed a line that even I had not expected. There was no doubt that Mother would levy swift and extreme measures to quash the threat of my dalliance. I took a deep breath and entered the room, knowing she had to be met head-on with bold action.

"I am here, Mother."

Crazed with fury, she spun around. I walked forward a few steps and stopped halfway across the room. Tess rushed past me to escape through the kitchen. Mother's nostrils flared as each breath she wheezed grew fiercer. She narrowed her eyes and came straight for me, screaming.

"You insolent animal, how could you?" Before I could react, her hand struck my face with enough force to make my ears pop. I stumbled sideways and she was on me again, her fingers squeezed against my throat.

"Mother, stop!" I cried out as I pushed her off of me. I reached for an iron poker that leaned by the fireplace and swung it between us. She jumped back, her teeth clenched.

"I must save you from yourself, Jacy. Your Negro impulses have been unearthed by spending time among them. Your defiance is fed by impure blood. For your sake, I will do all in my power to harness you."

"My sake?" I laughed bitterly. "Don't you mean *your* sake, Mother? You have never done anything out of care for me."

Mother lifted a calming hand toward me, but her trembling fingertips gave away her distress. She fixed an uncomfortable smile on her face while she reasoned with me. "Jacy, they could be hanged within the hour if I so decreed. I could easily report to McVey or Garrison that Rafe assaulted you and that Axel threw the rocks."

Mother paused, nearly giddy at the thought. "And I could order that Jerlinda be strung up by her neck along with them . . . simply *because*. But out of respect for your feelings, I am willing to compromise. They will be sold, all three, at the slave market in Smithfield as soon as Garrison returns. This way they cannot stir up the Negro in you. All can be as it was before your father died."

I laughed at her attempt to trick me. "Do you think I would trust your words? I suspect you would send them away, as if sold, only to lynch them ten miles down the road. Your hatred of Jerlinda is palpable."

Mother's eyes sparked. "She lured away my husband."

"They loved each other."

"Is that what the seductive wench told you?" Mother grinned. "She is a Negro, Jacy. She cannot feel love. She can only use carnal instincts to manipulate men in order to obtain an easier life."

I raised my chin. "I feel love, Mother. And as you keep reminding me, I *am* a Negro. One drop of blood makes it so; isn't that what you said?"

She squirmed to contain the hatred seething behind her thin smile. "Your unrestrained behavior has given me a severe migraine. I shall go to my chamber to regain my composure. I suggest you do the same. We will talk later."

Mother swept from the room. I had disarmed her momentarily with my firm stance, but the stakes were too high for her not to strike back quickly. I had little time to intervene before she regrouped and countered with a stronger assault. Every instinct in me drove me to protect the innocent souls she had targeted. If not me, then who? They were no longer chattel to me. I cared about them. Papa spent a lifetime safeguarding Jerlinda and Axel from Mother's wrath. His spirit urged me into action.

I rushed to the desk in the parlor. With ink and quill in hand, I scratched a brief but direct note and propped it on the desktop where she would be sure to find it.

Mother. Do nothing or our secret will be revealed. Jacy.

I slipped out of the front door and ran through the graying dawn to the cookhouse. The aroma of biscuits and gravy assured me Jerlinda would be there. To the surprise of the others, I grabbed Jerlinda by the hand and pulled her with me. We ducked behind a woodpile near the stable until I was sure Titus was not within earshot.

"Did missus find out about Rafe?"

"How did you know?" I whispered.

"Rafe told us what happened. His gut told him right off that Titus and Tess would use it to get in good graces with missus."

I touched Jerlinda's cheek. "I am afraid she will have you killed."

Jerlinda flinched, but remained calm. She followed me into the stable, where Rafe was brushing Eclipse. I had only to speak two words to convey my urgency.

"She knows."

Rafe reached out with regret and squeezed my hands. "I gotta run."

"All three of you must flee for your lives. There is not much time. Where's Axel?"

"He was about to ride down to the gristmill to fetch a load of oats for the troughs. He may still be in the barn."

"Hurry," I stressed.

Axel had just secured the horse to the wagon when we rushed in. Although I had no true plan, an idea struck me. "We'll take the wagon!"

"What?" Rafe said.

I tugged Rafe by the arm. "Pile some hay in the buckboard to conceal us. Your chance of escape improves with every mile gained before McVey realizes you have left the property. I will go far enough to see you safely on your way." Then under my breath I finished my thought so Rafe saw the sense of it. "Without the wagon, Axel cannot outrun McVey's bloodhounds."

The four of us hastily tossed hay into the back of the wagon. When a generous pile was mounted, Axel climbed onto the bench seat. "Axel, drive the wagon slowly along the lane that exits the farm. I will remain hidden until we are well beyond our property and then will join you at the reins. Without a day pass, you must look to be in the company of your mistress."

"Which way am I headed?"

I searched my mind for a direction and then it came to me. "We shall try to reach South Mills, where I can seek out Sylvan Firth. He is a man of good character and conscience. Now let's be on our way before Mother can intercept us."

We rolled east toward the sunrise. South Mills was a day's ride by wagon, and I prayed we would encounter no delay or confrontation. After we cleared our property and several neighboring farms, I crawled from the prickly hay mound and joined Axel on the bench seat at the head of the wagon. Jerlinda and Rafe pushed aside enough hay to sit upright and be comfortable, yet be prepared to burrow beneath the pile when approached by an oncoming traveler. Fortunately, the early-September weather was pleasant and the road to South Mills light of passersby.

Jerlinda dabbed her moist brow with a handkerchief. "Missus is gonna send a posse when she sees the wagon is gone along with you and three slaves."

"Maybe so," I said, looking over my shoulder at the empty road that stretched behind us. "But I hope that by the time she discovers the note I left behind, we will have traveled a hearty distance. I also played a trump card designed to make her hesitate."

Jerlinda looked up at me. "A what?"

"I turned her often-used threat against her," I said. "She may choose not to chase us out of fear that I'll reveal you as my birth mother. She would prefer to kill you to ensure her dirty secret is dead and buried. However, if you run away, her purpose will be served just the same. In her mind, if you are gone and I have no emotional ties in the slave quarters, her status and property will be preserved. Unfortunately, she can stall McVey only a short while, because once he realizes you are gone, hounds and patrollers will be unleashed."

We rode in silence while we contemplated the risks and consequences of potential capture. The impromptu exodus had not allowed for planning or preparation. They had left with only the clothes on their backs and no food or drink. Anxiety weighed heavily on me as I wondered whether Sylvan Firth was indeed an agent of the Underground, as Mother had suggested when he had visited our home. I had heard rumors about sympathizers who aided runaways with supplies and direction, but those whose treasonous activity was uncovered suffered dire consequences. The closer we got to South Mills, the weaker my loosely put-together plan seemed. In my attempt to save their lives, I might in fact be leading them to slaughter. Perspiration moistened my hair and clothing. What had I done?

"Here, Jacy," Axel said, handing over the reins. "Let me show you how to guide the horse so you can get back home safely."

"Thank goodness for your foresight, Axel," I said as he carefully folded my hands around the straps guiding the horse.

He smiled at my gratitude. "I reckon we been lookin' out fo' each other over the years, even when we didn't know we was kin."

I returned his smile, though we had little time to reflect on the quiet bond we shared. I had not yet thought about what would happen beyond South Mills. Axel was right: I needed to drive the wagon back to Great Meadow alone. What would I face when I returned? Would the countryside be crawling with slave hunters? Or would Mother be waiting to deal with me privately? Although dozens of questions raced through my thoughts, there was only one that tugged painfully at my heart.

How am I going to say good-bye?

I had just gotten to know my mother and brother. And though the initial shock and revulsion of my changed circumstance had rocked me, I was not prepared to part from them. In their presence, I felt their genuine care and selflessness. Gentle and kind, their hearts embraced me: never judging, never expecting. During the time I had spent sorting through the turmoil brought on by my secret, I had not realized how attached we had become. They were loving, like Papa, and it bonded me to them.

Then there was Rafe. Strong and tender, he healed me. He had opened my heart to what love should be, and I knew I would never be the same.

"Better give me back the reins," Axel said as the distant sound of horses' hooves sent Rafe and Jerlinda crawling beneath the hay for cover. Within minutes, a burly man on horseback was coming toward us. I tensed as he slowed his pace and raised a large, calloused hand to halt us.

"Good afternoon, sir," I said with a sweet lilt meant to please him. He pushed his evenly cropped dark hair behind his thick, protruding ears.

He looked warily at Axel. "More like good *evening*, lass. There is not much light left in the day. Where are you traveling to?"

"This hay is expected in South Mills by sundown."

"Delivered by a woman?"

I feigned insult. "Do I look like a common farmer, sir?"

"No, miss," he said, backing down slightly. "But I am not accustomed to seeing an unescorted lass side by side with a colored buck."

"He is my hired man. My husband fell ill with fever, but our debts require delivery of this hay. I do not trust this lowly slave to handle our money, so I must accompany him to assure the transaction is completed and our profit secured. However, I refuse to arrive in town perched on a haystack like a guinea hen."

The man tugged his hat apologetically. "That's your prerogative, miss, but you will not reach South Mills until after dark. Sunset brings the carousing of slave patrols, which ride fiercely in the night through this area. They are likely to harass your colored man, and I worry they may not be delicate with you either."

"I see." It was fortunate we had run into this man so that we were not taken unawares, yet I did not know how to protect us against the night.

He dismounted his horse and adjusted his bowler hat, which was adorned with a rabbit's foot. "Miss, I consider it my gentlemanly duty to escort you to town. I shall sit next to your colored man while you ride my stallion."

My anxiety twisted tighter. I did not want this stranger mounted on my wagon with two slaves buried beneath the hay behind him, but the threat of patrollers was a menacing alternative. I decided the lone man was the lesser risk.

"Thank you for your kind offer, sir. My name is Jacy Lane of Great Meadow."

"Ah, Jacy Lane," he said with a good-hearted grin. "Your name flows from my tongue like the chorus of a song."

His name was Caleb Briggs. He was stout in build, with a heavy beard and rough hands stained by a day's labor. He could not have been much older than me, but his creased face looked worn by a hard life. Caleb lifted me like a feather from the wagon onto his horse, allowing my legs to dangle sidesaddle.

"Are you from the area, Mr. Briggs?"

"I am, lass," he said. "My wife, Katherine, and I live in a cottage near Devlin Creek."

I could see from his appearance that he was not a man of means, but his strong arms and shoulders brought to mind the possibility that he was an overseer on one of the surrounding plantations. I grew anxious at the thought and needed to learn more about this stranger who felt compelled to escort me to South Mills.

"Are you a planter, Mr. Briggs?"

He laughed heartily at the inquiry. "No, miss, I have no use for the powerful gentry who bully the common man."

"You're a sympathizer, then?"

"I didn't say that," he interjected brusquely. "What a man does on his own land, and with those that are his property, is no business of mine. I have enough problems to busy my day without taking on someone else's cause."

I quickly changed the subject. "Won't your wife be concerned if you are not home for your evening meal?"

"She's in no hurry to see the likes of me."

Caleb hunched over the reins, his mood instantly soured. Silence fell between us as I decided I had prodded this man enough for now. Soon dusk was upon us. We rode together for less than an hour when several glints of light appeared in the distance.

"Looks like we have visitors," Caleb grumbled.

"Are they patrollers?" I asked the question loudly so Rafe and Jerlinda could curl deeper in the hay.

"Aye. Let me do the talking."

Within minutes six armed men on horses surrounded us. They carried torches and were dressed in worn trousers and suede coats much like the overseer McVey. Each man looked hard at Axel and then at me.

"Howdy, Caleb. Aren't you headed in the wrong direction? There are no lighters to be loaded this time of night."

"Aye, my work at the canal is done for the day," Caleb answered. "I am earning an extra coin or two by doing a favor for a friend."

The man closest to me laughed. "And is this the *friend*?"

"It's no business of yours, Patrick. Go on and leave me to my work."

"Hey, what's this?" croaked a man at the rear of the wagon. I nearly fell from my saddle when he swung off his horse and jumped into the wagon. He lifted a slouch hat from the hay. It was Rafe's.

"The hat belongs to my husband," I said, straining for the man's attention. "He misplaced it months ago."

The man held it to his face. "Smells like darky grime."

Caleb stood with one boot propped on the back of the bench seat. "Well, now, when did you grow the snout of a bloodhound?"

The other men laughed and barked at the man in the wagon. I held my breath when he scuffed aside a clump of hay and then another. "Can't be too careful."

"Get on with you," Caleb snapped. "What you're looking for is crawling in the thicket or slogging through the great swamp. Don't waste my time or yourn."

The man called Patrick spoke up. "Mount your horse, Spit. I would sooner court a gator than cross Caleb."

Caleb stared down the man in the back, who finally tossed the hat into the hay. He leapt directly into his saddle and spurred his horse around the wagon to approach Caleb head-on. He pushed his torch between Caleb and me. "No harm intended, Caleb. Here, the road ahead is dark. Use my torch to find your way to town."

The man called Spit tugged his hat in my direction, and to my blessed relief, they stormed off into the night. I knew nothing of Caleb Briggs except that perhaps he was some kind of canal man. But I was deeply relieved that he commanded the respect of the ruffians on patrol. I shuddered to imagine our fate had we faced them without him.

"You have been a godsend, Mr. Briggs."

"Oh, I'm no saint, lass. My wife would be the first to tell you so." His eyes fluttered with painful discomfort.

"I am sure you are wrong," I said with assurance. "A woman's heart can be misunderstood at times."

His deep green eyes were moist when he looked over at me. "Her heart is broken, miss. And if I was more of a man, I would know how to fix it."

"Love is the best remedy for a broken heart," I said softly.

"We have plenty of love." His voice cracked as he continued. "Six months ago, Katherine birthed a child before its time. Our firstborn, no bigger than a lifeless pup. The midwife said it had not formed in the womb as it should. She said it was God's way of ridding us of an oddity."

Tears filled my eyes. "I am sorry for your loss, Mr. Briggs."

"It was a harsh blow indeed," he said, shaking his head. "Katherine was devastated. I tried to be strong and not give in to tears. I told her we would have another and that what was lost was not truly a child. The more I encouraged her to put it in the past, the further withdrawn she became. Now we are like strangers."

I felt compelled to help him, as he had me. "Perhaps your wife needed your sorrow more than she needed your strength."

"What do you mean? Is it not my duty to be strong?"

"Strength isn't always toughness and mettle, Mr. Briggs. Tenderness is also a kind of strength, rooted by unwavering devotion. I have never carried a child, but I want desperately to be a mother. I imagine what my baby will look like and how it will feel in my arms. It's real to me, even though the newborn is only in my mind. I believe any woman who is with child is immersed in this same daydream. The child was complete and real to Katherine, even if only in her mind's eye. She needs to mourn her precious child, not be told its loss is God's will or that it can be replaced by another."

Caleb pondered my words for a long moment. "I never thought of it in that way. She must believe me to be coldhearted."

"Mourn with her, Mr. Briggs," I said, gently. "Mourn together so your hearts can heal as parents, and as husband and wife."

I said no more. Caleb's distant expression told me he was deep in thought. Ruminating about children made me melancholy as well. Perhaps I had tossed away my only opportunity to make my dream of motherhood come true. Another hour passed before we finally saw the lanterns illuminating the buildings of South Mills.

As we rumbled into town, I thanked Caleb for his assistance. "Axel and I can manage from here, Mr. Briggs. You have been a great asset. I wish I could pay you for your trouble."

"I would not have accepted money for a good deed," he said with a dismissive wave of his hand. "Tell me, who do you seek for delivery of this hay?"

I hesitated before answering. "Sylvan Firth."

Caleb eyed me from under his hat. "Aye, Mr. Firth is the lockmaster. He is a good and decent fellow. Sylvan was meant to be a minister, but his father tended the canal lock for many a year. It takes the entire family to keep the lock going night and day all year long, so Sylvan carried a lot of guilt when he left for the seminary. His father and two brothers were lost to a cholera epidemic just two weeks after Sylvan had been ordained. The good son returned to South Mills to step in as lockmaster so his dear mother would not be uprooted from her home. She passed to the other side less than a year ago." He pointed down the road. "His white-shingled house sits along the canal next to the lock station. Would you like me to escort you to his door?"

"Thank you for your time and trouble, Mr. Briggs. I do not wish to delay you. Go home to your wife. I am acquainted with Mr. Firth and need no introduction."

Caleb climbed down from the wagon and lifted me from his horse. As he settled me next to Axel on the wagon seat, Caleb tipped his bowler hat. "I owe you a debt of gratitude, lass. Fate must have placed you in my path."

When finally we came upon the canal, I was exhausted. We had not eaten all day, and tension had drained me of vigor. I asked Axel to pull the wagon into the shadow of a barn adjacent to the white-shingled house. When I approached the rear door on foot, all was dark except for the yellow glow of Sylvan Firth's hearth seen through the window. I knocked softly. When there was no answer, I knocked harder until I heard footsteps within.

I recognized Sylvan Firth's mouthful of sugar cube–like teeth as he peeked through the window, though his blank gaze told me my face was unfamiliar to him. "Mr. Firth, I need to speak with you."

He puzzled over me while I tried to figure out how to ask him for help without revealing the details. After all, if the rumors were wrong and he was not a sympathizer, I did not want him to confiscate Jerlinda, Rafe, and Axel as runaways. I was well aware of the generous rewards slave catchers collected for their efforts.

"Do I know you?" he finally said as he opened his door to examine me more closely.

"My name is Jacy. I am Bradford Lane's daughter."

"My goodness! Come in, Miss Lane. I did not recognize you."

It was not surprising. My clothing was dusty and smelled of perspiration. I had left so abruptly I wore no bonnet, which had allowed my thick hair to expand in the day's heat. Still, Mr. Firth was polite and accommodating, although he bit his lower lip nervously as I entered his home.

"This is not a formal visit, so please call me Jacy."

He offered me a chair at his kitchen table, where a single candle burned. "As you wish, Jacy," he said. "What brings you to South Mills and to my door in the dark of night?"

"I have some . . ." I paused to study his creased face. "I have a situation to discuss."

He slid a plate of biscuits toward me. "If you and your mother need me to conduct a business matter, I will be happy to oblige. However, I do not believe your mother finds me trustworthy."

"Mother does not know I am here." Quickly and without manners, I devoured a biscuit.

He leaned back in his chair. "I see."

I licked the crumbs from my fingers and took a deep breath. "I need help, Mr. Firth. But it is a delicate matter."

"Who directed you to me? Was it a *friend*?"

"No one directed me to you, sir. I have come of my own volition."

"Why me?" He leaned forward and folded his hands on the table. "What makes you think I can help you with this delicate matter?"

"I have heard you are a *sympathetic* man." I chose my words carefully to gauge his tendency without giving up my purpose.

His expression darkened with suspicion. "You believe gossip and rumor, do you?"

"No." I flushed. "I mean, I was hoping . . ." I stood abruptly. "Never mind, Mr. Firth. Excuse the intrusion."

Sylvan Firth intercepted me at the door and blocked my retreat. "You were hoping *what*, Jacy?"

"Please, I must leave."

He looked out the two windows nearest us; his stern expression softened with concern. "Did anyone follow you here?"

"No, but if I do not return to Great Meadow tomorrow, I may be sought after."

I was growing desperate. He was as guarded as I, but one of us had to risk revealing our hand so we could penetrate this impasse. "Mr. Firth, all I seek is a path."

I could see by the glimmer of understanding in his eyes that he had received my message. He raked his fingers through his flaxen hair as he paced around the table. Finally, he stopped and faced me. "You seem of good character, so I will trust my instinct." He placed his hand on my shoulder with fatherly care. "Do you wish to send a package to the North?"

I puffed a sigh of relief. "Yes, but there are three."

Sylvan raised an eyebrow. "Delivery is urgent?"

"Deathly so."

I heaved a shaky breath. Our fate was now in the hands of Sylvan Firth. I told him our wagon was alongside the barn at the rear of the house. He wrapped the biscuits and a few apples in linen for me to take to the others. He asked for no other details except whether the three were adults or children.

"We have steamers, lighters, and flatboats that come through the lock with cargo being moved north on the canal through Great Dismal Swamp. I can conceal your packages in a crate on a special lighter that is tended by a friend. From the canal, they travel on Deep Creek to the southern branch of the Elizabeth River. If all goes well, they then journey up the river to Portsmouth or to one of the other tidewater landings. Someone working for the cause will see that the crate is loaded onto a ship launching to one of the northern ports in Philadelphia, New York, or Boston. Instruction will be given, but my role ends where the canal enters the swamp. Beyond Deep Creek, Virginia, I no longer know their destiny."

The finality of the plan struck a blow to my confidence. "It sounds like a journey fraught with danger of discovery."

"I cannot sweeten the bitter truth," he said with pensive gentleness. "However, our methods are far less perilous than navigating the same journey on foot. By land, the swamp is a ruthless foe, though it is said that many runaways attempt to use its vast marshes and heavy thickets to ward off bloodhounds and slave hunters on horseback. There are even whispers of maroon settlements in the recesses of Dismal Swamp."

"Maroon settlements?"

"Rudimentary colonies where pockets of runaways live in the secluded safety of the inner swamp rather than risk capture on an uncertain path to the North. I cannot imagine that outlying runaways can survive for very long in the treachery of the Dismal, but I suppose escaping the horror of slavery makes anything possible. Now, let us see about those in the wagon."

We walked through the dark lot toward the barn. The sound of voices and music wafted in from the main road where homes, businesses, an inn, and a crowded tavern nestled sided by side. I hurried, knowing Jerlinda, Rafe, and Axel would fret over my lengthy absence.

"You are in safe hands," I said with hushed excitement as I approached the wagon. "And I have food."

The bundle of biscuits dropped from my hands when I found the wagon empty. I turned to Sylvan Firth. "They are gone!"

He stumbled in a panic to the barn. I followed him, whispering soft encouragement into the shadows. "No need to hide. It's me, Jacy. All is safe."

My heart sank in distress when they were not in the barn or in the surrounding lot. "We must locate them before they are discovered," I said to Sylvan.

He peered into the shadow of trees at the back of the lot. "Perhaps it is too late. The area of the great swamp attracts slave catchers from near and far. They pluck the poor souls before they can immerse themselves in the mangroves."

"We must keep looking," I pleaded. Following his gaze, I started toward the trees, but he caught my hand.

"Jacy, it's safer for you to search among the buildings on the street. I will look through the woods in the back."

We separated, he to the rear and I toward the lamplight down the street. The dirt road was soft from wagon wheels arriving and leaving the busy dock along the water. I knew little of the canal to the north, but below the lock in South Mills the waterway connected to the Pasquotank River, which flowed south to Elizabeth City, emptying into Albemarle Sound, and then onward to the southern tides of the mighty Atlantic.

A town of commerce, South Mills was not grand in size, but it flourished with merchants and tradesmen moving their wares from in-state regions, particularly those with timber interests. The nightlife along the main street seemed to belong to businessmen striking new deals and weary canal men drinking a day's pay.

At the moment, most of the activity centered in and around the tavern. Laughter and a lively piano tune poured from its open doors across the street. I scampered along the wooden planks lining the dirt road, poking my head into yards and alleyways. Hope faded with each step I took. How could I have come this far only to have the three of them vanish the moment I turned my back? Whatever the reason for their disappearance, it did not bode well. Something horrible had happened; I sensed it. Tears collected in my eyes as I looked up and down the street for a potential hideaway when the silhouette of a man appeared in the tavern door. His back was to me, but the bark of his familiar voice tore through my soul.

"Hold on to them until tomorrow," he snarled to an unseen partner in the tavern. "Come morning, I will pay you a fair price per head."

Garrison!

Chapter 10

I ducked into the walkway of an apothecary. Garrison turned from the tavern and crossed the street toward me. The enclosed side porch of the building was attached to the neighboring mercantile and offered me no path for escape. Pressed into the shadows, I watched Garrison stop beneath the flame of a streetlamp to look at his pocket watch. He had not seen me, but if he should, I would be in grave danger. I scampered to the wooden steps that rose to the rear door and pulled away a section of the wood lattice so I could crawl beneath the porch.

On my hands and knees, I scurried through spiderwebs and slimy grit to the back side of the porch. A feisty raccoon scrambled from my path and hid beneath the beams of the building's foundation. Pushing through the rear lattice, I rolled into a moist bed of ferns that covered a secluded lot behind the buildings. Before I could rise, rough hands grabbed me by my arms. I unleashed a terrified yelp, but a woolen hat was pressed tightly to my face to muffle my cry.

"Hush now, Jacy," a voice whispered. When the hat was lifted, there were Jerlinda, Rafe, and Axel gathered around me. Rafe helped me to my feet. "Where you comin' from?"

I flung my arms around his neck and pulled him to me. "Thank goodness you are safe." I tugged Jerlinda and Axel to me as well. I had never felt such utter relief and joy. "Garrison is here. I thought he had found you. Where have you been?"

"After you went into the house," Jerlinda said, "several men came through the woods toward the barn. We took off into the trees. I guess they weren't on the chase, but every shadow in the night feels like it's trackin' us. We tried to get back to the barn, but someone is creepin' around over there."

"He is Sylvan Firth, the man who is going to help us. When we found the wagon empty, we feared you had been captured." I hugged them again as my frayed nerves recovered. "Let's go to him."

Rafe, Jerlinda, and I held hands while Axel limped behind us. We stepped lightly through the trees to the yard behind the barn. When Sylvan saw us emerge from the shadows, he wiped his brow in relief. "Come with me."

Sylvan helped us move the wagon into the barn. "I must leave to make arrangements for you. When harboring fugitives, it's my custom to wear a distinctive butternut-colored jacket while on duty at the lock station to signal to my associates on the canal to be ready to receive passengers during the night. I believe there is a friend of the cause docked in the river below the lock, but he is not expecting me. Rest here until I return. Then we will move quickly and discreetly to secure you before dawn."

Stress and exhaustion quieted us. As the others ate the biscuits and apples supplied by our benefactor, I explained the plan of being smuggled by lighter up the canal as it was told to me by Mr. Firth.

"What is a lighter?" Jerlinda asked.

"It's a kind of boat," Rafe said. His time in South Mills with my father made him familiar with the canal and its trade. "Big enough to haul timber goods from the upper swamp, but light enough to float atop the canal water, which is no more than six or seven feet deep."

"How does the lighter move if there ain't no river current?"

"There are long setting poles attached to the bow and to the stern, which is the front and the back of the boat. These poles stretch to the canal bank, where pole men push the lighter as they walk a towpath that ain't much more than a log rail in most places."

Jerlinda frowned anxiously. "Sure don't sound like a quick escape."

We exchanged looks of trepidation. "Mr. Firth's methods are tried and successful," I said to bolster us, one and all. "Slow and safe is better than a blind sprint, is it not?"

We fell silent, knowing there was no gain in doubt and speculation. Rafe unhitched the horse from the wagon. I joined him in the corner of the barn while he watered and patted down the weary animal. Since we were unable to light a lamp or candle, we had only the moon beaming through the loft window above us to provide illumination.

"Will you be all right when you go back?" Rafe asked, his eyes strained with concern.

"Axel had me practice at the reins. I think I can handle the horse and wagon without trouble."

Rafe reached out for my hand. "I mean at Great Meadow. We are leavin' you in an awful mess."

I pressed my other hand to his cheek, amazed by his selfless care. "I have the easy part."

"We'll be fine," he said to reassure me. "If the plan works out for the best, the reward will be a dream come true. Freedom. Can't hardly imagine it."

If the plan works. The possibility of failure and its deathly consequences was too terrifying to linger over. So too was the unbearable thought that I would never know their fate.

Axel chomped the last of his apple, core and all. "If we get caught or are split up, I ain't sayin' who I am or where I come from. That way they can't prove I am a runaway."

"No, no," Rafe said, rejoining the group. "You got it all wrong, Axel. If any of us gets caught we gots'ta make sure we tell 'em where we ran from so they will send us back to Great Meadow. Otherwise, a slaver could sell us south and we wouldn't never find each other again. Even if missus has McVey whup our hide for runnin', at least the others will know where to find the one who got caught."

"What if they sell us south anyway?" Axel mused.

"Jes' keep on sayin', 'I belong to the missus of Great Meadow in North Carolina.' No marster wants to be accused of thievin' another man's property."

The creak of the wooden door caused us to spring to our feet. We held our breath against the silence. "Jacy, it's Sylvan."

His appearance was welcome and dreaded. The method of flight was arranged and ready to be put in motion. The gray cover of pre-dawn twilight hung like a veil of gloom. Sylvan gathered us together before leaving the barn.

"I have arranged for your transport on a cargo lighter carrying crates of pecans up the canal. You will be concealed in a small compartment beneath the hull. It is close quarters, but designed to allow air to pass through in abundance."

"Are you taking them to the lighter now?" I choked, realizing our moment of good-bye was fast approaching. In a matter of hours, they would be gone. They had occupied my world for my entire life, but their presence within me had only just begun. Sensing my anguish, Jerlinda entwined her fingers with mine.

"Water traffic begins soon after sunup," Sylvan said, looking from one anxious face to the next. "We must board you before the dock fills with laborers and other lighter men. Do not be alarmed if your vessel has not moved by day's end. We have had little rainfall and the water level of the canal is low. A feeder ditch will be opened north of here that will channel water down from Lake Drummond. You will be on your way as soon as possible."

Jerlinda pressed her hand to her breast. "Can't we wait here until the canal is ready to take on the boats?"

"It's too dangerous," he said. "Because of rumors, my activity and property are closely watched. Even now I must proceed carefully. You will be safe on the lighter. The canal man who captains it will provide you with water and open the hatch when no one is round-about." Mr. Firth held his arm open toward the door. "We must go now, before the golden glow of sunrise steals our cover."

We followed Sylvan Firth on a path winding behind his house to where the lock station stood. Wooden planks groaned beneath our feet as we hurried past moored flatboats. Through the thick mist swirling atop the water, there appeared the outline of a large, omi-nous presence along the dock on the opposite bank. My breath caught in my throat. It was Garrison's steamer, the *Southern Gale*.

"Here it is," Sylvan Firth whispered.

The lighter, though long and sturdy, was dwarfed by the *Southern Gale*, which loomed in the background. Chills resonated through me. Even now, Garrison was likely housed on the ship, a mere stone's throw from where I stood. If not for the haze of night, he could be gazing upon us or aiming a shotgun to thwart our effort. We all jumped back when a coal-skinned Negro in light cotton trousers and a sleeveless shirt stepped from the mist.

Sylvan shook the stranger's hand. "This is the lighter captain, Archie. He is a freedman and sympathetic to your plight. He will keep watch over you and give you instruction when you reach Portsmouth."

Suddenly, all was moving too quickly. Our flight from Great

Meadow had been so abrupt and dangerous; there had not been a quiet moment to gather words of farewell. No time remained to sort out and explain my feelings to Rafe. In truth, I barely understood them myself, but the tearing of my heart told me love had taken root.

Sylvan hurried us onto the boat. He and Archie pushed aside a reel of thick rope and lifted some loose boards in the hull. "Hurry; we've not much time."

Axel knelt to enter the hole, but was held back by my hand upon his shoulder. My voice cracked with emotion. "I am sorry I scolded you from the balcony that night, Axel. I spoke with disrespect when in fact you were looking out for my well-being. You have been a loyal brother even when I was unaware. Thank you."

Axel grinned. With a squeeze of my hand, he hobbled into the hidden compartment. I turned to Jerlinda, who opened her arms to me. Stepping into her embrace, I felt her devoted love envelop me.

"I cannot bear to let you go," I said, awash with regret. "After all these years, I finally have a mother who loves me. Why must it be like this?"

"Oh, baby girl," Jerlinda cooed. "Even though we feel the pain of lettin' go, sometimes we got no choice if we want what is best fo' our loved ones. There ain't no other way."

"Unless I go with you," I said, struck with a desperately impulsive thought.

Jerlinda's eyes clouded. "God bless you, chile, for wishing it. But you gots'ta stay."

"But why?" Tears rolled warm and heavy down my cheeks. "Why must I stay?"

Jerlinda smoothed wisps of hair away from my strained face and then braced my shoulders with parental firmness. "We must honor yo' father, Jacy. He gave you a privileged life so you would not carry the burdens of a slave. Chile, you have never lived as a Negro and cannot understand the measure of sufferin' as we do."

"Then I will go with you but maintain my white standing," I said, grasping at possibilities. "Perhaps my light skin will bring advantage and security to your relocation. I will stay with you until you are settled in your new life."

Grasping my muddied judgment, Sylvan Firth gently intervened. "Jacy, you are too sheltered and inexperienced to understand the danger of their journey."

"Mista Firth is right," Rafe said as he reached for my hand to steady me. "We ain't on a holiday trip. We is runaways. And I can't protect you when I don't even know that I can protect myself. Besides, if yo' horse and wagon are found in South Mills, they will know where to begin a chase for us."

He wrapped me in his arms, sweeping away what was left of my heart. "Believe me, girl. I would love to take you with us, but it is safer for you and for us if you go back to Great Meadow and make a good life for yourself."

I looked upon his pained face. "There is so much I want to say, things you need to understand."

I struggled to hide the heartbreak that blazed inside me when he ran his trembling fingertips along my cheek. Rafe pulled me closer and whispered, "I'm sorry I caused you such trouble. If I had been more careful in the stable, Titus would not have caught us."

"Rafe, none of this is your doing," I said as a numbing ache grew inside me. "You deserve a better fate, all of you."

Rafe ran his ardent gaze over every curve of my face as if etching it in his memory. "I won't never forget you, Jacy Lane."

"Nor will I forget you," I said, embracing him. "But I cannot say good-bye."

"Let's jes' smile and step away," he said, welcoming me into the fold of his body. He held me tightly against his broad chest before letting go. I quivered when his warm lips brushed my cheek as he eased from my arms.

Rafe climbed into the hull and held up a hand to assist Jerlinda. Before she descended, I pulled her into my arms. "Thank you for loving me, Mama. I will carry your love within me, always."

I dug through my pockets until I found the tiny pink hair ribbon she had saved from my newborn days. "You gave this to me, but I want you to take it with you. For luck."

"Thank you, precious girl." With glistening eyes, she touched my cheek. "The sound of yo' voice sayin' *Mama* will ring in my ears forever. Stand strong and proud, chile. You will always be Jacy . . . *Jerlinda's chile*."

The lighter captain, Archie, nudged her toward the open hatch in the hull. "We gots'ta get you below deck. Watermen is gonna be crawlin' the dock anytime now."

"You are in good hands," I said, brushing away my tears to force a smile. "Freedom awaits you." Parting with a sweet kiss to my lips, Jerlinda climbed into the compartment and was gone.

Sylvan Firth hustled me back to his house as the sun rose in the east. I bathed and was given fresh clothing from a trunk that had belonged to his deceased mother. With my hair washed and tucked into a bonnet, I was once again inconspicuous in my role as a respectable mistress. With Archie's cargo lighter still anchored near the lock, my heart was anchored there as well, but Mr. Firth encouraged me on my way.

"Garrison Yob will be in and around town until the *Southern Gale* leaves. If he sees you or your wagon, then our efforts will be for naught. I know it is difficult, Jacy, but you must go. I will have a trustworthy associate escort you home."

The journey back to Great Meadow was dreary despite the bright sunshine. Sylvan Firth's associate, Peter, was a husky, quiet lad of sixteen. He worked at the livery and was happy to tie his steed to the back of my wagon and take a day's jaunt. He squirmed a bit when I wept tears of heartbreak, but he was inclined neither to give solace nor to seek the reason. When he finally did clear his throat to speak, I was surprised by his words.

"My condolences, miss."

"Pardon me?" I wondered how much the lad knew of my ties to Jerlinda and the others.

"Your daddy dying the way he did was mighty sorrowful for all that knew him. Even though I'm still a sprout among men, your daddy always gave me a coin and a good word for helping him when he came to town with his horses."

I turned to the earnest young man. "Were you with him the night he died?"

"No, miss, but I was nearby," he continued. "Mr. Lane was bunked in the livery with the horses after he sent his colored men catfishing down at the canal for the night. He watched over them palominos like they was his own kin."

"Thank you for your condolences, Peter." His tender observation brought renewed tears. "It was a horrible stroke of misfortune to have a skunk wander into the stalls and cause my father to be trampled."

"Mighty peculiar too," Peter said absentmindedly. "Haven't had much of a problem with the varmints this summer, but they was coming out of the woodwork that night."

"Oh? How so?"

"Earlier in the night, I crossed paths with Mr. Yob from the steamer. He was behind the livery near the blacksmith forge carrying a sack with a skunk he said was letting off fumes near his ship and disturbing his crew."

My skin bristled. "Why would he bring it near the livery?"

"That's what I said!" Peter shook his head with annoyance. "I told him to keep that skunk away from the horses. If a herd got sprayed, the smell alone could break a business deal. I told him to release it into the woods east of the canal so it couldn't wander around town."

"And did he?"

"Don't know." Peter shrugged. "I went on my way. Can't think of a reason why he would ignore my warning and release it there purposely."

"Unless he had vengeful intent," I said.

The possibility outraged me. I remembered Garrison's fury when Papa struck him down in my defense. He had vowed to answer Papa's tirade. Two days later my father was dead. Garrison might not have meant to kill Papa, but he had a conniving hand in his demise. Every instinct in me knew it to be true.

Peter drove our horse harder than Axel had, and we rolled through the countryside at a steady pace. The closer I got to home, the more I dreaded our arrival. I had no way of knowing how Claudia had responded to my note, but since we had not encountered any patrollers or slave hunters, I believed she had not taken any aggressive action. When the fields of Great Meadow came into view beneath the sinking sun, I pointed to the lane leading to the main house.

"Peter, I insist you stay the night as my guest."

"Well, maybe I'll curl up in the barn and start back at daybreak."

"Nonsense," I said. "I must repay you for your kindness. The least I can do is to provide you with a warm bed and a hot meal."

"Ma'am, I am used to bunking at the livery. A blanket in the barn and a little grub would suit me just fine."

When he steered the wagon down our lane, I braced for the worst. I took solace in knowing Claudia could never again strike out at Jerlinda, Rafe, or Axel. I climbed down from the wagon, and while Peter secured the horse, I walked to the house. When I entered the dining room, Claudia rose from her chair.

"You!" The word hissed from her like a torched flame.

I was too exhausted and despondent to posture for battle. She crossed the room and clutched onto my arm. "You have put me in a precarious position. Where are they?"

"What does it matter?" I sighed. "They are gone. Isn't that what you wanted?"

"Your outlandish deeds have cost me dearly, and not just in profit lost on runaways. As soon as I found your note, I was forced to fire Virgil McVey before he discovered that three of our lot were missing. Had he known, I could not have stopped the slave hunt."

"What will you tell Garrison?"

"I will tell him that I suspected McVey stole some chickens, and with no overseer to keep watch, three ingrates slipped away. He will have no reason to suspect a ruse."

"And me?"

She glared at me with icy disdain. "I was prepared to skin you alive, but fortunately no damage has been done to our overall reputation. You are a Negro at heart. I should have expected a streak of defiance in you. But it is over now. With Jerlinda and the others out of our lives, we can build a prosperous future without threat or fear of being exposed. Nothing is changed. You will continue as before."

"Nothing is changed?" I could not keep from laughing in bitter amusement. "Are you insane? *Everything* is changed. I am changed.

The world around me is changed. And most of all, in my eyes you are changed, forever. You are not my mother. I will no longer allow you to demean and manipulate me. The secret used against me as a weapon does not pierce or frighten me anymore. It strengthens me, because I am full and complete, no longer diminished by your contempt. The lies you shackled me in were not made of iron and chain, but they enslaved me just the same. Never again will I be ordered to the fence or cursed as a feral quadroon."

Claudia was stunned. She lifted her hand to strike me, but lowered it when I raised my chin, daring the blow.

"Do not cross me, Jacy. I will watch you suffer before I allow you to impugn me."

At that moment, I realized I had made a grave mistake. My place was near those who loved me enough to let me go, not once but twice. There was no longer a life for me at Great Meadow. My hope for happiness was back in South Mills. Perhaps my white appearance would enable me to escort Jerlinda, Rafe, and Axel to the North in a safe and respectable manner. I remembered once hearing Garrison scoff at Papa, telling him there were places in the North where white families and free Negroes lived within a few miles of one another. If I began life anew in a state like Pennsylvania or New York, I could maintain contact with them while settling into an existence far from the reach of Claudia's threats and manipulations.

Jerlinda was right when she said I must honor my father. But I would honor him by living a life of love, even if it meant conceding privilege. I wished to love those dearest to him in a way he could not. I believed with my heart and soul that Papa would want it to be so.

I ran to Mayme's room. She was shocked to see me and gathered me in her thin arms. "I was not sure you would return."

"I cannot stay, Mayme."

Her lips tugged into a melancholy smile. "You alone will live with your choices. Make them with conviction and certainty."

"I have, Mayme," I said, kissing her hands. "Though it breaks my heart to leave you."

"Don't worry about me, child. My life has been lived. What is spun for you here by Claudia will be a web of unhappiness. Let my lasting gift to you be my blessing. Come, we must gather some heirlooms and valuables for you to take with you."

"There is no time, Mayme. I must leave before Mother finds a way to stop me."

"Here, then," she said as she reached for a small tin box on her mantel. She loosened the lid to show me its contents. "I found this in your grandfather's wardrobe closet soon after his death."

Using her delicate finger to nudge aside a broken pair of spectacles, a simple gold ring, and a pewter overcoat button, Mayme lifted a hidden keepsake from the box.

"Paper money!" I exclaimed.

"I have kept this box as I found it," she said wistfully. "A private remembrance that I have shared with no one else."

I touched the spectacles and imagined Grandfather's playful gaze. "Oh, Mayme."

"The keepsakes are of little value to anyone except an old woman reflecting on earlier days, but the cash can be used in your flight. It's only a dozen ten-dollar banknotes, a modest amount by our living standards, but it may prove to be a treasure trove if you find yourself in desperate straits."

I took the money and pulled her to me in one last desperate hug. "I love you, Mayme."

She eased me from her arms to help me on my way. Holding tightly to my hands, Mayme smiled tearfully. "You are never helpless, Jacy. You carry within you the blood of a daring father and a courageous mother, pure of heart and deed. I do not know what lies ahead for you, but when your journey seems impossible, remember . . . you are proof of the improbable. Go now, Jacy. Go and be happy."

I kissed her cheeks, but could not linger another moment. It was critical that I sneak from the house when Claudia was unaware. With so much at stake, she would surely chase after me when she discovered I was gone. When I crept down the stairs, I found the dining room empty. I fled with some cheese and corn bread that had not yet been cleared from the table. Bursting into the barn, I pulled Peter toward the wagon.

"Hurry, Peter. Return me to South Mills!"

Chapter 11

With Great Meadow at our backs, we rolled beneath the bright moon and brilliant stars. I felt raw and untried, having shed the lie I was living. But I also felt unencumbered and free to grow. Well after midnight, we pulled into a poplar grove and slept. At dawn we began again and arrived in South Mills before noon. I hurried down the road to Sylvan Firth's home. My frantic knocks went unheeded, so I ran to the lock station. I saw Sylvan before he saw me, so when I flung open the door he nearly toppled from his chair.

"Jacy!" he exclaimed, his face draining of color. "It is dangerous for you to be here. Garrison Yob has been searching all over town for you."

"Garrison?" Saying his name made me retch with fear.

Sylvan hustled me inside, looking around to see whether I had been noticed. The one-room building that overlooked the lock roared with the sound of rushing water as the lock emptied and lowered three shingle flats down to meet the dark headwaters of the Pasquotank.

"An acquaintance of your father saw you near the livery yesterday morning. He assumed you were in town with Garrison. The two men must have crossed paths, because by yesterday afternoon, Garrison had been to every establishment in South Mills, including here at the lock station, inquiring about you."

I clutched the lapels of his butternut-colored jacket. "Mr. Firth, I cannot let him find me! I have decided to retrieve those I left in your care and pay a sympathetic journeyman to take us by carriage to the North. For their safety and my peace of mind, I must see them delivered with my own eyes. Can you recommend a coachman who will consider this venture?"

Though no one was around, he closed the door and tried to soothe me. "Jacy, you must calm down. What you are suggesting is madness. Let them go."

My emotions unraveled like a poorly knitted sweater. "I can't let them go, Mr. Firth. They are all I have now."

"You are being foolhardy," he said firmly. "What life can you have with them? Even in the North, a white woman associating too closely with the Negroes will not be tolerated. You would be cast out by white society and rejected by the colored. Your presence would invite increased danger to an already precarious situation."

Absorbing his words made my head spin with uncertainty. I did not want to cause Jerlinda, Rafe, and Axel harm, yet I had no organized plan other than knowing I would not return to Great Meadow or remain in South Mills. Distance was my only hope of breaking free of Garrison's claim on my tomorrows. Perhaps Aunt Sarah in Charleston would take pity on me. We had never met, and I wondered whether she would take me in if I showed up, unannounced, on her doorstep.

"As you wish, Mr. Firth," I said, broken by despair. I reached into my pocket and held up the banknotes from Grandfather's tin. "But first I must give them this seed money to get them started in their new life. Then I will ask for your help in arranging a carriage to take me to Charleston as soon as possible."

"They are gone, Jacy. They left here by lighter yesterday afternoon. My guess is that they will arrive in Deep Creek sometime today. I'm sorry."

The frustration of having control over nothing in my life flamed into single-minded determination. "Then please put me on another vessel to Deep Creek. If I can catch up to Archie's lighter, I will entrust him to pass along these banknotes. Jerlinda and the others will benefit from having some cash when they arrive in the North."

Sylvan shook his head sympathetically. "The flatboats and lighters are pushed like gondolas up the waterway. They move slowly and rarely catch up to or pass one another."

"There must be some way to reach them," I said in desperation.

"Your best chance is the *Southern Gale*. She is a hearty steamer once used solely for passengers. She has fallen into disrepair and now is used mainly to transport shingles and timber staves from the upper swamp to Albemarle Sound. For a shilling or two, you can buy your way on board for her return up the canal. When Garrison questioned me yesterday, he indicated that he had just arrived from Elizabeth City and would not be traveling to Deep Creek."

"I cannot risk crossing paths with him," I said with a shudder of premonition. "If he finds me, all will be lost. Perhaps I can follow the canal towpath on horseback."

Sylvan put his arm around my shoulder. "Jacy, the towpath is far too narrow to traverse, even on foot. Besides, Dismal Swamp is a treacherous region and the canal banks go unprotected. Fugitive slaves of every demeanor inhabit the tangled thicket and are said to be as wild as the bears and panthers that roam the marshes. In desperation, they sometimes steal food and clothing from plantations along the swamp's edge or from boats moored along the canal banks at night. A woman alone would be easy prey for any rascal, Negro and white alike. If you fear Garrison's proximity to the *Southern Gale*, the only other avenue to the Virginia end of the canal is by way of the stagecoach road to the east."

A lone possibility emboldened me. "Maybe Peter has not yet unhitched the wagon. I will hire him to take me—"

"Jacy!" My heart dropped when Garrison's voice boomed through the open window. "What are you doing here?"

My throat clenched in panic. Fortunately, Sylvan was quick to give a reason as he opened the door of the lock station to keep me from being cornered. "She was looking for you, Yob. A canal man told her he had seen you near the lock."

Garrison grabbed my wrist. In his fury, he had not noticed the banknotes clutched in my fist. "You should not be in town unescorted. Your impetuous, unrefined behavior will be put to rest once we are married."

His words hit me with the force of a bullwhip. I yanked my hand from his grip, casting the bills into the air, where they fluttered around us like falling leaves. I waved my hands to catch the notes, but Garrison lunged to bridle me. His fingertips grazed my shoulder, but I slipped from his grasp and burst free of his restraint.

Fleeing the lock station, I heard Garrison follow in quick pursuit. "Jacy, I demand you stop and explain yourself!"

Terror drove my footsteps away from him. *What am I doing? Disobeying his command will infuriate him all the more.*

Still, I could not help but run faster. I raced across the street toward the livery. If I could reach Peter, maybe he would provide me with a horse for a quick escape. I ran through the stable calling Peter's name, then squeezed through a hole to the back side of the building and held still.

Between a gap in the slats, I saw Garrison burst into the livery. He walked along the stalls, twisting his head to examine every nook and corner. It was too late to cajole him. Besides, I could not mask my hatred in the wake of learning that my father might be alive if not for Garrison Yob.

"When I get you in hand, woman, I will tame your wild streak once and for all."

I panted frenzied breaths, hoping to compose the irrational thoughts driving me onward, but his nearness filled me with unbearable dread. *I cannot turn myself over to him. I will not!*

My only path of escape was from the rear of the livery toward the canal. My feet scampered through the high grass of a lumberyard and turned to where the canal stretched northward toward Dismal Swamp. I nearly made the cover of trees when Garrison bellowed again.

"I see you, Jacy! You cannot outrun me."

I could not let him catch me. He would overpower me and force me back to Great Meadow. Garrison's maniacal growl grew louder as he closed the distance between us. Winded and without hope, I nearly gave up until I saw a tunnel of trees where the canal disappeared into the swamp. I lengthened my stride like a quarter horse in a derby and ran for my life.

"Where are you going, you little wretch?"

Garrison's snarl made me sprint faster. The thicket began to close around me. I climbed an embankment of peat and mud. Vines and Spanish moss tangled the juniper and gum trees, creating a heavy web of greenery. I ducked and twisted through the thick vegetation while trying to keep within sight of the tea-colored water of the canal.

Garrison cursed and grunted behind me. His heavy, awkward frame could not navigate the damp trenches and tangled flora as quickly as my slight body. He fell farther and farther behind as I stumbled within the dense forest. Finally, his exasperated voice echoed from the distance. "To hell with you, you brazen fool! Let the swamp swallow you!"

Panting in sheer terror, I crouched against the base of a gnarled cypress tree. Birds screeched from the impenetrable treetops, and spiders crawled from my hair and clothing where torn webs clung and dangled. I swatted frantically at anything, large or small, crawling on my skin. Heat and stillness pressed against me. The canal was nowhere in sight; nor was the sun, even though I knew both were somewhere beyond the thick canopy and curtain of vines draped around me.

What had I done? I had allowed Garrison to chase me into oblivion. All was dank, suffocating, and, as promised, grimly dismal. I was free of Garrison, at least for the moment, but had I crawled into hell to escape him? Garrison's haunting curse enveloped me as I stood lost and alone, and swallowed wholly by the Great Dismal Swamp.

Chapter 12

I sat still for a long while. Exhausted by the chase, I needed to rest and restore my calm, an elusive task on both accounts. My ears remained alert to any rustle of underbrush that might indicate Garrison had continued in secret pursuit. Entombed in a fortress of needle-leaved cypress, junipers, and tall white cedars, I could discern no trailing footsteps. The sights and sounds around me were foreign, as if I were suddenly cast into a faraway land. The musty smell of peat and foul damps filled the air, along with an array of tumbling insects. I rose onto the tips of my toes to survey my surroundings but was hemmed in by the lush swamp forest.

"I must find the canal," I said aloud to ward off my sense of isolation. "This godforsaken terrain will be the death of me. I must regain my bearing and find the waterway so I can cross over, then hike my way to the stagecoach road. It can't be too far."

It was a simple plan, though I quickly realized the many dangers kicked up by my every step. Snakes of all kinds slithered from beneath my footsteps. Most were quick, harmless varieties I had seen hundreds of times in the woods and fields of Great Meadow, but others showed unfamiliar colors and markings.

"Aaaah," I moaned as I froze to let a thick black rat snake course its thick, scaly body along the rock on which I stepped. "This is bad," I whispered, beginning to understand the full scope of what I had done. Dismal Swamp was known for taking travelers in its grip. Men of experience, equipped for survival, often entered its mysterious underbelly and were never heard from again. Would I be the Dismal's next victim, my corpse lost to the appetites of swamp beasts?

The thought sent me pushing through the thicket in search of the canal, my breaths shallow with hysteria as I twisted through the grove of huddled cypress. Immediately the spongy earth gave way underneath me and I splashed waist-deep into a quagmire of dark water and green sludge.

"God help me!" I yelped as I latched onto a heavy vine.

A sound twittered from the thicket. I would have sworn it was a giggle had I not been so sequestered, but the noise was not threatening. Probably a songbird, I thought. Weighted down by my soaked dress, I struggled to crawl from the muck until I finally reached solid ground. I shook the slimy mud from my hands and curled up on the ground, weeping futile tears of surrender.

"This is hopeless!" I cried out. "How can I navigate the impossible? I feel like I am dressed in a leaden skirt and slippers."

I lay in a pool of sludge and self-pity for nearly an hour. Whining at the heavens for punishing me unfairly, I was eventually nudged by the terrifying realization that I had only myself to rely on. Tears and pleas would do nothing to help me find the canal.

Get up, I silently scolded myself. *I must have some of Jerlinda's fortitude in me.*

Drained emotionally, but rested from my extended collapse, I pulled myself from the dirt. My drenched clothing and the instability of the turf underfoot had me inching through the trees at a snail's pace. Occasionally, the rustle of scampering feet halted my steps. Usually, a squirrel or white-tailed deer could be seen retreating into the evergreen shrubs. At other times the culprit remained invisible. I shuddered with wonder at what beasts and reptiles might inhabit such a foreboding environment. Heat and fatigue burned throughout my legs and across my cheeks.

"Blast these bugs," I grumbled as I swatted away yellow flies and mosquitoes that came at me like bees to flowers. Some areas were nearly impassable and others opened into marsh heaths where I could at least glimpse the sun. It looked to be late afternoon.

"I feel like I have trod a hundred miles."

In truth, it was probably no more than a few hundred feet, but why dwell on the negative? I tried not to think about my high-laced boots rubbing sores on my tender feet, or the insect bites stinging my neck and arms despite the protection of collar and sleeves. I had lost my bonnet in my flight from Garrison, so the intense humidity thickened my long hair into a frizzy, woolen mat. My escape had been so sudden; I had brought no food, water, or even a single hairbrush. Perspiration and exertion parched my lips, but the tea-brown water did not look drinkable.

"Where am I going?" I huffed as I pushed away damp curls that stuck to my face.

The mangled array of trees looked no different from turn to turn, so it was difficult to gauge whether I had gained any ground. For the first time in my life, I had the humble experience of squatting in the dirt to relieve myself. The snap of a twig turned me around. I scanned the steamy jungle to no avail. Movement in the dense underbrush across a dreary bog caught my eye. I was dizzy with thirst and hunger, but I was almost certain I spotted a dark-skinned figure slipping between the trees and disappearing. Had I imagined it? Suddenly, voices echoed from the opposite direction.

"Keep your eyes peeled, mate." The raspy voice snickered.

Another man laughed in return. I followed the banter of conversation until I found myself overlooking the dark-water canal. It was a welcome sight because, unbeknownst to me, until I had heard the voices I had been stumbling in the wrong direction. Having once again found the canal, I could make the short swim across and seek the stagecoach road through the trees beyond.

I would not risk returning to South Mills, where Garrison lurked, but if I could talk my way onto the stage to Deep Creek, I could send a confidential note down the canal to Sylvan Firth. Both Archie and Caleb frequented the waterway, and I believed either man could be trusted to deliver a sealed note. My hope was that Sylvan would send Peter by carriage to escort me to Charleston, where I would seek shelter with Aunt Sarah. Mayme had told me she was kindhearted, and I prayed it would be so. My racing thoughts were pulled back to the challenge at hand when a second voice echoed along the canal.

"Load your pistol, brother, in case we see any runaways. They bring a high price, dead or alive."

I crouched lower as two poorly dressed white canal men drifted into sight. A man with strawlike hair and prominent freckles used a long wooden stave to nudge his shingle flat downstream. As they approached, I lay low and out of sight. The other man looked much like the first, only pudgier around the cheeks. He sat atop a load of stacked shingles, his legs dangling as he polished the handle of a pistol with his shirttail. When he finished, he tucked the gun in his belt and hopped down from his perch. Lifting another long pole, he speared it into the water and helped push the flatboat past me.

"I don't believe the stories of fugitive slaves running wild in the marshes," he grumbled. "The Dismal is fit for no man. They say even the buzzards don't go into the belly of this wretched swamp."

"Don't be so sure," the freckled man cautioned. "I knew a logger who said runaways come to the timber camps to help cut shingles in exchange for a few morsels of grub. He told me that some of them outliers have lived in remote settlements for ten or twenty years now."

"Ah, that's a tall tale if ever I heard one," the second said. "The darkies can't fend for themselves, especially in a hellhole like the Dismal. The ones that run into the swamp are either eaten by gators or swallowed by quicksand."

"Keep your voice low, brother," the first fellow said as he held a hushing finger to his plump lips. "You see that man on the shingle flat trailing us?"

My view up the canal was obscured by trees, so I could not see the canal boat in their distant wake, but the second man leaned forward to take a look.

"You mean the chap in the black fedora who boarded the flat that came through the lock with us?"

"His name is Quinn. He's a slave hunter who pays canal men a silver coin to let him ride up or down the waterway. He don't lift a finger in the work. He just sits facing west into the swamp with a shotgun propped on one knee and a sack with shackles and chains at his feet. If Quinn sees an outlier, he is off that boat in a flash and on the chase. When he has a wayward Negro in hand, he pays passage on the next boat passing through. That's how I met him. Quinn is a heartless gent, but he presented me the easiest dime I ever made."

The second man patted his gun. "All this talk about rogue darkies has made me jumpy. I'm glad I got a gun to see us to South Mills."

The first man laughed at the fellow who had doubted him earlier. "Since when do you shoot at *tall tales*?"

When the shingle flat drifted from sight, I began my trek through the tangled brakes along the canal. My ankles twisted and throbbed as the heels on my boots wedged in one gnarled root after another. I could barely draw breath in the vaporous heat that was making my head pound with depletion of body and spirit. I had to rest before I attempted my swim to the other side. To my dismay, the thicket to the east of the canal looked no less treacherous. My uncertainty about how far the stagecoach road lay from the canal began to worry me. Perhaps if I waited for a reputable-looking lighter man, I could catch a ride on a flatboat to Deep Creek. I thought about Grandfather's banknotes cast to the wind in my struggle with Garrison and cursed my misfortune. With no cash in hand, I worried about what type of payment a stranger would seek for his good deed. The risk was too great. My appearance in torn, dirty clothing, with my wild mane tangled with burrs, would not invite the respect and manners afforded a lady of good station.

I crawled between a bend in the trees where I could reach my hand into the tepid tea-colored water of the canal. I splashed my face but found no relief. I was desperate to take a sip to soothe my dry throat, but fought the urge to drink. The image of vultures and swamp beasts feeding on my poisoned carcass was all I needed to quell the temptation. Surely there would be a fresh spring amid this vast body of water.

I dragged myself behind some fallen cedar logs when the lap of water against wood warned me of another vessel approaching. No sooner had I tucked myself from sight than a small timber flat appeared. This one was poled by a weary young Negro and carried long wooden staves meant for the timberworks below. I was taken aback by the odd sight of a white man dressed in black trousers and vest sitting in a wooden chair faced to view the passing swamp. The white sleeves of the man's cotton shirt were rolled above his elbows, and a wide-brimmed fedora shaded his thick black brows, mustache, and goatee. Propped on one knee was the butt of a long-barreled shotgun, its length standing erect and ready for duty.

The slave hunter, Quinn.

He appeared exactly as the freckled canal man had described. His expression was hard and devoid of emotion, but his eyes were intense with scrutiny. Crouching to stay out of sight, I shifted around a stump covered with log fern when my foot slipped on the peat and I plunked down on my behind in a shallow pool of mud. Through the trees, I saw Quinn turn his head my way. His knuckles whitened as he gripped his gun and bobbed his head to scour the shadows with his keen glare.

I held my breath until movement on a rock next to me turned my head. There, coiled only an arm's length away, was the thick tan-and-brown length of a copperhead. The adventures of my youth taught me this was not a snake to tangle with. I sprang from the puddle and out of its poisonous reach, but my panicked reaction gave me away.

"You, there!" Quinn stood and aimed his gun. "Show yourself or I will strike you down."

I stayed low as I crawled along a rotted log. A shot rang out, his bullet nicking the gum tree to my right. I stumbled away from the canal and into the dense vegetation for cover.

He bellowed at the canal man who guided his boat, "Push us closer to shore, and be quick about it!"

The heavy splash of water and the pounding of boots told me that Quinn thought he had a cash bounty within his grasp. I pushed and twisted through creepers that clung to me like tentacles. Though they scratched my face and pulled at my hair, I pushed deeper into the briars, hoping they would provide me a path of escape that would be difficult to follow. I moved with great care in not making my position obvious.

Through the thicket, I saw Quinn stalking the marsh grass behind me. He did not have me in sight, but he was closing the distance between us. When I tried lifting my feet to continue, they were sunk in oozing mud. With great effort, I pushed forward, but my hair became snared in the briars that draped me. I tugged and pulled, but could not free my long locks where they twisted in the thorns and sticky creepers.

The rustle of my struggle caught the attention of Quinn. Now waist-deep in the bog and tangled by my hair, I watched him creep my way with his gun raised. All I could do was wait for him to find me in my prickly entrapment. When Quinn was less than twenty paces from the briars, the scamper of footsteps in the opposite direction sent him whirling away from me. He chased after the footsteps and disappeared into the trees.

After several minutes, the boom of a shotgun roused a heavy flutter of birds from the canopy. He had strayed farther away, so I moved quickly to free myself. I reached up and yanked my hair fiercely. It would not tear loose, nor would the briars uproot. I knew Quinn would return once he discovered he had been misled by a deer or squirrel, but the harder I fought to break free, the more securely I was clutched by the marsh thicket.

My heart leapt when the slosh of feet in water came toward me from beyond the bush. Was Quinn back already? I squirmed with what little strength I had left, but I was doomed. Braced to see Quinn's face, I gasped when a dark-skinned woman crashed through the bushes. Her yellow eyes were wide and wild. Barely clothed and wielding a knife, she burst toward me with her blade thrust fiercely toward my unprotected face.

Chapter 13

*B*efore I could cry out, the knife whisked past my cheek and up into my hair. With lean, muscled arms, she hacked through briars and snared locks despite my attempt to push her away. When what was left of my hair broke free of the briars, I realized her intent was to rescue me from Quinn. With a firm grasp on my shoulder, she pulled me from the mire and up onto my feet.

"Come."

The wild woman said no more. Stepping lightly, she led me into the knee-deep water of the marsh. My wet clothing slowed me to a crawl. Once again she came at me with the knife, this time slicing my skirt above my knees and carving away my sleeves at the shoulders. As the heavy material sank into the mud, my body broke free in movement. I raced after her, catching glimpses of Quinn in the distant trees.

Soon the water rose from my knees to my waist and then to my shoulders. I cringed at the thought of what lurked beneath the surface. Eels, cottonmouths, leeches! I shuddered with disgust, but my fear at losing the only guide I had forced me to keep pace in spite of the utter exhaustion and vulnerability I felt.

"Are there alligators in these waters?" I asked as my heart leapt and stuttered at every ripple that swirled around me.

The woman looked back sternly, then continued on without a word. I worried that the marsh bottom might fall away, but the woman moved deftly through the mangroves without hesitation. With our chins above the water and a heavy canopy of vines a few feet overhead, we navigated a tunnel of dense thicket that wound deeper into the swamp. The sounds of birds and Quinn's frustrated rants became muffled and distant. I had hoped this hidden channel would lead back to the canal, perhaps farther to the north, but when it finally opened, I was engulfed by marsh grass and sedge.

The woman pulled me from the water onto higher ground. Panting and gasping for breath, I sank onto a boulder. The slime and mud on the bank were thick with flies, but I was grateful to be out of the hazardous swamp deeps. The woman watched me as I feverishly picked sedge grass from my clothes. She dipped her hands into the dark water and held what she cupped to my lips.

"Here."

I shrank away before any dripped into my mouth. "We must find a freshwater spring," I said. "This may sicken us with dysentery."

The woman scowled at me and then slurped the water from her hands. She knelt by the water and motioned for me to join her.

"Be the cypress."

"Pardon me?" I said, wondering what to make of this swamp woman.

"It be the cypress that makes the water so dark. It ain't dirty. Every creature in the swamp drinks its water."

She was so adamant, and I so thirsty, I fell to my knees and slurped what I scooped against my lips. When no foul or bitter taste was left on my tongue, I scooped more vigorously until I was quenched. Hunched over the water, I cringed at my reflection. My hair had been unevenly chopped to just below my ears. Lightened of its thick length and sprung alive in the humid air, my short locks flailed out from my head in such disarray that I did not recognize myself.

Sitting back, I looked at the swamp woman, who stared at me with equal curiosity. Her brown eyes were set wide in her head and were yellowed like aged paper. She blinked with heavy lashes and lids, creating a sleepy countenance, though she crouched, keen and alert. With a nose neither broad nor narrow and full pink lips, her dark face glimmered with perspiration. She was crowned by a faded cotton rag folded along her hairline and tied atop her head, like those worn by most slave women working in the fields. Tucked along her head cloth was a line of purple flowers dangling small and limp from the heat.

"What's a white missy like you doin' in the swamp? You lookin' fo' runaways?"

"No," I said, a bit guarded. "I was traveling to Deep Creek."

Her eyes narrowed and puzzled over me. "Most folks go by boat or carriage. And not with a bounty hunter takin' aim on them."

Obviously this swamp woman understood that I was in some kind of trouble. I had become used to hiding my secrets, so I hesitated at revealing too much. However, the swamp woman seemed to be determining whether my presence was a threat. I owed her my life and my honesty with it.

"I am a mistress, but not completely white." I explained the circumstances of my birth and my attempt to help my slave mother. "I should have escorted them to the North myself, under the guise of business or holiday. After all, I am still viewed as a respectable Southern mistress."

The woman kicked her bare feet and chuckled loudly. "You sure don't look like no mistress now. Yo' skinny pale arms and legs look white enough, but yo' hair is gonna give you away fo' sure. When I seen you layin' tracks from that no-good varmint, I thought you was a light-skinned house slave on the run. It wasn't till I got up close and cut you from yo' dress that I realized you was white."

I was shaken with modesty at the mention of my exposed body. I folded my legs close to my chest with my knees tucked under my chin and my arms wrapped tightly around them. My stained dress, shorn of its sleeves and its length, looked more like the sack that she wore, though I moved more freely now that the cumbersome excess was removed. I tried smoothing my hair with my wet hands, but flattening it was hopeless.

"Don't get to feelin' shy. The ways of the swamp ain't nothin' like the outside. It is too fierce to do battle with. You gots'ta to blend in and become a part of it. Fancy clothes and manners got no place here. They be the death of you."

"You really live here? By choice?"

"The swamp is a harsh place, but once you become its friend, then it be yourn. No massas. No whips. No chains."

"Then you are one of those outliers I've heard tell of. Some people think it's folklore, but here you are."

"Call me what you want . . . outlier, runaway, wench, slave. Them words don't mean nothin' here." She stood proudly and poked her thumb against her bosom. "I am a survivor, livin' simple and free. When the sun rises, I go where I want and do what I want."

"Are you alone?"

"No." She seemed reluctant to say more. She peered across the marshes surrounding us. "Will yo' people send paddyrollers lookin' fo' you?"

"You mean patrollers?"

I had not considered the possibility. When I left Great Meadow, they did not know I was headed to South Mills. But with Garrison aware that I had entered the swamp, he might launch a search party.

"It's possible," I said.

"Well, they ain't likely to get too far," she mumbled. "The inner swamp ain't an easy trail. Why was the bounty man on the chase?"

"I was well hidden and he mistook me for a runaway. Anyone else searching for me will assume me to be in the area of the canal."

"Just as well," she said. "They're not likely to trudge this way, but it's best fo' me to know how far they will come in their look-see."

Though it bothered me to say so, I believed the effort would be minimal. "Claudia will be happy to declare me lost, and Garrison will not want the stain of embarrassment brought by my spurning his attention."

The swamp woman sat down next to me as though sensing hurt in my words. "I'll help you get to the north side of the swamp. We gots'ta stay inland, away from the canal, though. There's too many rascals on the hunt along the waterway."

I looked at her earnest expression and trusted her intent. Not that I had much choice, since I could never have found my own way through the vast junglelike forest that stretched in every direction. But her initial instinct to protect me from Quinn revealed her pure nature, and I was grateful for her kind offer of help.

"My name is Jacy."

"I am Violet." She smiled.

"Like the flowers," I said, pointing at the purple blooms that hung from her bandanna.

She touched her fingers to them. "Maola says they are African violets. Their kin lived in the faraway place where my kin lived too. We was rooted in the same soil, so that makes them my sisters. Letha was my slave name. I changed it to Violet when I came to the swamp."

"I like it." I grinned. "Thank you for helping me, Violet."

"We got a long way to go before thanks be given," she said, pulling me to my feet. I wobbled in the discomfort of my waterlogged shoes. The laces of one were torn open and the heel of the other flopped.

"Them shoes ain't gonna do you no good. Truth is, they will give you away as not bein' one of us meant fo' the swamp."

I tugged my shoes from my sore feet and let them sink into the water. Violet released the top buttons of my collar, then scooped up handfuls of dark mud and began smearing it on my arms and legs. After smudging my nose and cheeks, she nodded.

"The mud is a layer of protection. It will keep the bugs off you and hopefully ward off any fearful folks that might panic at the sight of white skin."

I looked down at my changed appearance. Without silk and lace to mark me as special, I was stripped of distinction and promise. Mud was my rouge instead of powder, and its coarseness served to remind me how far I had fallen. Covered in earthy muck and sticky with moist heat, I might have experienced an astounding rebirth. Frightened and confused, I grappled to make sense of it. The world around me was strange and threatening. Nearly naked, I was ill prepared to fend for myself, and even my barefooted steps were as tentative as a toddler's as I followed Violet. We traipsed across open, spongy heaths, then amid marsh grass and sedge until we came upon a patch of some kind of wild black grapes.

"You hungry?" Violet asked as she plucked some grapes and tossed them in her mouth. "They is a bit mealy this time of year, but still good to the taste."

I was ravenous and didn't care if they were end-of-season pickings. I yanked the grapes from their vines with both hands and ate them as quickly as I could. Before I got my fill, Violet grabbed onto my hand and pulled me to the ground.

"Shhh."

Her eyes were fixed across the marsh. I saw nothing at first glance, but then a large, muscled Negro emerged from the cattails. He wore no shirt, so his broad dark shoulders glistened in the receding sun. His trousers were torn at midcalf and secured to his lean hips by a length of frayed rope. The man's coal black beard was heavy, although his woolen hairline dipped back on his scalp, emphasizing his high, smooth forehead.

"That's Ox. We don't want him to catch sight of us."

We crawled from the bushes and into the trees as the man disappeared into the distant marsh. "Let's move quick so we don't cross paths with him again."

I followed Violet as she led me deeper beneath the canopy of cypress and vine. "Is that man an outlier like you?"

"Yes, but the swamp holds all kinds of creatures. Vicious cougars stalk the forest where harmless warblers sing. Ox can be meaner than a bear in a claw trap. I learned long ago to stay out of his way."

Suddenly, an agonizing pain pierced my foot. "Aaaah!" I cried out as I dropped to my knees. Blood gushed from a deep gash on my exposed sole. Violet squeezed my foot to slow the bleeding, but the pressure made me cry out again.

"Quit hollerin'!" Violet words were sharp and pleading. "The yelp of a woman is sure to attract attention. Don't want no restless man or hungry animal sniffin' after us. Now hold still and let me see how bad you been cut."

"Who dat, Violet?"

The man's voice chilled me. Was he the man called Ox? Violet shifted her body in front of me as the man came through the trees. He too was large and shirtless, but his hair appeared full and sprouted from beneath a slouch hat. He held a long stick that had been carved to a point at the end. He glared fiercely until Violet spoke.

"What you sneakin' around fo', Tupper?"

"Ain't sneakin'," he said, still staring at me. "I is huntin' marsh rabbit. Now, is you gonna tell me who dis mud-soaked fresh face is?"

"This here is Jacy. She is on the run, passin' through the swamp fo' freedom in the North."

"Dat right?"

I nodded, my throat clenched too tightly to utter a response. Tupper knelt and fingered my bloodied foot. "Looks like a piece o' shale sliced you good. Nearly slashed to de bone."

He untied a faded cloth worn loosely around his thick neck. After folding my torn skin over the wound, Tupper knotted the cloth around my foot. "Better take her to de backwater marsh and get her off her feet before dat cut gets plump and sore."

He looked from Violet to me. "You ain't runnin' nowhere till dat gash settles or you'll pull up lame and be nothin' more than a meal for de buzzards."

"We is much obliged to you, Tupper," Violet said as they helped me onto my feet. "Be on the watch while you is huntin'. Ox is on the prowl."

"Yep, I seen him. He say one o' his gals seen a white mistress out at de eastern edge of de swamp. Said she was prancin' around in her fine dress and shoes."

"Probably lost and found by now," Violet interjected quickly.

"Ox says she was makin' tracks inland. I told him dat was crazy. His gal most likely saw de ghost of a lost soul cloaked in white. No mistress is gonna stroll in de swamp. But Ox say if there is a mistress in de wood, den there's a massa not far behind. So if she ain't no ghost, she will be soon enough." My eyes blinked wide at Tupper's musing.

Violet wrapped my arm around her shoulders. "We'll leave you to yo' hunt," she said as she hustled me from the swamp dweller. I shuddered to think what might have transpired had Violet not altered my clothing and appearance.

More blood trickled from scratches clawed on my exposed legs as we pushed through the skin-ripping thicket. Violet helped me limp across a narrow rocky stream to where another marsh bed opened. "We gots'ta wade through the water to the high ground over yonder."

There looked to be several wooded island mounds at the center of the inner swamp amid dense cattails and saw grass. Once again, Violet walked confidently into the water, this time holding a stick to poke away water moccasins that slithered too close. I snapped a tall reed in half and anxiously followed suit.

"How do you know where to go? Every marsh pool and cypress grove looks the same to me."

"I been in the swamp near about two years. I know it better than the cotton plantation I ran from, because I can roam about and study the land. The curve of trees and the bend of the water are signs enough to follow. Gots'ta know them to survive."

My foot throbbed painfully as we finally dragged ourselves onto high ground. I leaned back on the peat to catch my breath. The swamp water around us glimmered in the orange glow of sunset, and for a moment its beauty made me forget the hell I had just navigated. I could barely walk, but with Violet's shoulder supporting me, I hopped on one foot along a path through a canopy of juniper and gum. We reached an area where the trees thinned. Despite my agony and desperate circumstance, I gasped in wonder. There amid the flora and fauna was a crude hut. Behind it was another, and two more within the trees to my right.

A maroon colony.

Chapter 14

The tales and folklore were true. Here in the belly of Dismal Swamp existed a rudimentary settlement of runaways living free and out of reach of the surrounding plantations. A few dark faces peered at me from behind trees and underbrush. As Violet waved and greeted onlookers by name, they shuffled tentatively back to small peat fires that sizzled with ash cakes.

When I was about to collapse with pain and exhaustion, Violet pulled me up a mossy embankment to where another hut was nestled beneath some scrub oak. Movement came from inside and two tiny faces appeared.

"Mama!" they squealed as they raced into Violet's arms.

"Children?" I muttered in complete shock. "There are children in the swamp?"

"Of course," Violet said. "This here is my Rose and little Lyle."

The slight girl, Rose, looked to be ten or eleven years old, with short braids tied with rawhide strips. Her unblinking gaze flickered with wonder. Lyle huddled behind his sister. He appeared to be only half her age and much shyer, though it was easy to smile at him, with his hair standing high like unshorn lamb's wool. Both children had their mother's wide-set eyes and were dressed in ragged sacks.

"But how? The conditions are so harsh."

Violet looked at me, perplexed. "We ain't in jail. We is livin' free and this is our home. It's true that the swamp is dangerous ground fo' chilluns. But no more dangerous than livin' as a slave."

I shook my head in amazement. "How do you protect them from the elements and the predators?"

Violet nudged her children toward a low-burning fire being tended by an old woman. She smiled as she watched them scamper away and then looked at me. "I got a better chance of protectin' my babies here than I do on any plantation. Trouble don't usually come lookin' fo' us here. And if it do, at least I can raise a stick to defend my family."

I swatted the aggressive flies that buzzed around my face and gazed at the stick hut in the shadows beyond the fire. "The conditions are so bleak. Certainly disease and starvation are your enemy."

"Maybe so, but we are free to choose our battles. Most folks here in the swamp would rather die in the brush by a natural foe than suffer at the hands of a slave driver day in, day out. That's the same as havin' no life at all."

My God, how tortured was a slave's life for them to choose Dismal Swamp as the better home? I shuddered at my own assumption that the Negroes were lucky to have such a fine life at Great Meadow. Their entire existence revolved around serving us. What had they left for themselves?

"Come and eat," Violet said as she sat between the old woman and her children by the fire.

The gray-haired woman was thin and deeply wrinkled. She had no teeth and moved around the fire, smacking the lips of her sunken mouth as if chewing a fine cut of beefsteak. Using a hoe blade, she lifted four charred disks from the ashes and set them on a rock. They did not look or smell appealing, but my empty stomach needed a meal. When I reached for an ash cake, my fingers were singed by their scorched surface. The children giggled as the cake flew from my hands and into the dirt.

The old woman curled her busy lips in annoyance. "You gots'ta let 'em cool."

The children giggled again. Violet raised a stern finger in their direction. They quieted but continued to watch me with big grins on their little faces. Violet picked the ash cake from the dirt, blew on it a few times, and brushed it clean.

"This here is Maola," she said, motioning toward the old woman. Violet snapped the dry cake in half and gave me a piece. "She looks after Rose and Lyle when I go off to forage."

"Is that what you were doing over at the canal?"

Violet's face hardened. "I wasn't there to steal, if that's what you mean."

"No, that's not what I meant, honestly." It was important to me that she know I would not impugn her character. She nodded as if acknowledging my remorse.

"There is crab apple at the swamp's edge this time of year. Occasionally, a light-haired townsman leaves a basket of blankets, clothes, and tools beside the remnants of a chimney tucked in the trees above town. My knife and this hoe come from that kindly soul."

I thought of Sylvan Firth and suspected he was the light-haired benefactor giving aid with his secret offerings. I smiled at the proof of his quiet commitment to the cause of freedom and understood more and more the motivation in his heart.

"Now, don't get me wrong," Violet continued. "There are plenty of swamp folk who steal a chicken from a plantation or an ax from a timber camp, but it be desperation drivin' their deeds. They take only what they need. Nobody is livin' a favored life out here."

The evening passed with me marveling at their quiet, simple co-existence with nature. I, on the other hand, fidgeted on a coarse log, swatting at the bugs that buzzed at my ears and climbed my legs. I flushed when I noticed the group watching my futile battle.

"I am not accustomed to the constant barrage of insects," I said in defense of my discomfort.

Violet blinked at me through the firelight. "We ain't no different. Don't know anybody who likes bugs crawlin' on them. Even a mule will use its tail to shoo a fly."

"I didn't mean to imply . . ." I hesitated, embarrassed by my presumption that they were oblivious to the same discomfort. Violet rescued me from my ignorance.

"Bugs are a nuisance, fo' sure, but we are on their turf. They can't help takin' notice of us. I figure if they can put up with us, then we ought to try to put up with them."

Maola clucked at my whining. With an exasperated shake of her head, she reached for Rose, who immediately stood and tugged the old woman up from her seat on a smooth stump. After a few labored steps, Maola's stiff legs loosened and she disappeared into the night.

A short while later, Violet led her children to the hut to ready them for sleep. I leaned back to gaze at the breathtaking blanket of stars that twinkled across the heavens above. Frogs and cicadas croaked in the marsh, and the songs of night birds came at me from every direction. I shuddered at the strange world that separated me from all I knew, though the whispering voices of those at other firesides comforted me in their nearness. Exhaustion pained my body and my foot throbbed sharply within the bandage provided by Tupper. Slowly, my eyelids bobbed shut.

"I made a place fo' you inside," Violet said as she poked me awake.

I was not sure how long I had dozed before Violet helped me into the dark hut. She nudged me into a dry, spongy corner. I had never slept on anything other than a feather bed; however, I was grateful that I was not lost and alone in this mysterious swampland. Though I was in unknown territory, nothing could prevent me from sinking into a deep and oblivious sleep.

The twitter of warblers and larks coaxed me awake. Sticks and vines twisted overhead like a jumbled woodpile, but the structure was sturdy, and only a few shards of sunlight penetrated the fortress. The dirt floor was covered in a thick layer of Spanish moss that provided a degree of softness, but the hut was too low for me to stand without bumping my head. Panic fluttered within me.

What have I done?

My life at Great Meadow was far from perfect, but had I traded it for a struggle I could not endure? I had never lived without advantage. I longed for the comfort of Mayme's arms and the innocence torn from me by a secret I could not outrun. Still, I had tossed my home aside to follow my heart. In one day, impulse and emotion had led me to this strange place where I found myself surrounded by wild, unknown Negroes.

I took a deep breath and looked over to where Rose and Lyle lay curled at my side. *These are families,* I reminded myself before unfounded terror could run away with my senses. I was not forced to hide in the swamp. My panic slowly eased with the knowledge that I would soon continue on to the civilized canal port of Deep Creek.

The creased moss where Violet had slept was now vacant. I crawled from the hut into a warm morning. My foot was severely swollen and the pain excruciating when I bore my weight on it. Again I thought of home. Whenever I had a bump or bruise, Papa would send Axel to the icehouse to chip two frosty corners from a frozen block; one was meant to provide cool relief from the ache and the other for me to suck on as a reward for being a *"brave little girl."* I longed to feel the soothing chill of ice on my tongue, but it was a delight that now seemed a thousand miles away, along with the memory of that brave little girl.

I limped over to sit on a log rolled next to the peat fire. Had I been at Great Meadow, my wound would have been cleansed with a boiled cloth and dressed with clean bandages and doctor's ointment. I was not accustomed to having an infirmity go unattended, causing me to worry that my foot would not know how to heal itself. Surely the seeds of sickness were sown in the dirt and mud that were now my floorboards. A sudden pang of doom shook me.

Violet was nowhere in sight. In the daylight, I had a better view of the island around me. More huts were visible amid the trees. I counted six of them from where I sat. Through the juniper and cypress branches on the lower banks, the mist-covered swamp was coming alive with wildlife. Several deer meandered on the far edge, and morning birds called from the cattails below. I scratched at an acorn-sized lump on my elbow before noticing my legs and arms were dotted with welts left by the swarm of flies that hummed around me.

"We'll rub some mud on those bites," Violet said as she came up over the hill with an armful of peat to toss on the warm ashes.

"Aren't you concerned your fires will alert patrollers to where your settlement lies?"

Violet puffed on the dry peat until it ignited into a low flame. "Tiny peat fires don't throw off much smoke, but they will keep a long, slow burn a-goin'. Besides, there are wildfires that scorch somewhere in the swamp all the time. Well, now, here comes Tupper. Did I tell you he is Maola's son?"

The man who had wrapped my foot the previous day walked out

from among the trees. He carried a long stick, and the old woman, Maola, followed on his heels. I flushed with renewed awareness of my bare limbs, but no one gave me a second glance. Stripped of my fineries and detached from home, I felt oddly removed from myself.

"Found a branch straight enough and thick enough to use as a crutch," Tupper said. "Whittled it smooth where it curves at de top to fit comfortable under your arm. I may need to shorten it."

"Thank you," I said as he held it against my body to measure its length.

"A thumb's length from the tip should do."

Violet smiled. "Tupper, that was right kind of you."

He tugged his hat toward Violet and grinned, obviously pleased by her gratitude. Perched on a stump, Tupper carved a nub from the bottom of the crutch. "I figured that nasty cut would be mighty sore today."

"It hurts terribly. Aided by this crutch, I am sure it will mend quickly."

"Let me see," Maola said gruffly. She knelt on the ground and examined my foot as a doctor would. "Better wash it clean. I'll go see if I got me some jimsonweed and boneset. Go on down to de swamp and scrub it good."

I followed Maola's instruction and hobbled to the water's edge. Violet came along and introduced me to a few tentative onlookers. My polite smile did little to alleviate their guarded curiosity about the stranger in their settlement.

"Do you always wear flowers?" I said to Violet as she plucked a few delicate purple blooms from the shoreline and laced them in her head cloth.

"Jes' because I live rugged don't mean I ain't a woman," she teased. "Soon the flowers will be bucklin' down fo' the winter. I get a bit low-down till they come back around in spring."

"If we can find a couple of flat pieces of shale, I can show you how to press and dry your flowers so you will have a supply to get you through the long, cool months."

Violet brightened at the idea. I winced when I dipped my foot in the tepid water. Violet gently loosened the bandage and rinsed the wound as best she could. When she helped me lumber back through the trees, two hogs ran squealing across our path, scattering a cluster of chickens that pecked the hillside.

"Hogs?"

"They run wild on the island," Violet said. "We have goats too, but we keep 'em penned so they can't feast on the vegetable garden."

"You grow crops on the island?"

"Jes' a small patch of corn, okra, and some peas. We tried potatoes and carrots but they don't take to the damp soil. Maola grows herbs to ward off sickness. She simmers tonics, teas, and root medicines when needed. She also mixes poultice ointments and cooks bark and root into syrup fo' swamp fever. She can doctor most anything."

While I would not call their existence a village, I was amazed by their ability to carve out a life in this crude environment. "I would not believe it possible had I not seen it for myself."

"Our swamp island may seem sparse to you, but it is rich in game, fowl, and fish. Our bowls don't go empty like they often did in the slave quarters."

"How many outliers are here?"

"We think of ourselves as settlers, not as outliers or runaways. I don't got a head fo' numbers, but there is a small collection of us on the island and in the surrounding woods. And there are other settlements deeper in the swamp. More settlers than I can count."

"Ouch!" The pain in my foot had spread to my lower leg. My ankle and calf were swollen and as hard as a rock.

"Let's get you off yo' feet. You ain't gonna be in no condition to traipse to the northern swamp until this foot is healed."

By the time we returned to Violet's hut, the children were awake and eating corn mush from a wooden bowl. Maola was hunched over a small pot of simmering water. She crumpled a white flower and a handful of leaves into the brew.

"What is it?" I asked innocently.

"You ain't never seen boneset, girl? Even a chile knows an herb like boneset." Her toothless mouth puffed as she poured the tea into a hollowed gourd. "Drink up. It will keep de fever from comin' on you while you mend."

The hot liquid was terribly bitter, but I forced down every drop for fear of being scolded by Maola. I forgot that those around me assumed I was a light-skinned slave; therefore I did not want to appear unfamiliar with slave practices. If I fumbled or hesitated, Maola would be keen enough to guess that I was not a runaway. Their survival depended on their not being discovered by outsiders. If I was exposed as a fraud, I would undoubtedly be deemed a threat. Even Violet could not protect me if the swamp settlers felt their freedom was at risk. When I finished my tea, Maola handed me two small green leaves. I shuffled them in my hands, not sure what they were for.

"It's jimsonweed," she said, motioning me to put it to use.

I folded them together to make them easier to chew and then stuck them in my mouth. Immediately Maola jumped at me and slapped my face. When I opened my mouth to cry out, she ripped the leaves from my tongue.

"Don't eat it, fool! Jimsonweed will kill you. You is supposed to rub it on yo' foot to bring down de swell."

I spit and slobbered onto the ground to rid myself of the poison. Shaking with anger, I could not believe this woman had the audacity to strike me and call me a fool. She had no right to be harsh with me; it was not my fault I had no experience with plants and herbs. But I was in no position to challenge her. Instead, I tempered my resentment and silently complied with her directive, rubbing moisture from the leaves onto my foot and ankle.

Maola paid no attention to my bruised feelings while she diligently concocted a poultice of gingerroot and tallow. She smeared the greasy ointment on my cut and rewrapped my foot with a fresh rag.

"This will do," she said abruptly. She gathered her things and scuffled away with no more fuss or bother.

Tupper handed me a gourd filled with water to rinse my mouth of tea bitters and jimsonweed. "Don't let Mama ruffle yo' feathers. She don't have no patience fo' those not practiced in common ways."

Violet sensed his suspicion and spoke up to explain my ignorance. "Not every plantation relies on herb remedies; isn't that right, Jacy? I bet yo' massa paid a doctor to tend to yo' colored, right?"

Her anxious eyes begged me to play along. Forced to lie to protect myself, I lowered my head. "Yes," I said, feeling the irony of hiding my white heritage to establish a Negro identity.

When Tupper had gone, Violet settled me by the fire with my foot propped on a log. "I gots'ta milk the goats. Stay put with the chilluns till I get back."

"We'll be fine," I said as she walked away. Like Violet, I believed it was best that I not wander the island without her. Lyle climbed onto my lap and blinked up at me with eyes as dark as the tea-colored swamp. As his thin frame nuzzled against me, pangs of despair rose up from within me. I had long imagined how a child would feel in my arms. Small and hungry for love, a child of mine would never want for care or affection. I held tighter to Lyle, his bushy hair tickling my chin, and felt my dream rush past me. Like so many other lost opportunities in my life, it was not meant to be.

The morning sun glistened atop the ripples of the marsh. With the trees speckled with colorful waterbirds, the swamp looked anything but dismal. But as the sun rose in the sky, the sweltering September heat returned. Intense sun rays gleamed against my face, arms, and legs. I thought about Great Meadow and remembered Claudia's obsession with my wearing wide-brimmed bonnets. Now, as my skin baked in the summer sun, I wondered how dark my complexion would tan in its natural state.

Thoughts of abundant breakfasts of preserves and almond scones made my stomach grumble with neglect. I missed the feel of fresh water in my tub and the convenience of a privy. Most of all, I missed Papa and Mayme. Tears rose in my eyes at how my life had fallen away. What was I doing in the middle of nowhere, bruised, bitten, and injured? Would I ever find my way from the Great Dismal? If so, where would I go? I certainly could not show up at Aunt Sarah's looking as I did now.

Would I dare to follow Rafe, Jerlinda, and Axel to the North, even though they had begged me not to? The love they so generously offered beckoned me. I turned the possibility over in my mind and felt an unexpected tug of hope. How would I find them? They had long left Deep Creek by now. Perhaps the lighter man, Archie, could tell me which ship had smuggled them.

A new pain twisted in me. What if their passage failed? They could be discovered a hundred different ways as they traveled the canal, and a hundred more if they made it to the tidewater landings in Virginia. I did not want to consider the possibilities.

"You look funny."

I opened my eyes and saw young Rose staring at me. I glanced over my bitten, bruised, and scraped limbs. "Yes, I am a mess, aren't I?"

Rose leaned closer. "I mean your face."

I touched my gritty cheeks, realizing that most of the mud from the previous day had dried and flaked away. "I guess I am what they call light-skinned, Rose."

"You look like my pappy before he be dead."

"Had he been sick?"

Rose nodded her head. Even at her tender age, she had taken notice of my unusually pale complexion. To her, I wore the ghostly mask of death. The remaining mud and blush of sunburn could not hide our difference. How long would it be before others questioned me too?

"How's dat foot of yourn?" I turned to see Tupper strolling toward me with a dead animal in his grip. "Got me an extra rabbit."

I leaned away as he shoved the limp animal toward me. It swung between us like a pendulum until I realized he was giving it to me. I took it, but I had no idea what to do with it. Years of frolicking with Louis had taught me a lot of things, but removing the hide of an animal was not one of them. Once, after trapping a squirrel, he had attempted to demonstrate the barbaric evisceration. The first cut that beheaded the defenseless animal had sent me rushing to the bushes to vomit. I had declared to Louis on the spot that I would not sit in witness to an act so bloody and vile. Looking back now, I wished I had paid closer attention.

Tupper handed me his knife. "Go on and skin it. Be quick about it, because I can't go back on de hunt without my blade."

Not wanting to admit that I had never skinned an animal, I returned his knife with a nod of gratitude. "Thank you, Tupper. You have assured us a fine meal. Take your blade and return to your tasks. Violet will return soon. Rather than delay you from your hunt, I will wait and make use of her knife."

Tupper cocked his head curiously as he slid the knife into a sheath on his belt. He started to turn away and then paused. "Where did you say you was from?"

My skin flushed at his sudden interest. "A horse farm in North Carolina. My mother was a house servant to the mistress."

"House servant, eh?" Tupper pursed his lips as he considered my response. "And you?"

"My time was spent at the main house as well." I prayed my half-truth quelled his suspicious inquiry.

"Den you was a house servant too." He nodded tentatively. "Guess dat's why you talk so fancy."

I exhaled a nervous breath when he walked down the embankment and into the trees. When Violet returned to the hut, I told her about the rabbit and Tupper's visit. "Shoot, you gots'ta get some know-how or folks is gonna figure you out right quick."

Violet proceeded to teach me the art of skinning a rabbit. After the first few cuts, she gave me her knife and guided me through the process. A woozy wave of nausea washed over me, though I squelched the familiar urge to spew. This was survival, and the faint of heart would not withstand the trials at hand. Resolutely, I followed Violet's instructions without protest.

"Separate the meat and spread the hide to dry on a rock," she explained patiently. "We'll use it when cool weather comes." Violet then hacked a foot from the animal and tossed it to me. "Here, it will bring you luck."

My hands and forearms were covered in blood, but I felt an odd sense of accomplishment. *If Claudia could see me now.* The thought amused and stung me at once. I was struck with the knowledge that I truly had no home anymore.

Violet's broad smile pleased me. I wanted to prove myself worthy of the risk she had taken in saving me. My determination to rise to any challenge, big or small, tickled her; however, we both knew that my ability to adapt was essential to my emerging from the Great Dismal. I still had a tremendous journey ahead.

I learned Violet had fled a cotton plantation in the southern part of the state. Her master had fallen on hard times and planned to sell all the slave children under the age of twelve to settle a debt. Violet had begged to be sold together with her children.

"He say, 'Letha'—because that's what he called me—'Letha, I can't lose no pickers. You got work to do here. Now, I know I sold away yo' man, but we'll marry you up to another sturdy buck, so you can start a new litter. Them pickaninnies of yourn ain't gonna be sold as a pair anyways.' That's when I knew I had to make a run fo' it. I'd rather die than have my babies scattered on the breeze. I run off that very night with nothin' but the night sky to show me the signs to the North."

I squeezed Violet's hand. "You made a brave choice."

"I was lucky to get a choice at all. Most folks don't get no warnin' that their babies is gonna be snatched. And those with a hankerin' to run don't usually get too far once the Negro dogs is on their heels. My prayers was answered when I crossed paths with Tupper, Maola, and Tupper's wife, Martha."

"Tupper's married?"

Violet leaned closer to continue in a hushed voice. "Tupper knew all about the swamp from an outlier that got caught raidin' a timber camp and then sold to Tupper's massa. Martha was powerful a-scared of the swamp. Not me—I hold this jungle to my bosom with love because it lets me hold my children to my bosom too. I am a part of the Dismal," she said, pointing to the freshly picked violets wound in her head cloth. "Can't say the same fo' Martha, the poor soul. She cursed the swamp and then it cursed her. She died of the fever last spring. Even Maola's herbs couldn't save her."

"Do you ever think about leaving the swamp?" I asked. "Perhaps you and the children can come to the North with me."

Her eyes flashed fearfully. "I ain't never gonna step from the swamp and risk bein' caught. I'd rather face snakebites and swamp fever than the rattle of a chain. I know how to be safe here, Jacy. Beyond the swamp, I can't choose or control anything I do. Can't even hold tight to my own chilluns."

Admiration for her courage and conviction washed over me. "I wish I could ease your burden."

Violet shrugged. "We got enough high ground to be safe when the rains come. Over time, we've made or collected most of the tools and utensils we need. I traded some of the blankets left fo' me at the swamp's edge fo' that cook pot. Gonna get me an iron skillet soon; then we'll have some fine fixin's."

"You certainly have a bright outlook, Violet."

"That's the freedom shinin' from me," she said with a smile. "White folks don't know what a beacon it is fo' those without it."

Within days, the laceration on my sole was much improved, although it continued to crack open when I walked. My strength was returning in spite of the fact that I was desperately hungry. Various forms of baked cornmeal along with fish and small game cooked on a stick did not agree with me. I ate only enough to keep my tummy from cramping too tightly. Violet noticed my sparse appetite and decided to venture across the marsh to gather some berries while I stayed in camp with Maola and the children.

"Get some ash cakes in de fire while I wash up dese chilluns."

Maola's order came with a sack of corn dropped at my feet. As she took Rose and Lyle by the hand toward the deep pools at the end of the island, I scratched my head in wonderment. Ash cakes could not be too difficult to prepare. They seemed quite rudimentary. I sifted my hand through the dry corn kernels.

"Hmm, this isn't cornmeal." I looked around for a hand mill like the one I used to see in the cookhouse but found none. "Maola brought me the wrong sack."

Instinct told me that Maola would not want me rummaging through her hut, so I decided to wait until she returned. As I stretched out in the hot sun, I noticed how much browner my arms and legs were becoming while exposed to the elements. I supposed my mixed blood made me susceptible to a tanned hide.

As I examined their changed appearance, I noticed a figure across the marsh. It was the man called Ox watching me from the bulrushes. I shuddered at his hard expression and immediately folded into myself to hide my bare limbs.

"Ain't you made dem cakes yet?"

I jumped when Maola stepped in front of me. "What?"

"You ain't done one thing while I bathed de young ones."

I leaned to peek around her. Ox was gone. I looked up into Maola's piercing eyes.

"There was no cornmeal."

"So grind some," she huffed. "You is de dumbest, laziest creature I ever knowed."

I flushed with embarrassment. "I could not find Violet's hand mill."

Maola scoffed at my explanation. "Hand mill? You ain't in de big house no more. Go on and grind it with a rock. There's a flat stone right behind you."

I scurried to heed her direction, but when I poured some of the kernels on the surface of the smooth stone half the bag dumped onto the ground. I gathered what was spilled as she stood over me with her hands on her hips. I pounded a rock against the kernels, shooting more into the brush than were crushed into dusty meal. With a quick swipe of her hand, Maola smacked me on the back of my head.

"Get out de way," she barked. "Don't got corn to waste on yo' foolishness. Empty-headed gal . . . can't even make a lowly ash cake."

I was humiliated by her insults. Lack of experience made me fumble, not lack of effort. Could she not see I was trying to please her? In spite of the cruelty and abuse I had endured at the hands of Claudia and Garrison, I had never been struck in anger. Now this woman hit me at every opportunity. I was not skilled in the ways she expected, but hitting me would not help me to learn.

Frustration burned in my eyes. "Stop being so cruel."

Maola's eyes sprang wide. "Don't you sass me," she said, slapping me again. "Get outta here while I clean up yo' mess. Go on. Go down to de marsh and wash de stink off o' you."

I grabbed my crutch and staggered down the hill. I seethed at Maola's unfair treatment of me, but she had the upper hand. I did not want to cause any trouble for Violet or for me. It was best to remain humble and compliant until I could leave this horrible place. I waded into the swamp and splashed my face with water. With my darkened hue, I no longer bothered to rub mud on my skin, so the trickle of water over my warm cheeks refreshed me. Breathing deeply, I felt my temper subside. I lifted my eyes to the beauty around me and breathed again.

I must not lose myself in all of this. I am still Jacy Lane, no matter my appearance, no matter my fate.

A loud splash of water came from the cattails behind me. Before I could move, there he was.

Ox.

As his ferocious glare seared into me, I turned to run. His large paw clamped down on my wrist. "You aren't fooling me, missy."

My arm pinched with pain beneath his rugged touch. "Unhand me, you brute."

"You don't belong here," he said in an unexpectedly articulate manner. With a fierce yank of my arm, he pulled me to him. "Come with me."

Chapter 15

"*L*et go of me!" I fought to break free of him, but he was too strong. When I stumbled, he simply dragged me through the marsh.

"Maola! Help!"

I didn't know if she heard me, because Ox shoved my face down into the sedge. He held my head beneath the water while I flailed my arms and legs. With a vicious jerk, he lifted me by the hair onto my feet. I coughed and spit out the water that regurgitated in my mouth.

"Hush up," he growled.

I reacted swiftly to his assault by biting his arm. Ox roared in anger as he released me. I stumbled backward, but he came at me again. From nowhere, Tupper stepped between us. The sharp tip of his hunting spear stopped my attacker in his tracks.

"Back off, Ox. I don't want no trouble with you."

The woodsman pointed a shaky finger at me. "She is white, Tupper. She is the mistress that was seen near the canal."

Tupper gripped my chin and turned it toward my accuser. "Look again, Ox. Did you ever see a ragtag gal like this on de arm of a massa?"

"She may be stripped of identity," he huffed, "but she knows who she is."

I was shocked by the accuracy of his instincts and his well-spoken candor. From his primitive appearance, I had expected him to grunt and snort in accordance with the name given him. My misjudgment reminded me how little I truly knew of this strange landscape and the people within it. He commanded a direct and respectful response from me, so I obliged.

"I am not wholly white," I said, fearful of my confession. "My slave mother fled north by way of the canal. I was lost and then injured in my chase to go with her."

Ox measured me with intense vigilance. "If what you say is true, then you must leave here and continue your pilgrimage. We will not allow slavers to penetrate this swamp fortress. If you are still here when I return, I will know you are a white liar and you will be punished as an enemy of freedom."

"She'll be on her way as soon as de gash on her foot heals," Tupper said in my defense.

"I will know," Ox stated ominously. He turned and sloshed through the saw grass without looking back.

Like a protective older brother, Tupper pulled some swamp grass from my hair and looked me over. "You all right?"

"I think he intended to drag me to a distant thicket and hand me over to the swamp creatures!"

"Probably so," Tupper said as he helped me to dry land. "Folks look up to Ox in de settlements. Some say he's been lyin' out since de big uprisin' in Virginny years ago. He preaches freedom at all cost, so them ain't empty threats he threw yo' way."

I shuddered. "I fear we haven't seen the last of him."

"Stay away from de bulrushes. You never know what's lurkin'. Wash in de deep pool down past those huts and draw water over at dem rocks."

"Bless you, Tupper. I don't know how to adequately thank you."

Tupper shrugged modestly. "Most swamp folks is good and decent people, layin' claim to de only patch o' freedom dey can find. But some like Ox got de love and trust beat out of 'em. It's best if you don't wander from de hut unless you is with Violet or me."

"I shall heed your warning, Tupper."

Tupper glanced back toward the huts. "Is Violet around?"

I sensed Tupper's warmth for Violet and smiled. "She went berry picking. Perhaps you can come around later and share a meal."

Tupper grinned. "Tell Violet I'll bring some venison. She likes dat."

I retreated to the hut but found no one there. I crawled inside and curled up on the peat in defeat. I had never felt so worthless or persecuted. My basic skills of survival were inadequate and my instincts dull. From my failure with Maola to being threatened by Ox, my naïveté was exposed as never before. In my privileged upbringing, I had had no responsibility in my own care and development. It was no wonder I felt bullied by Maola and Ox, just as I was bullied by Claudia and Garrison.

I cannot lie here whimpering. I must claim my life wherever it leads, much like Violet claimed hers in the swamp. If she can find peace and contentment within the Dismal, then surely I can find it in the world beyond.

By the time Violet returned, my outlook had become one of determination. I asked her to show me how to grind corn into meal and prepare ash cakes wrapped in cabbage leaves. I accompanied her to milk the goats, and when Tupper crossed the marsh on a crude raft with a slain deer on board, I helped butcher it for dinner. The abundance of meat brought a crowd to the large fire that burned in the night. Everyone contributed to the feast. Some brought ears of corn that were baked on hot ashes. Others offered chicken eggs and shelled peas. I took great pride in giving Maola a cooled ash cake of my own making that she ate without complaint.

Those around me had mixed feelings about the odd-looking stranger in their midst. Most maintained an uneasy distance between us, while some grew more tolerant. When the congregation grew to twelve, one of the elders finally approached me. He was a slight fellow with tight brown curls laced with gray.

"They call me Samuel," he said without idle pleasantries. "Do yo' massa own any properties named Betsy Ann or Timber Joe? They is my wife and son."

"No," I said, wishing I could ease the sorrow that glistened in his weary eyes. "I'm sorry."

A shy girl, who looked to be fifteen or so, handed me a gourd filled with tart cider. "How 'bout Addie? She my mama."

My heart broke as each shake of my head shattered one hopeful expression after another. All these families torn apart, not knowing the fate of loved ones. I had been apart from mine for only little more than a week and was tortured by worry. How does a spirit sustain itself when parents, siblings, and children are torn away? Yet in their faces I saw endurance, not self-pity, and I was awed.

They told stories and sang spirituals. When they filled their bowls, I noticed there was a pecking order of elders, men, mothers with children, and on down. I avoided any missteps by abiding my place as a newcomer. There was no disrespect in the order; it simply reflected the hierarchy of the colony. They were a community and no one went without.

Watching them filled me with an overwhelming need to leave

them with a lasting token of my gratitude. What did I possess of any value? An idea struck me.

The children.

I could introduce them to a basic freedom they had long been denied—education. I had neither the tools nor the time to teach them to read or write, but I could give them the building blocks, letter by letter. I smiled, feeling as if a part of me had been rediscovered.

Eventually, the blaze subsided and the group dispersed to their individual fires. The sky was clear and glazed with starlight. Violet crawled from the hut after settling the children on their pallet of peat.

"You have been a good friend, Violet," I said when she joined me at the fire. "You offered your hand when I was knocked down, then gave me the guidance I needed to grow stronger for the path ahead."

"You ain't been here long enough to learn more than a speck, but you ain't leavin' till I show you the knee-dropper."

"The knee-dropper?" I had no clue what she meant.

She moved closer as if sharing a secret. "Tupper told me what happened with Ox today."

"Oh." I flushed. "Thank goodness Tupper came to my defense."

"Jacy, you ain't a mistress no more. That means you ain't protected like fine porcelain locked in a china closet. Me and Tupper might not be around the next time trouble comes a-callin'." She tugged me to my feet. "Now, grab me by the hair and force me down."

"Violet, I will do no such thing."

She pressed my hand firmly against her head cloth. Several flower petals fluttered to the ground when she feigned being forced to her knees. She looked up at me with serious intent. "We is vulnerable out here on our own, but we got a hidden weapon."

"What's that?"

She jerked her fist up between the part in my legs, stopping before the blow buried into my groin. "The knee-dropper." She smiled. "Do it fast and fierce. Then you'll see how quick they fall to their knees."

"Violet, I am not strong enough to topple a man with one blow."

"Strong don't matter if you hit them here," she said, tapping her finger to her crotch. "A man's soft place is his one weakness. It's like snappin' a cornstalk at its base so that it falls and goes limp in the field. Even the most powerful man is cut down by a blow that hits his soft spot."

My cheeks flushed with embarrassment. I had never discussed a man's intimates and knew little of the subject, but Violet's eyes gleamed with the secret shared.

The thought of fending for myself in such a way frightened me. "I could never pull the trigger on an action so bold."

"If you can't protect yourself, Jacy, you can always stay here. It ain't fancy, but it's home."

"You have a kind and generous heart," I said, reaching to hold her hand. "But I have a need to find my family. I want to help them if I can and remain together if fate allows, just as you hope for you and your children."

Her fingers looped with mine in tender understanding. "Soon you will be ready to tread north. Tupper gave me a cut of hide and some guts from his deer. If I dry it and soften it with tallow, I can tie together a sandal for yo' foot. Won't be too sturdy, but it will give some protection. When you can step without pain, we will go."

"We?" I waved off her gesture of support. "I do not want to put you in any danger, Violet. If you point me in the right direction, I will take responsibility for the journey ahead."

"Yo' journey beyond the swamp will be burden enough," she said with serious caution. "I got the know-how to deliver you to its startin' point. Woodsmen more skilled than you lose their way in Dismal Swamp, never to be heard from again. Ain't gonna let that happen to you, girl." She laughed. "You are my sister of the swamp now, so I gotta make sure you get where you need to go. Tupper said he would take you, but I know the outer swamp better than him."

"Tupper is a good man," I said. "He is fond of you, Violet. I can tell."

Violet giggled. "He is a fine man indeed."

I smiled as she continued to stare at me with a sheepish grin. "What?"

"He asked me to visit him in his hut."

"And?"

I was surprised when Violet's eyes clouded with tears. "We is both mighty lonely. My man was sold south years ago, and Tupper's Martha has been dead long enough fo' his ache to turn to need. There was a time when freedom seemed too much to hope fo'. I feel the same about love."

I touched Violet's cheek. "Don't be afraid to reach out."

"You speak like you know somethin' about it," she said softly.

"By the time I realized how attached my heart was to another, it was too late. If fate allows me a second chance, my feelings will not go unspoken."

Days passed and my wound healed. No longer in need of my crutch, I helped Violet gather wood and dry peat for Maola to use when she watched over Rose and Lyle in Violet's absence. I shucked corn and ground meal so she had an abundant supply. When chores were completed, I led young Rose and Lyle to the soft ground beneath a tall cedar.

"These markings are called letters," I said as I scratched the alphabet in the dirt with a foot-length stick. "A . . . B . . . C," I said, carefully pronouncing the sounds.

Rose sat straight and attentive while Lyle danced around me, all the while peeking sideways at my lesson. He crawled onto his knees and joined his sister when I gave them each a stick of their own to copy the letters as I pointed to them. Soon, curious maroon children from neighboring huts came into our circle. They giggled when Lyle's rendition of the letter M looked more like a spider, then clapped when he drew a perfect T. I smiled at their enthusiasm and inquisitive nature. It occurred to me that these deprived children were no different at heart from the white boys and girls huddled in schoolhouses across the state.

No sooner had the revelation warmed me than a handful of boys who were gathered around little Lyle burst into laughter. In the peat, he had drawn a simple face with large eyes and sharp teeth. His impish personality was so innocent and endearing. He reminded me of Axel in his boyhood days. As I approached them, Lyle raised his hands and growled like an angry beast.

"That's a wonderful drawing of a bear, Lyle. Can you write B for *bear*?"

He crinkled his nose with glee. "No bear," he said, making his voice roar. "Maola."

Even I had to laugh, though I quickly looked around to see if the old woman was within earshot. I was still chuckling at the silly imitation when we settled around the fire that evening.

"Is we reading, Jacy?" Rose asked sweetly as she effortlessly carved the alphabet in the dark soil between her outstretched feet.

Using my finger, I wrote Rose's name beneath her string of letters. Without my asking, she spoke the letters aloud. "R . . . O . . . S . . . E."

"Those letters spell Rose."

The little girl's eyes popped open. "Me!" She spoke the letters again, then proudly declared, "Rose!"

I hugged her to me. "Now you are reading."

The evening passed with Violet and her children saying words and names for me to spell out, to their delight. *Lyle. Rain. Swamp. Mama.* The game went on and on. Violet watched intently as Rose repeated the letters, her face lighting up with a broad smile. Violet reached down and pointed to the letter J and then the letter C.

"Jay . . . cee," she said, excitedly. She looked up at me, her grin reflecting prideful achievement.

"That's right," I said, flooded with pure and simple pleasure. "Me."

"We're reading, Mama!" Rose squealed as she threw her arms around Violet.

"Yes, we is, chile," Violet said, nodding at me thankfully. "Yes, we is."

The next morning, the children accompanied me to the end of the island to bathe. We swam through the water and rubbed our hands vigorously beneath our clothes to freshen up. Maola came to the river's edge to keep a watchful eye. Since I had become a contributor to the camp, she no longer belittled me, though she still carried a subtle air of mistrust. Chewing her tongue with her toothless gums, she greeted the children with grandmotherly strokes of affection as they giggled and splashed around her knees.

I paused to bask in a brief moment of serenity. I sank low in the water with my face turned up to the azure sky. The warmth of the sun on my cheeks replenished me, but just as my eyes were about to droop closed, a sudden whoosh in the water rushed past my shoulder. I sprang to my feet in the waist-deep pool, alert for an unseen threat. The water around me was still; then, eerily, a dark, plum-sized head broke the surface a few feet away. The creature moved methodically atop the water, its trailing wake revealing the three-foot length of a water snake.

A cottonmouth!

I recognized it immediately as the species of wicked viper that had struck Rafe's father dead with its poisonous bite. It slithered toward the shallows, where Rose and Lyle frolicked without notice of the approaching danger. "Hurry to the pond bank, children. Snake!"

They did not hear me above their playful banter. My heart pulsed with terror as the snake did not alter its course from the children in its path. Beyond them, I saw Violet rise from her knees in the distant garden, her face ashen with horror. I screamed more forcefully so I would be heard.

"Be still, Rose!" I yelled. "Hush now, Lyle!"

Maola's wrinkled face scowled at my brusque command. Oblivious to the reason for my outburst, she nudged the children, who stood by her in the knee-deep water. "Dance, little ones. No white mongrel can order us silent. She hides her white ways behind her tawny skin, but she still thinks she's better than us."

With the snake nearly upon them, I picked up a stick and charged at the trio. Maola covered her face as I splashed in their direction and Violet broke into a sprint toward the water. The children screamed and clung to Maola. I swung the stick over my head. With a vicious swat, I landed a blow against the cottonmouth where it glided on the water a few feet from Rose. Violet plunged into the water and, with Maola's help, pulled the children onto higher ground. The snake submerged and then resurfaced. I walloped it again, causing it to slither into the lily pads. I tossed the stick aside and sloshed from the water to where the others huddled on the bank.

"Is anyone hurt?" I gathered the children into my arms. "I didn't mean to frighten you. If you had moved, you could have been bitten."

They wrapped their arms around my neck and hugged their little bodies to mine. The brush with tragedy shook me as well. Violet knelt beside me. Tears rolled down her cheeks as she put her arms around all three of us. She kissed the faces of her children, then kissed me.

"Bless you for bein' here."

Maola touched my hand where it squeezed Rose's shoulder. I looked up at her and she gazed upon me with soft eyes. She said nothing, but what was conveyed by the earnest pat of her hand said more than any words she could have spoken.

"The time has come," I said later that evening.

Violet nodded her head. My foot had healed sufficiently to allow our trek to where the swamp met Deep Creek. I had lost valuable time while I recovered and worried I might never pick up the trail taken by Rafe, Jerlinda, and Axel.

"It's probably best to get you outta here before the weather cools," Violet said softly. "We will leave in the mornin'. I'm gonna stroll over to tell Maola so she'll come for the chilluns."

Knowing Violet would likely spend some time with Tupper, I relaxed by the fire with Rose at my side and Lyle asleep on my lap. "Take all the time you need. I will settle the children."

When Violet left, I closed my eyes and let the cadence of frogs and crickets soothe my loneliness. Violet's relationship with Tupper made me think of Rafe. I ached for his tenderness and love. The memory of his gentle touch stirred my depths. Rafe had awakened my heart in ways I could have never imagined. He was so strong, kind, and caring. And he was *gone*. Thinking of him made me all the more confident in my decision to follow them to the North.

"I got a present fo' you, Jacy."

Rose's dark eyes blinked sweetly as she hid her hand behind her back. She reached up and looped a knotted string of rawhide around my neck. Tied firmly to the rawhide was the rabbit's foot that Violet gave to me the day she taught me the art of skinning the animal.

I squeezed her affectionately. "Thank you, dear Rose."

Rose stroked my hair with childlike care. "Maola helped me make it. Tupper said when you leave you is gonna need all the luck you can get."

I hugged Rose tightly so she could not see my apprehension. She climbed up on my lap next to Lyle. "What's it like outside the swamp, Jacy? I only remember Massa's place. When we ran off we traipsed in the dark and didn't see much 'cept the stars in the sky."

Her question was difficult to answer. I pondered my thoughts of the world and discovered I viewed it much like Violet viewed the swamp. Yes, it could be harsh and treacherous, but there was beauty in it as well. I thought of Mayme's and Papa's devotion to me. Jerlinda's lifetime of love from afar. Sylvan Firth's courage. Rafe.

"It's a place of both hope and hopelessness, Rose. What do you remember about your plantation?"

"I remember my straw pallet was nice and dry. There wasn't so many spiders. But mostly I remember bein' a-scared. I don't like white folks. Maola says they are devils."

I put my arm around the little girl's shoulders. "Some are devils indeed, but many are not. The good and bad of a person grows on the inside."

"Are you sure? Folks here is scared of 'em."

"They are frightened of the ones who come with guns and chains. Are you afraid of me?"

Rose giggled. "I ain't afraid of you, Jacy. You looked funny at first, but not so much anymore."

"Well, *I* am white."

Rose's mouth dropped open in disbelief. "You ain't colored?"

"I am Negro as well," I said, holding out my arm to display my deeply suntanned skin. "But most important, I am good on the inside. I love you and your brother. And your mother as well. That's your proof that not all white folks are devils. Someday, if you leave the swamp, that bit of truth might comfort you. It's a little kernel of hope to carry with you like a rabbit's foot."

Rose continued to stare at me with inquisitive interest until her eyes grew heavy. I helped the children to bed and curled up in the moss beside them. I knew not what lay ahead of me, but I would not miss this raw existence. Nor would I miss the muggy heat and torturous insects.

I would, however, miss the sanctuary these swamp settlers had created. They were bonded to one another and dared to keep hatred and oppression at bay despite the sacrifice it required. They embraced the life they had chosen because it was free of constraint and inequity. *That* would be *my* kernel of hope to carry as I reentered the outside world.

A twinge of anxiety pinched me from within. What if my journey was rooted in false hope? Until now, I had followed my heart and trusted my instincts. Brushing my fingertips over Rose's gift where it dangled from my neck, I wondered if the superstition of a lucky rabbit's foot would serve me better than the naive hope that I could begin a new life in the midst of unyielding prejudice and intolerance.

Chapter 16

I did not sleep as I awaited the sunrise. At first light, Violet appeared. She tucked a flint rock and her knife in a tiny sack tied at her waist. The only possession I had was my rabbit's foot. As we shared a farewell meal with Tupper, Maola, and the children, a thought occurred to me.

"Should we take some cornmeal?"

Tupper raised an eyebrow. "You can't cook or carry any food. De bears would be on you in no time."

"We are gonna travel light," Violet added. "Less chance of sinkin' in the swamp or gettin' tangled by the trees. We'll get by on berries and pine nuts."

We came together to bid our farewells. The children wiped teary eyes as I kissed their cheeks. "Here," I said, lifting a large, flat stone from the brush. "I have a surprise for you."

Rose and Lyle sidled next to me as I leaned the stone against the base of a bald cypress. "Letters!" Rose squealed as she admired the alphabet I had permanently scratched into the stone's smooth surface.

"Now the rain can't wash away what you have learned," I said, squeezing the two precious children to me.

Rose pointed to the words I had etched below the letters. "What's them words?"

I touched my finger to each word I read. "'Thank you. I love you.'"

Rose sniffled sadly as Lyle beamed at recognizing his name scratched on the stone. "Lyle," he said, patting the letters with his small hand.

"That's right, Lyle. You are a smart little man." I pointed to each of the other four names I had included on the rocky scroll as he recited them aloud.

"Rose, Mama, Tupper . . ."

When I pressed my fingertip to Maola's name he paused. Hers was a difficult name to spell and we had practiced it only a time or two, but before I could give him a hint, Lyle crinkled his nose and growled like a bear. I laughed through my tears at the comical gesture that eased the sorrow in our good-bye, and in that innocent moment, I believed for the first time that laughter and joy were not gone from my life forever.

The children clung to Violet while she hugged them and whispered words of love in their ears. Maola took them by the hand. "Yo' mama will be back soon enough." The old woman then nodded at me, her eyes warm with dignified regard. "Step safely."

Considering my run-in with Ox, Tupper wanted to see us through the first few miles of our journey. Using his log raft, he floated us to the opposite bank, then guided our hike through the marsh until the sun was high overhead. After crossing a flowered brake, Violet paused before entering the thick forest of white cedar ahead.

"Better turn back now, Tupper."

He surveyed the landscape around us. "Thought maybe I'd go de distance."

"That ain't a good idea, Tupper. Three of us will be easier to spot than two."

"Well, then, Violet," he said firmly, "let me be de one to take de risk. You got babies at home."

"Tupper, the swamp folk rely on you fo' meat and wood and keepin' harm from us."

I stepped between them. "Please, I do not want either of you taking risks on my behalf. You have done more than enough for me already. Just tell me which direction to tread and how long the journey. I shall pursue my fate without becoming a threat to yours."

"Gotta get you beyond Lake Drummond," Violet insisted. "Tupper, you mean well, but you never wandered the upper swamp like me. Jacy's best chance of gettin' there quick and without trouble is by followin' me. Go on back and keep my chilluns safe."

Tupper was torn by the decision, but he could not argue with the sense of it. Anguish tightened his face as he embraced Violet. "Don't brush too close to de timber camps."

He shook my hand and wished me well.

"Thank you, Tupper. You are a great man."

Tupper walked back across the brake, looking over his shoulder as we waved good-bye. When he disappeared into the trees, Violet looked at me. "He was right about the camps. Each step takes us farther into the timberland. The problem is the camps move around dependin' on where the loggin' is bein' done. So we gots'ta be extra careful."

We walked on in silence, stopping occasionally when the rigorous journey slowed my steps. With plenty of water to quench my thirst and Violet's encouragement to coax me through utter exhaustion, I walked farther than I thought possible. The sound of woodpeckers and warblers kept us company, although the eeriness of the dark woods caused me to feel watched and tracked. Perhaps it was Tupper's warning that put me on edge. We found no berries or wild grapes, so we foraged for pine nuts. Before the sun sank too low, we nestled in the hollow of a tree to wait out the night.

"Can't risk no fire, and the tree cover is too thick to follow the stars," Violet said.

This pattern continued for two more days. Occasionally the snap of twigs or the rustle of underbrush had us ducking for cover, but no threat showed itself. Late in the afternoon of the third day, we came across a hand-dug channel of water.

"The canal!" I exclaimed.

Violet shook her head. "Naw, that's what they call a feeder ditch. The canal men and bonded slaves dig ditches from Lake Drummond in the west so water can flow to the canal in the east. That way when we get a dry spell the boats can keep afloat."

We swam across the slow, narrow flow of dark water. As we shook ourselves off on the other side, a disturbing thought occurred to me. "Violet, what shall I do for proper clothing when I get to Deep Creek?"

Violet looked over my tattered appearance. "We can either steal some from a farm on the fringe or we can work out a trade with a bondsman."

"Why would a bondsman help us?"

"Bondsmen are nothin' more than field slaves hired out by their massas to cut shingles. Massas make good cash on a set amount of shingles cut by their bonded properties. The bondsmen work mighty hard, because any extra they cut beyond their day's allowance is cash in their own pocket. Most hope to earn enough to buy their freedom."

"I still don't understand why they would help us."

Violet stopped to sip some water from a ground stream. "They will help us because we will help them make their day's measure and then some."

"But Tupper warned us to stay away from the timber camps."

"We ain't goin' to the camps. Passels of bondsmen go into the cypress and cedar groves around the camps to cut the timber used fo' shingles. If we find one a-hustlin' like he is diggin' fo' treasure, we will offer him a hand in securin' his *extra*. Bondsmen will trade off food, clothes, and even tools to outliers who sneak from the trees to work fo' them."

"It sounds dangerous, Violet. What if one turns us in to his overseer?"

"Bondsmen got no grudge against the runaways. The truth is, some of the runaways was bondsmen who took off fo' the swamp when the other timbermen wasn't lookin'. Most slave catchers don't waste their time chasin' bondsmen into the swamp. They jes' send fo' more slaves to fill in fo' the runaways."

Violet laughed. "The owners don't like losin' their properties, but I guess the high price paid fo' shingles and staves is worth the risk. Every few months, a massa gets ornery enough to traipse a posse into the swamp, but they only get far enough to flush out a few runaways that stay near the camps. Slave catchers don't have the gumption and know-how to track their way to the inner swamp."

The trees around me now looked sinister. "If what you say is true, then we are in a very precarious area."

"Yep, we is beyond Lake Drummond and gots'ta be mighty careful. But we are almost to the swamp's end. We'll get you some clothes so you can be on your way."

The following morning we hiked more quickly, driven by the increased danger and nearness of my destination. The knock of an ax against wood echoed in the misty distance. Violet kept me close by, holding my hand and creeping a few trees at a time. By the time the warm sun burned away the damp mist of morning, the axman was closer. Other axes could now be heard as well, but they were far off in the trees. I sensed Violet's intent was to approach the axman nearest to us. When his squatty figure could be seen at the edge of a clearing, we stopped and watched him for a long time.

"Don't you think it is risky to believe the first man we see will help us?" I whispered.

"*We* are helpin' *him*. That's the attitude we gots'ta carry."

I rolled my eyes. "Even so, perhaps we should look around at some others."

"Strollin' around these woods is the last thing we should do," Violet said, squeezing my hand with certainty. "This here fellow was the first to lift his ax this mornin', so that tells me he wanted an early start to make the most of his day."

I understood her point immediately. "A bondsman earning extra cash."

"That's right." She smiled anxiously. "Let's get a closer look."

We crept through the trees and underbrush. Violet pointed toward the clearing, where low stumps of harvested cedar dotted the needle-covered ground. Several axmen chopped at the bases of trees across the open brake. What the man nearest us lacked in height was compensated for by huge round shoulders and powerful arms. His skin was dark and shiny, like a shelled chestnut. He grunted with each swing of his ax until finally he stepped away.

"Widow maker!" he called out to no one in particular. The whine of buckling wood began slowly and grew into a deafening crackle as the tall cedar swooshed through its neighbors and crashed to the ground. Without pausing, the timberman lifted his ax and started chopping the branches from the fallen trunk.

"Wait here," Violet said as she stepped from the shadow of a cypress. "I don't want him to see both of us. Even though you look more colored than on the day I met you, yo' light honey skin is enough to put him on edge."

I had not given my appearance much thought, but Violet was right. My shortened hair, made wild by the unrelenting humidity and lack of care, could not be disguised without a bonnet. That and the natural tan that came with my constant exposure to the sun over two weeks had me leaving the swamp a much different woman than when I had entered. It would surely bring challenges I had yet to consider. But now was not the time or place to worry about what would happen next. Escaping the swamp was not yet guaranteed.

"If I don't wave you over, it's the wrong man," Violet said as she continued to watch the bondsman. "If he ain't a friendly sort, then go on alone while I busy him from noticin' you. Keep the sun to yo' right till midday and then to yo' left toward evenin'."

This possible separation was far too abrupt. "Violet, I will not leave you in danger."

She gave me a nod of confidence, suggesting her directions were meant only as a precaution. She signaled me to stay low, so I sank down and watched her approach the man. He nearly dropped his ax with surprise when Violet appeared from behind a tree. She stayed beyond an arm's length as she tested his willingness to help us.

As they exchanged some quiet words, he twisted his head toward the clearing, fearful of being seen by the timbermen in the distance. Violet motioned toward the swamp and then to the direction we were headed. The man removed his broad straw hat and wiped his brow. When finally he spoke again, she waved me to her. This first contact with someone outside of the swamp made me feel exposed and vulnerable. He was equally guarded as I scampered to where they stood.

"Jacy, this here is Fulton. He ain't got much time."

I nodded, hesitant to speak. Remembering back to Tupper's innocent observation of *"dat's why you talk so fancy,"* I was keenly aware that my formal speech pattern set me apart.

The timberman looked me over. "Girl, you is de lightest yellow Negro I ever seen."

I lowered my head, wishing I had muddied my face, but Fulton did not dwell on my complexion. By the way he kept looking around, he felt as jumpy as Violet and me.

"I'll tell you de same as I tol' her," he said to me as he pointed to Violet. "We is glad fo' any extra stumpers or shingle getters to share de load. We don't mind puttin' swampers to work if dey don't cause no trouble. But stumpin' out here in de woods ain't woman work."

"There must be something we can do to earn a few threads of clothing. One simple dress is all I need."

Fulton laughed. "First off, there ain't no dress, simple or otherwise, within twenty miles o' here. The best I can do fo' you is a cotton shirt and a sorry pair of breeches."

"Fine, let me work for those."

"Like I said, we don't mind takin' on a few swampers when de need arises. Even Boss Man over in de camp likes cheap labor. But only men chop timber out here, and de timber camp ain't no place fo' gals."

Violet shrugged at me. "Guess we is gonna have to steal from a farmer's clothesline along the swamp edge."

"Dem border plantations is on de lookout fo' varmints like you. It be too dangerous to raid a yard fo' a simple fit of clothes." Fulton hemmed and hawed until finally he took pity on us. "You gals lay back in de woods fo' now. I'll come back tonight with a shirt and breeches; den you can be on yo' way. If you keep tiptoein' 'round here, Boss Man will snatch you up and add you to his slave gang. He loves cheap labor, I tell you. But *free* labor is even better. I'll say again, de timber camp ain't no place fo' a gal."

"Thank you, Fulton." I said as my insides twisted like a wrung-out washrag. "The clothing will be a great help."

"Go on now, before one o' these rascals sees you and offers you up to Boss Man fo' a shot o' corn whiskey."

Violet and I sank into the thicket and found a heavy cypress stand where the swamp water ran deep enough to flow like a stream. We quenched our thirst and collected some nuts, though not enough to unravel the hunger that throbbed in my tummy. I noticed a patch of purple violets, so I plucked a fistful and knelt next to my friend. Arranging the flowers neatly around the bandanna tied to her head, I looked into her deep brown eyes as they watched me.

"I want you to go now, Violet. Return to your family. I could never have survived had you not taken me under your wing, but you have brought me far enough. The risk is necessary for me because I am returning to the outside world. You, however, have nothing to gain in this vulnerable position. I will be eternally grateful to you, Violet."

Violet considered my words. "Guess you is right. Can't do much more fo' you." She touched her fingertips to the flowers braided in her bandanna and smiled. "I'll wait fo' Fulton to come back tonight. Then we'll say good-bye."

Anxiety tugged at me, but Violet could not be dissuaded. The steady chorus of axes popping against wood lulled us into a drowsy rest. Periodically, the axes would halt to another cry of, "Widow maker." The roar of the fallen tree was followed by a brief pause of the most silent silence I had ever known, and then the axes would begin again. There was also the whoop of, "Gad'dup," meant to rouse mules and oxen brought in to haul the logs to the timber camp located somewhere in the distant trees. The rise of smoke in the sky marked the encampment about a mile to the north.

The tickle of gnats against my sweaty skin awakened me from my nap. Violet was stretched across a blanket of ferns with her head resting on the curve of her arm. The chorus of axes still rang, but I could see by the sinking sun that it was late in the day. Dead gnats speckled my neck and collected around my eyes and ears. Desperate to rid my skin of perspiration and insects, I followed the stream to a small dark pool. The warm water did little to cool me, but as I submerged entirely beneath the surface, the tingle of fluid on my hair and body invigorated me. I surfaced and sank beneath the water several times just to feel its soft stroke through my hair. The rush of water reminded me of a hot summer's day long ago, when Jerlinda rescued me from the sweltering heat. I was twelve years old when she led me to the pond where the Negro children splashed and swam.

"Yo' daddy won't be home from Raleigh till tomorrow," she said as she nudged me to the water's edge. "With missus locked in her room in the grip of the low-downs, that leaves me to look out fo' yo' comfort."

She lifted a bucket over my head and rinsed the stickiness of the muggy August afternoon from my thick hair. I squealed with delight as the water cooled and refreshed me.

"Can I jump in with the others?"

The slave children were having so much fun I practically begged on my hands and knees. Jerlinda glanced up toward the house and then back at me.

"Missus would have a fit if she saw you in the colored pond. Besides, you aren't dressed fo' a swim, chile."

I stripped to my undergarments before she could protest. "There, I am as ready as anyone else here."

Jerlinda chuckled at my proud determination. To my dismay, she ordered the other children from the pond.

"Go on, chilluns! Step outta the water so Miss Jacy can have a quick swim."

The Negro boys and girls moaned as they traipsed to shore, looking at me as though I had stolen their marbles. Rafe was fourteen at the time. He plopped down in the mud on the far bank. Beads of water dotted his tight curls and water dripped from his chin as he watched me impatiently. I wanted all to see that I was as fun-loving as they were, so I grabbed onto a rope that hung from an old willow and swung myself from the bank, then plunked into the deep end of the pond.

Bubbles giggled from me as I drifted down, but when I planted my feet to push to the surface they sank into the mud-thick pond bottom. When I tried kicking free, I realized I was entrenched up to my knees. I flailed beneath the surface, and when I could no longer hold my breath the pain of gulped water burned in my chest. I heard muffled cries from above, then a loud splash. Rafe's arms were around me, but we were anchored by my submerged feet. Frantically, his hands traveled down the length of my bare legs and tugged at my ankles. I held on to him as he pulled me from the muck and carried me upward.

We both coughed up water and gasped for air when we broke the surface. He was as frightened as I as we clung to each other in the wake of the near tragedy.

"You all right?" he sputtered as my fingers groped the bare skin of his back.

Nose-to-nose with him, I nodded. "I think so."

He gently wrapped his arms around my waist and glided me to shore. Jerlinda was beside herself with panic as she helped to drag me onto the dry grass. She patted my forehead and chanted words of praise, but I was lost in the moment of lying side by side with Rafe, his hand still in mine. Motionless, we gazed at each other in a way that intimately connected us from that day forward.

A heartache stirred by the memory brought me back to the moment. Oh, how I wished I could feel Rafe's hand in mine now. Sufficiently cleansed, I floated toward the shallows. Movement caught my eye within the cypress downstream. It was gone in the blink of an eye, though my prickled skin remained raised. I hurried back to Violet, who jumped when I tugged her arm.

"What's wrong?"

"I saw something hidden in the cypress down through the brake."

Violet's eyes fluttered. "A timberman?"

"No, it may have been a bear," I said, still unsure. "Or it could have been a man, very dark, with bushy hair like Ox."

"I think I would rather it be a bear than Ox." Violet grinned, trying to ease my worry. However, her darting eyes gave away her distress. "Let's move back over to the timber stand. The stumpers sound like they is back across the clearin'. It'll be easier to catch sight of a bear between the cedars than it will be if we sit here. The underbrush is so heavy, an animal could pounce on us before we took two steps."

We crept lightly to the cedars and sank into the shadows. "I feel like we are being watched."

"Shoot," Violet whispered. "I felt like that fo' the last three days. Let's hope it's jes' fretful thoughts makin' us feel that way. Don't seem to be nothin' followin' us."

Violet was right. The woods behind us remained still, but I was so spooked, I continued to stare along the path from which we'd come. I could not shake the feeling that something was staring back at me. Dusk settled over the swamp. Mosquitoes began buzzing in my ears, and frogs croaked from every direction. The timberland grew strangely still as the axes ceased and voices receded into the distance.

I tried not to think about what would come next, because I had no way to plan for it. I had no knowledge of the upper canal or Deep Creek. All I could do was hope to find the lighter man Archie. Depending on what he told me of the fate of Rafe, Jerlinda, and Axel, I would figure out what, if anything, I could do from there. Each day lost increased my worry that I was chasing the impossible.

Perhaps I could send word to Sylvan Firth. I was certain he could deliver me another dress and bonnet by way of Archie's discreet travels on the canal. Maybe even shoes, although I did not know what size his mother had worn. Either way, I would make do. Always, there was the nagging fear that Archie would tell me that my loved ones had been captured by someone like Quinn, who made his living by outthinking runaways.

"Where is you?" Fulton's voice was low and strained.

I wondered now, Could we trust this stranger? I supposed that if he had wanted to turn us in, he could have done so immediately and not waited until the thick of night. We went to where he had axed the tree earlier. His silhouette moved through the cedars in the moonlight. When he saw us, he rushed over and shoved a bundle of musty clothing in my arms.

"Here," he said urgently. "There's some corn bread in de shirt. Now scat! I'm a-feared someone might be on my tracks."

No sooner had the words left his lips than the dreadful click of a shotgun being cocked came from behind me. As quick as my next breath, the hammer of another shotgun clicked in the darkness behind Fulton and then another to our right.

"Where do you think you're goin', Fulton?"

A thin, mangy-looking white man with a large cowboy-style hat and rotted teeth stepped close enough to press the barrel of his gun against Fulton's ear. At the same time, a shotgun poked my back between my shoulders, as did the third to Violet. My heart fell into the pit of my stomach. We were captured. I glanced at Violet, but she was too stunned to move, her eyes fixed ahead and her jaw dropped.

"Ain't goin' nowhere, Boss Man."

With a quick and mighty sweep of his gun, the man called Boss

Man struck a hard blow to Fulton's head, causing him to drop to his knees. Fulton held his hand against a gash that spewed blood between his thick fingers. Mercilessly, the man struck him again.

"I ain't no fool, you lyin' darky. Looks like you and your pals are makin' tracks for the swamp."

"No, sah. I ain't runnin' nowhere, Boss Man. I jes' took pity on a couple o' swampers. Brought 'em some food and clothes, but dey is from my own rations. I ain't took nothin' dat ain't mine."

The man snatched the bundle from my arms and looked it over. "What would a swamp rat want with your filthy threads? I think the three of you grabbed your stuff and thought you could disappear with the rest of the outliers. I am sick of losin' slaves to the wild. I'll whip you good to make an example of you."

"We are not your slaves," I said in support of Fulton's explanation.

Boss Man turned and drove the butt of his shotgun against my forehead. For a moment, everything went black and I heard Violet cry out. I tried focusing my blurred vision, but the pain swallowed me and spun everything in sight. It wasn't until I saw a fourth man coming through the trees that I realized I was flat on my back against the ground. He carried a lantern, and when his light shone over me, Boss Man snickered.

"Well, looky here. We got us a couple of wild wenches. No wonder you was hightailin' it to the bushes, Fulton."

"I ain't on de run, Boss Man. I work hard so I can buy my freedom."

"He speaks the truth," I implored as I struggled to sit up. "I begged him for some clothing."

Boss Man pressed the tip of his shotgun against my cheek. "What does a lowly wench want with a man's trousers?"

I looked up into his small mousy eyes. "I am not a runaway slave.

I am a mistress. I have been lost in the swamp and was aided by this kind woman. But as you can see, I am not dressed to appear in public. Though I would prefer a proper frock, I must settle for what is available by way of clothing so I can seek out assistance in Deep Creek."

I was relieved when I finished my confession. And although it exposed me in my mission, I had to protect Violet and Fulton. I was surprised when Boss Man did not lower his gun. Instead, he heaved a couple of low snorts.

"Well, boys," he spouted mockingly, "I didn't know we were in the presence of a *lady*. I should have known by your fine hair and soft appearance that you are of regal upbringin'."

The men who encircled us chuckled with disdain. One removed his hat and bowed. "We are pleased to make your acquaintance, fine mistress. May I offer you a drink from the master's well?" He opened the front of his trousers and a stream of urine rained down on me. The others burst out in laughter at my humiliation. Boss Man reached down and took hold of my hair.

"You stupid Negress. You obviously carry the blood of your master, but that don't make you less of a darky than Fulton here. You talk brighter than most, but you can't outsmart a white man."

"My name is Jacy Lane. My family owns a horse farm called Great Meadow near Camden County."

Boss Man kicked me in the ribs, doubling me over as pain buzzed throughout my belly.

"Do not insult me with more lies. One look at you tells me all I need to know. I claim you as my property unless I find you posted in Virginia as a runaway. I shall call you Bette." He looked at Violet, who was being held back by her arms to keep her from coming to my aid.

"What's your name?"

"Violet."

"And hers?"

Violet paused, as if knowing her answer would bring swift recourse. "Jacy."

Boss Man stepped over me. He whacked Violet in the face with his gun, knocking her limp in her captors' arms. He raised his weapon to drive it down upon her, but I screamed out.

"It's Bette! My name is Bette." I reached out to Boss Man in desperation. "Please let us go. We will not bother your timbermen again."

Boss Man looked down his long, thin nose at me. "Chain them, boys. We'll put these feisty runaways to work in the shingle yard."

"No!" I cried out. "You can take me, but please leave Violet in the swamp."

Boss Man leaned close enough for me to smell his stale scent and pungent breath. "Don't you ever dare to ask me for *anything*. I will take *you* and *her* and any other wild darky I please. You've been in the bush too long to remember your proper place."

He smiled coldly and raised the butt of his gun over my head. The last thing I recalled was the thump of his blow and the sound of my cry before darkness dropped over me like the lid of a coffin.

Chapter 17

I awoke to the rattle of chains as I rolled over onto my back. Through the thin veil of fog that swirled above, I saw a blurry sliver of moon as thin as an eyelash on a fingertip. The blackest sky I had ever seen hung over me. I lifted my head, igniting a firestorm of pain from ear to ear. I lowered my head back against the hard ground. Again I heard the rattle of chains.

"Glory be." Violet's face appeared over me. "Thought maybe you wouldn't come around."

I groaned as she gently placed her hands behind my neck and shoulder and eased me to a sitting position. That was when I felt them: heavy iron shackles clamped around my ankles.

"Where are we?"

"Boss Man's timber camp," Violet said.

She too dragged chains from her shackled ankles. Their links threaded through a chicken-wire enclosure and were anchored on the frame of a shed outside the pen. Violet's right cheek was swollen with a lump the size of a doorknob. Anguish twisted inside me.

"Oh, no, Violet. What have I done to you? I have led you back into bondage."

Violet's eyes glimmered with tears but she remained steady. "I escaped once. I can again." She paused. "If the right chance comes along."

I gripped Violet's hands. "I am so sorry, Violet."

"Tupper and Maola will watch over Rose and Lyle." Her voice trailed off as if she sensed the enormity of our predicament. "At least my chilluns is free."

In truth, I was more worried about her than I was for myself. Certainly I would be able to convince someone that I was in fact a free woman and a mistress by reputation, even if it meant returning to Great Meadow. I owed Violet her freedom. Maybe I could borrow funds from Mayme to purchase Violet after the matter was resolved, and return her to the swamp.

"We must stay strong, Violet. All will not seem so bleak after I talk with Boss Man in the morning."

My head throbbed and I lay back. Chained in leg irons, I felt like a beaten dog.

I am not a slave.

I looked over at Violet, who lay with her arm folded over her face. I wondered if she was thinking as I was: *I am not a slave.*

Did every Negro bound by chains or driven by whips harbor the same desperate outrage?

I am not a slave.

The fog closed in around us. Nothing was in sight except for me, Violet, and our chains. With that desperate image in mind, I succumbed to sleep.

The lonely cry of a mallard pierced my restless slumber. It honked with such urgency I could not help but open my eyes. The fog had thinned to gray in the twilight before dawn. "What is that sound?"

"It's the morning horn," Violet said as she pushed to her feet. She reached her hand toward me. "Better be on yo' feet when they come to the pen or we'll start the day with a whuppin'."

The gray mist seemed to lift in abeyance as well. Around us, the timber camp came to life. Negro men in straw palmetto hats shuffled from tiny shacks toward a trough adjacent to a large sawmill. They dipped tin cups into the trough and drank the thick, pale sludge. The cups were then tossed into a wooden barrel as they marched to a white overseer, who shoved an ax into their hands and pointed them toward the stand of cedars near the brake.

Two Negro women scrambled along the trough, emptying their buckets to maintain the supply of sludge until all the men were fed and had gone into the wood. Four men emerged from a building beyond the sawmill. Two were white and two were Negro. I recognized Boss Man as soon as he cocked his oversized cowboy hat on his head. The three men with him listened intently as he walked toward us with his hand tucked nonchalantly in his vest. Boss Man never broke stride as he walked past the pen and motioned the two white men in my direction.

"Take the yellow Negro to the shingle lot."

I hurried to have a quiet word with him, but tripped when my chains tangled my legs. From my knees, I watched him disappear into a large stable. Burly arms fell around me and wrestled me to my feet. The shackles around my ankles were unlocked and I was hustled from the pen.

We walked past the mill, where several pairs of slaves worked two-man saws as they cut timber into long staves. Droves of bonded slaves were stationed amid the staves, hard at work with mallets and froes, driving the cleaving tool into bolts of clear, straight-grained pine.

When a rough shingle was split off, it was clamped to a shaving horse, where another man smoothed and tapered it with a drawn knife. Teams of men piled the finished shingles into carts. These two-wheeled shingle carts were stacked to capacity and drawn by mules along a crude log causeway that disappeared into the wilderness.

When Boss Man reappeared, he carried a crumpled cotton frock. "Here, woman. Get out of that jungle sack and cover yourself before my young bucks get distracted from their tasks."

I looked over his shoulder and mine for a dressing area. He watched in smirking amusement as the rough white hands that held me now tore my swamp rags from my body. I stood before Boss Man shamed by my nakedness. He looked me over slowly and with interest before handing me the frock, which I pulled quickly over my head. The frayed, dusty frock was dyed brown and smelled of mouse droppings. It hung loose and was ill fitting, but I was thankful for the concealment it provided me.

"Remove your sandals. No women are afforded footwear here."

I glanced down at the deerskin tied to the bottoms of my feet by rawhide straps. I would hardly call them footwear, but when I saw his hand ball into a fist, I quickly slipped them off. I was hesitant to address him, but I did not know whether he would disappear again.

"Sir, there has been a horrible misunderstanding. You see, I am white."

Boss Man hissed with vicious contempt. "Listen, you light-skinned wench. A few drops of white blood might pearl your skin, but it don't save you from bein' a darky through and through. You are the most stubborn Negress I have ever plucked from the swamps. Uppity too."

"Sir, my name is Ja—"

The back of his hand cracked against the side of my face. "Take her to the whipping post, boys. Apparently she was not taught sufficient subordination yesterday."

Blood filled my mouth. I attempted one last plea, but was yanked by my hair across the lot by two overseers. They pulled my dress down around my waist and tied my wrists to bloodstained ropes secured to a thick wooden post.

"No, no," I cried out. "You do not understand. My name is—"

The first crack of the whip sliced open my back like a machete cutting through a tobacco leaf. My agonized screams filled the yard, yet no one halted their chores to gaze upon me. Warm blood streamed from the wound, soaking the dress hanging from my hips. The pain was murderous as the whip tore into my flesh again and again. My mind began spinning and I knew I would faint. Though fading from consciousness, I was keenly aware that each sizzling crack erased my identity piece by piece. The swamp had stripped me of my appearance; now the whip stole my soul. I was a slave, no different from any other.

I hung limp by my fettered wrists. Much like the roar of a sturdy pine felled by a timberman's ax, the sound of my inner voice whispering, *But I am Jacy Lane*, went silent. I lay still and waited for the stumpers to converge on me to strip me of bark and bough. Instead, warm water rushed over me. Its moistness instantly torched into a fiery hell. I screamed and wriggled from the hands scrubbing my back.

"Hold still," a woman's voice whispered. "It be over soon."

I knew at once that I was being washed with salt brine. I had seen the treatment inflicted on a slave in South Mills when he looked directly into the eyes of a mistress. They could have branded me with a glowing iron from a smithy's forge and I would have welcomed that lesser pain. When the torture was complete, I was left to throb and foam in the blazing sun.

"Well?" Boss Man's boot nudged my cheek where it stuck in the mud left by the flow of brine. I had been cut from the post and lay facedown, sprawled on my bare chest and belly. "My bold and uppity Bette, do you wish to blabber any more foolishness at me?"

When I closed my eyes in surrender, he yanked me to my feet. I covered my breasts with the front of my dress and did not meet his eyes. "That's better. Remember your place, woman, and things won't be so bad around here. Throw her in the pen and have the other one grease her wounds."

Violet wailed when they dumped me at her feet and tossed her a small wooden bowl thick with grimy tallow made from cattle fat. "Have mercy—what have they done to you? They beat you the same as they would me."

She pulled my dress over my shoulders, although she did not close the buttons on the back. "Lawd, I can smell the brine," she said, dabbing grease on my back where my lacerations continued to ooze fluid and blood. I was numb and trembling beneath her touch. When she finished tending my wounds, Violet leaned me against her so I could rest where I sat. Lying down would have been too excruciating. We were given no food or water until the next day, when Boss Man entered the pen with one of his overseers.

"Open your mouths."

When we obliged Boss Man emptied a bucket of water over our heads. Like a baby bird seeking nourishment, I stretched my neck to capture several swallows. The moisture that flowed down my back stung sharply, but I was grateful it did not burn with salt.

"Unlock the irons on the darker one," Boss Man snapped. When the shackles fell free of Violet, he took her by the elbow. "Listen, swamp rats. You can either be useful to me here or I'll ship you to market and profit on you by sale. You will share the work of the shingle Negroes and of the cookhouse women, dependin' on the need. I demand a hard day's work, but it won't break your back like a cotton pick or rice harvest. The timbermen carry the heavier load around here. Till I know I got you broke in good and am sure you won't take off for the swamps, one of you will always be chained. If the other runs off, I'll cut the throat of the one who remains. Don't think I won't. You seem attached like puppies from the same bitch, so I expect no trouble from you."

Boss Man stared extra hard at me, as if letting me know that he would be happy to do to Violet what he did to me if I did not comply with his orders. I said nothing. His whip and his threats had taken away my ability to speak, if not physically, then at least out of fear of reprisal.

Violet was led to the shingle lot while I was taken to the cookhouse. I was made to carry my chain as I shuffled my bare feet beneath the weight of the heavy leg irons. At the cookhouse, my chains were secured to a hitching post with enough loose chain to allow me to move in and out of the small building. Boss Man handed me a simple linen mobcap to put on my head like the other slave women in camp, including Violet. I attempted to push my hair up under the thin cloth crown, but it was not much larger than an oversized handkerchief with a floppy brim of ruffles. The short tight curls of the cookhouse women were well contained by the mobcaps; however, my hair had not been brushed since I'd left Great Meadow. It hung unevenly below my ears and was as wiry as a squirrel's nest because of neglect and the moist swamp air. Boss Man snatched the cap from my fumbling hands. He stretched it roughly over the top of my head and let my unruly tufts stick out from under the ruffles.

"You're gonna need a day or two before your back can withstand the weight of liftin' the wheelbarrow. Until then, Bette will put you to work at the cook fires."

When he walked away, I turned to the chocolate brown woman with smooth features and clear eyes. "Did he call you Bette?"

"What of it?" she asked matter-of-factly.

"He told me that I was to be called Bette."

The woman's eyes glazed over. "Any Negro he wants fo' his bed he calls Bette. Dat way no other mens, white nor black, can touch us. It ain't no honor. I can tell you dat."

I chilled at her remark, but she continued shucking corn with two other women. I recognized her voice as the one that had reassured me when I was washed in brine. "I do not know whether to thank you or strangle you," I said.

She looked at me coolly. "Better to be washed down by me. I am quick and soft-handed. If you wasn't a Bette, the overseer would do it and scrub mo' than yo' back. Besides, the salt wash keeps the cuts from festerin'."

"I thought I would die."

Her lips pursed in a snide grin. "You only got eight lashes. The whip hardly got a chance to loosen up to a good bite."

I decided to keep my thoughts to myself. This woman reminded me of Tess, and I did not want my words repeated to Boss Man. I wanted no more attention from him by whip or any other means. Therefore, I silently followed Bette's instruction to join the circle shucking corn. The heat of the cookhouse was suffocating, but I did as I was told. Supper for the timbermen was prepared from a store of bacon, salt fish, molasses, cornmeal, and sweet potatoes. The women ate only the castoffs, which were marginally superior to the fodder for the mules.

Several days passed, as did a degree of soreness in my back. With barely a whisper between us, Violet and I slept in the pen each night. We were exhausted by our duties and feared the shadows around us.

By week's end, I had my turn in the shingle lot. My back and shoulders ached trying to roll the shingle-laden wheelbarrow back and forth. Several times, I toppled my load to one side, requiring me to restack the shingles under the coercion of the overseer. Instead of drinking from my bucket when it was offered, I soaked my hands to ease the torn blisters on my palms.

One evening, the overseer took us to the slave quarters instead of the pen. Violet was directed to a modest open-sided shed close to the cookhouse, where she was chained to a tree. I was taken to a smaller hut outside the main circle of cabins. It was no more than a shack made of juniper poles. Inside, the far end was daubed with mud, where a fire flickered. The dirt floor was covered with wood shavings, and a small hole in the roof overhead allowed the smoke to escape into the night air. There were no shackles or chains in sight.

The overseer shoved me inside. "Don't run off or Violet will pay."

I could never have imagined that a rudimentary hut could lift my spirits. The pen was open and left us exposed to the elements. The autumn nights were increasingly cool, so I welcomed this little protective shell. The peat fire warmed the damp air and the straw pallet would be an improvement from the bald ground that had served as our bed. Even the thin woolen blanket folded on the pallet brought a tear to my eye.

I curled up on the rough straw and wrapped the blanket around me. The surge of a sudden downpour brought droplets of rain leaking from a dozen spots, though none dripped on me. My bones ached with utter exhaustion, and stabs of hunger in my belly were now the natural state. Eating corn mush and okra was simply another chore and did little to ease the pangs that never waned. For now, the pallet offered more of what I needed than did the trough.

I had dozed for what seemed like only a moment when the stick door of the shack was pushed open. The sight of Boss Man's wide-brimmed cowboy hat thrust me onto my hands and knees. I scrambled away from the door and so near to the fire that the sleeve of my dress became singed at the cuff. He stepped to the center of room and watched coldly as I cowered from him. Shaking the rain from his wet hat, he hung it on a juniper stick that protruded the wall. His comfort in the surroundings suggested this was not his first visit to the shack.

"Evenin', Bette." He smirked. The brown hollows of his stained teeth made me want to vomit. "Take off your dress and let me have a look at you."

I stared at him without moving. What was I to do? Thoughts of Garrison ordering me to the fence flashed in my mind. *"Be still; I am nearly done with you."* The flesh on my skin prickled at the memory of his unseemly words. *"Damn your thick mane."* I had vowed to never stand for that abuse again. The loving voice of my father echoed in my ears. *"Jacy, don't ever let anyone break your spirit."*

"I won't, Papa."

"What's that you say?" Boss Man's sharp voice brought me back to the moment. He had stepped closer to me. When I did not answer him, he reached down and tugged the mobcap from my head. "Go on; take down your dress."

He towered over me as I crouched at his feet. I would not look up at him. My eyes were fixed on the filthy clumps of mud caked to his boots. When I did not obey, he fisted his hand in my hair and pulled my face even with his belt.

"If not the dress, then open my pants."

My heart raced with terror. Boss Man's intentions reached far beyond those of Garrison. I no longer had Rafe or Jerlinda watching over me, prepared to use their wiles to thwart a forceful advance. There was only me. Outrage and determination sparked in my breast. The tighter he gripped my hair, the stronger grew the fury within me. I thought of Violet. I remembered the knee-bender she had demonstrated to me for such an occasion. I had to strike while in the perfect position. Balling my hand, I took a deep breath and, with all the force I could muster, I drove my fist upward into his groin.

"Ooooooh!" he yelped. With an agonizing groan, he collapsed in a heap. I sprang over him toward the door as he writhed in the wood shavings. "You insolent wench; get back here!"

With one hand between his legs and the other reaching for me, he grabbed my ankle. The power of his grip was compromised by his traumatized condition. I yanked free and burst into the storm outside. There was not much time. It would not take long for Boss Man to recover his legs and come after me. Lightning flashed around me as I sprinted through the slave quarters. I could not escape until I freed Violet from her chains. But how?

The axes!

Thunder echoed through the trees as I ran along the back edge of the camp, but the drenching rain did not slow my steps. I approached the sawmill knowing the axes were usually locked in a shed after dark. When I got there, the door stood open. I peeked in the building and saw the overseer standing over Fulton in the far corner where the grinding wheel stood. Dozens of axes were propped near him, their well-used blades in need of sharpening. Jagged bolts carved the sky above me, but also provided flashes of light for me as I ducked into the adjoining shed.

Bare wall space marked the spot where the axes should stand. All were in the mill with Fulton. Where were the froes that were used to cut the shingles? Was there another shed? Each blink of my eyes brought tragedy closer. In the next flicker of lightning, I saw the gleam of hatchets on the shelf. It was my one chance. I snatched a hatchet and ran across the yard to the quarters. When I burst into Violet's hut wielding the hatchet, the women scattered.

"Jacy!" Violet gasped. "How in the world—"

"The knee-bender," I said, pouncing on her chains.

"Oh, no." Violet shuddered. She knew there was no turning back. "Lawd, have mercy."

I could not free her of the shackle clamped to her leg, so I chopped frantically at the attached iron links. Thunderclaps marked the passing seconds as I cursed the chains that would not give her up. Seeing my futile struggle, Violet shook me by the arm.

"Get out while you can, Jacy!"

I did not pause or look up from my quest. "I will not leave here without you, Violet."

With six more fierce wallops of the hatchet, the chain link snapped, to my desperate delight. I grabbed Violet's hand and pulled her away from the camp and through the trees.

"Run, Violet! Run!"

The three remaining links on her shackle tinkled as we trampled in the mud. A loud bang behind us clenched my throat. Was it a gun or thunder? The cypress roots thickened and tangled our feet, but we pressed on. With all the twisting and turning, it was difficult to gauge our direction as we sought a route to the inner swamp. Lightning gave me a glimpse of a clearing ahead much like the one where we first saw Fulton. My heart leapt with excitement. It was our gateway to the swamp. Before I could shout my encouragement to Violet, a man stepped from behind a tree and caught me in his arms.

Boss Man.

"A stupid darky ain't gonna outsmart me," he said, clutching me around the waist and holding a pistol to Violet's head. "You are gonna watch this yellow Negress hang for what she done to me."

Instantly, we were knocked off our feet by an enormous dark figure. A painful gasp exploded from me as my back hit the ground with a thud. The figure lunged across my stunned frame at Boss Man. It was Ox! He and Boss Man grappled in the mud while I pulled myself from the fray. I writhed in the dirt, trying to restore my breath.

The ferocity of the battle going on next to me filled the night air with grunts and musky rage. I wriggled onto my knees as Ox rolled his massive body onto our overpowered assailant and clamped his hands over his throat. Boss Man's eyes bulged, though they never lost their glaze of hate. Suddenly, a shot rang out. I jolted upward onto my feet as the squawks of terrified birds echoed in the surrounding forest. The struggle between the two men fell still. My heart sank as I watched Ox's arms go limp. Boss Man pushed him off and stood up with his gun pointed at my heart. Rather than hang me, he would shoot me now. My body shook with terror as he paused to unleash a vengeful grin. Then, just as his finger twitched on the trigger, his gun was kicked from his hand. Before Boss Man could react, a rock thumped on his head and he fell backward into the muck.

"Tupper!" Violet yelled out.

He ran to us, his eyes wild with emotion. "Is you shot?"

"You saved us, Tupper," I said as he wrapped his arms around Violet and me. "You and Ox."

Tupper wiped the rain from his face. "When Violet didn't come back, I knew somethin' was mighty wrong, so I made tracks this way. I crossed paths with Ox, and he said he laid eyes on you near de timber camp."

"Then it *was* him by the stream," I mused. "I saw him the day we were captured."

"With de help of some timbermen, we tracked you here. Me and Ox have been tryin' to figure a way to get to you." Tupper looked around. "Where is he?"

I looked over at the fierce freedom fighter lying facedown in the mud. We huddled around him and pushed him over onto his back. His eyes blinked slowly, in contrast to his quick, shallow breaths. Flickers of lightning from the receding storm revealed blood mixed with the mud on his chest.

"Ox? Can you hear me?" Tupper pleaded.

His lips quivered to form words. "My name is Albert."

The man's eyes gazed at me with pride as his life drained away. I touched his cheek. "Thank you, Albert." His features turned to stone as the steady rain rinsed his lifeless face of dirt and blood.

With no time for pause, Tupper pulled us to our feet. "We gots'ta go!"

I bent over the dastardly Boss Man, whose eyes stared unblinkingly toward the heavens. "This muddy swamp is as close as you will get to salvation, you wicked bastard."

Violet braced her arm around my trembling shoulders. "Don't waste no words on a dead man, Jacy. His judgment will come at the hands o' the devil."

"We can't leave him here," I said. "If they find a dead white man in the wake of discovering us gone from camp, they may launch an intensive search into the swamp."

The rain had slowed to a drizzle and the night grew quiet. Tupper shook his head thoughtfully. "No need to fret. We'll throw Ox on top of dis rascal. When de timber men come upon 'em, dey will think dey killed each other. It would please Ox to know dat his last deed on dis earth protected de swamp. He was a man of freedom at all cost."

Violet and I nodded at the sense of it. "Let's get on with it," Violet said. "Don't never want to feel those chains again."

I looked down at the shackle still clamped to her ankle, then scanned the underbrush around us. "I dropped the hatchet when Boss Man sprang at me from behind the tree."

"Here it is," Tupper said, plucking it from the mud.

"Take it with you," I said. "Use it to break the shackle. I do not want Violet to carry a reminder of our time here."

Violet's hand trailed gently from my shoulder and down my back. Her touch was delicate, in care of the lash marks still healing beneath my dress. "Wish I could give you somethin' to take yo' reminders away."

I gathered her into my arms. "You have given me more than any living soul on this earth. You are brave and good-hearted in all you do, Violet. I shall never forget you. Any scars I carry from this horrid experience will be paled by the kindness with which you blessed me."

Violet wiped her tears, then joined them with mine as she pressed her hand to my moist cheek. "Well, you blessed me too."

I let loose a doubtful chuckle. "I have been nothing but a burden for you to carry upon your back. You will be glad to be rid of me."

Violet's eyes softened. She leaned in and placed a kiss on my lips and on both of my cheeks. "You are a good soul, Jacy. You showed me and my chilluns that it ain't white blood that causes the hate. That bit o' hope means more than you will ever know."

Tupper patted my shoulder. "Maybe you should come back to de swamp until we know there ain't gonna be no backlash."

I pressed my hand to his. "I have come this far, Tupper; I must continue on. Step quickly, the both of you, so you will be deep within your homeland by sunrise and the discovery of these corpses. You are a gentle man. I wish you peace and freedom, always."

Tupper's hand wrapped around Violet's, their fingers interlocking. As trickles of moonlight broke through the clouds dissipating overhead, I noticed a faint lavender smudge in the shadows. I plucked a single violet from the greenery and removed the mobcap from Violet's head.

Planting the flower amid the curls of her hair, I smiled tearfully. "You have shown me pure love and true courage, my precious sister of the swamp. I love you and thank you with all of my heart." I pulled her to me for one last embrace.

"Jacy, you are leavin' the swamp a different girl than the one who stumbled in. The blind ways of a mistress are gone. Everything about you is stronger and more knowin'. I hope you find yo' people," she said, sniffling against my cheek. "Be safe and happy."

"You do the same," I whispered back. "Reclaim your freedom and never let go."

Tupper eased Violet from me. "Let's get on home, girl."

Violet pointed toward the cloudless sky far to her right. "Go east to the canal, then follow it north the last few miles to the town where the boats enter the deepwater creek that leads to the great ships. Be on the watch for patrollers and slave catchers. The canal bank and water routes are thick with 'em."

Her parting words of caution shook me. Dismal Swamp was a treacherous underworld I would gladly leave behind, but watching Violet and Tupper stride across the timber brake, I shuddered with dread of the unknown journey ahead of me. I thought of Rafe and longed for the comfort found in the joined purpose of a couple like Tupper and Violet. When they reached the distant tree line, the pair raised their hands in the moonlight to bid me farewell. Then, like wisps of smoke, they disappeared into the shadows of the swamp, leaving me alone and unsure of what the new day would bring.

The pure joy of being free of whips and chains was washed over by trepidation when I gazed upon the two dead men lying at my feet. I was reminded that my obstacles could not be predicted nor my outcome deemed secure. I took off into the night without looking back, yet I dared not look ahead either. When I reached the outside world . . . if I reached the outside world . . . would they view me as white or Negro? And more important, how would I view myself?

I reached for the rabbit's foot Rose had given me for good luck. In all the commotion, it had been yanked from the rawhide around my neck. I had never been of a superstitious nature, but with no one and nothing else providing me support and confidence, I felt the curse of Dismal Swamp close in around me.

Chapter 18

The terror unleashed in me by the image of Boss Man's frozen, lifeless eyes drove me onward most of the night in spite of the weariness that burned in my legs. Though vile to the core, the man was dead because of me. Would an angry mob swarm the jungle for the "yellow Negro" who dared to run? I quaked at every turn, knowing that beast or man could be stalking me in the thicket.

Unseen night critters rustled in the brush, forcing me to change course several times. Deep within a cypress grove, hundreds of bats darted around my head as if I were being chased through a nightmare. I swatted desperately at the darkness around me as the flutter of wings swooped past in every direction. Fright choked my cries within me. Their sound would give me away, so I swallowed my sobs and escaped the onslaught.

I had to calm my panic before I made a fatal misjudgment. Fatigue and uncertainty slowed my steps. Once I had put a comfortable distance between me and the timber camp, I decided to find shelter in the dry pocket of a massive tangle of juniper roots. I needed rest and feared becoming misdirected in the dark disarray of the swamp. I crawled within the fist of roots and sat with my knees tucked under my chin. Every inch of my being, inside and out, trembled with uncontrolled horror. I was hopelessly alone and helpless.

Or was I?

The memory of Mayme came to me in a warm rush. *"You are never helpless, Jacy. You carry within you the blood of a daring father and a courageous mother, pure in heart and deed. I do not know what lies ahead for you, but when your journey seems impossible, remember . . . you are proof of the improbable."*

My tremors eased as I drew in a calming breath. "I am safe for now," I said, comforted by the renewed determination in my voice. "I will face tomorrow when it comes."

Sleep arrived in short intervals as the occasional cry of a distant wildcat kept me on guard. It was the first night I had truly spent on my own, so the first glint of sunrise greeted me like a long-lost friend.

Using the sun in the eastern sky as my touchstone, I began again. I gathered my damp dress above my waist and did my best to keep it from becoming further drenched and stained in the dark-water marshes. This was challenging because of the rise in water from the thunderstorm the previous night. More difficult was the task of keeping the briars and thorns from shredding the dress into complete tatters. My appearance when I exited the swamp could very well be the key to my survival, so I protected my dress at every turn. The white linen mobcap I had taken from Violet was tucked in my pocket to avoid being dirtied by mud and perspiration.

Fortunately, the season benefited me. Though I knew not the date, I guessed it was late in the month of October. The heat that had thickened the air weeks ago was now subsiding and the heavy underbrush was losing its vigor. This made me fleet of foot at times, but also wary of the thinning veil of cover as I moved toward the swamp fringe. I passed near enough to other timber camps to hear axes and

crashing cedars in the far-off jungle, but I took no chance at encoun-
tering another Boss Man. So I stayed low and away from any stumpers
and shingle getters.

Late in the afternoon of the following day, the putrid aroma of rot
and silt that hung over the swamp lifted when I came upon a wide
marsh where the canopy opened to the blue sky. I bathed in a pool of
deep amber water. A broad-winged hawk circled overhead, and for
the first time since I had entered the swamp, I saw flocks of crows. I
took it as a sign of my proximity to open fields or plantations. I leaned
against a fallen log and watched a green heron strut on its long yellow
legs, seeking a minnow or tadpole. Dragonflies buzzed between lily
pads, and two spotted turtles watched me from the opposite end of
the log where it broke the surface of the thick bog. For a moment, I
was at peace, but the feeling was short-lived. Voices echoed from beyond the tree line across the marsh brake. I scampered into the thistles and listened.

"Step it up," a man's voice called out. From the position of the
sun, I could gather the voice originated somewhere to the northeast
and a good distance away.

Another barked, "Let's go. I want to push off before sundown."

The canal! It had to be.

As natural as a deer in the bush, I scurried across the landscape.
The canopy was alive with birds returning to nest after a day spent
on the wing. Not more than five minutes from when I heard the
voices, I came upon a narrow path of split-rail tracks laid on a cordu-
roy roadbed. I remembered the same planks leading from the timber
camp where the shingle-laden wagons driven by mule and cart boy
moved the timber products to be transferred onto shingle lighters for
their journey from the swamp. Staying well within the cover of the
forest, I followed the path of the makeshift road.

The sun was low in the sky when voices became plentiful and

close at hand. I peeked from the curtain of greenery in which I hid
and gazed upon the dark ribbon of water that was my compass to the
north. Though no more than a stone's throw from one bank to the
other, its width and depth assured me this was the swamp canal and
not one of its many feeder ditches. The mild lap of water through the
tall reeds at the water's edge was all that remained in the wake of a
flatboat that had pushed off from a crude camp where a clapboard
shack stood next to a modest wooden dock. I sank back into the
thicket when a man came bursting through the trees on the opposite
shore.

"Hey, Rowdy! I brought us some whiskey!"

"Yee-haw," yelped a bare-chested young man who appeared on
the wooden dock twenty yards upstream. "I thought you got hung up
when you wasn't on the last lighter."

"Got into a scuffle with the captain, so I had to talk my way onto
the stagecoach." The man laughed as he sat down on the bank and
removed his boots. "I dozed off and nearly missed my jump-off spot.
Me and my bottle would have been up in Deep Creek and you would
have nothin' but swamp water to pour in your gullet tonight."

"What'chu takin' your boots off for? I'll row the dugout over and
get you."

The man across the canal scratched his whiskered chin, then
laced his boots closed. "Good idea. I was gonna swim it, but the
night air will feel mighty cool in wet clothes. Is anybody else around?"

"Naw, the last of the cart boys is headed inland and I don't expect
any more boats tonight. It'll be dark before we knock back our first
drink, so anyone on the canal will likely be tied to land for the night."

Darkness fell quickly as the two men lit a large campfire. The
aroma of catfish cooking on sticks over the open flame knotted my
belly with hunger. I had always been rather thin, but my time in the
swamp had made me a bit bony. I had learned to make do with little

sustenance, but the smell of fried fish moistened my tongue with a painful craving. I had never stolen anything in my life, but when the pair drank themselves into unconsciousness, I crept to where their unfinished scraps lay in a wooden bowl. Using my fingers, I devoured what could be sucked from the discarded bones.

I tiptoed to the skiff tied at the end of the dock and pushed off quietly across the canal. If I reached the stagecoach road, I could follow it through the forest to Deep Creek. The vegetation on the east side of the canal did not appear as impenetrable as it was on the swamp side. I would need to tread carefully, but across the canal I could avoid the timber camps and heavily traveled split-rail paths I would otherwise cross heading north through the swamp. I did not feel the least bit ashamed of scavenging the food or the ride on the boat. Instead, I was grateful for the good fortune of stumbling upon careless canal men. Once on the other side, I walked until I found the dark, deserted road, then traipsed northward in the dark. When I could walk no farther, I hid in the stretch of woods between the road and the canal. Somehow, being a few steps outside of the swamp made me feel closer to Rafe, Jerlinda, and Axel. I was no longer lost in another world. I was once again in their wake and I could feel their pull on my heart. I sank into slumber with renewed hope that I would find the path to them.

"Wake up, wench." Eyes of blue ice stared down the barrel of a shotgun that was poised over my face. "I hope you enjoyed your last night of freedom."

Beneath the wide-brimmed fedora cocked on his head, the man's thick dark brows, mustache, and goatee unleashed a dreadful shudder throughout my body. It was the slave hunter Quinn, who had chased me the first day in the swamp.

"Get up onto your knees," he growled.

I had barely risen from the pine needles when he came at me with an iron collar and clamped it around my neck. I shrank to the ground, but he yanked the chain and pulled me back onto my knees.

"I am not a runaway."

He peered down at me crouched in the dirt. His eyes moved over my thick, matted hair and stained frock. He smirked at my bare, scarred feet that smelled of muck and mud. "Stick out your hands."

I lifted them, but my cracked, filthy fingernails and scabbed blisters belied my words. He sniffed with annoyance. "I have never met a darky of any shade that wouldn't lie to save its hide."

"I am no slave, Quinn. My name is Jacy Lane of Great Meadow in North Carolina. I was lost in the swamp. Return me to Great Meadow and you are certain to be rewarded."

I cringed at choosing to be returned to Claudia, but I had no better choice. This man was evil. Claudia might disown me and turn me out, but I would not be whipped or defiled by someone believing I was an errant slave.

"Oh, you know my name, do you?" He nudged the barrel of his shotgun against my forehead. "Why would an innocent mistress recognize a man who sniffs after the colored?"

His question sparked with sarcasm, but he seemed interested in hearing my explanation. I had to convince him of my identity, so I stretched the truth to flatter him. "You are famous for your work. My fiancé, Garrison Yob, tells me of your exploits along the canal."

"Do not try to beguile me," he snarled as he struck the back of his hand across my cheek. "Your light skin and proper dialect do not fool me. You are the worst kind of Negro because you try to pass yourself as white. That makes you more dangerous than the lowliest ebony wench."

Warm blood trickled from my nose. "Return me to Great Meadow and you will see I speak the truth."

"You are just biding time, darky. Do you think I don't know there are armed Negroes in the swamp? Your story is meant to lead me into an ambush."

"No, sir. I would not lie to you."

He yanked upward on the chain so hard that my neck and jaw nearly snapped. My sudden yelp and the accompanying clank of chain links startled a flock of blackbirds from the trees. Their squawks and flutter dropped maple leaves around me as I stood nose-to-nose with Quinn.

"I don't need to drag you across the border into Carolina to know you are lying." He spit a thick lump of warm mucus between my eyes. I heaved with disgust as it dripped from my brow, but I dared not lift my hand to wipe away his scourge. His words sparked with anger as he continued. "I played poker with a man named Yob in South Mills two nights ago. He was a bit of a blowhard, but he was in high spirits. No mention was made of a fiancé or local mistress lost in the swamp. Guess you better come up with some other lie."

"But—"

Quinn whacked the barrel of his shotgun against the side of my face. It felt as though my right eye had been knocked from its socket. All in sight went gray as pain speared through my head and I struggled not to lose consciousness.

"Not another word from you or I'll blast what little brain is in your head from here to the canal."

I could not have spoken had I tried. Quinn continued ranting, but all sound around me was muffled as though I had plunged my head into a bucket of water. He dragged me by the collar toward the canal, where a flatboat was tied to the bank. I had not realized how near the canal I had wandered the previous night.

It was a grave mistake, because Quinn had seen me sleeping in the brush as he rode the boat north to Deep Creek. He threw me onto the shingle flat, where two Negro men, one old and gray, the other in his prime, were secured by leg and neck irons. I also recognized the straw-haired, freckle-faced brothers who manned the poles.

"Push off, boys," Quinn snapped at the white men who had sold their souls for a grubby silver dollar. "I want to be in Deep Creek by midday."

I lay on my back amid the chains, staring through my swollen eye at the white clouds floating across the sky. The beautiful scene was far beyond my reach, much like the civilized world around me. I heard the caution of Jerlinda's words on the day we parted.

"Chile, you have never lived as a Negro and cannot understand the measure of sufferin' as we do."

Oh, Mama, I understand it now. I have walked your path for only a few weeks and it has broken me. As a Negro, I am assumed to be a liar. I am chained and beaten like a worthless dog. My body is not my own and I am stripped of dignity, hopes, and dreams. I am drained, Mama. Nothing of me remains.

From the canal, Deep Creek looked to be a village of forty or so buildings. Lighters and flatboats were roped to wooden posts, waiting to be lowered in the lock to the waterway for which the town was named. Deep Creek flowed eastward to the southern branch of the Elizabeth River, which was the water route to the tidewater seaports of Norfolk and Portsmouth. This made the village of Deep Creek, which marked the canal's origin, a busy pathway for goods moving inland or between the larger ports on Chesapeake Bay and Albemarle Sound. The inland timberworks in and around the Great Dismal provided a steady stream of lumber used by the shipbuilders farther north.

Slave gangs loaded the wares of flatboats and shingle lighters onto larger boats and barges that would then transport the goods to the seagoing vessels. Quinn hurried us past the lockmaster to a slave pen that was no larger than a one-room shack. A tall, scrawny man rose from where he slouched against the trunk of a nearby oak tree.

"What'chu got for me, Quinn?"

By the time the man strode over to us, Quinn had already shoved us in the pen and yanked away our chains and iron collars. From the other side of the locked door, I heard him dump the hardware in his sack, where it would remain until his next human harvest.

"Had a good day." Quinn yukked. "Two bucks and a very light mulatto. I saw no postings for them here or in Carolina. Give me a fair price and you will turn a mighty fine profit for them over at the slave market."

I heard the clink of coins being counted. "I'll give you three hundred dollars for the bunch."

Quinn huffed. "I can make five times that amount by hauling them to market myself."

The man chuckled. "Listen, Quinn, I don't want to haggle with you. We both know you ain't gonna waste your time going to Richmond. Your money is made on runaways who are posted with hefty rewards. These no-names are small pickings for you."

"Make it three hundred and fifty and it's a deal," Quinn countered.

"The yellow wench looks frail. Let's say three twenty-five."

"Wash the dirt and blood off her acorn skin and she'll fetch more coin than the ashy buck. It's hard to tell in her state, but she may even be a quadroon. Perhaps I should up my price for such a fine breeder."

"You're a hard-driving bastard, Quinn. But you damn well know the market. I'll give you three hundred and fifty for the lot."

"A fine deal for the both of us," Quinn said. "I'll take the cash and be on my way."

The slave trader's voice softened as he shifted the conversation. "Where's your boy, Quinn? When you brought him around the last time you were in town, he was busting his buttons telling me about riding down the canal with you."

"I promised my wife I would encourage his schooling until he is fourteen," Quinn said, his voice no longer hard with intent. "He has another year before he rides steadily with me and learns the trade that will provide him a man's wage. He's a bright lad. I ain't raising him to be nobody's grunt, hauling lumber or loading skids at the port. I lost one son to a timber accident and vowed I would provide a path for my youngest boy to earn a living with the advantage of his wiles and smarts."

"You've done right by your son, Quinn," the trader said with a hint of admiration. "A good bounty man will always be in high demand as long as there are darkies who are fool enough to run. They just don't know any better."

Quinn cleared his throat as if needing time to settle his stirred emotion. "Slave hunting is a worthwhile trade and I am proud to say that my boy has his old man's instincts."

The trader laughed. "Well, he loves his pa. That's plain to see. Here's payment for your bounty. Buy the lad a new shotgun for his next ride down the canal."

Quinn glanced through the small window on the side of the pen before walking away with a jingle in his pocket. He could have just as easily been bargaining for cattle: a simple business deal, cash on the barrelhead.

I lay on the dirt floor in complete surrender. At every turn a new obstacle had been thrown in my path. First, Garrison. Then the swamp and timber camp. Now *this*. Fate had been a cruel companion since I fled Great Meadow. I had acted against the natural order of things and this was my punishment. All I had left to do was to lie here and die in the dust.

"Take some water, gal."

The older captive knelt over me. The top of his head was bald and looked like a shiny mahogany egg sitting on a nest of cotton. His white, bushy hair grew thick from the base of his neck, along the sides of his head, and then spilled down his jawline in scraggly whiskers that converged into a cotton boll at the end of his chin. When I did not respond, he let the water in his cupped hand trickle over my cracked lips.

"Leave her be, Henry," the younger man mumbled from where he sat hunched in the corner. "She looks to be at the end of her road. We all is."

Old Henry held a hushing finger to his lips. "Them words is poison, Joe," he whispered. "You can't never give up on freedom. Never!"

Joe leaned forward. "What's the point, old man? They is jes' gonna haul us back and whup us twice as hard."

"Hunters can drag me back in chains a hundred times and I will run a hundred and one if that's what it takes."

"They will sliver the backs of your heels before it comes to that, Henry. Or shoot you dead."

The old man scooped another handful of water from the narrow trough beneath the window. "Then freedom is mine, one way or the other."

Once again, he knelt over me and moistened my lips. His earnest care coaxed me to speak. "What will happen to us?" I asked weakly.

"In the next day or so, the trader will chain us to his wagon and march us to auction."

My throat was dry and hoarse, but I needed to know what to expect. "Where will we go from auction?"

"You'll go to the man who shouts the highest bid." The broad, dark man named Joe frowned. "Ain't you never been sold?"

"No," I said, sitting up. "Don't you want to be sent back to the plantation you ran from? You must have friends and family there."

Henry's wrinkled eyes clouded. "My wife and chilluns was sold away long ago. My last massa had me in the cane fields. If the heat didn't kill me, the overseer soon would. I'll take my chances with a new massa. At least until I can chase the stars north again. I gots'ta hope that no reward is posted for me at the blocks. If so, I'm likely to go straight to hell by way o' the cane fields."

"I was sold at the slave market twice before, though not as a runaway," Joe said. "Both times a headman from one of the lumberyards came to the pen and poked the bulk of my shoulders. I'm strong like a bull, so it makes me a good logger. That's why they call me Timber Joe."

I lifted my eyes to him. "Timber Joe?"

He patted the muscles on his arms. "I was always a big boy and an even bigger man."

I thought back to the swamp island and the many outliers at the maroon settlement who had asked me if I knew their loved ones. "Is your father named Samuel?"

Joe's body tightened with surprise. "You know my daddy?"

"I met him in the swamp. He asked about you."

"The swamp?"

"He is living free, deep inside Dismal Swamp. There are many others as well."

A swell of emotion revived my heart as heavy tears dropped from Joe's eyes. "I can't believe he is alive. If I ever break free again, I'm headin' straight for that dreary swampland."

"Praise be." Henry sighed. "You see, you can't never give up. Freedom can be found a hundred different ways. We jes' gots'ta keep tryin'."

The old man's spirit lifted mine. What would I gain by giving up? I dusted myself off and went to the shoulder-high window. It was no wider than my head, but through it I could breathe in fresh air. I gazed past the lock station to where boats and workers cluttered the dock. Groups of men walked a path between the moored boats and the village that lay through the trees on the other side of the pen that imprisoned us. No one so much as glanced our way. To them, our cage was no different from the chicken coop or pigsty.

I watched the activity carefully, wondering whether Archie was among the busy laborers on the dock. I scanned one side of the canal bank and then the other. My view was obscured by some outbuildings, but in the gap between two sheds far to my right I saw a steamer that twisted my stomach into a knot.

The *Southern Gale*.

I was barely recognizable as the girl who had gazed upon the ship in South Mills. I thought of Quinn's remark that Garrison was not seeking or pining for a lost lover. I was not surprised. Garrison would never allow his reputation to be stained by me. His interest in me was to secure his social position, not to court love, and he had cast me aside the moment I ran from him into the swamp. Any public disgrace would have made it harder for him to attach himself to another unsuspecting host like a tick to a fawn. His vile character would never seek reunion, but he was not above revenge. Oh, how he would love to see where my path had led.

The sound of laughter drew my attention to three men standing on the path several yards from the pen. "Get on with you, Patrick. You have a fine lass waitin' for you in South Mills. Don't let this rascal lead you astray in the whiskey hall."

Could it be?

I held still. The men had their backs to me, but when they shook hands and parted ways, a lone bearded fellow with thick ears protruding from his dark hair turned to walk the path toward town. His bowler hat, adorned with a rabbit's foot, was unmistakable. It was Caleb Briggs, the man who had escorted my wagon to South Mills on the night I smuggled Rafe, Jerlinda, and Axel to Sylvan Firth.

"Mr. Briggs!" I called out, hoping to maintain discreet control over my plea. He glanced over at me, but did not break stride. "Mr. Briggs, please help me."

He cocked his head my way and furrowed his brow. Clearly he did not recognize me. My heart sped up when he looked around and then strolled toward the pen as though he were admiring the birds in the trees. He stopped a few feet away and knelt to fumble with the laces on his boot. Without looking up, he spoke with hushed caution.

"How do you know me, Negro?"

"I am Jacy Lane. You once said my name flowed from your tongue like the chorus of a song."

His eyes shot to mine in disbelief. "That's impossible."

"It may seem so," I pleaded. "But if you come closer, you will see that it is me."

He came to the window and gazed upon my face. "You cannot be the same girl."

"I assure you it is me." I pressed my hands against my wild hair to frame my face as a bonnet would. My bruised eye, tanned skin, and unkempt appearance did little to alleviate his doubt.

"A white woman would not be imprisoned with fugitive slaves," he said, more to himself than to me.

"I was born of a mulatto slave, but raised by my white father. When first we met and spoke of your wife's grief over losing a child, you said fate must have placed me in your path. Now I pray that fate has given me the same courtesy. I have fallen on hard times, Mr. Briggs. Please help me."

A harsh voice shouted from the path into town, "Get away from my darkies unless you intend to buy."

"How much for the large buck?" Caleb said as he stepped around the building to meet the trader head-on. I could no longer see him, but his voice was surprisingly casual. "I could use a sturdy bloke down at the dock."

"I expect to get at least seven hundred for him at market," the trader boasted.

Caleb laughed. "Nay, that's too hefty a price for me. The pockets of a simple lighter man aren't so deep. I'll hang on to my coins and do my own lifting."

"Well, be off with you, lighter man. I allow only men with the means to buy to mill about the pen."

"Fine with me, lad. I got plenty of rats crawlin' in the belly of my boat. I don't need none of yours."

The trader snorted at Caleb's cruel joke. "It's a dirty business indeed."

"Let me buy you a pint at the tavern," Caleb said. "We'll raise a toast to the filthy varmints."

"The two-legged or four-legged variety?"

"Is there a difference?" Caleb huffed.

The trader chuckled and I heard what sounded like a smack on the back. "I never turn down the gift of a pint, especially from a man who sees the humor in life. Slave trading is a merciless profession, so a hearty diversion is a welcome break."

Their voices faded, as did my opinion that Caleb Briggs was a man of good character. The bustle of the dock waned in the long afternoon shadows. After I'd finally reached my destination, my anguish at being jailed as a runaway made me wring my hands in frustration.

"Sit down, woman," Joe said as he leaned in the shadows. "You is making me crazy with all your panting and pacing."

"Joe is right," old Henry chimed in. "You gots'ta to be patient and wait for the opportunity to come along again. Might take months. Maybe even years. All we can do is wait."

"Years!" The burning thought nearly melted me to the ground.

The old man used his hands to brush aside the whiskers on his left cheek. Beneath his patchy white beard was a scar the size of a plum, shaped like the letter X.

"I was fifteen years old when a cotton planter who owned my mama branded me for leavin' his property. Only meant to see a gal at the next plantation, but the *why* of it didn't matter to ol' massa. The pain of bein' sealed by a hot iron lingers longer than any whip that laced my skin. It marked me as a runner. Here I am, forty years later, still runnin'."

I folded my arm in the narrow window and rested my head on it. Although I had never been to Deep Creek, the sight of the canal somehow kept me connected to North Carolina. Where would I be tomorrow? Or the day after that? A dark figure on the far bank caught my eye. I watched him move along the moored boats. When he turned to lift a bucket of water onto his vessel, I was certain.

He was Archie, the lighter captain who was responsible for taking Rafe, Jerlinda, and Axel up the canal to a rendezvous point with another *friend*. Archie spent all his time going back and forth between the seaports and South Mills. He was the key to my finding them, since he would know onto which ship they had been moved. He stood in the distance, near enough to see, but too far to hear me call out. It would have been less tormenting had he been a thousand miles away. He disappeared behind a stack of large wooden crates. My eyes remained locked on the lighter, trying to will him to me with prayer. But my prayers went unanswered and night fell like black crape across Deep Creek. No moon, no stars, no hope.

Chapter 19

The jangle of keys banged against the door of the slave pen. I sprang upward into the pitch-blackness. In the distance, laughter and the jolly tinkle of piano keys underscored the gloom of my dungeon. Instinct set me on edge. At this time of night, there was only one reason for the trader to seek what was in the pen. If I raised my fists to protect myself, I would be beaten into submission. A bitter seed of anger burned in me at the humanity that had been stripped from me once I was labeled a Negro. With Garrison, I had allowed my choices to be dictated to me. Now I had no choices, only the impulse to survive. I would have to sacrifice everything, including myself, to do so. I braced for my fate as the door creaked open.

"Jacy," a voice whispered from the doorway. "Step from your prison, lass. We must be swift and alert."

It was Caleb Briggs!

"You have returned," I said as he reached for my hand. "I thought you had abandoned me."

"I didn't want the bugger suspicious of me. The only way to get to you was to fill him with ale. He's got a trollop on his lap and is distracted by the merriment of a tavern song. When he tossed his jacket over the back of a chair, I crept off with his keys. He thinks I'm at the privy emptying a night's drink."

Henry and Joe jumped to their feet. "We all go free together," I said firmly.

Caleb spread open his arms to block the doorway. "I'm not looking to start an uprising. I simply feel obliged to return a favor." Caleb looked over at me, his chin quivering slightly. "You were right about sharing my wife's grief. Katherine has opened her heart to me, and I to her."

In a sudden burst of desperation, Timber Joe drove his shoulder into Caleb's midsection, knocking him from the doorway. Joe was on the run before Caleb knew what hit him. As silent as a deer, Joe sprinted toward the shadows of the canal, waving for us to follow him. Henry and I helped Caleb to his feet and when I looked up, Timber Joe was gone.

"Off to the swamp," Henry said with a glint of admiration. "Guess he wasn't riskin' the chance that a white stranger would take pity on us."

Caleb rubbed his tender ribs. "Jacy, freeing one of you is risk enough."

"Sah, I ain't lookin' fo' trouble," Henry said, brushing the dust from Caleb's jacket. "I just want to walk out the door and disappear, no harm to no one. If you leave me here with the others gone, there ain't no tellin' what that ol' trader man will do."

I touched Caleb on the arm. When he looked down at me, I whispered, "Please have mercy on us, one and all."

Caleb's jaw clenched as he grappled with his conscience. Finally, he stepped from Henry's path. "Hurry on, then. I am taking Jacy with me."

"Where will you go?" I asked Henry.

"I'm gonna follow the signs to the North. Let's hope I make it this time."

"Maybe you should follow Joe," I urged.

Henry waved his hand. "Dismal Swamp ain't fo' me. It's not far enough from the whips and chains. I am gonna keep steppin' as far north as my feet will take me."

Henry shook Caleb's hand and then touched my shoulder. "I hope you get to wherever it is you is goin'."

"Where *are* you going, lass?" Caleb asked.

"I truly do not know yet, but there is a lighter man named Archie who can point me in the right direction."

Caleb's eyes widened. "I know Archie. He is an associate of Sylvan Firth."

"Yes." I smiled with relief. "I saw him through the window at the dock. I must go to him." I turned to Henry. "Come with me and see if there is an avenue of escape he can provide for both of us. I am certain your chances will be improved with an organized route rather than running blindly across two states."

Henry studied Caleb and then me. "I reckon it's worth the risk."

Caleb hustled us toward the dock. He instructed us to wait for him behind several stacks of shingles that lined the loading dock. He ran to the tavern to return the trader's keys without notice. To our good fortune, the keys were returned to the trader's pocket just before he excused himself to the upper room in the company of his young harlot.

"The scoundrel's debauchery is both your nemesis and your deliverer," Caleb said when he found us huddled in the lumberyard. "Be grateful he is more lecherous than most."

Caleb led us past the lock station to where the swamp canal and the currents of Deep Creek were divided by a tall gated chamber like the one in South Mills. Except for the lap of water and the knock of wooden hulls against the dock, the levee full of boats was eerily silent. Caleb directed us onto the lighter where I had noticed Archie earlier. He held up a halting hand and then delivered a series of taps using his heel against her deck. Seconds later, Archie appeared from the rear of the boat.

"Who's there?" he said, straining his eyes in the night.

"It is Caleb Briggs. I have a friend of Sylvan Firth's in tow."

Archie stepped closer. "Don't usually pick up here. I am headed back down the canal with shingles meant for Elizabeth City."

I stepped from Caleb's protective shadow. "Archie, do you remember me? We met more than a month ago in South Mills. You transported a woman and two men at the request of Mr. Firth. I need to know where they went."

Archie looked me over, but like Caleb, he saw nothing familiar in me. "Don't know what you mean. I carry lots o' goods to and fro. Can't remember every package."

He was very guarded, but I was too desperate to be discreet. "One of the men had a significant limp."

"Ah, the threesome meant fo' Philadelphia."

My heart leapt. "Is that where they are? Safe in Philadelphia?"

He motioned us to the rear of the boat, where we could speak more candidly. "They were left in the hands of a trustworthy boatswain who sails on a merchant ship carryin' lumber to the shipyards in Philadelphia. The winds weren't favorable, so they sat at anchor fo' nearly a week. After they finally set sail, I don't know what became of 'em. But I promise you, Philadelphia was their jump-off point."

For the first time in weeks, I felt hopeful. "Can I talk to this boatswain?"

"From Philadelphia, his ship carries Northern goods back through Southern waters to Savannah. I don't expect 'em in Portsmouth fo' weeks, dependin' on the weather. Besides, yo' folks ain't gonna be sittin' at the port fo' you to stumble on. They are passed to another friend who helps to disperse 'em. The more time that passes, the colder their trail is gonna be."

"Then I must follow quickly to Philadelphia. I am already at a severe disadvantage."

Archie shook his head at my naive declaration. "It ain't like buyin' a ticket, miss. We only got friends on certain ships, so there is not always one in port. And even when we do, it's mighty dangerous gettin' you on board."

Caleb sensed my disappointment. "Maybe you should consider turning back, lass. Archie can take you down the canal and away from Deep Creek's slave trader. I'll see the colored man Henry to one of the tidewater landings. He can try to stow away on any ship headed north."

Though frightened by the unknown, I had learned to trust my instincts. I declined Caleb's offer with a nod of appreciation. "My journey is no longer driven by impulse, but rather by the belief that I must move forward."

Caleb searched my eyes for doubt, and when he found only solid resoluteness, he turned back to the lighter man. "Archie, is there another way? By land, perhaps?"

"They say there are threads of the system inland. Takes a lot longer and mostly on foot. But my contacts are only here on the coast. Maybe Sylvan Firth can find another way. Unless . . . ?"

"Unless what?" I asked, ready to cling to any possibility.

"The *Southern Gale* is moored below the lock waitin' to come through at daybreak. She was up in Portsmouth yesterday. I was shootin' the breeze with a coal man that works her furnaces and he said there is a ship called the *Bonnie Sue* that needed some unexpected work on her hull before shovin' off. She should have set sail four days ago. The coal man says there was a grumble on the docks because the longer the *Bonnie Sue* sits at anchor, the greater the delay of those awaiting her berth."

"Where is the ship headed?"

Archie smiled. "Philadelphia."

"Do you think she is still in port?"

"Let's go down to the *Southern Gale* and I'll see what I can find out. One thing I know fo' sure is Captain Scruggs of the *Bonnie Sue* is a friend of the cause."

Caleb took my arm as he motioned Archie from the shingle lighter. "We'd better move on before the dock comes alive with the sunrise."

The mention of Garrison's steamer, the *Southern Gale*, cloaked me in an ominous chill. Deep Creek was only twenty-two miles north of South Mills, but I felt as though I had traveled a thousand miles to get here. To brush so close to the hateful source of my journey seemed as if I were daring fate. However, the *Southern Gale* stood between me and a possible avenue to Rafe, Jerlinda, and Axel. Therefore it was a risk I had to take.

Every creak and bump along the dock lit a wildfire of panic within me. I needed only to think of Quinn and Boss Man to remember how easily freedom could be snatched away. Archie, Caleb, Henry, and I crept quietly down the column of steps along the descent of the lock. My breath caught in my throat at the sight of the *Southern Gale* moored at the front of a row of boats waiting for the lock to lift them from Deep Creek into the swamp canal. Archie pointed to the shell of a dilapidated shingle flat splintered within some trees along the bank.

"Take cover in that skeleton," he whispered. "I can't step aboard the *Gale* without bein' took fo' a thief, but I'll meander around her mooring until the coal man stirs. If the fellow says the *Bonnie Sue* did not raise her sail yesterday, then you may have a chance to catch her.

But I wouldn't go there if she's gone. Portsmouth is infested with slave hunters pokin' around for stragglers intent to stow away on the northbound ships."

Caleb secured me and Henry beneath a carefully stacked pile of weathered slats. "I will seek out a trustworthy acquaintance for use of a carriage. If the ship is in port, I will get you there swiftly. If she is not, I will take you as far from Deep Creek as possible. When the trader wakes with a whiskey headache and an empty pen, patrollers will spread through this town and surrounding thicket like hornets from a downed nest. You must be far from the swarm by sunup."

From within the buckled shell of lumber, I heard Caleb's boots jog toward the heart of town. Through a small gap in the slats, I overlooked the dock that stretched beside the *Southern Gale*. Every few minutes, Archie's silhouette paused near her bow and then disappeared again. Though Henry and I spoke no words, I was glad I was not alone. Suddenly, the sharp click of boots coming up the dock spurred my heart into a gallop. Caleb would be more secretive, so I knew it was a stranger.

I broke into a cold sweat when the paunchy figure stopped next to the plank that rose onto the *Southern Gale*. He struck a match and raised it to a pipe clenched in his teeth. The flickering match revealed the broad bulldog face of a man who was no stranger at all.

Garrison.

My heart dropped into the pit of my stomach and throbbed there as if mortally wounded by an unexpected shot. The familiar scents of sulfur and tobacco swirled in my head. It was all I could do to keep myself from bursting from the woodpile and into the trees. My shoulders trembled with such unbridled intensity that Henry had to put his arm around them to still me. Terror singed across my skin when another figure crept from the shadows.

"Quinn, you startled me," Garrison said with an uncomfortable hitch. "Why are you skulking around before dawn?"

Though Quinn had his back turned to me, the outline of his wide-brimmed hat was undeniable. "Oh, I always watch the dock for any early-morning activity. I saw someone over this way. I wasn't expecting it to be you. You don't usually come up the canal with your steamer."

"I heard there are quite a few eligible women in Portsmouth, so I went up to have a look."

"Is that right? And did you find the excursion worthwhile?"

"Not too promising, but the tart I laid down with last night made the trip more than satisfying."

Quinn chuckled. "So that's what has you on the dock in the chill of early dawn."

"Just dragged myself from her bed. The *Gale* is headed down the canal as soon as the lock opens. You are welcome aboard if you are heading south."

"Thank you, Yob, but my work is best done from a lighter. I can be off the water and in pursuit before a darky can blink its glassy eyes."

"There must be decent profit to keep you trudging this hellhole."

"Decent enough," Quinn said. "Brought in three from the canal bank yesterday. As a matter of fact, one claimed to know you. She was a wild swamper and the stupidest yellow wench I ever came across. Tried to claim she was your fiancé. Imagine that?"

Garrison's posture stiffened. "What's that you say?"

"I found the ignorant thing lying in the mud, bugs crawlin' in her thick matted hair, and the stink of the swamp soaked into her skin."

"Are you sure she was colored?" Garrison's voice was sharp and urgent.

Quinn paused before responding. "She was light-skinned. Probably mulatto or quadroon, but definitely a darky."

"Where is this woman?"

"She's in the pen down the road as far as I know. What's it to you?"

Garrison pushed past Quinn, leaving the man cursing under his breath. My view was obstructed, so I could only hear Garrison sprint up the road as the creak of an approaching carriage came our way. In the graying sky of dawn, Caleb appeared with a plum-colored buggy drawn by a lone horse. I was surprised when he waved Quinn over to him.

"Hello, good fellow," Caleb chirped. "I bargained to have this carriage in South Mills by noon and the ferryman won't be at his station until sunrise. Will you do me a favor and crank the ferry for me so I can cross over and be on my way south?" Caleb's burly appearance made him a formidable man to say no to.

"Let's be quick about it," Quinn huffed. "I got my own business to attend to."

I could not believe that Caleb had tricked the feared slave hunter Quinn into unwittingly aiding us in our escape. As soon as Caleb steered the carriage down the path to the creek side of the lock, where the rope-pulled ferry operated downstream, Archie scooted across the dock to where we hid.

"The coal man says the *Bonnie Sue*'s repairs were close to done, but she definitely did not sail yesterday."

"Caleb is crossing a horse and carriage on the ferry," I said. "We'll leave at once."

"You got a long ride," Archie said, scanning the area around us before pushing aside enough slats for Henry and me to climb out. "Luck be with you."

Henry put his hand on Archie's shoulder. "Thank you, friend. Now we gots'ta swim to meet the carriage on the other side."

Archie led us up along the canal beyond the dock. "Stay low in the water like an otter so you don't splash and cause a ruckus. Cut through them poplars on the other side, and before long, you will find the dirt path that joins to the stagecoach road to Portsmouth. I'll signal to Caleb so he knows where you is headed."

I reached out and shook Archie's hand. "Bless you."

Archie nodded. "Don't forget, Captain Scruggs is the man you seek. Don't trust no one else."

He saw us into the water and then turned down along the dock as if he were taking a relaxed morning stroll. For all I knew, this was how he spent every morning. Praise be for the courage and conviction of men like Archie and Caleb.

The sting of the chilly water took my breath away. Gauzy mist swirled from the surface as Henry and I labored across the canal using only our submerged feet and hands to propel us. Initially, my dress floated atop the water. This made it easy to keep my chin above the surface. However, halfway across, the weight of the saturated cloth sank it around me, dragging my body under and obstructing the movement of my legs. I spit and sputtered as I gulped canal water in my struggle.

Remembering my mobility in the swamp, I slipped off my dress beneath the water and pulled it along as my legs kicked harder. With Henry's assistance, I climbed the peat bank on the opposite side. The fight for survival eclipsed my impulse for modesty. We ran into the trees, where Henry quickly helped me back into my dress. I was neither threatened nor made to feel vulnerable in my natural state. We were allies, respectful of and dependent on each other, sharing a common goal of life in the free North.

As we ran in the direction Archie had instructed, I glanced over my shoulder at Deep Creek. Somewhere in the belly of the town, three men would soon learn of our escape and seek our path: the slave trader, Quinn, and Garrison, each vile in his own way. We had managed to wriggle through their fingers, yet I knew there would be others ahead of us who would be just as determined to thwart our effort. For now, all we could do was run clear of the swarm we had stirred up behind us. When I saw Caleb's carriage beyond the tree line, I kicked a trail of fallen poplar leaves as I ran to him.

"Here," he said, handing Henry and me each a bundle of clothes. "They aren't fancy, but they are dry and sturdy. The fellow who lent me his carriage has a wife who is sympathetic to your cause. There are biscuits and honey in the carriage."

Henry ate while I ducked into the trees to change from my wet frock. The bundle included a simple dress of brown linsey-woolsey, stockings, and suitable undergarments. Humble tears fell when I found a pair of soft ankle boots within the folded bundle. They were well-worn and a loose fit, but the joy of having shoes on my ravaged feet made me feel ready to step back into the world.

Caleb nodded approvingly when I emerged from the wood. "You are nearly presentable, Jacy."

He handed me a small tin, which I recognized as face powder. I opened the lid and touched my finger to the pearl flakes inside. How was it that the sheen provided by a layer of dust held in the palm of my hand could change the course of my life? I snapped the tin closed and gave it back to Caleb.

"My journey has brought me very far, Caleb. I will not tread backward."

Caleb's green eyes sparkled with understanding. "I didn't think to ask for a hairbrush."

I raked my fingers through my shorn and knotted hair, but it was no use. Caleb tied an ivory-colored bonnet on my head. "There," he said with an encouraging smile. "You no longer have the soft look of a mistress, but I am confident that you will pass as my sister and Henry as our driver."

Henry changed into trousers and a patched woolen jacket as I shoved biscuits dripping with honey into my mouth. They were the most delicious morsels I had ever eaten. I licked the sticky crumbs from my fingers and gulped the cup of buttermilk that Caleb offered. With milk running down my chin, all I could do was grin.

Soon we were on our way. Driving into the sunrise and then north along the southern branch of the Elizabeth River, our carriage rolled swiftly, with Henry acting as our coachman at the reins. Caleb and I sat in the carriage. To avoid scrutiny, I kept the wide brim of my bonnet pulled snug around my face. Most of the travelers we encountered were slaves or farmers hauling wagonloads of goods to and from the wharves. Consumed in their tasks, none was inclined to give us a second look.

The mouth of the river opened into an ever-increasing body of water. I sat in awe of the size and number of ships anchored in the distant harbor. I was an inland girl and had never gazed upon the magnificent sight of a seaport, though I had heard much about the ships from Garrison's grandiose accounts.

"Are we clear on the details of our plan?" Caleb asked as the passing of wagons became steady.

Before I could answer, a horse and rider came around the carriage from the rear and strode aside us. The man's dusty, shoulder-length hair whipped in the sea breeze, and a week's worth of whiskers darkened his cheeks. I folded my hands in my lap and lowered my head away from his hard stare.

"What business have you in Portsmouth?" His question smacked of stern curiosity, though Caleb answered casually, as if in pleasant conversation.

"I hear the port city is an excellent place to strike up business prospects."

The man stayed beside us. "You are rather rough and rumpled for a businessman."

"And you are rather nosy for a man I could knock from the saddle with one swing of my fist."

"Don't get ornery, mate. I don't care what business brings you here as long as it's not underhanded."

"You're the law, then?"

"The only law that interests me is meant for coloreds who are on the foot," he said, plodding his horse closer to Henry. "We get a lot who think they can stow away on ships leaving the tidewater landings between here and Norfolk. Is this your darky?"

"Of course he is mine. Do you think he is headed to Portsmouth to meet his ride to the North and I came along to kiss him good-bye?"

The man laughed, although his inquisition unnerved me. "And who is the young lady?"

"If you must know, she is my sister. What's it to you?"

"Seems a bit shy is all."

Caleb disarmed the man with a frightening show of agitation. "Back off, bugger. Our only wish is to have a pleasant visit to your city. If you continue to prod us for no reason, I'll be happy to give you the fist I promised you earlier."

"I don't sweat you, you backwater grunt. And my eyes won't be the only pair on you, neither." The man spurred his horse into a trot, blanketing us in a cloud of dust.

When he rode on, Caleb turned to me. "We have to be very cautious. What we are doing is all the more difficult because we are on unfamiliar ground. Had I not a grieving wife who needs me by her side, I myself would deliver you north by wagon."

"Your place is with Katherine," I said, touched by his compassion. "Besides, the trip by land is too long and no less hazardous. My goal is not simply to reach the North. It is to locate the family who passed through this port. I believe this route may be my only chance to find them."

"Very well, Jacy. Let's find out if the *Bonnie Sue* is still in port."

We rode through a crowded square where farmers and marketers sold their wares. The muddy street adjacent to the wharves was lined with wagons and dockworkers. Several cargo schooners sat like royal statesmen, being filled and tended by a stream of Negroes and seamen. Countless hogsheads of sugar along with those of flour and tobacco waited with other bales and crates to be loaded onto the skids of passing drays. I could not keep from staring at a group of weatherworn rummies gathered on the steps of a dram shop sharing a bottle of drink.

Moored farther down Water Street was a smaller, less regal vessel. Painted on her bow were two words: *Bonnie Sue*. I could not take my eyes from her as we rolled by. The relief at finding the ship still at anchor in Portsmouth was a godsend. A lone woodworker was tied at the waist by a rope strung from the ship's bow, applying turpentine to a row of newly cut slats that scabbed her hull. Henry glanced at me over his shoulder, his eyes glimmering with a mix of excitement and fear.

"Ahoy, mates," Caleb called to a pair of Negroes hauling water up the plank of the ship. "Can you tell me if your captain is aboard?"

One man swung his bucket down the road. "He's gone to the lumberyard to settle a bill."

Henry snapped our horse into a trot until we came upon the gates of a massive lumberyard. Nearby were several partially built ships sitting above the water in dry dock. We stopped near the gate and watched an array of wagons come and go. Looking at the neat piles of timber staves and shingles, I found my thoughts drifting back to the swamp, where these wood products were harvested on the backs of slaves and bondsmen. Perhaps some of the shingles on a nearby flat had been touched by my own hand, driven in an environment of misery.

Violet's eager face came to mind. I prayed she was safe on her swamp island and that she and her children would be watched over by Tupper. I would never have forgiven myself had she lost her freedom in helping me. If not for her and Ox, the mysterious bushman who had both threatened and saved me, I would not be here. Yet my journey was far from over.

Caleb nudged me with his elbow and pointed to a gentleman walking through the gates of the lumberyard. He did not strike me as a captain. He wore no three-cornered hat or jacket adorned with ribbons, though he exuded an air of confidence and dignity. Dressed in blue pantaloons with a golden stripe dropping from each hip, the man strode proudly as he buttoned his neatly tailored matching blue coat. Caleb climbed from the carriage and addressed the man as he passed us.

"Would you be Captain Scruggs?"

"I am Scruggs." The man paused warily. "Who is asking?"

Caleb offered his hand in greeting. "My name is Caleb Briggs. I am a lighter man on Dismal Canal."

"Ah, no doubt treacherous work," the captain said. "You look able-bodied, but I must tell you up front that my crew is complete and I need no others."

Caleb raised his chin discreetly in the direction of our carriage. "I am not here on my behalf."

"What business do you have with me, then?" the captain said, purposely looking in the opposite direction.

"A *friend* told me that you are willing to . . ." Caleb hesitated, choosing his words carefully . . . "Willing to transport cargo of a delicate nature."

"And what friend would suggest such a thing?"

My heart wobbled with uncertainty at revealing the contacts that had led us to him. If he was not of a sympathetic nature, he could cause these good men much anguish. Caleb glanced at me as if wondering the same. I spoke up, knowing we had no choice but to trust the system.

"I am a friend of Sylvan Firth and of a lighter captain named Archie. We could not wait for his escort, since his vessel is on the float down the canal. We are desperate, sir."

"I see," Captain Scruggs said. He surveyed the waterfront while contemplating my words. All activity around me seemed to fall still as I waited for him to speak. He folded his hands behind his back and stared ahead. "And how many packages do you wish delivered?"

Caleb answered. "There are just the two of them in the carriage."

Captain Scruggs glanced over at me curiously. The tawny hue of my suntanned cheeks was less evident with my face and hair concealed by my wide-brimmed bonnet. He took a moment to look closely at me, then turned away, his confusion abated. He asked no questions; nor did he seek reward.

"Do not be seen around the wharves or near the *Bonnie Sue*," he said hastily. "We are watched even now for any suspicious activity that suggests the movement of fugitives. There is a pier on High Street where the ferry runs to Norfolk. Next to that pier is a partially collapsed dock. When darkness falls and the lampposts are lit in Market Square, go to this dock. A man on a skiff will await you. He will carry you by water to the aft of the ship, where you will be unseen by the hunters who crawl these wharves like scavengers at low tide."

Caleb seemed uncertain. "How will we know we have approached the right man?"

"He will ask if you are seeking a friend," the captain said. "Now I must demand that you put your hands on me as though we are in disagreement. I assure you there are eyes on us and I must remain above suspicion."

Though he kept his words soft and kind, Caleb grabbed the captain by the lapels and shook him, "Bless you for your compassion, sir."

The captain pushed Caleb off and struck a hard blow to his face. Caleb's knees buckled and he crumpled to the ground. Captain Scruggs straightened his coat and brushed the dust from his hands.

"I return the compliment with great remorse for my rough display, but our lives depend on my unstained reputation." He scuffed his boot so that a divot of mud thudded against Caleb where he lay curled in the road.

The captain turned curtly and marched to the wharf. When he disappeared into the mass of workers who wailed and strained beneath heavy loads, Caleb lifted himself from the mud and climbed into the carriage.

"Are you hurt, Caleb?"

The brow of his right eye was puffed and reddened. Guilt washed over me at the discomfort he endured on my behalf. However, he gave me a half grin.

"Oh, I've been on the receiving end of many a plug worse than that one. Captain Scruggs was merciful in his delivery. Besides, it is a bargain price to pay for two seats on board."

I patted Caleb's arm in gratitude. "Maybe we should get out of harm's way while we wait for nightfall."

"Good idea," he said, rubbing his swollen brow. "Let's find the ferry landing on High Street so we will have no trouble locating it by lamplight. Then we'll wait outside the city, where no one will bother us. Give those reins a hearty snap, Henry."

As Henry urged our horse and carriage away from the busy wharf, I caught a glimpse of the long-haired stranger who had harassed us when we rode into Portsmouth. He was leaning against a wooden post along the wharves, his eyes fixed on our retreat. Captain Scruggs was right: We were being watched, and perhaps by more than one man. Danger stalked us, seen and unseen, from every direction. I turned my collar up against the chill; however, it was not the cool breeze that quaked my arms and legs with tremors. It was the impending night, and wondering whether its shadows would launch me toward liberty or into doom.

Chapter 20

The skiff bobbed in the moonlight, its mooring rope strung to the crippled dock. An eerie stillness quieted the landing as if all around us held its breath. Carousing seamen on evening liberty ashore could be heard along the wharves at Market Square. With a long day's work behind them, the merchant sailors made the taverns and gaming houses their nightly hubs of activity. This left High Street deserted from dusk till dawn, until the ring of the next morning's work bell would begin a new day's flow of merchants and watermen.

"I see no man aboard the skiff," I said as the three of us looked upon it from a hollowed shanty along the landing. "Do you think his actions were found out?"

Caleb lifted his hat and scratched his head. "Hard to say."

"Don't matter how many times I run"—Henry clucked mournfully—"moments like this still tear my guts out. Our next move either gets us one step closer to freedom or brings hell down upon us."

Henry's words prickled me from head to toe. When would this boulder of fear be lifted from me? But my journey thus far had taught me that shrinking in fear from the path ahead would bury me in an avalanche of hopelessness. I stood from my crouched position and straightened my shoulders.

"If Captain Scruggs's confidant is out there, he will not stay indefinitely. Our opportunity will be lost if we continue to hesitate."

No other words were needed. We moved as one from the cover of the shanty and ducked from one shadow to the next until we descended the steps that led to the splintered dock. A lazy bell clanked from a buoy floating in the darkness on the shrouded water that stretched in front of us. We stood looking around the nothingness, not knowing where to turn or take cover. Movement in a pile of broken rigging farther down the dock had me grabbing Henry's arm. A man appeared from the shadows and came directly at us. His face was pale beneath the wide brim of a tarpaulin hat, but his eyes were sharp and glimmering.

"If needed, I can offer you a ride to a friend," he said with a throaty voice that belched from him like a frog.

My panic-stricken heart eased. "Yes, we—"

He held up his hand to silence me. "Say nothing until we are where we need to be." Signaling us to hurry, he motioned his hand toward the skiff.

I turned to Caleb, who looked gray and shaken. I hugged him when he wrapped his arms around me. "Thank you for being a man of great courage and decency."

He released me from his arms and loosened the rabbit's foot adorning his hat. But before he could press the lucky memento into my hand, our parting was cut short by mumbled voices coming from the landing behind us.

"Check every nook and cranny," said a voice I recognized as that of the long-haired ruffian who had been watching us since our arrival in Portsmouth. "The carriage that is hidden in trees by the fishermen's wharf belongs to the bugger I was tellin' you about. Something about him and his so-called sister didn't sit right with me from the moment I laid eyes on them."

The seaman waved his arms for Henry and me to follow him to the skiff. Caleb squeezed my hands. "Aye, get on with you, lass. I'll hold off these bloodsuckers."

Henry whisked me along the slick, creaky dock and into the skiff. Our attempt to move in silence was denied us by the unsteady planks beneath our feet. The seaman motioned for us to sink low in the boat as the pace of unseen boots spread across the wharf.

My heart dropped when a voice barked, "Who's out there? Show yourself at once or I shall raise my gun on you."

"Where do you see 'em?" a second voice grumbled. "I can't make out nobody in this inky pitch."

An urgent whisper followed. "Over there. I saw movement on the far dock. Let's close in on them."

"This is your last warning," the second voice called out. "Step out into the open now. Better to be chained in the slave pen than blown into a hundred bits of tar by the blast of my shotgun."

Before I could grasp the gravity of the moment, a raucous commotion exploded on the dock. Though I could barely discern his silhouette in the night, I sensed it was orchestrated by Caleb. Clutching a broom handle, he ran the length of the pier, raking the stick on the planks. The slave hunters could not help but be drawn into the chase.

"There he goes! Get after him!"

I peeked over the side of the skiff as the men ran past our dock in pursuit of Caleb's shadowed figure. Immediately, the seaman scrambled for his oars and began rowing. His strokes were smooth and mighty. The wafting fog closed around us as we glided into deeper water. Any relief stirred in our exodus was shattered by the scene that played out in our wake.

"Is that him?" bellowed one.

"Where?" cried out the other.

The blast of two shots boomed from the landing. Henry grabbed my waist as I sprang to my feet. He pulled me down and into his arms as I gasped with terror. His hand clamped over my mouth to muffle my cries. Betraying our silence could not help Caleb and would most certainly turn the hunters on us. I eased from Henry's grip and dropped my face into my hands. Tears puddled in my palms as I wept quietly for our brave and selfless friend. The skiff continued its offshore path along the wharves where the cargo schooners were berthed. The experienced hands of the seaman dipped and raised his oars from the water in a practiced motion that released a mere trickle of sound in our backwash. Clearly he had made this run more than once.

I shuddered nervously as he passed by the darkened sterns of lumber barges and other seagoing vessels. Finally, the seaman lifted one oar from the water and used the other to steer us as we drifted quietly toward the *Bonnie Sue*, where she rose from the fog like a veiled cliff.

The seaman whispered in his croaky voice, "When we climb aboard you will be helped into a compartment belowdecks. Move swiftly and silently. More will be revealed later."

We bobbed where the ship's anchor was dropped. The seaman held the anchor line as he whistled three mournful notes. With that, a rope ladder toppled over the taffrail above us. The seaman caught the dangling hemp, which remained secured on the upper deck, for us to climb aboard the aft of the *Bonnie Sue* in secrecy. I was the first to crawl up the ladder, but I nearly slipped into the water when the rope twisted and twirled in my awkward ascent. Henry and the seaman used their weight to steady the rope at their end, making it easier for me to scale the remaining distance.

Near the top, several hands came at me and pulled me over the rail. I hadn't the chance to look around before I was shoved into another set of arms a few feet away and lowered by my wrists into a small cabin no more than five paces wide. Though a wooden ladder climbed one wall, I was not given time to secure my foot on a rung. I was dropped into the compartment and let out a whoop when an unseen man caught me in his arms. His dark face never changed expression as he tossed me aside and helped Henry behind me. No sooner had Henry's feet hit the floor than the wooden hatch above us slammed closed. A large crate was pushed over our entrance point and footsteps receded in the night.

Four of us stood motionless, measuring one another in the dim glow of a tallow candle that burned on the floor between us. With wary eyes, a Negro couple studied Henry and me. As the elder of the group, Henry took the lead.

"They call me Henry," he whispered, offering his hand to the lanky fugitive, who shifted protectively in front of the woman who clutched his arm. "This here is Jacy. I guess we is all headed in the same direction."

The young man's face was the shade of molasses, with nary a whisker. He wore a slouch hat, a wool shirt, and threadbare trousers. His woman's skirt and blouse were of stone gray cotton, as was the bandanna that wrapped neatly around her head.

"I am Deacon. Dis here is my wife, Bette."

Her name chilled me with thoughts of Boss Man and his harem of Bettes. It was astounding how abuse and hate could stain even a name. The woman peeked from behind her husband. Though her youthful face revealed a tender age, her eyes were pained, as though she had witnessed uncommon horror.

"Dis hole will fill with smoke befo' long, so we ain't got much time fo' candlelight. De hatch is usually propped open at night so de candle can burn, but dey will close us up till dey know dat nobody follered you."

"How long have you been here?" I asked, since he sounded as though he knew the routine of the ship.

"Near about two weeks. Captain said de ship had bulkhead damage near de bow, but tomorr'y we is finally shovin' off."

"Two weeks! What a harsh confinement to endure."

Deacon motioned for us to sit. "Ain't too bad. We is safer here than on land. During daylight, de hatch is closed while de seamen gots run of de ship. Every afternoon, de captain clears de back deck and opens de hatch to give us some fresh air, food, and water. Once we is at sea, he is gonna let us on deck fo' a spell. Too dangerous to try such a thing in port."

"We got blankets, candles, and a bucket fo' our necessaries," Bette said softly. "We ain't had no trouble, but we sho' will feel better after we cut loose from them slave catchers and port agents."

Henry looked over at me, his eyes brimming with emotion. "It took forty years of tryin', but I might make it to freedom after all."

The bitter scent of smoke thickened the air around us. Deacon leaned over the tin that held the candle. "Time to go dark fo' a while."

When he blew out the flame, we were engulfed in blank darkness. I leaned back against the wall to gain my bearing. The black pocket seemed endless, though I knew our compartment was snug. Deacon's voice came through the abyss.

"It's best to sleep when we is closed tight. It passes de time and leaves you rested when we get a glimpse of de world again."

Deacon spoke from experience, so I wrapped myself in a blanket and curled up on the damp floor. The small compartment smelled of musty clothes and scorched tallow. Here in the darkness all I had were my thoughts. Caleb's bearded image appeared in my mind.

What fate had we delivered upon him? Guilt roared in my ears. Its ferocity caused me to ache with heartbreak.

To ease the tears that rose and fell, I tried to think ahead. Conjuring Rafe's image took all my concentration. The distance between us felt as endless as the black hole that entrenched me. Sadly, I had no touchstone to assure me that I was gaining ground to where he stood, but I was awash with comfort when I brought him to me in memory.

Can he feel me like I feel him?

My need for authentic attachments and genuine affection had me running after him as if he were a kite torn from my hand in a merciless gale. He had remained my focus and intent since the moment we had parted. On the other hand, when Rafe had let go of my string, he had done so willingly. I wondered—in releasing me, had he also detached himself from the tender feelings that could hinder his journey? Perhaps he had vowed never to look back, our bond and admiration set adrift on the breeze as well.

I chose to believe our bond could not be so easily broken. For me, it grew ever stronger as I traced his journey. But he alone was not the reason I pressed on. I was pulled to Jerlinda by yearnings I had yet to understand. In her, I sensed something I desperately needed. Thinking of her eased my anxiety and I drifted into sleep.

The grinding sound of the crate being pushed off the hatch stirred us. The hatch swung open and a figure climbed down the ladder. The rush of cool night air was intoxicating. I breathed it in and let it caress my cheeks. The man struck a sulfur matchstick and touched it to our candle. The return of light was as welcome as the gust of fresh air. He was a seaman dressed in wide, baggy trousers and a blue fearnought jacket. A gold-colored kerchief was tied loosely around his neck. He was of hearty build with shoulder-length brown hair tied in a tight queue at the back of his head. I did not recognize him until his croaking voice revealed him as the seaman who had met us at the dock.

He handed Deacon a bucket of water and a ladle. "Captain Scruggs says this bucketful has got to carry you through a few days. Same goes with these rations. He'll supply you with more along the way."

I took the satchel that held strips of dried beef, four green apples, a generous portion of cheese, and several biscuits. "When will we leave?"

"We will set sail tomorrow. We have already been inspected stem to stern by port officials, so when the sun clears the horizon, we'll be under way. Save them apples to ward off seasickness."

"How long is we at sea?" Henry said as he helped himself to a biscuit.

"Depends," the seaman said. "A fair-weather voyage will bring us to port in three or four days. You can never predict the swell, but I promise you once we're at sea nobody can lay hands on you."

His words of assurance bolstered me. "Thank you . . . Um, is there a name I can call you?"

"Best for all if we remain nameless. Call me Sailor, if you like."

I nodded gratefully. "Thank you, Sailor."

"I'll keep the scuttle open for an hour or so," Sailor said as he climbed the ladder to the upper deck. "I'll have to close her before dawn. Then we'll batten down the hatches and be on our way."

"Can't wait to get outta here!" Bette's words squeaked with excitement as she threw her arms around Deacon's waist. "No more frets and jitters."

Deacon hugged his wife. "Don't count yo' chickens, girl. Bold thoughts might hex us."

Deacon was right. After all the obstacles I had encountered, I dared not let confidence lower my guard. We settled around the candle and devised a plan to stretch our rations over several days. The perishables would be eaten first: biscuits, cheese, and dried beef, in that order. The apples would be saved, though I couldn't imagine why.

It did not take long for me to find out. Shortly after our hatch was closed, a bell rang to announce daybreak. Sailor's voice boomed above us.

"All hands on deck, mates. It's sailing day!"

His order released a flood of footsteps across the top deck. We had barely snuffed our candle when cries of, "Haul anchor," and, "Loose the sails," were bantered back and forth with dozens of others. Shards of sunlight gleamed through razor-thin gaps in our wallboards, allowing me to see Henry's hopeful grin through the dim haze. We listened to the extended whirl of commotion until the shift of the ship caused Bette to clap gleefully. She would not have done so had there not been so many noises and bellowing voices to shield the sound.

The *Bonnie Sue*'s movement was slow and labored as she left her berth. As her motion increased, I swooned with a tingle of light-headedness. Perspiration broke out on my forehead. Suddenly, the small cabin seemed suffocating. My panting breaths alerted Henry to my discomfort.

"Stay calm and breathe deep," he said, patting me. "You'll get used to the rise and fall of the ship. When I was a boy, I worked on an oyster boat in Albemarle Sound. Took me a couple of days to get sea legs under me. Stand up and hang on to the ladder from time to time. It might help."

Eventually, the excited yelp of, "Set sail," raised a cheer from the seamen on board and sent me scrambling on my knees to empty the modest contents of my belly into the necessary bucket. Not long after, Deacon joined me.

"What a waste of rations," he mumbled as we lay on our sides, still retching.

Henry chuckled. "Maybe you ought to try one of them green apples."

I stumbled to the ladder and clenched the rail. The sway of the ship left me woozy, yet the crash of waves against her hull exhilarated me. We were free of Southern soil. Were I not so drained, I would have laughed. I imagined Garrison's livid expression when he realized I had escaped him a second time. No doubt he was thinking he was close to finding me, but little did he know how far I would run. I shuddered at the thought of ever crossing his path again.

On the second day of our voyage I claimed my sea legs. Sailor had opened our hatch for a considerable part of the previous night, which gave me the chance to clear my head and regain my composure. Though our sanctuary offered no more than the bare essentials, it provided more comfort than I had known in some time. Most of all, I felt safe in its shell, even if by way of false courage.

"Would you like me to brush the thistles from yo' hair?"

Bette rummaged through a satchel that held the pittance of belongings she and Deacon carried. She lifted a hand carder from her things and gestured to me as though asking permission.

I had never seen a carder outside of the spinning house. The device was no more than a simple wood-carved handle mounted to a rectangular paddle about two inches wide and four inches long. The flick card affixed to the paddle face was made of steel-wire teeth and was used to tease out wool for spinning.

"It may be beyond hope," I said, touching my fingers to my tangled clumps of cropped hair.

Bette went eagerly to work. As she peeled burrs and briars from deep within my locks, I felt humbled at being groomed like an animal. Bette's determination in ridding me of my swampland residue had me biting my lip in agony. Tangles of hair and marsh grass fell around us like milkweed in an autumn breeze. She tugged and scratched the carder from the frayed ends of my hair to the matted middle. My scalp burned and bled as knots that could not be disengaged were unceremoniously torn at the root. Bette used her teeth to shed me of a particularly unyielding nest of debris.

"Girl, when was the last time you brushed yo' hair? I swear you is crowned with last year's harvest."

I giggled, because I definitely felt as though I had been plowed and raked over. Fortunately her strokes became smoother and less forced. Closing my eyes, I tilted my head to savor the unencumbered carder in my hair, its massage and gentle pull now bringing me infinite pleasure. I had forgotten how comforting it was to be fussed over. Bette eased her rhythm to allow my indulgence.

"I would have never known it by first look," she mused, "but yo' hair is mighty soft and straight now that it's brushed out."

"Yes," I said with self-conscious hesitation. "It was much longer but had to be cut when it was snared during my escape."

She rested her hands on my shoulders. "You is lucky you only lost yo' hair. I know folks who lost fingers, feet, children, and their last breath. De road from hell is paddyrolled by de devil."

I ran my fingers through my hair as though getting reacquainted with a forgotten friend. Instead of mourning its tattered condition, I would hold my head high and feel lucky, as Bette suggested. After all, I might be stained and scarred, but I had emerged from the battle and secured a place on a vessel to freedom. We were four lives tucked in an unseen womb, waiting to be reborn.

Several days passed, each bringing a degree of challenge. None was so great as the fierce thunderstorm that engulfed us one afternoon.

The ship was tossed and battered from all sides. All we could do was cling to the ladder for dear life. Frigid seawater seeped into the compartment, rising slowly over our ankles. Henry kept us alert.

"Tie the blankets and satchel with our rations to the highest rung of the ladder. If they get drenched, they will be of no use to us."

"Henry's right," I called over the roar of the ocean's fury. "Even our clothing will bring a death chill if the seawater soaks us through."

Bette and I gathered our skirts to our waists. The men rolled their pants to their knees.

"We gots'ta stay on our feet," Henry yelled when Bette lowered onto one knee. "The bite of this cold surge is our enemy. If we bow to it, it could beat us!"

Deacon eased Bette onto her feet, but her face was ashen and her legs unsteady. The storm raged most of the night, leaving us exhausted. Pure survival instinct kept us standing. We all wrapped our arms around Bette to support her limp weight, but she struggled against us and eventually sank to the floor to rest in the corner. Water sloshed over her legs and around her waist, releasing waves of tremors throughout her chilled body. When the sea calmed and the water receded from our chamber, I gently stripped Bette of her wet clothes and wrapped her in blankets.

"Rub her arms and legs to get the blood a-flowin'," Henry instructed as we took turns massaging warmth back into her limbs.

Never leaving her side, Deacon held Bette in his tight embrace. He whispered and encouraged her to be strong, but the storm had left its mark on her. The return of sunshine on the deck was a welcome blessing, but our compartment remained cool and damp. Bette stared through hollowed eyes as I brushed her hair. My hand against her cheek told me what I had already suspected: She was hot with fever.

"Let's get you into the open air!" Captain Scruggs's voice jostled us from our restless slumber.

The hatch above us opened, revealing a clear night sky sprinkled with stars. Climbing from the hole was like shedding an ill-fitting corset. I could move. I could breathe. I could stretch my arms to the heavens! My elation fizzled when Deacon carried Bette onto the deck. The captain looked her over.

"We have fresh blankets and a steaming pot of chicory to warm your bones," he said.

Sailor poured each of us a tin cupful and exchanged our damp blankets for those that were dry. "We have entered Delaware Bay."

Unfamiliar with the eastern ports, I did not know what that meant for us until Captain Scruggs added his account. "We will dock in Philadelphia tomorrow."

He motioned to Sailor, who promptly deposited a large sack at the captain's feet. The captain reached inside and removed four sets of seamen's rigs: baggy trousers, fearnought jackets, and woolen caps.

"Ladies, you will have to remove your skirts, but other than that you can put these on over the clothes you wear."

My elation at hearing "Philadelphia" sank into confusion. "I don't understand."

Captain Scruggs's brow creased with concern. "The port ahead may be the most dangerous part of your journey."

"But we will berth in the free state of Pennsylvania," I stammered. "What have we to fear?"

Sailor poured us another round of coffee. "Unfortunately, the slave hunters don't abide by boundaries. They sniff the Northern cities like bloodhounds."

"The ports are especially at risk," the captain added. "Slave speculators seek to intercept any runaways who travel by way of the trade waters and capture them before they can disappear into the countryside or follow inland routes farther to the north."

"The bounty men are an aggressive and well-numbered bunch," Sailor huffed.

Henry slipped on one of the jackets. "Are these clothes meant to disguise us?"

"Yes," the captain said. "Once we are in port, you will escort me to a carriage. Uniformed men with their captain will attract no second glances. When we are clear of the vile web cast by the bounty men, you will be taken into the city. Return the rigs to the coachman and seek your freedom. Now I must ask you to go below. We are near enough to land to encounter unexpected sea vessels. We cannot risk being discovered."

Sailor helped us back into the compartment. "I'll open the scuttle later tonight for a breath of air. After tomorrow, you'll need no one's permission to gaze at the moon."

The evening passed quickly, although Bette's condition deteriorated. Even with the dry blankets, her shivers did not abate. Bette's skin remained hot to the touch and her eyes filled with terror. I spread my seaman's jacket over her and tucked it under her chin.

"Tomorrow you will be free, Bette. Onshore, we will find a doctor to treat your fever."

When his wife closed her eyes in sleep, Deacon folded his body around hers. "We is almost there, sweet Bette. Don't you give up now."

I paced eagerly while Henry crouched in the corner, as if fearful of giving in to excitement. Soon midnight was upon us and the hatch opened. Sailor dropped a satchel of boots into the hole. "These are castoffs from the crew. You'll need them to go ashore. We don't want the wrong footwear to mark you as a fraud. Captain Scruggs says you can keep 'em, though the gals ain't likely to find a decent fit."

"Sailor, may I borrow the satchel?" My question was answered by the wave of his hand.

"Take it with you. You'll need it more than me."

While the others slept, I sat on the floor and gazed up at the pearled night sky. My thoughts whirled with restless anticipation. I tugged the wool seaman's hat down over my ears and poked my head from the hole. My breath rolled into the cool night air like a puff of smoke. I was careful not to climb high enough to reveal any more of myself as the gentle rocking of the boat told me we were at anchor.

"You weren't thinking of jumping ship, was you?"

Sailor's croak nearly caused me to topple from the ladder. I flushed at being caught in my curiosity. "Oh, my . . . I was just . . . Well, I wondered why we were not moving."

Sailor sat on a bulwark with his leg propped on a barrel. He studied me as he puffed his pipe. "Land ahoy. Do you want to see?"

He scanned the deck behind him, then motioned me to follow him to the rail. When I stood, I could see in the distance the lamplights of Philadelphia. The promise of freedom took my breath away.

"We are so close," I murmured. "It makes me want to dive into the sea and swim to the city's shores."

He chuckled. "Philly is a rough-and-tumble place like any other."

"Ah, that may be, but it's the gateway I seek."

Sailor looked out across the bay. "You and many others. But the gateway can become a trapdoor if you're not careful."

"I am deeply grateful for your assistance, Sailor."

"Oh, I ain't no martyr, miss. I risk my neck for the glint of a silver dollar, not for a stranger's freedom quest. Captain Scruggs is the log-roller. He makes it all happen with nary a suspicion upon him. And he ain't alone. See them green and white lights off the port side?"

I looked in the direction of his pointing finger to where two dim lights, one white, one green, flickered in the waves. "What is it?"

"It's a rowboat coming from the eastern shore of Delaware. There's another like it off the starboard."

I looked the other way and saw identical green and white lights, no more than specks in the surf. "Runaways?"

Sailor nodded. "They are transported across the bay to South Jersey. Some by watermen, some by freedmen. Many a soul has drowned in the drink when confronted by a turn in the weather or an ornery bounty man. The fate of most runaways is as precarious as the toss of a coin."

I gazed across the rolling waves with admiration for this secret brotherhood, until I sensed Sailor's eyes upon me. I hesitated to look at him, but when I did, his hungry gaze did not reflect the pure awe I felt in the quiet actions of the night. He reached out and touched my cheek with fingertips that sought more from me.

"If you wish to thank me, save your words and share your warmth with a lonely seaman."

When I stepped back, Sailor pulled his hand away. "Didn't mean to be bold, miss. I thought you Negros enjoyed the attention of a white man. You must think I am a crusty fellow."

"I am a respectable woman, Sailor. My dignity is no less precious to me than it is to the finest lady."

"Sorry, miss," Sailor said contritely. He lowered his head with genuine embarrassment. "I thought a friendly understanding might suit both of us."

"My heart belongs to another," I said softly. "He made this journey weeks ago and I hope to find him." I looked out at the vast city stretching along the waterfront. "Now that I am here, I fear I was naive to think his footsteps would be easily traced."

"It's a big world." Sailor smiled, attempting to redeem himself by sharing his wisdom. "But his tracks are still fresh. I hear tell of organized groups in the city that offer aid to fugitives. Quakers, perhaps.

Or the Mennonites of Germantown. South Philly's Lombard Street is home to a few, as is a place known as Paschall's Alley. Seek them out and perhaps someone will know which path your man has taken."

He furrowed his brow with an afterthought. "Don't just stroll up to the doorstep of a Negro-aid office. Bounty men are clever enough to watch the comings and goings of an address that attracts needy runaways. Never let your guard down."

I gazed toward the city lights with heavy trepidation. Were my loved ones out there among the twinkling luminaries or was I chasing the wind? I trembled with a mix of excitement and utter terror. Sailor tapped me on the shoulder and motioned toward the hatch.

One more night in the hole.

I was not a slave, but freedom of a different kind awaited me on the shores of Pennsylvania. Closing my eyes, I drew in a deep breath.

Please let happiness be awaiting me as well.

Chapter 21

The whirl of activity began at first bell. Henry and I leaned against the compartment wall, staring at the hatch that would soon open and release us.

"Where will you go, Henry?"

His quick answer revealed that he had given great thought to the matter. "Years ago, I heard a cotton planter say that Philadelphia is the nearest Northern city to Southern soil. That ain't free enough fo' me. I'll track as far north as my feet and goodwill can carry me. I waited a lifetime to step on free soil. Ain't gonna risk havin' slave speculators grab me up and sell me south."

"We gonna do the same," Deacon said from the corner, where he sat huddled with Bette. "We'll move on when Bette's fever passes. Fo' now, the most I can hope fo' is a safe place to lie down and maybe find some tonic fo' her sickness."

I prayed Bette had the strength to continue. It was strange to think that after several days at sea clinging to one another for comfort, we would soon scatter to the wind. "I will feel forever bonded to each of you and thankful that I was not alone on this voyage."

Hours passed. We had been docked for an extended period when finally the hatch was opened and Sailor stood over us. "I see you are dressed in your rigs. Ladies, be sure to tuck your hair beneath them caps. Good luck to you, one and all."

By the time we climbed from the hole, Sailor was gone. The ship's crew was nowhere in sight, and I wondered if they had been ordered belowdecks or relieved of duty and sent ashore while the secret business of the ship was attended to by Captain Scruggs.

"Welcome to the free North." His greeting was guarded and his expression was darkly serious. "Our next steps will be the most treacherous thus far. If navigated properly, we will have you on a safe route in ten minutes' time."

He pointed to two wooden boxes at his feet. "Men, carry these sea chests, while the women lift those bundles onto their shoulders. Not to fear, ladies; the bundles carry mostly feathers and straw, so you'll suffer no burden. However, their bulk will serve to shield your tender faces. Walk as a tight group. Stay on my heels and speak to no one."

Within moments, he led us down a plank and onto the bustling wharf. Seamen and dockworkers pushed their way around us, though a path parted for Captain Scruggs to pass. I averted my eyes and held my bundle against my cheek as a hard-looking man with pocked skin and a heavy mustache squirmed through the mass of activity. His meandering made it obvious that he was not in the business of coming or going. He was sifting the crowd for runaways. My heart pulsed wildly beneath my oversized woolen coat.

Keep walking. Keep walking.

From the corner of my eye, I saw Bette wobble. She moaned softly and began to wilt. Deacon braced her around the shoulders, but she had fainted. I dropped my bundle to help hoist her upright. The commotion caught the attention of the pock-faced hunter. He pushed curiously through the crowd, his stare locked on our little group.

With discreet purpose, Captain Scruggs stepped in the man's path while keeping his back to the hunter. But instead of whisking us from the man's scrutiny, our captain raised his voice to the crowd.

"If any of you seeks work, give your name to the boatswain on the *Bonnie Sue*. This drunkard has been cast from my crew for stashing a bottle in the galley. I allow no rye or rum on board. The sea is no place for a whiskey haze."

The captain boldly turned to the hunter, who was on his toes seeking a clear view of Bette. "You, sir. You look to be an able-bodied man. Do you wish to go to sea?"

The captain's engagement startled the man, and his attention was successfully drawn to the question at hand. He dismissed the captain with an impatient wave.

"I make plenty of coin on dry land, and my whiskey is measured by no other man. If it's a haze I want, then it's a haze I'll have." The crowd burst into laughter at the bounty man's sarcasm as his tight lips curled into a smirk.

Unbeknownst to him, he had been hoodwinked. Turning away, he noticed my sack on the ground, where I had dropped it while catching Bette. My innards twisted with panic when he leaned over to retrieve it for me. Its light contents would surely reveal our ruse. From nowhere, Henry's shoulder blocked his path before the hunter laid his hands on the sack. Feigning a well-conceived groan, Henry hoisted the sack onto his shoulder.

"Watch it, boy!" the hunter barked while being brushed back by Henry's movement.

Henry lowered his head in obedience. "Sorry, sah. Just tryin' to please the captain."

The hunter spit in Henry's face and walked away. I was stunned. Our first steps on free soil felt no different from those we had trod in the South. If Henry felt the same, he did not show it. Perhaps this was because he had no point of reference to gauge respectful treatment. He wiped the spittle from his cheek and handed me the sack.

"Come," Captain Scruggs urged. "You are not safe on the docks. There are dozens more like him on the prowl."

I glanced warily at the faces we passed. No one looked twice at us. Our seamen's rigs blended inconspicuously among the hundreds around us. We exited the docks to a busy street, where an enclosed coach awaited us. Captain Scruggs opened its door.

"Hurry on. Mr. Davis will deliver you to Mother Bethel."

We climbed into the coach, but when I turned to give thanks to Captain Scruggs, he was gone. He had vanished into the crowd without fanfare or acknowledgment. He was a hero of the greatest kind.

Our driver, Mr. Davis, was a neatly dressed man of powerful build. His mahogany skin glistened beneath a fedora tilted smartly to one side of his head. With a crack of his reins, we were on our way. The clip-clop of our horse along the city streets comforted me. I felt a part of the world again and welcomed the return of civilized order.

Mr. Davis leaned from his perch to address us. "Deposit your borrowed rigs in the sack on the floor. Our destination is a moderate ride ahead."

We peeled away our disguises. I removed my skirt from the seaman's chest that Henry had carried from the ship and slipped it on. Helping Bette with hers, I realized that her weakened state had worsened. I ran my fingers over the heavy seaman's coat I had worn.

"Mr. Davis, might I implore you to seek a doctor for my friend's malaise? I have no money, but perhaps the donation of this warm jacket would cover the cost. I am sure Captain Scruggs would be willing to part with it in these dire circumstances."

"You are right," Mr. Davis answered. "The captain would gladly spare a jacket for the sickly, but there is no doctor en route who will allow a Negro through his door. Not to fret; Mother Bethel will see to her needs."

Mother Bethel. I marveled that a woman could wield such power and influence.

Our coach ride through the city entranced us with a landscape far different from anything we had ever seen. Even Bette opened her eyes to gaze at the busy streets where Negro men and women walked among the whites. The disappointing first impression left by the danger encountered at the wharf was forgotten as we rolled into the heart of a free black community within the city. Along one street alone, I saw a barbershop, bakery, and haberdashery operated by Negro entrepreneurs. Henry's eyes filled with tears.

"I always tried to imagine what freedom looked like." He turned to me with an awe-inspired grin. "Now I know."

Soon after dusk had fallen, Mr. Davis turned our coach down a side street. The lampposts had not yet been lit, so we rolled slowly down the dim corridor. The coach halted in front of a darkened doorway adjacent to a glass window where a bright lantern burned. Mr. Davis tapped on the door. An old Negress, full in figure, cracked the door slightly.

Mr. Davis removed his hat. "The friend of a friend sent me."

The woman nodded. Mr. Davis rushed to open the coach door. "Follow her to Mother Bethel."

We bade farewell to Mr. Davis and followed the woman down a long hallway that led to a rear door. Outside again, we rushed across a narrow alleyway between the buildings and finally came upon the darkened basement entrance of a church. The woman announced our arrival with a series of knocks. We were waved inside by a Negro clergyman.

"Welcome to Mother Bethel," he said as we helped Bette onto a bench. "I will send for Sister Lenora immediately. She is versed in the ways of medicine and can nurse this woman to health."

Mother Bethel is not a woman. She is a church.

I smiled in response to their blessed outreach. The clergyman who stood before us was enveloped in an air of dignity and confident leadership. "I am expected at a meeting tonight; therefore Sister Lenora will watch over you in my absence. I will make arrangements to get you to the next safe house."

When he lifted his lamp to leave, Henry stepped forward. "Is we free?"

The clergyman smiled. "You are, indeed, brother. And it is Mother Bethel's mission to keep you that way."

He climbed the basement stairs and disappeared onto the main level of the church. Several candles burned around us to give light to our sanctuary. We waited silently until lone footsteps could be heard rushing above us. I held my breath as the basement door creaked open. A round woman, who looked strikingly like the one who had led us to Mother Bethel, stepped inside. Steam rose from beneath the lid of the cast-iron pot she carried. She set it on a small wooden table and began spooning a hearty soup into bowls that she took from a corner cupboard.

"This here is pepper pot," she said with a gentle voice. "It will fill your bellies."

The soup, thick with potatoes and beef, warmed me considerably. While we ate, Sister Lenora spoon-fed Bette and tended to her needs. She also had Bette swallow two mouthfuls of elixir. Once Bette was settled under some blankets on a pallet, the kindhearted woman joined us at the table.

"Are you traveling together as one family?"

"No," I said, wanting to confide my intent. "We are devoted companions brought together by fate. However, our destinations are separate. Henry, Deacon, and Bette wish to continue north, but I do not yet know where my path will lead. Perhaps you can give me direction."

"How so?"

"Within the past month or two, did you provide shelter to a group of three? A woman named Jerlinda and two men, one of whom has a pronounced limp?"

Sister Lenora gave thought to my description, then shook her head. "A steady stream of freedom seekers flows through Mother Bethel, but I remember no one of that description. I am a common presence here, so I am certain our church was not their vessel."

I deflated at the lost possibility, but Sister Lenora was quick to offer encouragement. "There is a network of antislavery societies beyond the church. One of them may hold the answer you seek. Rest now and await instruction in the morning."

Sister Lenora checked on Bette before going upstairs. My pallet was dry and warm beneath my blankets, a wonderful improvement from the damp hole of the ship. Oddly, as I lay staring at the ceiling, I could still feel the occasional roll of the sea. My joy at arriving in Philadelphia was tempered by the coming sorrow of parting from my companions. Soon I would be alone again. I had come so far, yet did not know whether I was any nearer to Rafe, Jerlinda, and Axel. For all I knew, they could have been recaptured and sold south, or perhaps far along a road to Boston or Canada. I closed my weary eyes and vowed never to stop looking.

We slept long and well. The clergyman who had welcomed us the previous evening rustled us awake. "Plans are in motion to move you out of the city. We have fresh clothing for you to begin your new lives. Sister Lenora has prepared griddle cakes and scrapple to give you strength. I will blanket you in prayer to give you faith. May God watch over your footsteps wherever they may lead."

Our clothing was simple and hand-me-down, but, re-dressed in clean skirts, trousers, and frocks, we were shed of our fugitive rags. Sister Lenora fitted us with shoes donated or collected by her congregation. Looking over the group, I realized that while our threads could blend us into the neighborhood, we still had desperation and uncertainty blinking in our eyes. We were dressed for freedom, but had yet to garner our *sea legs* for this new and untried turf beneath our feet.

Bette and Deacon were the first to leave us. "You will travel by milk wagon to a farm outside of the city. There is a hidden room built beneath the dairy where you will be safe and given time to recuperate from your bout with fever. When Bette regains her strength, you can move onward."

I embraced Bette. Her petite frame had diminished greatly during her illness. "I will pray for you, my friend. Grow strong and be free."

Bette sniffled. "Look at you, all cleaned and polished. Don't you never forget dat wild-haired swamp girl you was when I met you. She is de reason you is here today."

I touched my hair and laughed. "I shall never forget her, Bette. Nor you. Your gentle touch restored me, first in hair and then in heart. You reminded me that tenderness can heal a ravaged soul."

"The secret is to grow strong in yo' journey, Jacy. Don't let it harden you."

I kissed Bette's cheek and hugged Deacon. They followed Sister Lenora through a side door and were gone. Henry came and sat next to me. "Guess this is the end o' the road fo' us. Are you sure you don't want to go farther north?"

I squeezed his hand. "My destiny will be determined somewhere in this city, one way or the other. My hope is to pick up their trail and follow. If I fall short, I will remain here in hope they pass this way again. Perhaps I am meant to aid the cause that delivered them and you to freedom. Mine is a different kind of liberty that has awakened a deep understanding in me. One I could never have fully realized without the hardship and abuse I endured to get here."

"You have a broad way of seein' things, Jacy. You been on both sides of the coin now."

"It's strange, Henry. When I first learned I was born of a slave, I was ashamed of the Negro in me. Now I am shamed by the white in me."

"That's nonsense, gal. Shame ain't rooted in what you are. Shame comes from what you do. It's yo' heart that makes you who you are, good or bad. Stay true to yo' heart, Jacy, and you will never live a day in shame."

I held tightly to Henry's hand. "Your optimism in the face of hopelessness is a gift to me. In the slave pen, you challenged me to never give up. Had it not been for you, I would likely be in bondage or worse. I will remember you with warmth and thanks for the entirety of my life."

Henry grinned. "Same goes for me. I been tryin' to get to this side of the line since my first whuppin' as a boy. You found the path that got me here. Every free breath I take I owe to you."

"Not me, Henry. It was a network of goodness and courage that delivered us."

The clergyman entered the side door. "Okay, Henry, the next leg of your freedom run is about to begin. I will take you on foot to the Cedar Street corridor. You will be given forged papers, so decide what name you would like to claim as your own. You will pose as a coachman for two white women traveling the northbound road to Bethlehem. Once in the Lehigh Valley, they will direct you to a safe house. From there arrangements will be made to move you to New York, where a caboose man will give you access to a train going north."

"All them miles stretchin' north sound good to me," Henry said with excitement. "As for a name, I think I'll choose Caleb to honor an old friend."

Tears dampened my eyes at Henry's sweet remembrance of brave Caleb. "You must have a surname as well," I said.

"Hmmm," Henry pondered as he stroked the white whiskers on his chin. "I think Caleb Freeman fits me fine. What do you think, Jacy?"

I pressed my hand to his cheek. "I think it's perfect, Mr. Freeman."

Henry's chest swelled with pleasure and he left the room as Mr. Caleb Freeman. For a moment I felt lost in the hollow of the empty room.

Sister Lenora returned with a basin and a washcloth so I could bathe. "I have made preliminary inquiries, but have yet to find anyone who remembers the three you seek. We are watched closely, so I must be discreet with my interactions."

"Perhaps I can inquire for myself. Is it safe for me to walk the streets?"

"You are not likely to be bothered if you move with caution. Reveal your search only to those who identify themselves as friends. Unfortunately, both white and black can be enticed by the coin of a bounty man's bribe, particularly if they seek a fair-skinned woman. You will be remembered and at risk."

I left the sanctuary of Mother Bethel by way of the rear door. Sister Lenora believed I was less vulnerable if I were not seen in her presence. She directed me around the block and past the front of the church, where Lombard Street stretched in both directions. I recalled Sailor telling me that Lombard was known for antislavery activity. Sister Lenora had suggested I begin my search with a Negro woman who owned a cake shop down the street.

I was invigorated by my unhindered stroll in the brisk afternoon air. After a short walk, I found the cake woman washing her store-front window. I admired her baked goods through the window as I addressed her nonchalantly.

"I am sent by a friend to seek your counsel." The rag she rubbed against her pane slowed in response to my words.

"You have found a friend," she said, staying focused on her chore.

"In the two months past, have you been visited by three on the move?"

"I have been a friend to many but ask no names."

"They were a woman, a skilled horseman, and another with a heavy limp."

She wrung the water from her rag into a bucket at her feet. "They did not visit me. Try the barbershop farther on."

I thanked her and hurried down the street. The barber had a gent in his chair, so I did not approach him. I lingered on the street and waited for the freshly shaved customer to leave. The barber shrugged his shoulders at my description and directed me on to a man selling newspapers on the corner. When he shook his head empathically, the magnitude of my quest struck me. I was searching for the proverbial needle in a haystack.

My day was spent tracking contacts. I spoke to a gentleman as-sociated with the Free African Society and another involved with the Convention of Free Negroes. Each lost lead deflated me a bit more. I wandered the black community, where at times my light skin made me suspect. I was far from Mother Bethel when night fell. The piercing eyes of dark strangers on shadowed streets forced me to abandon my attempt to find my way back to Lombard Street. I slept in an alley and am ashamed to say I plucked my breakfast from a garbage pail.

The next day began with the same results. "Sorry, miss," a chimney sweep said. "But over yonder is Mr. Purvis. He is a leader in the cause and heads the new Vigilance Committee in the city."

I rushed to meet the handsome gentleman who strode with confidence and purpose. From across the street, I assumed him to be white. However, as I greeted him, I suspected he was of mixed blood like me. After I explained my plight, he asked me to walk with him.

"Do you know the name of the ship they arrived on?"

"No, sir," I said.

He gazed at me with kind eyes. "Those you seek have not crossed my path, but I have many contacts. I will inquire on your behalf. Where are you staying?"

My blank expression revealed my transient state.

"Have you eaten today, miss?"

"Only discarded scraps, sir."

"Come with me." His long strides quickened. "I am dropping literature off at the home of a friend. She is a Quaker woman of great character and will surely welcome you to her table. Her home is also a safe house. Perhaps she knows of whom you speak."

When we arrived at her doorstep, she was introduced as Lucretia. She wore a muslin dress, a shawl, and a silk bonnet. "Sister Lucretia wears no cotton cloth harvested by slave labor; nor does she use sugarcane in her household."

"Free goods only," she said. "A protest of conscience."

Mr. Purvis shared my story with her, but she regretfully shook her head. "They have not passed through here. However, the ladies in the next room provide safe haven. Join them at the table while I meet in private with Mr. Purvis."

I was welcomed to the table by three white women and a fourth who was a Negro. They were busy sorting through pamphlets and papers. All were sympathetic to my plea, but could not help me. As we sipped tea and ate apple fritters, I learned they were members of the Philadelphia Female Anti-Slavery Society founded by my hostess, Lucretia Mott.

"Pardon me," I said innocently. "This is a free state. Why do you need an antislavery society?"

The Negro woman, whom they called Rachel, spoke up. "It is our duty."

Lucretia stepped into the room. "Our voices shall not cease until the scourge of slavery is reaped from our land along with the hatred it inspires."

"Even here in Philadelphia," Mr. Purvis added. "Just last year, an orphanage for Negro children was burned, as was a church."

The thought sickened me and made us all take pause. After a moment of reflection he excused himself. I followed him to the door.

"Thank you for bringing me here, Mr. Purvis. I believe I will take up temporary residence with one of the ladies, so I can help with the cause while continuing my inquiries. If you learn that one of your contacts gave refuge to my family, please leave word with Sister Lucretia."

He tipped his hat and opened the door. I was impressed with this man of dignity and education.

"Excuse me, Mr. Purvis. May I ask of what race you consider yourself?"

He lifted his chin and unleashed a prideful smile. "Miss, I assure you we are one and all of the same human race." Recognizing my turmoil, he added, "Like you, my blood flows from mixed heritage. Do not fear the Negro in you. Embrace it. Embrace the whole of you."

As though I were splashed with baptismal water, his words bathed me with promise. My thoughts swirled as I watched him traverse the street. A handful of men and women greeted him as he passed. His words, *we are one and all of the same human race*, resonated in me. Lost in thought, I hadn't noticed the dowdy woman

SHADOW OF A QUARTER MOON   281

coming at me on the cobblestones. Her hair was as ivory as her skin and all that she wore was dyed a rich indigo blue.

"Greetings, sister," she said, stepping around me in a manner that told me she was a steady visitor to the residence. "It is wonderful to see a fresh face lending effort to the cause."

The chorus of women cried out, "Emma!" as she entered. They were pleased to see her, and each woman rose to hug her warmly.

Rachel clapped her hands gleefully. "When did you return, sister? We have missed you." Rachel turned to me in explanation. "Emma has been in New Jersey for several weeks."

"I was visiting relatives in Camden County," Emma said. Then, opening her arms to the group, she laughed. "I daresay, sisters, that I am truly a city girl. The rural life is far too quiet for me."

Rachel noticed me tensing at the mention of Camden County. "Jacy, you look like you just crossed paths with a ghost."

"There is a county near my home by that name," I said, releasing a nervous breath. "Hearing the name spoken stirs passions, good and bad, in me. Some very remarkable people helped me pass through her rugged wilderness."

"That is behind you, girl," Rachel said with a smile. "You are on a different path now."

I politely returned her smile, but the edginess remained within me. My surroundings were indeed different, but my path remained unchanged. It was as elusive and unknown as it had been from the start. My hope was that I had not reached an impasse.

The women settled at the table with renewed vigor as Emma shared stories of her trip. When they learned I could read, they invited me to assist them in arranging their literature and handbills for distribution. I was taken aback by the bold inscriptions and call to action on the side of abolition. Such open opinion in the South would be met with harsh consequences.

"Jacy is new to the city, Emma. She's come by way of schooner."

Emma raised her brow in surprise. "From the South?" She studied me closer when I nodded. "Ah, then you know firsthand of the horrors of slave labor."

I flushed with the knowledge that I had lived more on the wrong side of the cause than on the right. "My background gave me only a glimpse of the true burden, but my brief experience with chains, whips, and terror has changed my very being."

"Can you tell us anything of plantation life?"

"We were not sustained by the harvest of a cash crop like cotton or tobacco. I grew up on a horse farm in the eastern region of North Carolina."

Emma shuffled through a stack of papers to my right. "I recently harbored a gentleman from North Carolina who was quite versed in the care of horses."

My heart wobbled to a standstill. I lifted my eyes to her in wonder.

"North Carolina?" My breath quickened. "Was there only one man?"

"Hmm?" she responded absentmindedly as she counted a neat pile of handbills.

Heat tingled across my cheeks and scorched within my bosom. "The man from North Carolina . . . was he traveling alone?"

Sensing my strain, Emma looked up from her work and stared at me from over her reading spectacles. "He was not alone, Jacy. There was also a woman and a quiet lad with a deformed leg."

The room fell silent when I sprang to my feet. "They are my family! They are alive!"

Lucretia came to steady me. "Emma, do you know what route they were to follow?"

"They followed no northern route, Sister Lucretia. They are in New Jersey. I took them there myself."

My head swirled in disbelief, causing my legs to give out from under me. If not for the sisters of the Philadelphia Female Anti-Slavery Society huddled around me in tender support, my stunned frame would have collapsed into a heap.

Chapter 22

T ears of elation spilled down my cheeks. "Are they well?"

"They were grossly underfed," Emma said. "However, the bounty of my kitchen was a sweet remedy, though the gentleman with the bad leg ate little and slept long. If you wish, I can have my coachman take you to them. It's a little more than a day's drive."

Emma took me to her home on Broad Street. It was not as large as the main house of Great Meadow, but it was far more luxurious. "Make yourself comfortable in the guest room," she said as she opened one of five polished oak doors in her mint green second-floor hallway. "Take all the time you need to rest and refresh. I will send for a new dress and have a warm bath drawn for you."

"Thank you, Emma," I said, amazed by my turn of fortune.

Alone in the room with walls the color of pearl, I felt as if I had stepped into a daydream. The scrubbed floors and washed windows sparkled with glorious cleanliness. No mud, no bugs, no dank swamp stench. I ran my coarse palm lightly over the smooth bedposts and crisp linens, expecting them to feel foreign. To my surprise, the familiar sensation of my former life assured me that my inner self had not been lost, despite the fact that my heart remained strongly bound to those denied these simple pleasures because they were enslaved, body and soul. My perilous journey had expanded the horizon of my understanding and I had grown to be more, not less, in my meager existence.

Oil lamps, hairbrushes, and other necessities I had once taken for granted sat neatly in place. I paused as I walked past the looking glass. My physical changes were obvious and too numerous to count, yet the changes within me were far more life-altering. I was ashamed of the misconceptions I had once carried. How could I ever have believed that slaves were not capable of deep feelings? If not for the strength and inspiration of loving hearts like Violet and her children, Deacon and Bette, Tupper, Henry, and even stern Maola, I would never have conquered my demons, seen and unseen.

Abundant vases filled with flowers decorated the room, and a yellow canary sang merrily from a gilded cage in the corner, making me think of the wild swamp I had left behind. The memory did not comfort me, but I realized now that my experiences in the swamp had become the foundation for my newfound fortitude. Surrounded by fineries reminiscent of my previous life, I did not long for Great Meadow. Instead, my thoughts continued to chase after Rafe, Jerlinda, and Axel.

I crawled beneath the fragrant sheets and sank into the soft feather mattress. Laying my head down without fear or threat filled me with intoxicating peace. Delicious sleep swept me away until the morning light brought Emma to my door.

"I peeked in on you last night, but didn't have the heart to wake you for dinner. I have a bath and a hearty breakfast waiting for you. My hired coachman, Gabriel, will take you to the home of my nephew, Thomas, in Camden County. Thomas agreed to secure employment and living quarters for the group you seek. You see, he breeds horses and was very interested in adding a skilled horseman to his stable."

I kissed Emma's hand with gratitude that was impossible to express in mere words. I hurried to ready myself and when I left she gifted me with a satchel that held a second dress, a bonnet, and an ivory-handled hairbrush. Emma also presented me with a basket of corn bread, pickled eggs, cheese, and a jug of cool tea sweetened with mint for the journey east into New Jersey.

The coachman, Gabriel, looked to be fifty, with hazel eyes that gleamed against his smooth dark skin. The thinning hair atop his head was offset by a boyish grin that revealed a wide gap between his two front teeth. We rode from the busy Philadelphia streets to a ferry landing near the mouth of the Delaware River where it narrowed north of the great seaport.

My light appearance was the only disguise I needed. With my hair brushed smoothly beneath a bonnet and my body covered in a neat frock and cloak, I would not be noticed by any rogue slave catchers. In truth, there would be no handbills posting me as a fugitive slave, though one look at my calloused hands, cracked feet, and whip-scarred back would suggest otherwise. As the ferry carried us along with our coach across the river separating Pennsylvania and New Jersey, I shared some corn bread with Gabriel.

"Just call me Gabe, Miss Jacy. Only the highfalutin ladies call me by my given name."

"Then you must call me Jacy. There is no need for formality."

Anxiety tightened my belly when Gabe's light eyes detached into a submissive gaze as the ferryman collected our fare.

"Back so soon, darky?"

Gabe stared ahead. "Miss Emma sent me back with an urgent delivery fo' her kin."

The ferryman looked me over, then grumbled as he moved on. I could not help but wonder if, when he looked at me, he saw a young white woman or a light-skinned Negress. His gruff demeanor suggested the latter. I dismissed my curiosity in order to learn more from Gabe.

"Do you run human cargo very often?" I asked in a low voice.

Gabe looked around to be sure we were far from suspicious ears. "Usually just to other safe houses around the city. Other folks carry them upriver or to Jersey City. It's a rarity for us to come east. But since Mr. Tom has stables on both sides of the river, he needs all the good horsemen he can get."

"Rafe is very skilled and has a natural rapport with the horses. My father relied on him completely with our herds."

Saying Rafe's name aloud released a wave of excitement within me. I was on my way to him. I could have never imagined when I stepped from Sylvan Firth's doorstep in South Mills that my journey would take so long. Or that it would impact me more profoundly than did the moment I first heard the word *quadroon* hissed at me. When last I saw Rafe, I was still grappling with my fear of how the world would look at me. Now I found myself grappling with how I looked at the world.

Gabe and I spent the night in the carriage house of a *friend* and were on our way after breakfast. We drove into a brisk wind, the approaching winter sharp on the breeze. I marveled at the harvested farmlands rolling in every direction from both sides of the road we traveled.

I said to Gabe, "My first impression of the North was of crowded wharves and noisy streets, but beyond the city, the landscape is not much different from North Carolina."

"The winds may blow cooler up here," Gabe said, chuckling sarcastically, "but the direction ain't as different as you might think. North and South are much the same. You'll see soon enough that it's not just chains that hold the Negro down. It's the beliefs harbored in the souls that use them. Here, words and ways don't leave strap marks, but cripple us just the same."

His words hung heavy in my heart, but my immediate joy pushed all sorrow from my mind. I felt nearer to Rafe, Jerlinda, and Axel now. Even closer than when we had lived as part of Great Meadow.

Will they recognize me? Will they welcome me?

My questions twisted inside me as Gabe turned our carriage onto a long dirt lane. The sight of the expansive fenced pastures dotted with blanketed horses caused me to tremble with anticipation. When we pulled into the yard of the manor house, a man dressed in gray trousers and a matching vest strode from the carriage house. His blond muttonchops flowed from beneath a derby that sat atop his thick blond curls.

"Gabriel! I did not expect you. Has Aunt Emma been stricken?"

"Not to worry, Mr. Tom. Miss Emma is just fine."

Gabe climbed down from the driver's bench to hand Thomas a letter sealed by his aunt. He read the note carefully and then opened the coach door.

"Welcome to East Acres, Miss Lane. Please step inside where we can talk."

I expected him to escort me into his parlor for tea, and was taken aback when he led me into the carriage house, where we spoke among his buggies. "Only one of the three is on the property. Aunt Emma asked me to assist her in placing the wandering trio. I had no need for a cook or maid, so the woman was taken to my wife's aunt. She is a spinster living alone on a country estate five miles south of here. She provides shelter and a good wage to the Negroes in her employ."

"Is Jerlinda well?"

"Well enough," he said. "Though their journey was taxing. The lame one fared the worst when drained by seasickness and dehydration. I had room for only one more stable boy, and Rafe was well equipped for the task. Axel could not be put out for hire until he regained his stamina; therefore he has been staying in the colored bunkhouse. As he's grown stronger, he's been of great help around the stable since Rafe's been gone."

My heart sank. "Rafe's gone?"

"Nearly a week," Thomas continued. "But only temporarily. You see, I have a larger stable, West Acres, over in Pennsylvania's Brandywine Valley. Rafe's superior skill with the horses became evident within days of his arrival. I entrusted him to move a herd of broodmares on the hoof to my other property."

"He did the same for my father, many times."

Thomas nodded respectfully. "He has quickly become invaluable to me. The horses respond to his soft touch. My headman, Murphy, bullies the mares. He grumbled mightily when I sent Rafe in his place."

"When will Rafe return?"

"By week's end." Thomas smiled. "Aunt Emma mentioned in her note that Jerlinda is your mother. I shall have Gabriel drive you and Axel to Aunt Delfina's estate, Cloverfield, where you can reunite with her. Axel is in the barn. Let me take you to him."

Walking past the stable made me sway with emotion. The scent of hay and manure would be offensive to most refined noses, but it dizzied me with warm memories. Our stable had always been a happy retreat for me, and it was no different now. After traveling hundreds of miles, I felt connected again. Connected to the part of me that came before.

As we walked into the open door of the barn, I saw Axel limp from the rear of the building. Triumphant excitement rushed through me. He wore a slouch hat and carried a heavy loop of rope around his shoulder, the image of the quiet farmhand I had seen countless times over the years. He straightened to a halt when he saw us in the doorway.

"Beg yo' pardon, Mr. Tom. I didn't see you there. I'll get on outta yo' way." Axel averted his eyes from us, as was common when a slave was in a white presence. He did not recognize me, so I removed my bonnet.

"Don't go anywhere, boy," Thomas said. "Your sister has come looking for you."

Axel turned in disbelief. His eyes squinted as if needing to refocus. "Jacy?"

I walked toward him with my arms extended. "Axel, I feared I would never find you."

Relief moistened my eyes with emotion. Still in shock, Axel took my hands in his. "I can't believe you is here." He shook his head slowly, trying to understand.

"I had to follow," I choked out. "My life is no longer rooted in Great Meadow."

Axel grinned widely and then started laughing. "Mama's gonna melt into a pool o' tears when she lays eyes on you."

Thomas wrapped his arms around our shoulders. "Gabriel has a coach in wait, Axel. Take your sister to Jerlinda."

We needed no prodding. We hurried to the coach, where Axel greeted Gabe. They were acquainted because Gabe resided in the Negro bunkhouse during Emma's visits. Gabe marveled at me as he spoke to Axel. "So Jacy is the gal that Rafe was reminiscin' over?"

My breath hitched at the mention of Rafe's name. "He spoke of me?"

"One night in front of the fire, we got to talkin' about people lost or left behind. He said there was a gal he wanted, but could never have. Said the miles put between them didn't ease his ache. But he also said that life rambles on and he got to begin again."

Tears rose in my eyes at knowing I was not easily purged from Rafe's heart. I understood the yearning, because I lived with it as well. But the thought of him acknowledging his need to begin again rattled me. Had he moved forward? Had a woman of less complication comforted him in his loneliness? I could not blame him if it were so.

"Hey, gimp!" a voice barked. "Why is you jawing when there's chores to be done?"

Axel spun around to face a flush-faced fellow leading a gelding across the yard. He was not much taller than Axel, although his arms and shoulders bulged with muscle. Dark hair hung around his ears; his whiskers were thin and boyish.

"I am on an errand for Mr. Tom."

"Well, your work will be waiting for you, gimpy. Ain't gonna put no darky chores on the others."

When the man disappeared into the stable, I could not hide my look of distress. Axel lowered his voice to a hush. "That pasty-face is Murphy. He is kind o' like the headman around here. Mr. Tom is a gentle sort, but Murphy and the white boys don't take kindly to the coloreds. They think we is sittin' in jobs meant for other white folks. He is spittin' tacks since Mr. Tom gave Rafe some headman chores. Especially when it calls for Rafe to give orders to the white farm-hands."

Murphy's demeanor and derogatory way of addressing Axel as *gimp* disturbed me. It seemed no different from the abusive tones of an overseer, minus the whip. Gabe sensed my discomfort and hustled us into the coach.

"How did you track us here?" Axel asked excitedly as we rolled from East Acres.

"By way of Portsmouth. My chase began only a day after you left South Mills, but the Great Dismal snatched me."

Axel's jaw dropped in amazement. "Lawd, I thought only devils and ghosts could survive the swamp."

I thought of Violet. "Oh, there are some angels there as well. I had been in Philadelphia a few days when I met Emma."

"Miss Emma." Axel nodded. "Bless her soul. I don't know if I could have made it another day. Our sea voyage nearly killed me. We was kept in the hollow of the bilge, soaked to the skin most o' the way. I told Mama and Rafe to keep goin' north without me, but when Miss Emma heard Rafe talk about Great Meadow, she got the idea to bring us here. We was mighty grateful we could stay together."

"You look quite gaunt, Axel. However, your spirits are high."

"It's been a slow rise, but each week I'm a bit stronger. Mr. Tom knows a fellow at the train yard who is lookin' to hire a coal man to shovel on the steam engines. He said he would look me over when Mr. Tom thinks I'm ready. Now that Rafe is bein' groomed to be more than a stable boy, I think Mr. Tom may keep me on to work here at East Acres. Can't wait to feel a coin in my pocket. That's when I'll know I am a true freedman."

The ride to Cloverfield passed quickly. Sitting next to Axel, hearing his voice as he spoke, brought me comfort beyond measure. I didn't know if it was because he was my brother or simply because we were rooted in the same past, but I felt protected, much as I had on the day he had reached out to me on the cliff. The bond that had begun at Great Meadow had survived the miles in between.

Red and golden leaves covered the ground as we emerged from a wooded grove that echoed with the peaceful trills of cardinals and jays. "This is it," Gabe said as he turned the coach through the gate of a stone entrance. "Cloverfield."

Within the walls of the neatly groomed property stood a beautiful two-story home that glimmered with a coat of fresh white paint. Rich blue shutters brightened the facade, and an expansive porch wrapped around the dwelling to a side yard. Fields stretched in both directions; an apple orchard lay to the left and a grape arbor in the side yard between the manor and carriage houses. I was pleased that Jerlinda had settled in such a serene environment, but my experiences told me that appearances were often deceiving.

When we exited the coach, Gabe went to the side entrance to announce our arrival. My heart pounded with anticipation. Axel put his arm around my shoulders as I swayed from a sudden rush of emotion. Before Gabe rang the bell, he was distracted by activity behind the house. He peeked around the porch post to the backyard and then waved us toward him.

When Axel and I reached the steps to the side porch, soft humming caught my ear. I teetered on jittery legs when I saw Jerlinda hanging washed linens on a line tied between two trees. She had her back to us and paused momentarily when the linens lifted and smacked in a gust of wind. I stood motionless, overcome by euphoric relief. Axel squeezed my hand and nodded for me to go to her. As I closed the distance between us by half, all thought drained from my mind. Her pull on me was stronger than ever, and once again seeing her gentle movement filled me with joy.

"Jerlinda," I squeezed from my tight throat. Not hearing me, she continued to arrange the sheets on the line. I took a deep breath. "Jerlinda," I said louder.

Her shoulders hitched at the unexpected voice behind her. She turned to gaze upon me from across the yard. "Yes, miss? Is you looking fo' Miss Dee?"

I realized my bonnet was still in my pocket. My short-cropped hair and improbable appearance made me a stranger to her. I stepped closer.

"Jerlinda, it's me."

She cocked her head to study me, but remained puzzled. Tears filled my eyes as a wave of need and emptiness crashed down upon me. I opened my arms in an aching plea. "Mama."

Her eyes opened wide. "Jacy!"

The pillowcase she held in her hands dropped to the ground as I raced toward her. I threw myself in her arms and was overcome by deep-rooted sobs. We clung to each other and wept. A lifetime of maternal separation melted away as she absorbed my need. The loving embrace of my true mother welcomed me to her. She held me like none other, and I knew my journey was finally over.

She lifted my chin to wipe my tears with her apron. "How can it be, chile? How can it be?"

"Oh, Mama." I sniffled, pressing my cheek to hers.

She rocked me in her arms. "If I was asleep, I could dream no sweeter dream than this. My baby girl is in my arms again. It's like I raised my hands and touched heaven."

We did not release each other even when a grandmotherly voice floated down from the porch. "Jerlinda, I have never seen you so light in spirit."

Jerlinda pulled me to the rise of the porch. "Miss Dee, this is my girl. The one I told you about."

The chalky face of the petite woman was deeply wrinkled, but her pale blue eyes glimmered with delight. Her gray hair was pinned neatly atop her head, though several loose strands fluttered across her face in the breeze. Slightly hunched by age, Miss Dee pressed her hand to her bosom in surprise. "The light-skinned daughter from North Carolina?"

"Yes," Jerlinda said, still beaming. "This is my Jacy."

Miss Dee smiled as though she already knew me. She pulled her shawl around her frail shoulders. "Please come inside. I just warmed some cider."

Axel and Gabe joined the three of us at Miss Dee's kitchen table.

Sitting next to me, Jerlinda continued to stroke my hand, her eyes fixed on me with disbelief. I gave them a brief and gentle description of my journey.

"I was delayed in Dismal Swamp, but when I finally reached Portsmouth I was blessed to find a captain willing to take me aboard. The blessing continued when I was introduced to Emma."

"Speakin' of Miss Emma," Gabe said as he finished his cup of cider, "I need to start back to Philadelphia. Axel, I'll drop you at East Acres on the way."

Axel shuffled reluctantly. "Where are you gonna stay, Jacy?"

Before I could answer, Miss Dee interjected. "She will stay right here with us."

"Oh, my, that is very gracious of you, Miss Dee. I do not want to be any trouble."

"Nonsense, child," she said with a wave of her hand. "Jerlinda's room is down that back hallway. It's spacious enough for the two of you and will afford you some privacy while you become reacquainted."

Axel gave me a shy hug. "I'll come back fo' a visit in a few days."

"Thank you, Gabe," I said when he lifted his hat in farewell. "Please thank Emma as well. I will send her a letter when I can collect my thoughts and emotions."

We stood to clear the cups from the table, but Miss Dee shooed us away. "The housekeeping can wait, Jerlinda. Go and settle Jacy in your room. Enjoy some time alone as mother and daughter. From what you have told me, it's long overdue."

I expected to see a snug servant's quarters at the end of the rear hallway, but Jerlinda's bedchamber was roomy and pleasantly decorated. The feather mattress on the oversized bed was well dressed with blankets of brushed wool and a quilt folded across its foot. The vanity and wardrobe were simple in design, but built of fine oak, as were a small desk and chair in the corner. A rocker sat next to the hearth, where a low flame crackled, giving the room a warm, cozy feel.

Jerlinda sat down on the edge of her bed. "Never was surrounded by such fine things except when I was on duty at the main house. Can't quite get my head right with it. Axel and Rafe got nothin' more than a bunkhouse shared with three other men, while I am livin' here like a queen."

I sat down next to her. "You deserve to live in comfort, Mama."

Jerlinda smiled. "The sound of *Mama* coming from yo' lips is a lullaby to my ears. I could curl up and listen to it from sunup to sundown and still it would prickle my skin."

"It seems natural to me now," I said softly. "As if I've found my way to you, not just physically, but emotionally as well."

She placed her hand over mine. "I'm glad, Jacy. So thankfully glad."

"Miss Dee is unusually generous with her help," I said, unbalanced by an intimacy I was not used to.

Jerlinda chuckled. "She is an odd bird fo' sure. Never met nobody like her. She don't care what others think of her ways. Even Mr. Tom says she shouldn't be so familiar. But Miss Dee treats us like we is nearly kin. Her coachman and gardener have separate quarters out back that are dressed and maintained as fine as this room. She says she can't right all wrongs, but she'll try her best to right what she can."

"From what I have seen of the North thus far, you are fortunate to be in the employ of someone righteous in her beliefs."

Jerlinda nodded. "Truth is, I only do some light housekeepin' and cookin'. More often than not, she joins me in the kitchen when I am stuffin' chicken or snappin' beans. I think she needs the company of another soul more than she needs the help."

When Miss Dee ate with us at the kitchen table instead of in the dining room, I understood Jerlinda's observations. In the South, I had never seen a white man or woman move among the colored with such unassuming ease. Miss Dee laughed sweetly when she told me that Jerlinda had slept on the floor instead of in the bed during her first week at Cloverfield.

Jerlinda's smile was bashful. "After a lifetime on straw pallets, I couldn't bring myself to muss up the fine bedcovers."

"When I discovered your mother curled on the rug one morning, I threw back the blankets of her bed and refused to leave until she climbed in. The feathered mattress must have agreed with her, because she fell back asleep for more than an hour."

"I wasn't sleepin', Miss Dee." Jerlinda giggled. "I jes' closed my eyes and imagined that this must be how a weevil feels on top of a cotton boll. My bones didn't know what to make of all that soft."

I smiled at Miss Dee's appreciation of Jerlinda's innocence. I also liked when she referred to her as my mother. Jerlinda liked it as well. Each time Miss Dee used the words *your mother*, Jerlinda's chest heaved with pleasure. Her eyes remained on me the entire evening. Whenever I looked her way, she released a joyful smile that assured me I had been right in following her. We retired to our room early, though neither of us was ready for sleep. Miss Dee gave me a nightgown, since the only belongings I carried in my satchel were a dress given to me by Emma and the one I had worn on the *Bonnie Sue*. As I slipped my dress from my shoulders, Jerlinda gasped from across the room. I turned to see her walking toward me, aghast with horror.

"What have they done to you?"

She touched her hand to my exposed back. My skin tingled where she ran her fingertip along the scars left by Boss Man's whip. Her voice was tight with rage. "You was supposed to be protected from this."

Chapter 23

I lowered my head. "My journey changed me, Mama. I am not the same girl you remember from Great Meadow."

Jerlinda came around to face me. She placed a gentle hand on each of my cheeks and lifted my gaze to hers. "Don't you never hang yo' head over a hardship endured. Mended scars are proof you survived. They are a part o' the fabric of you now."

Anger burned in my brimming eyes. I had not allowed myself to dwell on the bitter fury within me that had been seeded by the cruelty of those who looked on me as an animal. Instead, I had fought for survival and clung to the hope provided by those who treated me humanely.

"My scars are not only of the skin."

"That's usually the way, Jacy."

Jerlinda helped me into my nightgown. With an arm around my waist, she led me to the vanity, where she set me in front of the looking glass. I watched my reflection ease beneath the brush she stroked through my hair and I remembered Bette restoring me as well. Jerlinda's soft eyes watched my reflection.

"Tell me what happened to yo' hair, chile."

"For me to survive Dismal Swamp, my entire identity was stripped away in one form or another. An outlier cut my locks to untangle me from some brambles. Those around me said that I entered the swamp as a mistress, but left it as a Negro."

"Yo' opinion is the only one that matters. Is that how you see yo'self?"

"I don't know how to view myself," I said with a silent plea. "When I learned you were my mother, I tried to hide the Negro in me as if it were a curse. I am ashamed to admit it, but it's true. However, the dangers I encountered on my way north made me proud and determined to protect who I am, whatever my label."

"Raising you white was meant to lead you on an easier path," Jerlinda said softly. "The choice was not made to scourge you of a black devil. You is a grown woman now, Jacy. Walk the path of yo' own choosin'."

"Mama, you once told me that I could not understand your suffering because I had never lived as a Negro. Well, I have now. My experiences lasted only a few blinks of an eye compared to a lifetime, yet they made me stronger and better prepared for the days ahead. I know fear and hate like never before, but I have also gained compassion and pride. Being white no longer matters. What I seek is happiness."

"Sweet Jacy," Jerlinda cooed. "There is no need to shed the white in you to honor the Negro. Nor do you have to deny the Negro in you to maintain the white. Yo' heart is what matters. Everything else is window dressin'."

Jerlinda tucked herself beside me beneath the covers. "Let go of yo' wonderings for tonight and give thanks that we are safe and free to talk about it another day."

She was right. I was awash with gratitude. Against great odds, I had found them. They were well, as was I. Many who attempted a freedom run met with a different fate. I had much to be thankful for. We lay in silence collecting our thoughts. My eyes were heavy, but Jerlinda had a wondering of her own.

"Did you see Rafe?"

His spoken name nudged me awake. "No," I said, turning over to face her. "He is in service at Thomas's farm in Pennsylvania. He will return in a few days."

"You are anxious to lay eyes on him," Jerlinda whispered with a knowing nod.

"Yes. How did you know?"

Jerlinda touched my cheek. "I remember how young love feels. Is he why you left Great Meadow?"

"My life there had fallen apart," I said in a hushed confession. "I want to rebuild it on a foundation of love. I cannot do that without you, Rafe, and Axel. Great Meadow is no longer my home. You are."

Jerlinda snuggled me into her arms. "We is family, chile. Nobody is ever gonna take that from us again."

At peace and exhausted by the emotion of the day, I drifted into a deep slumber. But the ghosts of my past were still unsettled within me. I dreamed of seeing Rafe on the opposite shore of a slow-moving river. My spirit lifted at the sight of him smiling at me as he entered a rowboat and stroked its oars toward me. I waved happily as he closed the distance between us. Suddenly, the river's current flowed swifter, north to south. Rafe rowed harder but was pushed past me, unable to reach shore. I ran toward the river to toss him a rope, but the slave catcher Quinn appeared beside me, groping at my arms. I screamed for Rafe as he drifted away downstream. When Quinn's apparition changed into that of Garrison, I screamed louder. He laughed at my cries and clutched my hair, which was once again long and flowing.

Damn your thick mane, he growled. As soon as the words were spoken my long tresses began falling out in clumps. Garrison bellowed in fury at the hair left dangling in his hands as I ran to the water's edge and watched in horror as Rafe disappeared around a distant bend of the river.

I awoke with a jolt. Jerlinda was already up and out. By the bright gleam of sunshine through the window, I guessed it was midmorning. Squeezing a feathered pillow to my breast, I calmed the rapid breaths unleashed by the disturbing dream. By the time I washed and dressed, my composure had returned, although a heavy foreboding remained anchored in my chest. Miss Dee was alone in the kitchen when I emerged from the room.

"I am pleased you slept well, my dear."

I nodded. "The trip drained my body and spirit more than I realized. It has been a long time since I have lain down without the threat of peril or the burden of worry."

"From the little that Jerlinda told me, you deserve the slumber."

The kindly woman's genuine care moved me. "Thank you, Miss Dee. Thank you for allowing me to spend the night and especially for providing my mother with a respectful home."

"I provide nothing she has not earned by her addition to my household," she said with a smile. "Besides, you and I know that any kindness I show her does not change the injustice that has directed her life until now."

"Did she tell you I was raised as a wholly white mistress?"

"Yes, weeks ago. Leaving was a brave choice."

I shook my head. "If I were brave, I would have recognized their plight long ago and spoken out on their behalf. Perhaps I could have appealed to my father's compassion. He might have freed them. I did not understand the horror of slavery until I bore the weight of shackle and chain."

"Each of us follows a unique path to enlightenment. What matters is that we arrive."

My smile of admiration was generous and heartfelt. "Northern women are quite different from those in the South."

"Don't underestimate your Southern sisters," Miss Dee said as she patted my hand. "There are dedicated and active hands throughout the slave states. They are more readily seen here in the North because our livelihoods are no longer dependent on slave labor. But you will find that hardship and prejudice live here as well. My family does what it can to enlighten our neighbors, north and south."

"Are you not shouted down by opposition?"

"Oh, people shake their heads and sneer, but no one bothers me." She laughed. "They think of me as an eccentric old lady who collects stray Negroes the way some biddies collect cats. Let them think what they will, as long as they do not interfere with my helping former slaves find a place to take root. Thomas, on the other hand, must be more discreet. Men of commerce can be destroyed if their business associates suspect they are too Negro-friendly."

I heaved a sigh of disappointment. I had assumed freedom would mean opportunity for the colored, but obviously there were still many ways to deny opportunity. What a discouraging prospect.

"Where is Jerlinda?" I asked.

"She wanted to gather seeds from the herb garden before winter's first snow is upon us." Miss Dee pointed through the rear window of the kitchen. "Follow the path along the maples to the pond."

A satchel of dried plants hung from Jerlinda's shoulder when I found her at the water's edge. She smiled when she heard my footsteps approaching. "I was jes' turnin' yesterday over in my mind and prayin' it wasn't a dream."

I looped my arm through hers. "It's the best kind of dream, Mama. The kind that doesn't end when you wake up."

"This pond is my special place here at Miss Dee's. It reminds me of the pond at Great Meadow."

"How can you be nostalgic for Great Meadow?"

"Thoughts of Great Meadow kept me connected to you," she said wistfully. "And to yo' daddy."

I breathed in the scent of pond marsh. "Do you miss him?"

Jerlinda closed her eyes. "With all o' my heart."

"So do I." I sighed. "What do you think he would say if he saw us standing here together?"

"Oh, he sees us, Jacy. And he is beaming his big, happy grin. He whispers on the breeze to let me know he is here with us. He is a part of me . . . in the only way the world will allow."

Tears stung my eyes. "It's sad that he could not claim his family when he was alive."

"We had love. That alone was a miracle."

"If he loved you," I asked, "why didn't he give you your freedom?"

Jerlinda contemplated my question as though she had never considered it. "Bradford thought he was takin' care of us. He knew it would break my heart to leave the plantation, because it would mean leavin' you. Maybe Bradford thought it would be cruel to offer me the choice. I don't know."

"Part of me is angry with Papa," I said brusquely. "You were made to suffer in his absence."

"Jacy, I don't think yo' father ever knew how much I endured at the hands of Claudia."

"Why didn't you tell him?"

"Had I complained, Bradford would have struck down Claudia's rough way with me."

"Exactly," I said.

Jerlinda pressed a tender hand to my cheek. "And who do you think would be made to pay fo' my betrayal?"

I stepped into her arms and held her to me. All those years I had ached with need for a mother's love when all along I had unknowingly been blessed by the purest, most selfless devotion a child could be given. Jerlinda allowed me a moment to thank her with my embrace, then shook me off to lighten the mood.

"Let me show you a trick I taught Axel when he was a boy."

She picked up a flat stone at the pond's edge. Leaning to one side, she flicked the stone sidearm, skipping it along the surface nearly the length of the pond.

"Five skips," she said, clapping playfully. "That was a good one."

Her enthusiasm warmed me. "Where did you learn to throw like that?"

"Yo' daddy taught me," she said proudly, with her hands on her hips. "Comes in handy too. Especially on moonless nights when lowdown dogs think they can corner my daughter."

I immediately thought back to the night when Garrison was pummeled with rocks by the fence. I burst into laughter. "That was you?"

She shrugged and smiled coyly as she headed for the house. Getting to know her dizzied me. I followed after her like a puppy waiting to be tossed another biscuit. When we reached the back porch, Jerlinda noticed the carriage parked in the side yard.

"Mr. Tom is here. I better put some water on fo' tea."

I left Jerlinda in the kitchen as I went to greet our visitor. I heard voices coming from the parlor, and though it was not in my nature to eavesdrop, I paused when I heard Thomas mention Rafe's name.

"The situation is not as clear-cut as you suggest, Aunt Delfina. I agree that Rafe is far more skilled than Murphy, but to advance a Negro to lead horseman will create a dry-land mutiny."

"As he is now, Rafe is nothing more than an indentured servant, only a fine line's difference from a slave."

"Be fair, Auntie," Thomas moaned. "I entrust Rafe with the care of my finest."

"Then he should be rewarded accordingly."

Thomas's footsteps paced back and forth. "These are delicate times, Auntie. The influx of freedmen has created an agitated mood among their white counterparts who are threatened by the competition for wages. The animosity is palpable on the farm."

"Most of the long-timers at East Acres are working for whiskey money and nothing more," Miss Dee huffed. "The freedmen are trying to settle and begin new lives. Give him the chance to earn true independence."

"That sounds wonderful in theory. However, Murphy and men like him will grind Rafe beneath their boots to maintain their place above him. They could bring serious harm to him and to the farm as well. I would have fired Murphy last month if I did not fear the backlash against Rafe or me. My hesitation is not motivated by greed. Without my income, my ability to help anyone is severely diminished."

His words frightened me. Yet I had no doubt his concerns were warranted. Not all Northerners were sympathizers. When in Philadelphia, I had overheard many conversations that debated colonization, whereby freed Negroes would be removed from the country altogether. Fear of the unknown was an ugly thing. Rafe's abilities should be celebrated, not vilified by those wanting more than they had earned.

"Be creative with your resources, Thomas." Miss Dee's voice was eager and encouraging. "That which Rafe values is not measured in coin."

"I don't understand, Auntie." Thomas sounded intrigued by Miss Dee's declaration, and I must admit I was equally captivated.

"Pay him in acres, nephew."

"Land?"

"Yes," she said firmly. "You have more land than you can manage in Brandywine Valley. Send him there to expand the stables. Can he earn you grand profit with his skill and experience?"

"Surely he can," Thomas said, thoughtfully sorting out the possibility in his head. "Rafe's expertise is unmatched in the region. If I can procure other freedmen or white laborers who are willing to work for a fair boss regardless of his color, then Murphy and his boys will ease off to reclaim their pecking order here in New Jersey without threat to Rafe, who will be a hundred miles away."

"You will have to ask Rafe," Miss Dee continued, "but I am willing to bet that he would seize the opportunity to have a place to live with his family, especially if he were allowed to apply his wages to acreage selected for his purchase. Both you and he would be served well by such an arrangement."

Thomas was no longer pacing. "You have outlined an interesting option, Auntie. I believe you are the cleverest negotiator in the family. And the truest innovator of ideals."

Drawn to their sincere desire to provide us with a mutually beneficial beginning, I entered the room. "Jacy," Miss Dee sang out. "I was hoping you would join us. Thomas has some good news for you."

Thomas was quick to abate my curiosity. "One of the men who accompanied Rafe to West Acres rode in last night. The herd has been delivered and stabled, so I expect Rafe to arrive back here tomorrow."

I pressed my hands to my face as Miss Dee put her arm around my shoulder. "I suggested that Axel come by carriage tomorrow morning and escort you back to East Acres to greet Rafe upon his return."

I was awhirl with elation and panic. The thought of seeing Rafe thrilled me, but much had changed for each of us in the two months since we had been apart. His new life had already begun, and I did not know whether or how I would fit into his expanded world. Physically, I was different, hardened and scarred. His attachment to Great Meadow was shed when he escaped up the Dismal Canal. Had he purged me as well?

"I have not seen much of Rafe since we settled in New Jersey," Jerlinda said when I posed the question to her later that night. "During our journey, we were so fearful that we spoke only of what we needed to do to survive. There was no lookin' back. We certainly never expected to see you again unless we were caught and returned in chains."

"Does that mean he has calloused over any feelings for me?"

Jerlinda reached out to comfort me. "You were never truly looked at as a possibility by him, Jacy. I don't know how Rafe has reconciled it in his heart. Remember, yo' father loved me dearly, but it was impossible for us to build a life together. He had to establish a life separate from me."

"Your words sound as if you know he has found someone else."

"I only want to protect you from hurt," she said. "Axel may know more than I do. But I understand the sting of lovin' a man from afar."

From dusk till dawn, I stared at the ceiling. Its blank facade revealed nothing. I ached with a pain as sharp as any I had ever known. Without my realizing it, the yearning I had first felt in the stable at Great Meadow had grown into love. In the shadow of Garrison's aggression, I had never understood *wanting* a man, but as I dreamed of all the tomorrows yet to come, not one was imagined without Rafe at my side.

I was dressed and ready to go when Axel arrived the following morning. Jerlinda chatted with him as she poured a cup of coffee, but

I could only stand in the doorway, unable to sit or talk. When we were on our way he looked at me, perplexed.

"Why is you so down in the mouth?"

Axel's eyes flickered with brotherly concern. I no longer saw him as a young slave boy hobbling around a plantation. He was a sensitive man with an unyielding sense of family. I confided in him, as I had often imagined siblings would do.

"I am afraid, Axel."

"Afraid?" He gave me a half grin. "After all the trouble you scraped through to get here? I figured nothin' could scare you now."

"I fear Rafe will look upon me with cold eyes. He and I had an awkward parting. Did he ever say anything to you about our interactions?"

Axel held loosely to the reins as he glanced my way. "Rafe said he had feelings that he had no right to act on. He said you pulled away, as any mistress would when brushin' too close to a slave."

"My reaction was in response to my experiences with Garrison. I did not know how to receive intimacy because I had only learned to defend against it. I panicked because Rafe is a man, not because he is Negro. You have witnessed my struggles with Garrison, so you must see the truth in what I say."

"Rafe was crushed," Axel said gently. "He had grown mighty softhearted toward you and thought you felt the same."

"I *did*, Axel," I said, dropping my head into my hands. "And still do. I have longed for his touch ever since. But I never got the chance to explain. That's why I am afraid. Even if I have no right to hope that he loves me, I cannot bear the possibility of Rafe hating me."

"Rafe don't hate you, Jacy. He ain't made that way."

I wiped tears from my cheeks. "Is there any chance he may still love me?"

Axel squirmed in his seat. His hesitation in answering said more than any half-truth he could speak.

"Is there someone else?" I uttered while bracing for what I could read in Axel's silence.

"The washwoman at East Acres has fussed on Rafe since the day we arrived. Charlene is a bossy gal with three chilluns who need a daddy. She can ooze like honey when she wants to."

The thought of another woman disheartened me. In my present state, I had very little to offer. My face was still yellowed with fading bruises. Add to that raw feet, cracked hands, and brittle hair, and Rafe would likely find little of the girl he left behind. I was unsure and inexperienced in ways that a woman of my age should be seasoned, and worst of all, I was now regarded as an outsider by black and white alike. Yet, in spite of the sadness welling in me, I wanted to see Rafe and wish him well in his freedom.

When we arrived at East Acres, Axel took me to the stable. Walking among the horses was bittersweet. When Axel introduced me to Charlene, I sensed her immediate resentment. She was a bit standoffish and intimidated me with her confidence as a woman with a clear plan in regard to Rafe.

Her lips pursed. "You say this is yo' sister?" she said to Axel. "She looks like she fell in a bucket o' whitewash."

"No need to be brash, Charlene. Jacy is here to see Rafe."

"Well, don't hold him up from dinner," she said with a huff. "He'll be hungry when he rides in, and I intend to surprise him with something hot and tasty."

Axel mercifully led Charlene away toward the springhouse while I stroked the muzzle of a large chestnut horse with black marble eyes. I felt close to Rafe among the horses, which both pained and pleasured me. I thought about Eclipse and wondered whether she felt my absence. Or was my affection as easily replaced as it had been in Rafe's life?

Much of the afternoon passed with me talking to the steeds. Axel paused in his chores to check on me but was called away by Murphy to help mend a fence in the pasture. He was gone quite a while, so when I heard their wagon roll into the yard, I walked to the stable door. Activity drew my attention to the barn where the wagon halted.

"Secure the horses while I take these geldings to the corral."

The voice sent shivers of excitement through me. I tried to step from the doorway but my feet would not move. Emotion swirled in my heart until my heaving breaths could not keep up.

Rafe.

Chapter 24

Rafe stood on the wagon bed, his back to me. In one easy motion, he leapt from the wagon onto the saddle of a horse tied to the buckboard. My heart raced at the sight of his composed, confident face. A light shadow of whiskers accentuated his aura of poise and quiet wisdom. Yearning fluttered within me, making it clear that tenderness had grown into adoration during our separation.

Without the haunted look of a slave, Rafe was a commanding presence. He glanced my way, nonchalantly looking past my greatly altered countenance. He was preoccupied with several beautiful golden palominos that were secured to the rear of the wagon. Elation burst from my depths as I opened my lips to cry out, but before I could call his name, Murphy stomped from the stable twirling a whip.

"Leave them spirited mares to me," he growled. "Go haul the bales to the loft with your colored pal."

The tension created by Murphy's attempt to bully Rafe from his responsibilities unsettled the palominos. His overzealous whip nipped the haunch of a young mare. The animal reared up and danced nervously, then bolted down the lane that exited the farm. Amid a rumble of hooves, Rafe spurred his horse in vigorous pursuit. I jumped from his path as he thundered from the yard, his burning eyes fixed on the frightened palomino. The power of his nearness swept me away like an uprooted sapling in a rush of floodwater.

I could not stop myself from stumbling down the lane after him. My journey to him had been so long and arduous, and now as I sprinted the distance between us I felt as if I too were riding the current of a swollen river. Still on horseback, Rafe slipped one arm from his loose brown jacket as he closed in on the errant mare before she could escape the property. He cut off her path toward the open road and redirected her along the white fence posts of the upper meadow. Most men would have thrown a lasso around the animal's neck and wrestled it into submission, but in full gallop, Rafe calmly stood in his stirrups, slipped one leg over his own mount, and then leapt onto the back of the terrified horse.

I gasped when the palomino slowed to rear up, but Rafe yanked off his jacket and tossed it over the mare's face, successfully obscuring her vision. The horse shimmied and bucked as my desperate footsteps continued to close the gap between us. Now Rafe's firm yet gentle voice could be heard soothing the animal. I kicked my heels faster, impassioned by the sound of him.

Rafe's expression softened as he leaned forward on the blinded mare's back to tenderly stroke her neck and shoulders. He carefully removed his jacket. "Easy, girl. You is safe now. Rafe won't let nobody hurt you."

He looked my way, startled by the sound of my frantic steps rushing up the hillside toward him where he sat on the calmed horse. Rafe stared with dismay when I slowed as I neared him, my face wet with tears. His puzzled gaze struck me like the blow of a sledgehammer.

There was no warmth or recognition to welcome me. My legs wobbled from the strain of the emotional and physical exertion needed to reach him. I fell to my knees.

"Thank God I finally found you," I said, opening my weary arms in his direction. His entire body tensed at the words of this frenzied woman kneeling on the moist sod in front of him. I tugged the bonnet from my head and pushed back the short crop of hair that crowded my face. "I have been chasing you since the moment we parted."

My words jolted Rafe forward on his perch. His eyes, once distant, darted over every corner of my face. "Jacy?"

Tears streamed down my cheeks as I leaned back against my heels and raised my arms to the heavens in splendid relief. My journey was truly over. He was my destination. Rafe sprang from his horse and came to me. Tossing his hat aside, he dropped to his knees and gently collected me in his arms as I wept.

"I love you, Rafe. I would have spent the rest of my life looking for you just to whisper those words in your ear."

He pulled me tight to him, his embrace now as desperate and frantic as mine. I laughed as he stroked my hair and kissed my face. "You crazy girl," he said, clutching me. "You crazy, crazy girl! How is it possible?"

My hands trembled against his face as he eased me to my feet. The feel of his strong arms and the scent of his skin welcomed me like the blaze of a rekindled hearth.

"Forgive me, Rafe," I muttered hoarsely. "I was afraid that day in the stable. I flinched at your touch because until then I had only known Garrison's abuse."

I looked up into his glimmering eyes as words continued to tumble from me. "You left believing that I had pushed you away. My hesitation had nothing to do with you or our differences. All that matters is our sameness. I want you to know that I will never regret the moment you reached out to me in the stable, because in that moment my heart came alive like never before."

Sensing my anguish, Rafe pulled me closer. "Easy, sweet girl. You are safe now. Don't need words to tell me what yo' heart feels. You are here. That says more than a hundred words spoke a thousand different ways."

He paused to gently cradle my face. Emotion swirled in me when he ran his tender fingertip along my cheek. My lips parted slightly, not to speak, but rather to invite him to me. Rafe's trembling mouth closed over mine and the miles of my journey seared through my mind. Dismal Swamp, the timber camp, the slave pen—all deepened the well within me, and I would draw from those waters for the rest of my life. Rafe clung to me, and I to him, until a gruff hand shoved us from behind.

"You damn darkies can't be trusted," Murphy barked. "You're so busy groping your yellow wench you forgot that there are horses to corral. The entire flock of you is the same: animals and good-for-nothings."

I spoke up in our defense. "I apologize for the interruption, Mr. Murphy. However, I have traveled all the way from North Carolina and—"

Rafe held up his hand. "We owe this man no explanation, Jacy. He is not a boss or an overseer."

"Though I should be," Murphy grumbled. "Thomas will regret the day he gave over the skilled labor to you instead of me. And you'll regret it as well."

"I have been threatened by worse than you," Rafe said, stepping nose-to-nose with Murphy.

"Don't be so sure about that, darky." Murphy twisted his lips into a crooked grin. "Carolina, huh? Didn't you tell us you was from Ohio?"

My heart sank when I realized my attempt to help had revealed a dangerous detail of a past Rafe had obviously kept hidden. In my excitement, I had let down my guard, a mistake that must not be repeated.

"Get back to the business of the farm, Murphy," Rafe stated. "I must report the news of West Acres to Thomas."

Murphy glared fiercely at Rafe before stepping away to rope the runaway palomino that grazed along the fence. Rafe lifted me onto his horse and then mounted behind me in the saddle. I held firm to his arm where it wrapped around my waist, securing me in the warm pocket between our pressing bodies. Our horse plodded slowly down the lane to the main house. Neither of us could speak. We simply let the wonder of the moment bind us together.

"Rafe!" Thomas called out as he stepped into the yard. "Welcome back. I look forward to your update on West Acres."

When the men shook hands, I noticed Murphy sneering at them as he tugged the runaway in the direction of the stable. My concern over Murphy abated as Axel smiled at us from the hayloft, where he was stacking bales brought in on the wagon. This was a time to rejoice. And yet instinct prodded me to be cautious.

"Jacy." Thomas bowed with dignified courtesy. "Do you mind if I steal Rafe away for a brief business discussion? Charlene is about to serve the hands an afternoon meal in the barn. You are welcome to join them."

Rafe squeezed my hands before we parted. "When I am finished, I will come for you. We got lots to talk over."

In the barn, a long bucksaw table had been pushed to the center. Axel and three Negro farmhands sat watching as Charlene ladled stew onto tin plates in front of them. I slid onto the bench next to Axel while Charlene looked me over with disdain.

"Why don't you run yo' pale-skinned behind over to the dining room."

"Pardon?"

"This table is for hardworking coloreds," she said with mocking politeness. "I am sure you would rather sit at the white table, where biscuits and a warm fire accompany the meal."

I squirmed at her bold challenge. "No, thank you. I am quite comfortable here."

"Well, maybe we are the ones who ain't comfortable," she said, still unwilling to fill my plate. "You come riding in here with yo' delicate features and acorn skin, falling all over Rafe. You ain't doing him no favor. Or us neither. We got no use for a wannabe white gal."

"The only thing I want is to be a friend to all," I said. "And to live my life as I am."

Charlene huffed. "You are a friend to no one, you tawny mutt. The whites will never have you and we coloreds don't want you neither. You carry the devil in yo' blood no matter where you sit yourself." She slammed the pot of stew in front of me. "Don't expect me to serve the likes of you."

Charlene stormed out. The men around me chuckled, although I could not tell whether they were laughing at me or at her. Axel dipped some stew onto my plate. "Ugly comes in all shades, Jacy. Don't pay her no mind."

Their conversation turned to matters of East Acres. I pushed the voices from my thoughts, along with Charlene's bitter outburst and Murphy's threats. When Rafe emerged from the main house, I hurried over to him.

"The sight of you still knocks me sideways," he said. "Jerlinda must be over the moon with joy. I can't believe you're really here."

My eyes filled with tears. "I can't believe it either. I just want to hold you and talk to you."

"I am thinkin' the same," he said, taking my hand. "Thomas has given me use of his coach so I can take you back to Cloverfield. Axel will drive, so we can be alone inside the carriage." He touched his finger to the scar on my lip where Boss Man's fist had split it open. "I want to know everything."

When we were on our way in the carriage, Rafe wrapped a blanket around me and waited for me to gather my thoughts. "I should have gone with you the night I left you in South Mills," I said. "I had no idea how much of me was filled by you. The feeling parts of me went with you, and all that remained was a hollow shell. If I had been smarter or braver, I would have insisted on going with you."

He slid his arm around my shoulders. "We would not have let you, Jacy. It would have been like lettin' you dig yo' own grave. We could barely protect ourselves. Protectin' you would have been impossible. Let's be thankful that fate found a way to bring us back together." He untied my bonnet and ran his fingers through my short locks. "I am afraid to ask what hell you stepped through to get here."

I pressed my cheek to his chest. The chronicle of my journey tumbled from me like a haunting fairy tale. He said nothing, but steadily stroked my arm to ease the anger and heartbreak unearthed in my recounting. I spit the names of villains and wept those of friends, all the while braced in his loving grip. Tears brimmed in his eyes when I finished. I could not read his thoughts or wonderings, so I whispered a hushed confession.

"My unorthodox journey has delivered me to you, though I have arrived a damaged package. Perhaps there is no place for me in your new life."

Rafe's lips quivered, yet he could unleash no words. His warm fingers gently opened my palm to expose the calluses brought on by grinding corn and shingle work. He lifted my hand to his face and caressed its roughness with his lips. Then with delicate care, Rafe ran his hand down my leg and lifted my foot onto his lap. I blushed when he untied the lace of my boot and slipped it off. He removed a can of ointment from his jacket pocket and massaged it into the cracks and carbuncles left from my barefoot days in the swamp.

"This is saddle soap," he said as he soothed my wounds. "It will soften the crusty sores that continue to bleed. Given proper care, you will mend."

I knew he was not talking only of my feet. He let his tender touch say what words could not, and I was flushed with warmth and yearning. I believed he could heal me, inside and out, allowing us the possibility of a new and beautiful journey together.

"I want to see where the whip struck you," he whispered as he slid the blanket from my shoulders. He helped me from my jacket and unbuttoned the back of my dress. He pressed his soft lips to the scars on my back and stroked them with saddle soap until I shuddered.

After absorbing each of my wounds into his heart, he eased me back onto the blanket and held me tightly. "This is why I feared you comin' with us, sweet girl. Even here in the North the colored are cursed with a hard life. Livin' white would be the better choice. Thomas and Miss Dee could help you."

"Living white might be the *easier* choice," I said through steadfast tears, "but I do not consider it the *better* choice. Not if it separates us as it did before."

Rafe was clearly concerned for my well-being. "But as you are, your tormentors will be doubled. The whites will view you as Negro and the colored are likely to target you as an outsider who can't be trusted. Our children would be caught in between as well. I'm not sure I can protect you."

"Just as I am not sure my light appearance can protect you, Rafe," I said, raising my chin to show him my wounds had not defeated me. "All I know for certain is that I love you. I do not fear a hard life. I only fear a life without you. Have you room in your heart for me? Charlene seems to think—"

He cradled my face in his hands. "I love *you*, Jacy. We have always been connected, even when there was no hope that we could build a life together."

"There is always hope, Rafe," I said, touching my fingertips to his lips. "The breadth of my pilgrimage taught me that hope is always one step ahead of us. We must press forward to keep it within reach. I do not seek the impossible. I seek only a home, family, and love."

Rafe's lips brushed over mine as he whispered, "Marry me, Jacy. And we will heal each other. Thomas has offered me the chance to own land in exchange for expandin' his stables in Pennsylvania. Come with me, Jacy. We will raise a family in freedom. Jerlinda and Axel too."

I answered with a yelp of joy. Breathing in his kiss, I could never have imagined such a glorious possibility. I thought of Mayme and her blessing of happiness. My past and my future seemed at peace within me.

We remained in each other's arms and announced the news upon our arrival at Cloverfield. Jerlinda hugged me as Axel slapped Rafe on the back.

"I'll send for the parson tomorrow," Miss Dee announced, beaming. "We shall have your wedding ceremony here in the parlor. All will be right with the world, even if only for a day."

Then, as if her proclamation tempted fate, our revelry was halted by a fist pounding against the front door. All in the room fell silent when Murphy stepped inside.

"Thomas sent me to fetch you."

"Is there trouble at the stable?" Rafe said, approaching his nemesis respectfully.

"I don't ask for explanations, you uppity chestnut." Murphy sniffed. "His instructions were to bring you home with me. I'll leave my horse with Gimpy and we'll take the carriage."

"Axel should come with us," Rafe said as he slipped on his jacket. "We may need him if there is a pressin' matter on the farm."

Murphy held a hand up to Axel. "He stays here. Thomas said only to bring you."

Murphy's insistence put me on edge. "Perhaps I should return with you, Rafe."

I saw the concern in Rafe's eyes. He shifted uneasily. "That won't be necessary. I'll be back by noon tomorrow. No rightful circumstance will keep us from bein' husband and wife."

As he embraced me, Rafe whispered in my ear, "No rightful circumstance, Jacy. I promise."

Those words haunted me that night when I crawled into bed beside Jerlinda. *No rightful circumstance.* I shook my head to release my anxiety. It had been a magnificent day and I wanted to savor the dream realized. Jerlinda sensed my restlessness.

"Ain't never lived a day without bein' on guard fo' the bad," she said softly. "But that doesn't mean the bad is always meant to be."

I rolled on my side to face her. "Murphy frightens me. He harbors a great deal of hatred and resentment."

"Him and a thousand others." Jerlinda sighed. "But Mr. Tom has great plans fo' Rafe."

"I worry that may be the problem."

Jerlinda stroked my hair. "We can't let fear cripple us. Think about the good that tomorrow will bring. You will be married to a man who loves you, and soon we will have a home to call our own. Who could have imagined such a thing a few short months ago? Let that miracle comfort you and rock you to sleep. You will learn soon enough that the peace of a carefree slumber is no more the right of a Negro in the North than it is in the South. I wish I could spare you that truth."

I dozed beneath Jerlinda's touch. When morning came, I greeted the day with enthusiasm. Jerlinda and Miss Dee had already begun preparing the afternoon meal that would follow my wedding. I bathed and tied my hair with ribbons. Miss Dee had hung a simple ivory gown over the chair, and when I stood in front of the looking glass, I was struck by the woman gazing back at me. I thought of Papa and Mayme. Would they recognize me as I was now? Would they love me? Their warm presence stirred within me, answering the questions I pondered. I missed them, but knew they would be proud of the strong and complete woman who had chased and found her destiny.

"You look beautiful, sweet girl," Jerlinda said as she entered the room, her eyes bright with pride. "Yo' papa is smilin' down on you today. I can feel him."

I gently hugged her. "I feel him too, Mama."

"Now, let's finish gettin' you dressed." Jerlinda led me by the hand to the desk. She reached inside the top drawer and with delicate fingers held up the pink ribbon I had worn as a child. A rush of tears flooded my eyes as she tied it into the short tufts of hair at the side of my head. It was an overwhelming moment between mother and daughter that I would always treasure.

The parson was an amiable man who upon being introduced to me began to pontificate about his sympathies toward the "enslaved masses to our south." I could not concentrate on his long-winded chatter as my eyes kept watch on the gate. It was nearly noon and Rafe had yet to arrive. Axel came to the window where I sat and handed me a glass of cider.

"I sho' will feel better when he gets here," he said as he glanced out the window.

"As will I, Axel. I can't shake the feeling that our good fortune is an illusion."

Axel nodded. "Like when folks say somethin' is too good to be true?"

I pressed my hand to my forehead. "I don't want to say it, Axel. It may curse us. I don't even want to think it. I just want Rafe to ride through that gate so I can cast aside these feelings as rootless jitters."

"Looks like you may get yo' wish." Axel pointed toward the stone wall. The crest of a hat bobbed from the other side where a horseman rode to the entrance. I sprang to my feet, toppling the cider from my grip.

"He's here!" I squealed. But my glee evaporated when Thomas galloped his stallion through the gate. He smiled broadly as Miss Dee opened the door to allow him entrance.

"My goodness, am I late for a party?" He chuckled, then paused at the roomful of anxious eyes looking to him for answers. I pushed my way through the group.

"Thomas, where is Rafe?"

Thomas cocked his head. "Is he not with you?"

My heart tightened like a vise in my chest. Miss Dee stepped to my side. "Your man Murphy took him away last night. He said he came at your directive to bring Rafe to East Acres."

"Oh, no." Thomas grimaced, his face draining pale. "If Murphy came for Rafe, it was of his own volition. I did not send for Rafe, nor have I seen him at the stable. Jacy, I do not know where he is, but if Murphy has Rafe, he is in the grip of hate."

Chapter 25

I gasped in horror. Jerlinda grabbed my elbow to steady me. "I don't understand," she said. "What business does Murphy have with Rafe?"

"Murphy *knows*," Thomas moaned as he clawed at his hair. "I told him that his duties would expand when Rafe moved to Brandywine. I thought it would please him to be in charge again. Charlene served tea to Rafe and me when I offered him the land deal. She must have told Murphy the details of our arrangement. Murphy would be outraged at learning a Negro would rise in station over him. It would not matter that it was well deserved."

I clutched Thomas's arm. "Would he strike out in violence?"

The hesitation in his response told me what I feared. "I have not seen Murphy since last night," he sputtered. "I must return to East Acres at once. Perhaps Charlene can reveal more."

"I am coming with you," I said.

Miss Dee motioned to Axel. "We will take my carriage so Axel, Jerlinda, and I can escort you."

Jerlinda and I ran to our room to get our cloaks. The sight of the unused wedding dress slipping from my frame and onto the floor gave us fretful pause, but Jerlinda helped me into my travel clothes and we were on our way. Thomas spurred his horse into a gallop. His urgency filled me with dread. Though our carriage could not keep pace with his sprint, Axel pushed our horses to their limit. When we entered the lane at East Acres, Thomas's horse was already tied in the yard. Through the open doors of the barn, I saw Thomas shaking Charlene by her shoulders.

"Stop avoiding the question, Charlene! Tell me what you told Murphy."

Charlene was in tears. I would have felt sorry for her had her actions not been so vile. Her eyes sprang wide when she saw us rushing toward her.

"I didn't mean no harm to Rafe. I swear, Mr. Tom. But it soured me when I heard you say you wanted him to settle on yo' place in Pennsylvania. Especially when Rafe said it would be the perfect place to start a life with *her*." Charlene's cold eyes shifted to me. "If she hadn't shown up, it would be me."

Thomas shook her again. "What did you do, Charlene?"

"I poked Murphy's temper by sayin' Rafe stole his chance at fortune by pleadin' to yo' sympathetic nature. He was furious that you rewarded Rafe over him. I didn't know Murphy would do what he did. I just wanted him to demand to be given the position instead of Rafe. I wanted Rafe to stay here so I could have a fair chance at winnin' his heart."

I blinked back hot tears. "Charlene, what did Murphy do to Rafe?" I demanded.

She turned away, not wanting to say. I pounced on her, knowing that every minute she delayed meant Rafe would be in greater peril. Axel and Jerlinda tried to pull me off of her, but I held tight to her hair until she bellowed.

"When Murphy brought him back from Cloverfield, he and his boys beat Rafe and hogtied him in the wagon. They rode off last night and ain't been back since."

"Blasted hooligans!" Thomas cursed.

I pushed Charlene aside. She collapsed at my feet as I tugged desperately at the lapels on Thomas's topcoat. "We must find them before they kill him."

"They could have gone in any direction," he said, straining to formulate a plan.

"The wharves," Charlene said, sobbing. "They took him to the wharves."

"The wharves?" Miss Dee intervened. "Why would they take Rafe there?"

Charlene looked up tearfully. "Because the wharves are thick with slave speculators on the hunt."

I sank into Jerlinda's arms, needing no further explanation of the grave consequences wrought by Murphy's actions. Barraged by re-membrances of the hard eyes and determined intent of the slave hunters perusing the wharves when I disembarked from the *Bonnie Sue*, my entire body trembled. Murphy would be assured a hand-some fee for turning over a runaway to a bounty man who was eager to return fugitives for reward or profit by selling them back into bondage at the nearest slave auction south of the Pennsylvania bor-der. Either way, Murphy would be rid of Rafe and paid well for his vengeance.

Thomas threw his hat down in frustration. "Stay here, one and all, while I try to intercede. Time is against us. These deals are usu-ally struck quickly so captured freedmen can be hustled to neighbor-ing slave states before their capture can be challenged."

When Thomas took the reins of the carriage, I climbed in beside him. He raised his brows in surprise. "I have come too far to sit by idly while others dictate my fate," I told him. "I will face it head-on, whatever it may be. The vows have yet to be spoken, but my heart is already committed until death do us part."

Thomas took one look at my raised chin, firm with resolve, and knew I could not be swayed. Jerlinda and Axel stood stoically as Thomas guided our carriage down the lane and onto the dusty road that stretched across the countryside toward the eastern banks of the Delaware River.

"The wharves on the Jersey side of the river are not as extensive as the port in Philadelphia," Thomas said after we had ridden several miles in silence. "I hope that will be to our advantage."

The reality of what had happened settled over me as the carriage bounced along in the direction of the sinking sun. In a matter of hours, I had gone from the highest high to the lowest low. I heard Jerlinda's voice from the previous night.

"Ain't never lived a day without bein' on guard fo' the bad."

Her words haunted me and now seemed a premonition. But I also remembered the words that had followed. I spoke them aloud to bolster my ability to hope. "But that doesn't mean the bad is always meant to be."

"Pardon?" Thomas leaned his ear toward my mumbling.

"Oh, nothing." I blushed. "Are the river wharves much farther?"

"Probably another ten miles," he said as he tugged the horses to a halt. "But we may not have to go that far." He pointed to a small tavern built of stone at the crossroads in front of us. "That's my wagon roped to the hitching post."

My heart lifted. "Murphy?"

Thomas nodded. "Let's hope his desire for a pint was stronger than his need for revenge."

There were only three men in the tavern, including the old gent behind the bar. Murphy and a seaman were hunched over half-empty glasses with a bottle between them. His watery eyes were emotionless when he looked up at us.

"Well, here he is now, the darky-lovin' backstabber."

Thomas grabbed Murphy by the collar and pulled him to his feet. "Where's Rafe?"

"Ain't this milky wench with you a chestnut in disguise?" Murphy's drunken fog did not soften the bite in his words. "Darkies ain't welcome here. But if you step out back, I'll gladly have a taste of the white in you."

Thomas shoved him into the corner with so much force that an unlit oil lamp fell from a shelf on the wall and crashed at their feet. Thomas pounded his fist against the wallboards next to Murphy's left ear as warning of his fury. "Tell me what you did with him."

Murphy's eyes glimmered with equal rage. "I gave you four long years, Thomas. Then you hand over prime acres to a darky you've known for barely two months."

"I handed over nothing. I merely presented Rafe with an opportunity to earn what most men would deny him. His skill and experience make him deserving."

Murphy snarled in amusement. "What he *deserves* will come by way of the whip, Thomas. Rafe is a runaway slave. Did you know that?"

"I do not believe in the institution of slavery, so the word *runaway* is irrelevant to me."

"Well, it's not irrelevant to the bounty men who thrive by retrieving another man's property. I found one who was happy to take Rafe off my hands."

Thomas slammed him against the wall again. "Damn you, Murphy. You had no right to steal his freedom. Do you place no value on a human life?"

"I have more right to take his freedom than you had right to give it. He's chattel and has no value unless shackled to a chain."

I could no longer harness my anger. "Where can we find this man to whom you ransomed Rafe?"

"It's too late," Murphy said with a sneer. "They crossed over the river at sunup. They'll be in Maryland before you step foot from the farmlands of New Jersey. Rafe is in slave country, where he belongs."

Thomas clenched his teeth as he hissed, "You are a selfish bastard, Murphy. Did you think you would benefit by removing Rafe from the farm? If so, you are as much a fool as you are a scoundrel. For this betrayal, you are dismissed from your duties at East Acres. May you choke on the whiskey purchased with your blood money. Once it's gone, you will have nothing."

"Don't be so sure," Murphy said, shaking Thomas off of him. "My gut tells me that Rafe's gimpy pal and the woman at Cloverfield might bring a handsome penny as well." Murphy snickered as he made an ominous accusation. "Tell me, Thomas. Is your business breeding horses or is it stowing runaways?"

If Thomas was as panicked as I, he did not show it. Instead, he bored his eyes into Murphy's without flinching. "You greedy bugger, are you dim-witted enough to believe that every colored within fifty miles is on the run?"

"Could be," he said, walking to his table to fill his glass. "Could be not. But I aim to find out. Then we'll see who the dim-witted fool really is. I bet this yellow Negro would fetch almost as much silver as Rafe."

"Jacy is not nor ever was a slave." Thomas was on his heels now. He took my elbow and backed us toward the door. Murphy raised his glass to us.

"Every colored is a slave at heart. It takes only a chain to make it so."

Thomas steered me out the door into the cool evening air. "We have to get back to East Acres immediately."

"What about Rafe? I cannot give up on him."

"Catching up with him will be impossible," Thomas stressed. "He is likely to be auctioned at the nearest slave market."

"I will try to find him with or without your help," I wailed.

Thomas turned the horses in the direction of East Acres. "I will do all in my power to help you, Jacy. But first we must send Jerlinda and Axel to safety. Murphy is sure to come for them when he awakes from his bender and finds both his bottle and pockets are empty. A man without conscience is a ruthless foe."

How could it have all gone wrong so quickly? We barely had the chance to celebrate our reunion when senseless hate tore us apart. Jerlinda wept when we told her and Axel of our confrontation with Murphy. Miss Dee braced my mother's shoulders.

"Don't fret, Jerlinda. We have several solid networks that can move you to safety."

"Jes' when I dared to hope fo' a good life, we have to scatter on the breeze. We came all this way to find out that chains are still only a heartbeat away. I can't bear thinkin' of Rafe cast back into the darkness."

Thomas huddled with us at the bucksaw table in the barn. "At least we've been warned and can take action before it's too late. We can send you northeast toward Connecticut or up the river into the lake region of New York. Do you have a preference?"

Jerlinda looked over at Axel and then to me. "Don't matter as long as we stay together."

I reached across the table and squeezed Jerlinda's hand. "Mama, it can't be so. I cannot go on without trying to find Rafe."

"Jacy, your loyalty is admirable," Thomas said, his eyes soft with sympathy. "But searching for Rafe would be a futile act of desperation. And one that could cause you great harm. Rafe is likely to be sold into the Deep South and perhaps given a different name by his new owner. What you are suggesting is impossible."

I bristled at the thought. "I do not believe he will be lost into the bowels of the slave markets." I turned to Axel. "Do you remember what Rafe told you in South Mills before you were hidden on the shingle lighter? You and he discussed what to do if you were caught during your escape."

Axel thought for a moment, then lifted his head with excitement. "Rafe said to make sure we told 'em where we ran from so we would be sent back to Great Meadow."

"That's right." I nodded. "No man is going to purchase a slave who openly claims another man or woman as his rightful owner. Rafe will be returned for reward. I am convinced of it."

Jerlinda's face was ashen. "What are you sayin', Jacy?"

"I am saying that I am going back to Great Meadow."

"But, Jacy," she said, her hand trembling in mine. "You can't go back. Claudia will crush yo' soul fo' choosing us over her."

"Don't worry, Mama. I will return to Great Meadow a stronger, more composed woman than the frightened waif she terrorized. There is no other who can intervene on Rafe's behalf. Any consequence Claudia levels on me will be less in measure than what she will deliver on Rafe for his role in my life."

Thomas stood and paced the room. "If you are determined to return to North Carolina, I will take you there by carriage. The journey is too perilous to attempt alone."

"Because I am a woman?"

Thomas paused. "Because some will look upon you as a woman of color. Including the woman you once called Mother."

Jerlinda and Axel were distraught that they could not go with me.

"It is far too dangerous," I told them. "If you were captured, I would never forgive myself. Knowing you are safe is my only comfort."

Jerlinda's eyes grew moist. "If we go farther north, we may never see you again. I had to bid you good-bye when you was a baby being taken to the main house. Then I had to say good-bye again after I finally got to hold you in my arms as a young woman. I can't say good-bye no more. I can't!"

I came around the table and laid my head upon her shoulder. "I know, Mama. Your heartache is also mine. The evil of others has made life unfair for those of us who wish only to be left alone."

Miss Dee's delicate hands fisted in frustration. "Thomas, there must be more we can do."

"Perhaps there is," he said as he checked his pocket watch. "Rather than send Jerlinda and Axel into the northernmost part of the region, I will transport all three of you to Brandywine Valley. If we leave before sunup, Murphy will find you gone and assume you are running north. If he is determined to cash in on your capture, he will conduct the chase in the opposite direction."

"Will West Acres be a safe haven?" I asked.

"No less safe than here." Miss Dee sighed. "Sadly, a carefree life can be guaranteed nowhere. But at least you can rejoin them regardless of Rafe's fate, though I pray for your success. Then you can settle there as planned or continue to safer ground if necessary."

I kissed Miss Dee's cheek, causing her to blush. She and Thomas confirmed my belief that good and evil were not defined by race. They were rooted in conscience and deed.

"Let's leave immediately," I said to Thomas. "Miss Dee can send our belongings at a later date."

———

We traveled a route that led us south of the crossroads where we had encountered Murphy. I was settled in the carriage with Thomas. Still, I watched the dust in our wake for any riders in pursuit. Axel sat on the driver's bench, managing the horses, Jerlinda at his side. After crossing the river by ferry, we steered clear of the Philadelphia port and its host of slave speculators. It was a long day's journey, although the anxiety knotted between my shoulders loosened the farther west we rode.

"Is we still in the free states?" Axel asked as Jerlinda gripped his hand. They glanced back, the dread of recapture glazing their faces with strain.

Thomas looked at them assuredly. "We are still in the state of Pennsylvania. The border that separates the free North from the slaveholders is to the south."

"My skin is prickled at what lies in wait over the horizon," Jerlinda said with a shudder.

"I wield a great deal of power in this region, Jerlinda. You are safe with me."

As the tranquil farmlands of Brandywine stretched in front of us, I turned my thoughts to Rafe. What if Murphy had lied? What if he had lynched Rafe and fabricated the story of selling him to a speculator? The thought chilled me to the core. I closed my eyes and imagined him alive. The tug in my heart assured me that Rafe was thinking of me and willing me to him as if trusting that I would not allow him to be lost or forgotten.

"West Acres is beyond the next hill," Thomas called to Axel.

As we rolled over the gentle crest, I was staggered by the wealth of property that filled the belly of the valley. Thomas had been modest when he had said West Acres was larger than her sister stable in New Jersey, and all looked golden in the glow of the setting sun.

"This makes Great Meadow look like a corner cabinet," Axel muttered as his jaw fell open in awe.

Several farmhands waved to us as they walked toward the heart of the property, where an array of barns, stables, and outbuildings stood with collective dignity. Equally impressive on the hillside was the main house. Built of brick and stone, the two-story home was simple in design, yet commanded the same attention given to the highly adorned country manors we'd seen along the way.

"I will take you to the adjoining property that was proposed to Rafe as compensation for heading my stables," Thomas said as we continued on. A mile or so down the road, Thomas turned the carriage onto a narrow, rutted lane. "The property is a bit neglected. I bought the homestead and land from a widow who moved west with her son and his wife. I wanted it primarily for its grazing acreage, but with some work it will make a fine home. The furniture, linens, and other necessities were all a part of the bargain, since the family had no need to double their load."

By the time our carriage pulled into the overgrown yard, dusk had surrendered to night. Thomas lit a lantern and led us into the quaint cottage. "A local merchant lived here during the summer while his house was repaired after a fire, so it should be well equipped."

He was pleased to find logs in the timber box next to the stone hearth. With Axel's help, Thomas started a warm fire burning and two additional lanterns glowing. "Make yourself at home. It's a bit dust laden and in need of a good airing, but it should prove to be of adequate comfort."

Stiff and sore from the long ride, Jerlinda eased into a rocking chair angled toward the low, crackling flame. Her hands delicately stroked the smooth cherrywood arms of the rocker. She looked up at Thomas and me. "How can a place I ain't never been till now feel so much like home?"

"Because you *are* home, Mama," I said, kneeling beside her to place my hand over hers. "Sometimes our hearts know what is right for us before our sensibilities do."

"Like with you and Rafe?" Her voice was soft and sympathetic to my pain. Heartbreak knotted inside me. All I could do was respond with a shaky nod and fight back the tears that threatened to spill.

Fortunately, Thomas bolstered us by lightening the mood with some gentle humor. "Well, it looks like Axel has made himself comfortable."

Jerlinda and I looked over to where Axel was curled on the woolen rug next to the door. With his arm tucked under his head, he inhaled the deep breaths of heavy slumber. Jerlinda chuckled. "That fine boy has earned his rest. He works twice as hard as most."

I smiled. Axel had indeed worked diligently to claim his manhood. Papa would be pleased with the fine son that Jerlinda had raised. Axel was a young man who had quietly become someone we relied on. He reminded me of Papa, and I was proud to call him brother.

Thomas unloaded a few supplies he had purchased when we passed near Kennett Square. Exhaustion trumped our hunger, so the cornmeal, sugar, molasses, and tea leaves were placed on the pantry shelf. I offered Thomas a grateful hand.

"Thomas, we will be ever grateful for your compassion."

"I was raised in a family that did not believe in turning a blind eye," he said, touching my cheek. "What you see as compassion will someday be the natural flow of kinship between all people. I am simply doing my part to shift the loathsome current."

I smiled. "Much like a lockmaster attempting to join two divergent headwaters."

"Yes." Thomas nodded thoughtfully. "A seemingly difficult task, but not impossible."

Jerlinda stood as Thomas walked to the door. "We is proof of the possible, ain't we, Jacy?"

"Yes, Mama, we are." I put my arm around her, hoping she didn't notice the rush of anxiety that flushed my cheeks. I hoped that the obstacles ahead would not be insurmountable.

"The well is behind the cottage, and the outhouse is next to the woodshed," Thomas said to Jerlinda as he opened the door to leave. "I must go to the house at West Acres and make arrangements for my housekeeper to deliver more supplies to you while Jacy and I are gone. She is a trusted Negro woman who will see that you have all you need. The valley is home to an abundance of Quakers. They are a peaceful and sympathetic lot, so you have nothing to fear in their presence. I will return at first light with a fresh horse and carriage."

"I will be ready to leave when you arrive," I said, following him onto the porch.

We looked tentatively at each other, knowing the road ahead would stretch where conscience and consequence could not be predicted.

Chapter 26

When morning came, my good-byes with Jerlinda and Axel were more solemn than those in South Mills. Our reunion had bonded us all the more, making the fear of separation heart wrenching. Jerlinda wept as I untied the pink ribbon from my hair and asked her to hold on to it until I returned. Our little family of three held tightly to one another until Thomas urged me into the carriage. My steps would lead me back into the belly of the beast, and there was no disguising the trepidation felt by all.

We were midway through Maryland by the following afternoon. Dressed in a warm bonnet and heavy cloak provided by Thomas, I was assumed to be a lady of fine upbringing. We were blessed with mild weather, which allowed us to move swiftly through long days. When Thomas secured us each a room at an inn north of Alexandria, Virginia, the innkeeper smiled sweetly at us, as though we were a couple on holiday. However, as we traveled farther south, the looks we attracted from others along the way became more scrutinizing. By the time we reached Richmond, leery glances were cast in our direction at every turn.

"Get that darky off my doorstep!"

"Pardon me?" Thomas said as he stepped in the path of a road-house proprietor who charged at me with a broom.

"I recognize a half-blood when I see one," he barked at Thomas. "I pegged you for a honey-dipper the moment I saw you help her from the carriage. What you do under the veil of night is your business, but you ain't doing it here. Keep her bare-bottomed in a hayloft, where she belongs."

Thomas grabbed the broom handle wielded by the scrawny man and used it to plow him into the corner. "Mind your manners, sir, or I will be forced to throttle you."

A soot-covered man with a droopy black mustache got up from a table across the room. "What's goin' on, Spunk?"

"This here honey-dipper is parading his colored wench through my front door like she is fit—"

Thomas choked off the proprietor's words by pressing the broom handle against his throat. The mustached gent rushed at Thomas and wrestled him off of the man he called Spunk.

"Where you from, mister? We don't take kindly to strangers throwin' their weight around town."

"I am from the great state of New Jersey, where vulgarity is seen as the measure of a man's ignorance."

"Well, ain't you fancy? I may be a common chimney sweep, but no highbrow Northerner is gonna walk in here and insult my friend."

His fist hammered Thomas under the chin. Before Thomas could recover, Spunk tackled him onto the floor. I screamed for help, but the half dozen men drinking at the bar watched in amusement. The chimney sweep kicked Thomas in the ribs, while Spunk landed several blows to his face. Not knowing what else to do, I threw myself onto the grappling men. Spunk pushed me away as the chimney sweep pulled him to his feet.

"She don't look colored, Spunk."

"I'll show you," he said, taking hold of my bonnet. Before he could yank it off, I slapped his hand away. His eyes sparked with fury, but the chimney sweep held him back.

"Let's just ask her," he said while stroking his slick mustache. "Tell us, woman. Is you colored?"

I had vowed never to deny my heritage, but fear of reprisal made me vague. "Is this how you treat your women in the South? You unfairly accuse and brutalize them?"

My frankness disarmed them, and though I tried to hide it, the remnants of my Carolina lilt added to their confusion. Fortunately, the chimney sweep remained unconvinced by Spunk's accusations.

"We treat our women with care and dignity, miss. But we got no use for Northern upstarts treatin' us like hayseeds."

He and Spunk tossed Thomas into the street. I hurried after him and helped him into the carriage. I did not look back or invite any further inspection of us. I wanted only to get our horse trotting as quickly as possible.

"Get on back to darky-lovin' Jersey," Spunk spat at us. The small crowd that had gathered erupted into laughter. "You got no place down here among real men. You are all a bunch of sympathizin' winks. Turn tail and run home."

Thomas pressed a handkerchief against a cut in his lip. Welts on his chin, forehead, and cheekbone swelled into purple bruises. "The social climate is far more volatile than I anticipated," he said.

"It's true." I dabbed at a nick that trickled blood from his brow. "We must tread carefully. But do not judge the whole of the South by plantation standards. Just as there are men like Murphy in the free North, the Southern landscape includes wonderful, kindhearted people who impugn slavery and its abuses. I owe my life to a handful of brave souls, Negro and white alike."

The ride from the lower Piedmont region of Virginia across the border into North Carolina stirred emotion in me I had not expected. I had run away from my life here only a short time ago, but the pull of the familiar beckoned me home. My eyes filled with tears when I thought of Mayme and the many times she had comforted me as I knelt at her feet with my head in her lap. Though she would embrace my return, no amount of grandmotherly love could protect me from my choices. Hard as I tried, I could not play out in my mind the scene of confrontation that would soon take place with Claudia.

Was Rafe there? What was the nature of the backlash caused by my exodus? Had Claudia admitted my heritage to Garrison or did she even now maintain that secret?

Anxiety quaked within me, so I turned my thoughts to the east, where the sun fought to break through the morning haze. I was grateful we had followed the inland route back to Carolina. It stayed west of the tidewater ports and canal banks, where I could be recognized. Unseen across the miles lay Dismal Swamp, its treachery and magnificence entwined as tightly as the briar patches and creepers that isolated the secret colonies that inhabited its belly. I wondered if Violet was safe and wished I could tell her that I now understood her choice of freedom even in the harshest of environments. Thomas noted my reticence.

"We are near, aren't we?"

I pointed to the fields stretching to our south. Shards of sunshine pierced the morning mist as Great Meadow lay spread before us. My heart clenched as we turned into the lane that led to the main house. The property was eerily still, with no horses grazing in the fields or prancing in the corrals. Even the yard looked ragged and deserted as we rolled to a halt. The flower beds along the front porch had gone to seed and a plow lay disassembled by the tack room entrance.

Thomas helped me from the carriage. "I shall secure the horse and then we will face Claudia together."

Footsteps came from the barn. I turned to see Titus emerge carrying a pail of milk in each hand. His eyes widened and when he flinched, one of the buckets slipped from his grip and spilled its contents over his shoes. He said nothing, but turned on his heels and retreated into the barn. Thomas looked over at me for an explanation. Instead I touched my hand to the lapel of his coat.

"Allow me to face her on my own," I said, bolstered by a sense of self I had never known while living on this property. "She will find me a changed and determined woman."

Thomas studied the resolve in my expression. "As you wish, Jacy. If you need me, I shall be in the barn watering the horse. I am sure I will have no trouble procuring a bag of oats on a horse farm."

"Titus will supply you with all you need."

Walking across the yard, I was struck by a peculiar sense of uncertainty about how I would be received and in what mental state I would find Claudia. I did not dwell on my questions, because as I stepped onto the porch, the door opened.

Claudia wore the same black dress as when I had left. The lines around her tight mouth and sharp eyes were darkened and more pronounced. She was noticeably thinner beneath the layers of crape. I was not sure if the months had drastically changed her or if it was my growth as a woman and survivor that made her appear more pathetic than intimidating. Nevertheless, she was quick to go on the offensive.

"I knew you would show up sooner or later," she said with bitter satisfaction.

I fought back the impulse to shrink from her. "Where is he?"

Her lips curled with disdain. "That's why you are here?"

There was no confusion or question in her response. Obviously, she knew I was referring to Rafe, which meant he had been returned to her, as I had suspected. Claudia stepped back to signal me into the house. The hall was as silent as a tomb. My eyes followed the stairs to the second floor, where I had last embraced Mayme.

"She's dead," Claudia said, her voice devoid of emotion.

My heart sank. "When?"

"Does it matter?" She sniffed.

Sorrow blanketed me as I thought of Mayme. I worried that her will to live might have faded after losing my father and then me. Before guilt could take hold, Mayme's words came back to me.

"You alone will live with your choices. Make them with conviction and certainty. . . . Let my lasting gift to you be my blessing. . . . Go, Jacy. Go and be happy."

Claudia looked at me keenly. "Where have you been all these months?"

I turned my head when she reached for my bonnet, but she snatched it before I could stop her. She looked me over, her eyes wincing as if in pain. "You are living as a Negro?" She seemed more intrigued than angry.

"I am living as myself, Claudia."

She quivered at my use of her name. "Claudia, is it? You have cast me aside as your mother?"

"You cast *me* aside long ago," I said, weary of her game. "Tell me where Rafe is. I know a ruthless speculator brought him for reward."

"That is true," she said. "But what makes you think I would pay for a runaway who tempted you into a deviant life?"

"Because you need him," I countered. "Your stable cannot thrive without his expertise."

"Stable?" She walked away. When she stopped to lean on the post at the base of the stairs, I noticed her hands were trembling. "Did you notice when you rode in that there are no horses? They have been sold."

Though this was no longer my home, the thought of the horses being gone ripped my father's spirit from the land. "Why? Did you think it would punish me?"

"You said it yourself, Jacy. Without Rafe's expertise, I could not generate profit for the farm. I rehired Virgil McVey and he suggested planting the fields with tobacco. It is a popular and profitable crop that needs only diligent hands. McVey herded the horses to Charlotte for auction and used the profit to increase our slave force to support our transition to field labor."

"Great Meadow, a tobacco plantation?"

The thought horrified me. Suddenly, Claudia came across the room. She reached out to me as if pleading for approval.

"You left me no choice. Our survival depended on Garrison. He would have stepped into your father's role as Great Meadow's proprietor."

I disengaged from her desperate clutching by retreating into the parlor. "What you do with Great Meadow is your business. I have come only for Rafe. Where is he?"

Claudia stumbled after me and latched onto my elbow. "It's not too late, Jacy. You can get Garrison back."

"Have you gone mad?" I uttered in astonishment.

Claudia's eyes sparked with excitement as she pawed at me. "We can use gloves to hide the coarseness you have wrought upon your hands. I can iron your hair until it grows long and heavy like before."

She paced the room, throwing ideas into the air. "Your cheeks are a bit bronzed, but an extra layer of powder should conceal that. You really must stay out of the sun, Jacy. I will ask Garrison to dinner. Yes, a reunion dinner. I have not told him you are of Negro blood. We can tell him your erratic behavior was induced by the shock of your father's death. We will beg for mercy and forgiveness."

Her hysteria alarmed me. "Stop, Claudia! Stop and listen to me."

She paused. Frantic tears dripped down her face as I gripped her by the shoulders to keep her focused on my words. "I no longer cower like a mongrel. Nor do I conform to servitude because I am a woman. Do you know why?"

Her expression sank with shame as I raised my chin with pride. "Because I *am* a quarter moon, Claudia. At first glance, I may look like a piece of this or a sliver of that, but look closer. Revealed in the shadow of a quarter moon is its wholeness waiting to emerge. It's true. You can see its completeness. Only a dim outline at first, but slowly it sheds its shadow and glows with magnificent fullness."

"But you will forever be marked as a Negro. You *cannot* believe that is a better choice."

"The choice I make is to be loved for who I am, wholly and without compromise. Jerlinda, Axel, and Rafe have embraced me like none other. We are building a life together. Rafe is a good and decent man. I am in love with him. If necessary, I will drop to my knees to plead for his freedom."

Claudia walked to the window, taking time to absorb all I had said. "You have left me in ruin."

Her words were not spoken in anger or bitterness, so I gently continued my appeal. "For all the years we lived as mother and daughter, I beg you to have mercy on Rafe."

"If you love him as you say," she said, "are you willing to barter for him?"

My heart raced with elation. "I will do all in my power to procure his freedom, even if it means asking Thomas for a loan. He will gladly invest in Rafe's return."

"I do not want money, Jacy." Claudia's stare was earnest with intent. "I want *you*. An even exchange. Rafe can go if you stay. Tell me, Jacy. Do you love him enough to trade your freedom for his?"

Chapter 27

My mouth dropped open in disbelief. "You can't be serious."

"Oh, but I am." She nodded vehemently. "It brings me no pleasure, Jacy. But my freedom is at stake as well."

"*Your* freedom?" Her self-pity infuriated me.

"Without you or your father, I have no way to secure the income needed to run this property. Virgil McVey is a capable overseer, but he is ill equipped to negotiate business arrangements. I am too old and settled to find another husband who can take over my affairs. With some careful manipulation and humble pleas, I can repair the damage you have done with Garrison."

Anger burned my cheeks. "I will never succumb to that ogre again."

"Then we will forget Garrison," she said, waving her hands in the air as if erasing him from the discussion. "You have youth and fine features that will entice a better man. There is an abundance of suitable bachelors in Raleigh. We will make an effort to travel there for social functions."

I grabbed Claudia's shoulders and shook her. "You cannot force me to be a concubine for your comfort."

Her eyes grew tired and her face drained of expression. "Daughter, I am not forcing you to do anything. I am giving you a choice. Your cooperation for Rafe's freedom."

I pulled at my hair in frustration as I flopped onto the settee. "Do not call me *daughter*. A mother would not ask her child to toss away her life. Does your cruelty have no end?"

"What I ask is not cruel," Claudia said, dropping to her knees in front of me. Her glassy eyes darted over my face, desperate to find the submissive child I once was. "A daughter's purpose is to sacrifice for her family. I wed your father to secure comfortable station for my mother after my father died. As the eldest daughter, it was my duty, not that my sister ever uttered a word of gratitude."

"Perhaps Aunt Sarah believed you married for love," I countered calmly.

Claudia rocked back and forth, still grappling to restore me as her bargaining chip. "You will lead a good life here with me, Jacy. And your reward will be in knowing you gave that worthless slave you care so much about his freedom. I will even vow to never pursue Jerlinda and Axel as runaways."

Her words twisted in my depths. "What you ask will lynch my soul," I said, feeling a noose of compromise tighten around my throat.

She reached out and grasped my hands, trying to offer tenderness, but her groping fingers felt like the claws of a predator. "My offer is generous, Jacy. It is the only scenario in which Rafe will leave a free man."

She had me and she knew it. I despised her pompous ignorance. Claudia truly believed she was charitable in her barter for me, yet her self-preservation came at an outrageous price. How could my incredible journey end where it had started? Perspiration moistened my cheeks, or was it tears? I would not stand in the way of Rafe's freedom. With no other option, the outcome was predestined. I suddenly felt cold and alone.

Wiping tears from my eyes, I stood with straightened shoulders to show the resolve in my decision.

"I will remain at Great Meadow if Rafe is released immediately. Please take me to him."

Claudia crossed the room to the rolltop desk. She removed a brass ring with two keys from the top drawer. "He is in the icehouse. Bring him here and I will sign his free papers."

With keys in hand, I rushed from the house. I called out for Thomas as I ran, but he was nowhere in sight. I wanted to get to Rafe as quickly as possible, so I continued down the path through the lower fields to where the icehouse stood near the pond. My hands were shaking when I reached the windowless building and fumbled to slide the key in the padlock securing the door.

"Rafe, it's Jacy," I called out as I jiggled one of the keys in the keyhole. "I am here."

In spite of the crisp morning, my palms were moist with sweat. I heard no movement inside, which unleashed a searing wave of panic within me. "Please do not let me be too late," I pleaded as the key finally turned and the jaws of the lock released.

The building was set atop a ten-foot hole with crude wooden steps leading into the hand-dug pit. The cold, dank interior smelled of ice and wood shavings. Only a few blocks of ice remained stacked in the pit, most having been used during the summer and autumn months. Soon, the frigid return of winter would begin the cycle of replenishing the ice supply for the coming year.

The light from the open door was all that illuminated the shadowed pit. There, curled and shackled in the damp sawdust, lay Rafe.

I scrambled down the steps and knelt over his limp body. Touching Rafe's cold, tight hand, I cried out as the biting chill of death clung to my fingertips.

"No! No!"

Inconsolable horror ripped through me, but shockingly, my screams caused Rafe's eyes to flutter. I frantically rubbed my hands up and down his clammy arms to give him warmth until, finally, his eyelids peeled open.

"Rafe!"

His chains clanked when he lifted his cold palm and pressed it against my cheek. "Am I dreamin'?"

I pulled him to me. "You are not dreaming, my love. You are waking from a long nightmare. But it's over now. Let's remove your chains. You are free."

My heart skipped when I heard footsteps behind me. It was Thomas.

"Help me, Thomas. Take this key and remove Rafe's shackles."

"You have found him!" Thomas scurried into the pit and went to work on the locks anchoring Rafe in the makeshift prison. The reel of the chains falling away thrilled and sickened me, but with Thomas's help we carried Rafe into the late-morning sunshine.

"We must take him to the house to warm him with tea and blankets," I said.

Rafe regained his footing and wits by the time we got him to the main house. As we crossed the porch, Claudia opened the door, but stood squarely in its frame.

"You are not bringing that lowly slave into my house."

"Stand aside," I said.

"Unless a Negro is in service, he has no place in my home."

"I am a Negro, Claudia. Was I not in your home a few minutes ago?"

She cringed at the point I flagrantly threw in her face. "Besides, Rafe is not a slave," I continued. "It is a fact by your own decree."

Claudia was clearly flustered. She looked at Thomas guardedly, then stepped back to allow us to enter. Bracing Rafe under his shoulder, I led him to the dining room hearth, where a fire blazed. Thomas threw several logs on the flames while I gathered blankets to wrap around Rafe's shivering body. Tess appeared from the kitchen with a tray. She carefully avoided my gaze as she poured two cups of hot tea meant for Thomas and me.

"Bring one of those cups here," I said with my arm around Rafe. "And simmer some broth for him as quickly as possible."

Tess glanced at Claudia as though questioning my authority. Claudia nodded for her to follow my directive, which sparked a flash of surprise across Tess's terminally solemn face. She disappeared into the kitchen and returned a short time later with a steaming bowl of consommé. As I spooned it into Rafe's mouth, he stared at me.

"How did you know where to find me?"

"I remembered you telling Axel that if any of you were ever caught, you were to confess to belonging to Great Meadow. You were right in your contingency tactic, because when Murphy mentioned that you were in the hands of a bounty man, I knew in my heart I would find you here."

"Jacy was hell-bent on following your tracks," Thomas said from across the room. "But we still have a prickly issue to resolve." He turned to Claudia. "Mrs. Lane, I will never engage in the purchase of another human being. However, I will compensate you generously for Rafe's document of ownership, which will be turned over to him upon signing."

Claudia leaned against the archway of the dining room. She stared at me as she spoke to Thomas. "My needs are long-term, sir, and cannot be satisfied by a simple monetary payout that will dwindle in the face of debt."

"But I am willing to negotiate a generous settlement."

Claudia retreated to the parlor and returned with a piece of folded parchment. "Jacy and I have already reached an understanding. Rafe's papers are signed and his to keep."

Rafe's face lifted from his teacup. "My free papers? Just like that?"

"Just like that," she said as she handed the document to Rafe. "And with no fee or delay. You may leave at once."

My heart melted at Rafe's prideful grin. It was so pure and unexpected. He gathered me in his arms and spun me around. "I can't believe it! When Murphy held that gun to my head and handed me over to the slave hunter, I thought all was lost. Now no one can call me *runaway* or chain me as a fugitive from the law."

Rafe's elation touched my soul. Biting my lip to keep from crying, I smiled weakly when he brushed back the locks that dangled along my brow. His giddiness slowly dissipated and guarded intuition clouded his face. "What aren't you tellin' me, Jacy? Deep in your eyes, I see pain. There is more to know; isn't that right?"

"Some concession was required," I said as I clenched my jaw to steady my smile in a desperate masquerade. "But your freedom is guaranteed."

He turned to Claudia. "What price did you demand for my release?"

"I require only that Jacy remain at Great Meadow," she stated flatly. "Everyone's needs are served."

Rafe shifted his frame to stand poised between Claudia and me. "All, except for Jacy's. What about her needs?"

"Her life here will not carry hardship, as would a life with you. I mean that not as an insult but as an observation of the truth."

"Is this what you want . . . to stay?" Rafe's dark eyes caressed me with care. He stepped closer. "Don't be afraid to say if your heart tells you so. I will love you no matter your choice."

His willingness to let me go made me love him all the more. Rafe deserved to be free. Knowing he would take care of Jerlinda and Axel helped me to bear the pain of the lie that was needed to seal the deal. I lowered my head to shield him from my sorrow. "Take your paper and go before she changes her mind."

Rafe slipped a gentle finger under my chin and lifted my tearful gaze to his. "Now answer me with your heart."

I felt his loving eyes peel away my guilt and conscience so the devotion in my soul could not hide. He smiled tenderly, then stared at the signed document in his hand. My heart sank as his chin quivered with anger and determination. A calm aura of uncompromising pride slowly inflated his broad chest. I read his thoughts, and my eyes sprang wide.

"Don't do it!" I cried out, but it was too late. Rafe looked over at Claudia and watched her gasp as he crumpled the parchment and tossed it into the fire. "True freedom should allow me to live life on my own terms, and that does not mean leavin' Jacy behind."

"Rafe, no!" I reached to grab the paper from the flames, but he held me to him.

"We'll stay here together, sweet girl. Neither of us will be free, but we will have each other."

Claudia pulled me from Rafe's arms. "You cannot live here as a Negro, Jacy. If anyone suspected the truth, it would ruin me."

I pried free of her and returned to Rafe's side. "I will never again deny who I am. If Rafe will not leave without me, then I will stay here as your slave, not as your daughter."

The creak of floorboards came from the front hallway. I reached for Rafe's hand when Virgil McVey stepped into the room with his shotgun raised and aimed our way. "Is everything all right, Mrs. Lane? I noticed a strange carriage in the yard."

Claudia's breathing grew shallow. I expected her to launch into a venomous rant and order the vicious overseer to apprehend us; instead she began to tremble. Claudia was as shaken as I at McVey's sudden appearance. Panic flashed in her strained eyes. How much of our debate had he overheard? She squirmed to respond, but when words failed her, McVey came to his own conclusions based on her agitated demeanor.

"Looks like I got here just in time," he said, pressing the barrel of his gun to Rafe's cheek. "What kind of fool would I be if I let a brazen Negro run off for a second time?"

Rafe released my hand when the overseer shoved him against the wall. I tried to intervene, but McVey shook me off his arm. "It's not what you think, Mr. McVey," I pleaded.

Anger curled the overseer's mouth into a snarl. "I should have seen you was under their spell that day I found you in the slave quarters. That's how these uprisings start. A few bold ones trick you into thinking they're harmless; then they come back to fire up the rest."

Thomas's hands fisted with distress, but he and I were both held at bay by the sight of the cocked gun pinning Rafe helplessly against the wall. Any quick movement could spark a tragic response.

"Sir, Rafe poses no threat to you or to this woman," Thomas stated, his voice tight with caution. "I can vouch for his character."

"Character?" McVey huffed. He looked Thomas over from head to toe. "You don't look like no bounty man. That makes you either a sympathizer or a dirty dog. Which is it?"

"I am here to negotiate—"

McVey raised his aim from Rafe's cheek to the back of his head. "The only negotiating in this room will be done by my shotgun."

I spun around to Claudia. "Mother, please! Don't let him do this!"

Claudia's hand trembled against her breast. In her stunned expression, I saw years of lies and manipulation unraveling at her feet. She wobbled as if ready to faint. "Oh, it's Mother again, is it?"

I hurried across the hallway to where she wavered in the entrance to the dining room. I slipped my arm around her elbow, partly to support her before she wilted, but mostly to bring her near enough for me to whisper, "It's over, Mother. Life as you knew it cannot be salvaged. A violent incident will only draw attention to the whys and hows. Nothing can be gained by holding us hostage."

Claudia did not look at me. She stared blankly ahead, her shoulders heaving under the weight of inescapable duress. Her head moved slowly from side to side, as if conflicting thoughts were embattled within her, until finally she shifted her gaze to McVey.

"Lower your weapon, Mr. McVey," she said weakly.

"But, Mrs.—"

"I said lower your weapon!" Claudia's bark got his attention, even though her pale face was drained of expression. "This is still my home and my property. You will do as I say and ask no questions. Go and see to the fields."

McVey relaxed his finger off the trigger. He held his threatening pose for a moment more before finally lowering the shotgun to his side. He glared at me with a measure of disdain so thick and heavy, I thought it might ooze from his pores. A sudden chill set me to trembling and did not recede until McVey stomped from the house, slamming the door behind him.

I stepped toward Claudia, but she turned her back to me. "Get out, Jacy. You no longer have a place here."

"Will you release Rafe?" I said, touching her arm in a gentle plea. "Without condition? We simply wish to begin a life together."

She glanced back at me, her eyes awash in defeat. "Take him and be gone. I am too exhausted to care what happens to any of you. I could reclaim you and Rafe, maybe even track down Jerlinda and her son, but what would be the point? You are all sad reminders of my misery." Without a hint of remorse or sentiment, Claudia stepped into the dining room and closed the double doors between us.

Time was of the essence. We did not want to risk Claudia changing her mind, so Rafe and Thomas rushed to ready the carriage as I hurried upstairs to gather a few personal items from my bedchamber. The room was as I had left it, though damp and chilly with no fire in the hearth. I quickly tossed some clothing and a few keepsakes in a trunk and dragged it into the hallway. I paused outside Mayme's room, feeling her spirit call to me.

Opening her door, I was hit by a wave of sadness. I took a moment to sit on her bed, just to let her memory gather around me. From the corner of my eye, I noticed her small tin box on the mantel and remembered her showing me her precious keepsakes on the day we parted. When I lifted the lid, a tearful gasp escaped me. Added to the spectacles, button, and ring belonging to my grandfather was Papa's gold pocket watch and a brooch he had given me on my sixteenth birthday. Remembrances Mayme had held dear in our absence.

Her closet and drawers were emptied, no doubt by Claudia, the contents possibly sold. However, Mayme's lace night bonnet was folded neatly on her bedside table. I placed the bonnet in the tin and tucked it under my arm. Hurrying down the stairs, I stared at the closed doors of the dining room as I crossed the front hallway and stepped out the door.

"There is a trunk in the upstairs hallway with some of my belongings," I said, rushing into Rafe's arms.

Thomas stepped around the carriage. "Stay here with Rafe. I'll bring down the trunk."

Rafe embraced me. "Are you okay? I know you are losin' a lot by leavin'."

I kissed him tenderly. "What I am gaining far exceeds any material loss brought by my exodus." I leaned close to kiss him again, but was distracted by the shrieking whinny of a horse inside the barn.

Instinctively, Rafe turned to seek out the distressed animal, and I followed after him. Old suspicions stirred in me. Could Titus be luring us into a trap? Rafe took my hand as we rushed across the front yard toward the ruckus. By the time we reached the barn, Rafe and I were gripped in tension. When the barn door swung wide, my breath heaved from me in a wild yelp. There was Titus holding the reins of a neglected Appaloosa.

"Eclipse!"

I ran to stroke the mane of the young horse that had first connected Rafe and me. She had filled out and matured into a sturdy filly, but her haunches were bruised and scarred—evidence of abuse.

"She's been cryin' out back o' de barn," Titus said, jiggling the reins nervously. "I think she sensed you was here."

Horrified by her battered condition, I ran to soothe her. Rafe joined me in greeting our old friend, who stomped restlessly as Titus handed over the reins to Rafe. Titus said nothing more, though I could see regret in his eyes. Behind him was an old wagon hitched to a carriage horse. I assumed he would climb aboard the wagon and head to the fields; instead he glanced toward the house, then strode away along the fence to the lower pasture.

As soon as Rafe and I placed our hands on Eclipse she began to settle. We stroked her from head to tail, carefully avoiding her wounds. Tears filled my eyes when her muzzle explored my neck.

"You're safe now, girl," I whispered in her ear. "No one will hurt you ever again."

I returned to the main house and opened the front door just as Thomas came out with the trunk. "Jacy, we must not linger here. No good can come of it."

"I shall be along in moment, Thomas."

Inside, I stepped tentatively toward the dining room. I cracked open the doors and saw Claudia hunched in a chair by the fire. She did not acknowledge me when I approached, and I spoke matter-of-factly so as not to antagonize her. "I thought you sold all the horses."

She gazed into the flames. "All except the workhorses, of course."

"And Eclipse," I said, causing her to look up at me. Claudia's eyes were sunken and dazed. She had no idea what I was talking about, though it did not take much to jog her memory. "The horse that Papa gave me."

"Oh, the Appaloosa," she said reticently. "Garrison insisted that I not sell her. I don't know why. He hates the animal and beats her incessantly. He rides out here every now and then to see if I have received any word from you."

"I am taking Eclipse with me."

I braced for an argument, but instead tears trickled down her ashen cheeks. "Take her. She is of no use to me. No one will believe her to be a suitable breeder in her condition."

Claudia seemed so vulnerable and alone. I could not help but respond. "What will you do, Mother?"

"I honestly don't know," she said. "I have spent a lifetime fighting to secure a reputable status. I am tired, Jacy. I am just so tired."

"It is never too late to lay claim to the good in your soul," I said, kneeling to offer my encouragement. "Perhaps you can sell Great Meadow and buy a modest home near Aunt Sarah in Charleston. If you embrace family with an open heart and mind, they can fill your emptiness and make you stronger. My experiences have proved this to be true."

Claudia's lips creased into a weak smile. "I wish I possessed your naive optimism, Jacy."

"Mother, we are no longer bound to a secret that forced us both to withdraw in fear. We are free to live without the burden of hidden shame."

Claudia scoffed in bitter amusement, yet her eyes shone with a hint of admiration. "I was always so focused on hating what you were," she said softly. "It left me unable to love." She motioned toward the large oak table that stood at the center of the room. "I have prepared another set of papers for Rafe, as well as for Jerlinda and Axel. I assume you know where they are. Their freedom will be as legitimate as yours."

Claudia paused to pat her cheeks dry with a handkerchief. "Your father's love makes you deserving of an inheritance," she said as she straightened in her chair to regain the appearance of dignity. "If nothing else, I have earned what Great Meadow can provide me, but I will send you off with a horse and wagon to use in your new life. I have instructed Titus to bring them to the front yard. Leave before McVey takes matters into his own hands."

Suddenly Claudia's life appeared emptier and less open to possibility than that of my slave mother. I was awash with pity as her bitter shell fell away and her humanity was revealed. When I touched her hand, she lowered her head and brushed her thumb along the tip of my finger. The gesture was ever so slight, but it was sincere.

Perched next to Rafe on the bench seat of our wagon as it rolled in the midday sun, I was no longer the broken woman I had been the first time I had left Great Meadow. Rafe stared at the papers Claudia had signed and sealed declaring him, Jerlinda, and Axel as free. He bit his lip as he struggled to find words, but could not. From time to time his eyes brimmed with emotion while we followed in the tracks of Thomas's carriage. I rested my head on Rafe's shoulder, not ever wanting to be out of reach from him again. I understood our fate was unique. Countless slaves were separated from loved ones every day, lost to one another forever. Very few ever secured free papers, even in the North. With gratitude swelling inside me, I vowed loyalty to the network that had aided us. When we reached the next crossroads, I was nudged by an irrepressible need.

"South Mills is a short distance to the east. There is something I must do before going north."

Rafe sensed my urgency. "You sure?"

"There is a former slave who lives in a maroon settlement in Dismal Swamp. Violet saved my life at great risk to herself. Sylvan Firth will know where to leave supplies that may find their way to her hands. If not, they will still help someone like her who is in need. I promise we will not linger."

Thomas was anxious about our change in course, yet he resisted Rafe's suggestion that he continue on without us so his return to Pennsylvania would not be delayed an additional day. "Even with free papers in hand, you are not guaranteed safe passage," Thomas said. "Let us stay together, unified in purpose."

I grew queasy as we rode swiftly toward South Mills. I owed Violet a great debt, and like so many benefactors who had reached out to me in my journey, I was compelled to take a risk to do what was right. However, as the town and swamplands appeared on the horizon, Claudia's haunting remark about my naive optimism prickled my skin like gooseflesh.

Chapter 28

I lowered my head as our wheels rumbled through the heart of town toward the lock. With wagons hauling supplies to and from the lighters along the canal, no one had the time or inclination to take notice of us. The danger in our return was palpable now. Garrison could cross our path at any moment. If my reputation had been maligned by scandal, it would take only one familiar face to put a whirl of small-town gossip into motion. I could endure the scuttlebutt, but I feared it could derail our relocation to the North. Thomas followed as we pulled our wagon behind the livery.

As we approached the canal, I saw Sylvan Firth at work in the lock station. His light hair was longer and more wind-tossed than when last I saw him, but his familiar butternut-colored jacket was a welcome sight. The water level of the South Mills lock was raised from the Pasquotank River so that two shingle lighters could begin their journey up the canal to Deep Creek.

"Good afternoon, Mr. Firth!"

Sylvan nodded at me without recognition as he cranked the mechanism that opened the lock gates. Then, as if he'd been struck by a revelation, his head snapped back in my direction. Horror darkened his expression. He motioned for me to wait for him to finish his task so he could leave the lock station to speak to me.

"Thank goodness," I said to Rafe as we walked along the canal next to the open lock. "I see no sign of the *Southern Gale.*"

I started to tell Thomas of Garrison's steamer when a bearded man on the lighter that exited the lock caught my eye. I grinned in amazement at the thick, protruding ears and evenly cropped hair of the burly canal man who moved to secure ropes at the rear of the vessel.

Caleb Briggs.

He was alive! I thought he had been shot when Henry and I escaped to our rescue ship, the *Bonnie Sue.* I hesitated to call out because it might implicate him in my escape. Besides, if he had seen me as the lighter nudged away, he would wrongly assume I had been captured and his effort gone for naught. But the sight of him riding out of view lifted my spirits with relief and gratitude. A tap on my shoulder spun me around.

"Jacy Lane? Can it be you? You have changed considerably since your abrupt departure."

"I have indeed, Mr. Firth," I said. "We are about to begin our second and final journey to the North, but first I need to speak with you."

Distress paled his cheeks. "I will instruct my apprentice to attend to the lock so we can talk in private. Go to my barn and I will follow in a few minutes."

When Sylvan arrived, I eased his worry by explaining the reason for our unexpected appearance.

"Thank goodness your journey to the North was successful. I have thought of you often and pondered your fate. Rafe's recapture was a cruel twist that has become an increasing occurrence, with the lucrative rewards paid to slave hunters. You are blessed with a positive outcome, but I fear you are tempting fate by being here."

"Is Garrison in town?"

"I have not seen him in a few days," Sylvan said with a puzzled shrug. "He divides his time between South Mills and Deep Creek. Some say he's got a new lady there, but our friend Archie says Garrison spends a great deal of time prowling the canal."

"For me?"

"For something that slipped from beneath his arrogant thumb," he said with ominous warning. "His conceit makes him obsessed with vengeance."

I recognized Garrison in Sylvan's words. He did not love me, but had arranged to *have* me. He'd be damned if a woman, any woman, was going to throw that offer back in his face. His obsession with finding me had little to do with reclaiming me. He needed to humiliate and reject me on his own terms.

"Then let us not waste another minute," I said. "An outlier in the swamp told me you occasionally leave supplies at a secret location for those in need to find. I wish to do the same before returning to the North."

Sylvan sketched a crude map in the dirt with a stick. "November dusk comes early and is the best time to slip in and out of town unnoticed. Follow the canal bank to where it meets the swamp forest. There are remnants of a stone wall that leads to a crumbled chimney where a cabin once stood. The area is grown over and well hidden. Leave the supplies at the base of the chimney. They are usually gone by the next day. Gather your bundles behind the livery, where you will have easy access to the swamp without notice of townsmen milling about the street. When your task is complete, come to my home by way of the back door. I will provide you shelter tonight so you will be rested and well fed for your journey home.

Now I must return to my duties at the lock before someone comes looking for me."

"We are indebted to you again, Mr. Firth." I tugged on the sleeve of his symbolic butternut-colored jacket. "I see you are still active in your secret cause. Our thanks will be given by way of support in the freedom network that delivered us. Ours will be a safe house to others."

He bowed respectfully. "I can think of no finer payment."

We scattered to make some discreet purchases. Thomas bought a hammer, a machete, a few suckering knives, two axes, and a bag of nails. Rafe was forbidden to enter the shops, so he waited outside as I carried my small tin of heirlooms into the mercantile. I browsed the shelves for supplies I thought would be the most helpful. I leafed through several children's books, including a basic schoolbook that devoted each page to one bold letter and a corresponding picture.

A . . . Apple. B . . . Bear.

I smiled, thinking of Rose and Lyle. After much consideration, I placed an iron skillet, two hand mills, several satchels, and two books on the counter. One was the picture book of letters and the other the Bible. I had faith that Rose would someday read one as easily as the other.

The short, redheaded woman at the cash register watched me poke through the contents of the tin for payment. Each keepsake had special meaning, but Papa's gold pocket watch would carry the most monetary value. Besides, I still had the brooch he had given me on my sixteenth birthday. That would be keepsake enough.

"Will this gold piece cover the cost of these items?" I said, showing her the watch.

The woman tapped her fingers impatiently on the counter as she looked over my selections. She took away one of the hand mills and waited for my reaction.

I did not have the time or the talent to barter, so I nodded in agreement. As I handed over the watch to the shopkeeper, I noticed a stack of stationery paper neatly etched with deep purple violets in the corners.

"My daughter is quite artistic," the woman said when she saw me admiring the design. "Her personalized letterhead is widely sought after."

"Can my purchase include one sheet of paper?" I asked. "And the loan of a pen?" The shopkeeper rolled her eyes and rustled through the shelves beneath the counter.

I brushed my thumb over the violet. It was a silly thought, but I was deeply warmed by sentiment. The shopkeeper set an inkwell on the counter and handed me a steel-nib pen. With two broad strokes, I curled the letter J and the letter C across the paper. The shopkeeper pursed her lips with sour disapproval as though I had ruined her daughter's precious artwork, but I blew it dry and tucked it in my pocket.

Behind the livery, Thomas lit a small fire to keep us comfortable as we watched the waning sun disappear. He crouched to warm his hands, then looked to where Rafe and I huddled. "Let me deliver these goods on my own. Going as a group might draw a suspicious eye on us."

"I agree," Rafe said as he wrapped a blanket around me. "But I should be the one who takes the risk. You have done more than enough, Thomas."

Thomas put his hand on Rafe's shoulder. "If someone comes upon a Negro carrying axes and knives in the night, you would be hung without question. As a white man, my motives are more easily disguised."

"Then we will go, the two of us, on foot," Rafe countered. "It should take no longer than an hour."

·

I grudgingly gave in to the sense of it. I placed the stationery in the satchel with the skillet and watched them trudge into the night. The moon was full and would aid in their swift return. Having previously run the path to the swamp's edge, I knew they would be back in no time. And yet the subtle hint of decay floating on the breeze from the Dismal stirred a strange foreboding in me. Using a stick, I poked the smoldering logs to unleash new breath into their flames. As the wood hissed and cracked, Eclipse snorted and shuffled at the hitching rail where she was tied. I walked over to pat her neck and shoulders.

"Look at us," I sang into her ear. "Together again, as we should be."

Eclipse jerked her head. She was unsettled in spite of my affectionate caress. My heart sank when boots shuffled somewhere beyond the fire's halo. I surveyed the shed and smithy forge next to the livery. The movement paused. I held my breath and waited until the scuffing of heels resumed. That was when Garrison stepped from the shadows. His smirk oozed with contempt and satisfaction.

"Well, well, if it's not the mysteriously missing Jacy Lane," he hissed, "speaking words to an orphaned horse that should be spoken to me. What was it you just said to her? 'Look at us, together again as we should be.'"

Chapter 29

A bolt of terror shot through me when Garrison stepped toward me. I backed up as though I were a frightened colt. "Stay away from me."

"I didn't believe it when Spit told me he saw a gal who looked like you ride in with a Negro. I thought you were either dead or long gone."

"I *will* be after tonight," I said, cornered, with my back against the building.

"You will be *what*?" His plump lips curled wickedly. "Dead?"

His innuendo made me shudder. "I will be gone. You will never have to see me again."

"You humiliated me, Jacy. Your mother said you were crazed with grief when you ran off, a breakdown caused by the loss of your father. But I learned the truth from Titus. He said you invited the hands of a darky to caress your flesh."

"That's not true," I said, hoping to appease him. "Besides, you and I were never a suitable match."

He glared at me with rage and disgust. "All those evenings you stood frigid against me, yet you gladly gave yourself over to a Negro?"

"I love him," I said with bold confidence. "And he loves me."

Garrison grabbed me by the hair and dragged me away from the livery. I tried to scream for help, but his rough hand clamped over my mouth. He snatched a branding iron from the shed adjacent to the forge and pulled me back to our fire. Plunging the iron into the embers, he sent sparks bursting in every direction. He pinned me on the ground and laughed as I wriggled beneath him, each of my arms crushed under the weight of his straddled knees. I retaliated by biting the thick fingers he squeezed against my lips.

"Damn you!" he barked as he yanked his fingers from my mouth.

"This is the place where my father died," I snapped with thinly veiled accusation. "Will you kill me as well?"

His expression grew dark. "He had no right to dissolve our engagement. Our union would have released me from serious debt. I wanted your father to feel an equal financial loss. My only misdeed was coating those palominos with stench. The fact that your father died in the accident was an added bonus for my effort."

"The events of that night were no accident!" I cried out. Unable to wriggle free, I delivered my outrage through a forceful shot of spittle that was spat up into his face with vengeance.

Instantly, Garrison's eyes lit with fury. He pulled the branding iron from the flames. "The events of tonight are no accident either, but who's to know?"

I cringed as he lowered the searing orange tip of the brand near my cheek. Once again, his sweaty palm muffled my screams and also kept me from turning away.

"You have deviant impulses, Jacy. Your feral behavior denigrates my spotless reputation. Now you will be marked with permanent proof of the animal that you are."

As the heat of the iron hovered over my skin and I braced for the agony of his persecution, from nowhere Rafe came hurtling in at full gallop. He drove his shoulder into Garrison's ribs, knocking him off me and into the dirt. The branding iron bounced to my left, its red-hot glow only a few feet away. I scrambled for it as the two men engaged in violent fisticuffs.

Rafe lifted Garrison by his collar and slammed him into the wall of the livery. But before Rafe could land another blow, Garrison pulled a knife from a sheath tied to his belt. With a ferocious snarl, he plunged the blade into Rafe's side. I screamed as Rafe toppled sideways. Garrison raised his knife to stab him again, but I swung the branding iron and struck him in the head. Thick blood streamed from his temple.

Garrison turned from Rafe's writhing body and came at me. "You infernal—"

I swung the iron again, but he deflected it with his hand, causing its molten tip to plunge squarely against his groin. He fell to his knees, bellowing in agony. The bitter smell of burned cloth and seared flesh filled the air. The excruciating pain caused him to pass out midscream. I scrambled over his limp body to get to Rafe. Blood stained his shirt above his left hip.

"I won't let you die," I vowed as I desperately pressed my hand to his wound to slow the bleeding.

"Help me to my feet, Jacy. We gots'ta let Sylvan know what happened."

I managed to get Rafe upright. He groaned when I braced him around the waist to guide his staggering footsteps. When we arrived at Sylvan's back door, we were bloodstained and shaken.

"Garrison discovered me! He stabbed Rafe."

"Blast that cursed devil," Sylvan seethed. "Hurry! Ease Rafe onto the daybed so I can examine his wound."

I removed Rafe's shirt to reveal the gash in his side. Though blood still oozed, Sylvan pressed his fingers to the surrounding flesh. "The knife appears to have penetrated only the meat of him. If we pack it with sulfur, the bleeding will cease."

Sylvan quickly gathered the powder and bandages he needed. As he cleansed the wound, Sylvan questioned us anxiously. "Is Thomas holding Garrison in hand?"

Rafe's nostrils flared as he endured the painful procedure, but he remained steady with strength. "Thomas is deliverin' the supplies to the swamp chimney. I turned back to check on Jacy."

I stroked Rafe's bare shoulders to comfort him as Sylvan applied the sulfur. "How did you know I was in danger?"

"The *Southern Gale* must have come upriver when we were at the mercantile. I saw her stacks in the moonlight on the downside of the lock. My gut started crawlin' with worry, so I came back."

I pressed my lips to his brow. "Thank heaven you did."

Sylvan eased Rafe to a sitting position and wrapped a heavy layer of bandages around his waist. He met our eyes with a grave look of concern. "Where is Garrison?"

"He is unconscious behind the livery." I described the confrontation and the nature of his injury. "His intent was to brand me. Now, through his own vile actions, *he* is the one who wears the permanent mark of the animal that *he* is."

"Let's hope he has not regained consciousness and sought out help." Sylvan pulled on his coat. "Rafe, be still and rest while Jacy leads me to Garrison."

We darted through the night to where Garrison lay curled in the dust. He twitched and gurgled when Sylvan attempted to assess the damage. "He is incoherent with shock, which is to our advantage."

We found a stack of blankets in the livery and used them to spin a tight cocoon around Garrison, from the neck downward. I jumped to my feet when the thud of boots interrupted our task. The approaching figure was upon us before we could scatter. To our relief, it was Thomas.

His eyes grew wide. "What's happened? Where is Rafe?"

"He is at Sylvan's, injured but safe," I said, folding the loose corners of the blanket around Garrison's legs.

Sylvan motioned Thomas to us. "With your help, I believe we can get Garrison out of town without anyone knowing there was an incident. It matters not that Garrison is at fault. Injury at the hands of a Negro will always be viewed as mutiny."

"You have my total support and cooperation," Thomas said as they lifted Garrison into the rear of Thomas's carriage.

"Take him to the plank of the *Southern Gale*. Tell the captain you came upon him in the livery and that he looked to be trampled by a horse. Garrison is too dazed to articulate any detail."

"Won't they examine his injuries?"

"It's not likely, since there is no doctor aboard to treat him. Explain that he is in shock and needs to be taken downriver to Elizabeth City as quickly as possible. Garrison owns the steamer, so the captain will not balk at making a night voyage on his behalf."

Thomas climbed into the carriage. "Sounds like a solid plan, Sylvan."

"I would do it myself except that I am known to the captain. You are a stranger and will be safe in the North before they piece together the night's events."

"Take Jacy back to Rafe's bedside," Thomas said. "I will be along after I have playacted my part."

Sylvan and I hurried to the house. Rafe opened his eyes when we entered the room. He agreed that Sylvan's plan allowed us the advantage of time. "It will give us a chance to be well on our way before he can accuse us of any wrongdoing."

"It could be days before he is in any condition to report his lies with clarity," Sylvan said. "But if I were you, I would leave by first light."

"We will, Mr. Firth," I said, nodding my understanding of the imminent danger around us.

Huddled over Rafe, Sylvan had the chance to study me more closely. My short, thick hair. My rough hands and almond skin. His shaken expression revealed sympathy for my altered appearance, but I neither sought nor desired his pity. I carried no sorrow in my heart. Sylvan had no way of knowing that I was reborn. Nor did he realize the depth of my relationship with Rafe. So when he spoke, his fatherly concern did not insult me.

"Jacy, I have a distant cousin in Ohio who can take you in and reestablish you in the white community there. No one will know you, and with the right amount of lace and powder you can recover your birthright."

I looked down at Rafe. He was watching me intently, gauging me for uncertainty. Sylvan's gracious offer was meant to save me. But I was already saved. Stroking Rafe's cheek, I smiled. "Mr. Firth, *this* is my birthright. Love and family. There are no greater gifts I seek."

"I want you to be happy, sweet girl," Rafe said as he touched my hand where it now rested on the muscled curve of his chest, "even if it means giving you up to Ohio."

I tucked myself next to him with my head on his shoulder. His dark skin glistened in the candlelight and his eyes drooped with weariness. "We will never be parted again, Rafe. After all we have overcome, a quiet life in your arms will be a blessing."

Sylvan's face warmed into a grin that flashed his sugar cube–

shaped teeth. He nodded his head and said no more. He was a man who understood conviction and matters of the heart.

Rafe stroked my hair. "As soon as we are home, we will have the wedding that Murphy stole from us."

I smiled at the thought. I was at peace and soaking in the happiness between us when an idea struck me. "Why wait?"

"Why wait for what?"

"To be married," I said gleefully. I turned to Sylvan. "The day you came to Great Meadow with news of my father's death, you told Claudia you had attended the seminary and could administer funeral rites."

"That's correct," he said with a glint in his eyes that suggested he knew what my next question would be.

"Can you administer marriage vows as well?"

Chapter 30

Thomas was surprised to find us standing at the hearth, awaiting his arrival. "Your plan went off without a hitch, Sylvan." He set his hat aside and extended his hand to Rafe. "I am relieved to see your wound has not leveled you. In fact, you look exuberant."

"That's because I am about to marry the woman I love." Rafe grinned. "Now that our witness has arrived, we can get on with it."

Sylvan held a closed Bible in his hands. "I never had the honor of performing a marriage ceremony before leaving the ministry, so the formal vows are not fixed in my memory. Since time is of the essence, I will keep it simple yet heartfelt." He paused to clear his throat and then smiled warmly. "Do you, Jacy, take Rafe to be your husband?"

"I do," I said tearfully.

"And do you, Rafe—"

Rafe swept me into his arms. "I do. I will. I promise!"

He pressed his lips tenderly to mine, releasing a swirl of precious joy within me. The shadow of my inner quarter moon lifted forever as my completeness shined back at me in Rafe's eyes. A few short months ago, this moment would have been inconceivable.

Now I could not imagine my life in any other form. I thought of my mother, the mother who had loved me from afar and waited for me to find my way to her. I closed my eyes in poignant anticipation of sharing our good news with Jerlinda and Axel when they welcomed us home.

"You all right, girl?" Rafe asked as he folded his arms around me, and I smiled up at him.

"I am blissfully all right," I said, rising on my toes to kiss him.

Sylvan Firth toasted us with a glass of sherry. "Here's to the hope that every journey up the canal ends so well."

Rafe and I gazed at each other, understanding that our journey together had only just begun. There would be countless challenges ahead, but with Rafe at my side, I knew we could traverse even the roughest of roads.

The four of us talked long into the night about ways we could aid the network that had delivered us. Sylvan was pleased to have another safe house toward which to direct those in need. All too soon, the coming of dawn interrupted our celebration.

"I do not wish to rush the honeymoon," Sylvan said with a wry grin, "but it is safest for all if you leave town before night grays to dawn."

As a token of farewell, he filled a satchel with food and drink for the long road home. I embraced him for his friendship. "You are an inspiration, Mr. Firth. As one last favor, please tell Caleb Briggs that I am well and thankful he is alive."

Sylvan kissed my cheek. "He will rejoice at the news."

Beneath a stream of moonlight, we returned to the rear of the livery. Thomas kicked dirt over the spot marked by Rafe's spilled blood. The branding iron used in my defense lay in the dirt, clumped with remnants of cloth and flesh. Thomas tossed it in the carriage.

"I'll throw this in the first pond we pass," he said.

I tied Eclipse to the rear of the wagon and patted her gently. "We are going home, brave girl. Together as a family."

Rafe climbed onto the bench seat, then offered me his hand as I climbed up beside him. My breath hitched with dizzying astonishment at the sight that met me as I stood on the buckboard. Rafe scratched his head in wonder as he muttered, "What's all this?"

Scattered across the seat and floorboards were violets. Dried and tattered, but violets nonetheless. They had been pressed and saved at their peak. Though faded and brittle, to me they were as brilliant as the first blooms of spring.

"They are a sign of thanks from Violet. She has found our supplies."

I smiled as I lifted her broken shackle from where it lay amid the flowers. "She wants me to know that all is well."

I gazed to where moonlight cascaded over the distant swamp. My rebirth within its savagery and magnificence had led me to this moment of fulfillment. I sensed Violet was somewhere in the thicket watching me. I pressed a handful of flowers to my breast and raised my hand in acknowledgment. She was safe and still free . . . as was I. The joy in knowing each other's fate was a ray of hope that would gleam eternally.

Rafe put his arm around me. "Let's begin our journey home, Jacy. The moon is full and shining bright enough to illuminate our path."

"Indeed, it is." I smiled. "And ever more shall be."

Long intrigued by the transitional period just before the Civil War, **Eileen Clymer Schwab** found inspiration in the courage of those who sought freedom, and in the spirit of joined purpose among those who provided aid during their journey. She resides with her family in northeastern Pennsylvania. Please visit her at ecschwab.com.

Author's Notes

Dismal Swamp. The name immediately conjures up images of a dank, foreboding, and treacherous wasteland. I stumbled upon the Great Dismal during the research phase of *Shadow of a Quarter Moon* as I read material about the history of the Underground Railroad in North Carolina. As a writer, I could not overlook a name so vivid and descriptive. I knew immediately that I would mention it during the journey of my main character, Jacy Lane. At the time, I had no idea that the bleak-sounding region was so rich and storied in Underground Railroad history, or that it would play such a significant role in my novel.

This is a good example of how research can often shift plotlines or shape characters in unexpected ways. For me, research is a process of discovery—not just of historical facts, but of tendencies, beliefs, undertones, and nuances of a particular time period. Through this process, I become better acquainted with my characters and the world around them. The mysterious Dismal Swamp was too alive and complex to remain simply a lush backdrop of scenery; it became, in essence, a kind of womb for Jacy's rebirth.

I had the pleasure of visiting Dismal Swamp during the early stages of writing *Shadow of a Quarter Moon*. Contrary to its name, it is a beautiful National Wildlife Refuge that straddles the border between eastern North Carolina and Virginia. This natural wonder stretches approximately thirty-seven miles long, twelve miles wide, and is home to a rich variety of plant and wildlife.

The twenty-two-mile Dismal Swamp Canal runs along the eastern edge of the swamp from Deep Creek, Virginia, to South Mills, North Carolina, where functioning locks continue to service the canal. These days, the area of the welcome center and park along the North Carolina stretch of the canal is bustling with hikers, bicyclists, kayakers, and visitors enjoying the educational facility and trails that provide access to the swamp. The canal itself is designated as an alternate route for the Intracoastal Waterway, making it common for visitors to stop in their tracks to watch a beautiful sailboat or yacht glide along the serene ribbon of dark water.

Just as Jacy describes in the novel, the water of the canal and swamp is dark brown—not dirty with silt, but the color of a robust cup of tea. The water is made acidic by the leaching of cypress and juniper trees, therefore allowing for little of the bacterial growth that is usually found in swamp environments. Because of this purifying component, it is said that in earlier centuries casks of tea-colored water from Dismal Swamp were taken on long voyages by seamen like Blackbeard and Commodore Perry. But for me, it was the allure of the swamp's mysterious history of harboring runaway slaves that struck me when I first dipped my hands into its dark and peculiar depths.

By some estimates, upward of a thousand runaway slaves, or "maroons," passed through or inhabited Dismal Swamp for varying lengths of time during the years before the Civil War. The true number of maroons who adopted this foreboding sanctuary as their home will never be known, but Dismal Swamp is believed to have been the site of one of the largest maroon colonies in the United States. It was a desperate existence, but the swamp's dense and treacherous terrain provided a barrier between outlying former slaves and the bounty men who chased them. Horses and tracking dogs could not penetrate the forest with any degree of success, and slave hunters on foot often gave up quickly in the dank, vaporous interior, where panthers, bears, and poisonous snakes threatened them in their search. It simply wasn't worth the risk.

During one of my visits to Dismal Swamp, I was fortunate enough to meet the longtime Deep Creek lockmaster Robert Peek. On his day off, he took me by boat up through the lock at Deep Creek and then south on the Dismal Swamp Canal as far as Feeder Ditch. We traveled the narrow Feeder Ditch to the edge of Lake Drummond, within the swamp's interior.

Along the way, Robert shared his extensive knowledge of the canal and swamp. The canal was completed in 1805, dug almost entirely by slave labor. The waterway was used primarily to move timber goods harvested from the swamp via flatboats and lighters that were pushed like gondolas to the rivers that connected to the seaports, north and south. A legendary hotel was built along the canal where it crossed the state line from North Carolina to Virginia. Known as the Halfway House, the hotel was a popular site for duels, because with one shooter standing in one state and the second shooter standing in the other, neither could be prosecuted for murder. There are no remnants left of this hotel, though its mystique remains.

Adding to the folklore of the area is young George Washington's association with it. He invested in swamp acreage during the 1700s with the intention of draining areas of wetland to be used for farming. When the task proved too daunting, he made a tidy profit by producing juniper shingles. During the Civil War, the canal was used by both the Union and Confederate armies to move supplies and troops.

One of the more touching stories I encountered was that of Moses Grandy, an enslaved canal man who worked diligently to save six hundred dollars to buy his freedom, only to be duped by his master and sold to another man. Moses struck a bargain with his new master and again paid six hundred dollars for his freedom, only to be cheated a second time. Finally, on his third try, Moses Grandy purchased his freedom and eventually settled in Boston. He continued to work tirelessly until he was able to purchase his wife and several family members. Sadly, though, he was unable to locate some of his children, who had been sold away and forever lost to slavery.

The reputation of Dismal Swamp as a fortress of freedom was no secret. Even in the 1800s, the region's legacy of concealing freedom seekers stirred intrigue. Did you know that after writing *Uncle Tom's Cabin*, Harriet Beecher Stowe wrote *Dred—A Tale of the Great Dismal Swamp*? I had no idea! The haunting desperation of a runaway was also captured in a poem titled "The Slave in the Dismal Swamp" by Henry Wadsworth Longfellow.

Though the legends of the swamp have grown dormant over the years, I am not surprised others were inspired by its storied past. I felt honored, through this novel, to give new life to the distant bogs and long-held mysteries of this historic region, as well as to pay homage to the daring freedom seekers who claimed this "dismal" existence as a better choice than that of bonded servitude. Research is an act of discovering and remembering. There is much about this period of time we would like to forget, but it is a pivotal part of our growth as a nation. Those who carried the heaviest burden should not be forgotten; nor should the activists of the Underground Railroad. Though most remain nameless, they are true American heroes. My hope is that through the life-altering journey of Jacy Lane, we will remember.

EILEEN CLYMER SCHWAB

SHADOW OF A QUARTER MOON

A CONVERSATION
WITH EILEEN CLYMER SCHWAB

*Q. America's Underground Railroad is present to varying degrees in both of your novels—*Shadow of a Quarter Moon *and* Promise Bridge. *Do you feel a responsibility to "shine a light" on this period in history?*

A. I am certainly very inspired by the courageous men and women who followed their conscience and took action despite the threat of severe consequences. Remembering the spirit of the Underground Railroad is a way of acknowledging and paying tribute to this incredible freedom movement and its legacy of trust and shared purpose. I loved having the opportunity to take my readers on a journey that immerses them in Underground Railroad activity. In my previous novel, *Promise Bridge*, the secret network remained hidden through most of the story, but in *Shadow of a Quarter Moon*, Jacy's experience puts us in the shoes of a woman on the run. This allowed me to dig deeper into my research and breathe life into characters who face the fears and dangers inherent to their flight.

Q. Characters move in and out of Jacy's life as she flees to the North. Did this make it difficult to develop relationships between Jacy and the secondary characters?

A. Much like any runaway's, Jacy's encounters are brief. Her life often depends on the compassion and integrity of strangers, but on the move, she has no time to get to know anyone deeply, even though these characters have a huge impact on her destiny. Those who assist her have different reasons for aiding the cause. In truth, their motivations do not matter as long as they provide food and/or shelter. Even though Jacy does not spend a lot of time on the page with most of these characters, they each become a part of her in some way and she will never forget them. Many of us recall people who passed quickly through our lives, but left a lasting imprint in one way or another. Imagine if that person truly held your life in their hands. I did not want these secondary characters to be veiled in shadows or hidden behind closed doors. I wanted Jacy (and the reader) to see their faces and to feel their conviction.

Q. Jacy's life-altering journey is both internal and external. How does one affect the other?

A. Jacy's internal journey begins the moment she hears the word *quadroon* instead of *quarter moon*. Learning the secret of her birth destroys her world and eventually motivates her into making a physical journey that further challenges who she believes she is. The farther Jacy travels on her road to freedom, the more evolved she becomes. She arrives in Philadelphia a much different woman from the helpless girl in the opening scene. In many ways, her physical journey is the embodiment of her inner growth and discovery.

Q. How likely was it for a mixed-race slave to be viewed as white?

A. Because of widespread sexual abuse of enslaved women by masters and overseers, the presence of mixed-race slaves was quite common. Though light-skinned slaves were often favored for house duties and personal service, they still suffered the cruelty of servitude. It's impossible to know how often the ruse of pretending to be white was successfully perpetrated, but there is no doubt of the advantage of passing as white. In a well-known account, Ellen Craft, a light-skinned slave from Georgia, disguised herself as a sickly white man traveling to Philadelphia for medical attention. Ellen's husband, William, accompanied her, posing as the man's servant. After traveling first by train and then by steamship, the couple arrived in Philadelphia on Christmas Day, 1848. Ellen's successful masquerade had won their freedom.

Q. Any other true-life inspirations?

A. The main characters of *Shadow of a Quarter Moon* are composites of fact and fiction. Jacy does, indeed, cross paths with some historical figures of her day. I love that my characters pass through Philadelphia. The city is so rich in Underground Railroad history. Lucretia Mott was an outspoken abolitionist who founded the Philadelphia Female Anti-Slavery Society. She and her husband, James, believed slavery was an evil and they often sheltered runaway slaves in their home. At that time, Robert Purvis was also active in Philadelphia's Underground Railroad and abolitionist activity. As he says to Jacy during their encounter at the home of Lucretia Mott, Mr. Purvis was known to comment, "In the matter of rights there is just one race, and that is the human race." Members of the Bethel African Methodist

Episcopal Church (Mother Bethel) were also central to African-American abolitionist activity. Since these historical figures were outspoken in their fight for the abolishment of slavery and were active players in the Underground Railroad, Jacy was destined to benefit from their commitment to the cause.

Q. Was it challenging to break away from the traditional plantation setting of the time period?

A. Not at all. In fact, it was important for me to show that life in the South stretched beyond the confines of plantation life. It is easy to associate the South as a whole with slavery, but most Southerners were not slaveholders. Throughout Jacy's story we get to see the heroes as well as the villains of the time. The same is true when Jacy arrives in the North. To her dismay, intense prejudice continues to be an ominous presence in the free states as well.

Q. As with your previous novel, Promise Bridge, *there is significant meaning behind the title,* Shadow of a Quarter Moon. *Is this purposeful?*

A. I love when a title hints at the very essence of a book, even if a reader does not realize it until the end. It's like a secret between the author and those who have finished the book. My hope is that afterward, just hearing the title brings all the emotions rushing back, and that the deeper meaning within the title resonates with readers as much as the characters do.

QUESTIONS
FOR DISCUSSION

1. Do you think Jacy's father is wrong to hide the truth about her origins from her?

2. Why is Claudia so desperate to secure Garrison as Jacy's husband?

3. Do you think that, witnessing Claudia's mistreatment of Jacy, Jerlinda wishes she had kept her daughter in the slave quarters?

4. Is Claudia's bitterness justified?

5. Why do you think Jacy is drawn to Jerlinda in spite of the upheaval caused by their secret?

6. Do you see Mayme as a stabilizing presence in Jacy's life? How so?

7. Which character do you think has the most impact on Jacy during her journey?

8. What signs did you see of Jacy's internal transformation?

9. In Dismal Swamp, Jacy is stripped of her identity. In what ways does her experience in the swamp help her to rebuild her sense of self?

10. Violet saves Jacy when she is chased into the swamp. Other than Violet, what outlying maroon has the most impact on Jacy? How so?

11. Contrary to Garrison's behavior toward Jacy, Rafe's gentle care for her is apparent throughout the book. At what point do you think Jacy realizes she is in love with him?

12. Why is Jacy so attached to the horse Eclipse? How are their plights similar?

13. How is Jacy different when she arrives at Emma's house in Philadelphia?

14. What did you learn about the Underground Railroad during Jacy's journey to the North?